I0670451

WRAITH

An Andrea Kelley Mystery
The Archivist Book 3

ELLE ANDREWS PATT

Blue Beech Press
Knoxville, Tennessee USA

Cover design by Alexandre Rito

ISBN (PB AMZ): 978-1-960974-00-6

ISBN (PB D2D): 978-1-960974-97-6

ISBN (EBK): 978-1-7347544-9-0

ISBN (HB): 978-1-960974-01-3

Published by BLUE BEECH PRESS

5923 Kingston Pike #161

Knoxville, TN 37919

Wraith/An Andrea Kelley Mystery/The Archivist Book 3 -- 1st ed. MARCH 2023

"Fairy Lullaby" is an old English take on the Irish lullaby, "A Bhean Úd Thíos" from the 1500's and in the public domain. "There Be Love" is an original folk song written by the author.

Publisher's Note: This is a work of fiction. Names, characters, places, and incidents are a product of the author's imagination. Locales and public names are sometimes used for atmospheric purposes. With the exception of public figures, any resemblance to actual people, living or dead, or to businesses, companies, events, institutions, or locales is completely coincidental. Any historical personages or actual events depicted are completely fictionalized and used only for inspiration. Any opinions expressed are completely those of fictionalized characters and not a reflection of the views of public figures, the writer, or publishers.

ALSO BY ELLE ANDREWS PATT

NOVELS

GHOST: An Andrea Kelley Mystery

(The Archivist Book 1)

SPIRIT: An Andrea Kelley Mystery

(The Archivist Book 2)

BLIND MICE BITE: A Matt Loose Mystery

NOVELETTES

MISSING: PRELUDE TO A MURDER CONVICTION

The Prometheus Saga: MANTEO

The Prometheus Saga 2: REMUDA

Return To Earth: SOMEDAY LOYAL

The Masters Reimagined:

REGARDING MR. BULKINGTON

The Masters Reimagined 2:

AMONG THE BLUE HORSES

CONNECT: https://linktr.ee/elleandrewspatt

For my mom and dad, who have always known that no matter what else I may be doing, I have always been and always will be a writer to my core.

ACKNOWLEDGMENTS

The journey to getting Wraith on the page and published was a long one for many reasons, the tail end of the pandemic not the least of them, with the many adjustments all of us had to make. But also, Andrea Kelley's world has reached the point of life that all stories hit if you stick with them long enough: the characters want a say. Sometimes where you, the writer, think the story should go is not where your heart and gut say the story should go as you listen to those character voices you've created and let loose into the world.

All that to say I had a couple of false starts on Wraith before I found the emotional groove the characters needed based on what's come before. And the emotional groove is what makes a story come to life. But false starts upset production schedules which are already dicey and open to interruption due to life in these trying times. I wrote at least twice the number of words than I needed for the final version of Wraith you have in your hands now! In fact, my keyboard is so worn out that I'm constantly deleting doubled 'e's and missing 'r's.

Thank you so much to Victoria Gerkin for her kind patience and advice, to ever-helpful First Reader Kelley Rebori for her honesty, and to eagle-eyed Lindsey Patt, who compiles my Archivist series bible that lets me keep track of all the story universe details. Thank you to former literary agent Paul Stevens for his trust in my storytelling, belief in this series, and the helpful research-related call related to his new industry.

Oh, the research! Wraith was no exception in the research department. Thank you to the many who have so enthusiastically shared their knowledge and personal stories of Charleston and West Virginia, Appalachian lore and culture, eastern West Virginia, law enforcement, avenues of adoption and guardianship, ghost stories, and all the other tidbits that get tucked into a story like Wraith. Whether through answering a call or email or sharing your story and knowledge online, please know how much I value your willingness to document and share both the most mundane and most arcane details of both modern and historical life.

Thank you to my fellow writers, especially the #5amwritersclub, Ralph Walker, and the participants of the Fall 2021 Unforgettable Characters and Incredible Journeys workshop, where the basic beats of Wraith in progress were re-shaped for a more resonant story. While it was always meant to be the wrap-up of the foundational Archivist trilogy, reshaping the thought process behind the original beats made the story richer than it might have been, and gives the Andrea Kelley universe new energy to draw from for the next four books.

Most of all, thank you dear reader, for taking an interest in my fictional world and loving the characters and storylines of The Archivist series. Thank you for your honest reviews online, comments on social media posts, and emails that share your thoughtful feedback and love for the books. I couldn't continue to share Andrea Kelley with the world without you. Special thanks to Ruthie Kuhlman for keeping me writing, and Elaine Sweatman, Mickey Noel, Carmen Colwell, and Ivy LeDonne for their steady encouragement.

As always, thank you to my family for giving me the space, time, and patience that allows me to write. And for this book that broke my brain, extra cheerleading, homemade cookies, and a much-needed break in the form of a Saturday trip to the Jack Daniels and Nearest Greene distilleries.

—EAP

WRAITH

1

The young woman perched in the backseat of Andrea Kelley's little Infinity FX seemed unaware of her surroundings. Although the windows were closed, her red hair blew around her face and licked her bare shoulders above her billowing white dress as her voice droned on. "Then Tucker says to me, them green beans need a'pickin' now. Go on up to Leah Beth's and fetch her girls down here'n. But when I get up in the holler, them girls ain't there."

Andrea glanced over at William Taka, her best friend, sitting bolt upright in the front passenger seat, his hair wet from a shower and jaw clenched, tee-shirt on inside out, jacket in his lap. Scott was working late so Taka had simply stayed after dinner, like so many times before. She reached over and grabbed his tight fist.

"They's gone a'sangin' down on Winslow crick. Ever-body knows that 'bandoned homestead's got haints that'll scare the skin right off'n yourn..."

In the rearview mirror, Andrea glimpsed the woman's thousand-yard stare again, before returning her attention to the road.

"Ever-body knows why them crossvines a'grow so thick down there at the homestead."

Taka took a deep breath, opened his hand, and threaded his fingers through Andrea's. "Was Jimmy okay?" he croaked through a tight throat.

"Yes, I think? He didn't say he wasn't." Andrea had dated Jimmy, a state cop, for a couple of months before they settled into a close, affectionate friendship. But Taka and Scott, who met at roughly the same time, had formed a tighter bond.

"There's love and then there's fate and then there's Robie Dawkins and that slip of a girl from Copper Ridge," the ghost said.

Taking her hand back, Andrea threaded the FX from Timber Way onto Greenbrier which ran south down through the hills where she lived and then straight across the flat valley of Charleston, West Virginia, all the way to the north bank of the Kanawha River.

"Take sixty-four, it's faster," Taka said.

She nodded. The hospital lay to the west, on Route 60, which Greenbrier intersected, but that way lay multiple stoplights and Friday night traffic through historic East End. I-64 would let the FX fly west with a short jog south to General, the Charleston area's only Level 1 trauma center.

"Dewey?"

Ignoring the ghost as she chattered on, Andrea illegally passed a green Ford Galaxy poking along at pot-head pace before she answered. "He's in surgery."

Scott worked for Dewey Sanderson, Charleston's own business magnate. Dewey and Taka had a complicated relationship that had once been intimate. They'd politely ignored each other for years until recently, when they'd both suffered at the hands of a man Andrea still didn't regret killing, though she did regret her inability to stop dreaming about it and, despite reassurance, her worry that he'd come back to haunt her. Literally.

As if answering that thought, the rambling ghost said, "... might could, missy, he might could. You'd be smart to be a'feared of that one. He slinks across the skin like cold water, liftin every hair. Leah Beth claims him breathe on her nape one . . ."

The ghost's hair whipped harder around her face and shoulders, like the FX were a convertible with the top down. Her full train dress streamed right through the backseat and trunk of the FX, catching Andrea's eye in the side mirror.

"What's her name?" Taka said.

"Whose name," Andrea said over the ghost, braking for a stoplight.

"The ghost in the kitchen. Before I went up to shower."

"She hasn't said," Andrea replied, her gaze drawn back to the rearview as that spectral wind calmed, but still tugged and pulled at the ghost.

"Do you know the damage bullets do internally?" Taka said, hands again fists on his thighs. "They cavitate. Do you know what that means?"

"Yes." She did. Bullets cause a shock wave that blows body tissue outward. The tunnel they create displaces everything around it, shifting tissues that should never be moved that far from where they attach to everything else. Massive trauma. "I do."

He shook his head. "I don't know how I feel about either one of them. But I can't lose them, Andrea."

Looking over, she noted how tired he looked, the tight line of his mouth as he pressed his lips together. She hoped her busting in on his shower with news of the shooting wouldn't set him back in his therapy. She'd already caused him enough pain.

"Wait. Is she here?"

"She is. She's talking and talking. I don't think she sees us."

He frowned at her. "How is that possible?" None of the ghosts Andrea had seen before communicated well verbally. Or traveled with them. The light turned green. Andrea pressed down on the accelerator and the FX shot forward into the intersection. Keeping her eyes on the ramp to westbound I-64, Andrea shrugged. How would she know? She just wanted her to stop talking.

" . . . 'cause that girl from Copper Ridge sees the future. Ever-body says so, but I don't believe that. Now throwin' the bones, that there's different, but just a'closing your eyes and saying sumpthin' what rise up on your tongue . . ."

TAKA ASKED for Scott at the emergency room reception desk and then they sat for ten long minutes. He leaned forward, elbows on his open knees, watching everyone who came and went, though he couldn't have described a single one even a minute later. A woman in a wheelchair was doubled over, arms wrapped around her middle and crying in quiet, hiccupping breaths. A small boy seated directly across from Taka caught his eye, but then his bright-eyed gaze slid past Taka and froze. He stopped swinging his feet, staring.

Taka's skin prickled, his heart giving an uncomfortable lurch. "Did she come in with us?"

"Yeah. She's sitting on the other side of you, still talking." Taka flushed cold but forced himself to remain still.

Andrea leaned into his shoulder, her phone in her hand, the text screen open. "Jimmy's upstairs with his boss. They're waiting for word on Dewey. Chet's arm is broken."

Chet was Dewey's main bodyguard. They knew each other in passing, what with Chet lurking behind Dewey for at least the last three years. When Scott joined Dewey's security team, Taka had learned Chet was competent and street smart. That made the impossibility of an attack at the Coliseum, Dewey's club, even more incredible. Taka couldn't stop his mind from leaping straight to a connection with the murder of Dewey's dad, Senator Dante Sanderson. Dewey had been there, too. Taka wondered now if his hunch that Dewey held the reins in that situation was wrong.

A man in blue scrubs stepped through a secure door next to the reception desk. "Detective William Taka?" They both jumped up, but once at the door, the man shook his head at Andrea. "He okayed Detective Taka. You're welcome to wait right here. It'll only be a few minutes, anyway."

Taka's stomach dropped. What did that mean?

"Is that good or bad?" Andrea asked for him.

The man gave them a thin-lipped smile and stepped back, giving Taka room to enter.

"Go check on Jimmy," he said, trying to ease the worry on her face. "I'll text you when I know." He hoped the ghost stayed with Andrea, even though he knew now that when it came to ghosts whatever he wanted didn't really matter.

JIMMY PACED THE SECOND-FLOOR HALLWAY. His West Virginia State Police supervisor, Maddox, stood near the windows on one side of the large, open, surgical waiting area, barking as quietly into his phone as he was capable of. Uniforms, both state police and Charleston Police officers were posted where they were needed, including the trooper keeping an eye on Jimmy, and everyone else was still at the Coliseum processing the scene.

He shoved his hair off his forehead, smoothing it back with both hands. And then noticed the dried blood on his shirt. Scotty was his responsibility. His field agent. But Andrea and Taka were on their way, and he needed to pull his shit together, so he didn't blurt that out. He and Maddox had agreed that Scott's true identity and his undercover status would remain in place unless Scott tapped out. Although he hadn't managed to collect any concrete evidence against their target, Dewey Sanderson, WVSP had made investigatory inroads into both arms and drug networks based on leads Scott furnished them through his proximity. Jimmy couldn't blow that for them no matter the circumstances.

"Jimmy," Andrea called out behind him as she entered the hall.

Jimmy spun on his heel, opening his arms as she rushed at him. Her warmth shocked him. He didn't realize how cold he was until she pressed against him and wrapped her arms around him.

"What happened?"

He wasn't supposed to tell her anything, but Scott would almost certainly tell Taka. They had hopelessly tangled their personal and work lives like damn rookies, both of them lying to Andrea and Taka. But Charleston was a small city in a state of small towns, and it was a rare cop that didn't have some sort of relationship with someone he shouldn't be talking to—a brother, a best friend, a sister-in-law.

They'd settled into a steady friendship that he still hoped might become more. But she wasn't the sort of woman to forgive a lie easily.

And he hated that disappointing her seemed inevitable in this rat's nest he and Scott had built during their investigation of Dewey without much thought towards the real-life consequences.

Andrea pushed him away enough that she could see his face. "Jimmy?"

He glanced at Maddox, but he wasn't looking at them and the trooper shadowing them was too far away to hear. He wanted to reel her back in so he could hide from her, but he sucked it up instead, meeting her dark brown eyes as he said, "I shot him."

"Dewey?"

"Scott. I shot him."

"Why?"

Now was the time to come clean. That Scott was an undercover officer borrowed from North Carolina's State Bureau of Investigations. That he was Scott's handler. "It was an accident," he said instead, which was true. "There was an active shooter at the club. Not inside," he added when horror crossed her face. "Out back. Someone was trying to kill Dewey."

Andrea glanced down the hall at the scurry of nurses, a middle-aged couple with their heads together down the way, but no one was paying them any attention. "Were you on surveillance?"

She knew his team was interested in Dewey's activity and a few months ago when Taka had been kidnapped, she'd seen them in action. "No, we've moved on," he lied. Because he really needed to lay any more thoughts she might have about that to rest. "I'd actually gone for a beer with Scotty and just left out the front when I heard the initial shot. Scott thought I was part of the attack and when I saw his gun pointed at me—I reacted."

"Is this related to Dewey's dad?"

Jimmy shook his head. "Too early to know. Dewey could have most anyone after him considering his activities." Suspected activities. Despite Scott being embedded for several months, despite the cover story of a long-term friendship between Jimmy and Scott as an unspoken invite for Dewey to try and corrupt Jimmy, they still had damn all hard evidence to prosecute Dewey for anything.

"The shooter?"

"Got away."

———

"…WHAT'S this? 'nother fair-haired boy. They's be a nickel to every dark-haired dime down Jackson way. But he's not a'one. Not a'one them those bones be chatterin' and clatterin' on aboot."

Andrea's gaze shot to the ghost. Was she referring to Jimmy?

"I really fucked the pooch on this one," Jimmy said to the floor.

The ghost had her head lifted, as if scenting the air. "No one's so bright as them dark-headed lads what's been gone from Winslow's crick so long."

"You made a mistake," Andrea said, tone firm, still watching the ghost side-eye. They'd all just been through an officer-involved investigation with Taka. The suspect Taka shot had died. Please, God, let Scott be okay.

"None's them touch don't feel it. Them bleeding-vines don't lie."

"What's wrong?"

Besides everything? Andrea tilted her head toward the ghost.

Jimmy raised his brows. "Visitor?"

"Chatty one."

"It's a hospital, I guess that's to be expected."

"Tucker sez they's just a'moved, gone away, but Leah Beth heard tell how's that one's a wraith and ain't it been seed a'sanging in the holler, diggin' and pickin' like it was still a'this world."

Andrea forced herself to ignore the ghost. Jimmy needed her. "She showed up at the house, a little while before you called."

"Nobody else?"

"A couple in the ER lobby."

"Where's Taka?"

The thing about Taka was, he acted as an amplifier. Whenever they were together, the ghosts she saw came through clearer, with more agency, and she saw more of them. They also saw more of her. Taka dialed up all the spirit room lights.

"They let him back, Scott gave them his name."

The red-haired ghost's reality and volume remained undimmed

through the several feet of concrete between the ER and the second floor. Andrea's attention drifted back to her. She was wandering from wall to wall in the hallway as she talked on, turning circles when she strayed too far from Andrea. Two nurses and a worn, anxious woman walked right through her. And she kept walking through a state trooper standing further down the hall, pretending not to watch them.

Jimmy straightened up, looking past Andrea. "Doctor."

Andrea followed him closer to the waiting area. The doctor stepped onto the carpet and asked for Dewey's family.

An older man in a wrinkled suit and sporting a moderate beer gut drifted over from the windows, his cell phone still pressed to his ear. "I'm Major Maddox, state police."

A subtle shift of focus rippled through the small groups huddled together in the area. Maddox dug in his suit jacket and brought out his badge to flash at the doctor. She stayed his hand and took a good look.

"Mr. Sanderson has no family present?"

"His mother lives in Florida, she's being contacted. I'm the lead state investigator on the shooting and we very much would like to speak with Mr. Sanderson."

"He's headed into surgery. There's a high probability he'll fully recover, but you won't be able to speak with him until late tomorrow at the earliest."

"Tomorrow is what Tucker always sez," the red-haired ghost piped up louder than before. "Tomorrow. Tomorrow. Tomorrow, Madeleine. I'll be a'taking yous home."

Was her name Madeleine?

"...trooper outside treatment," Maddox was saying. "We'll need him present at all times."

"He accompanied Mr. Sanderson to the OR and is standing in the hall to recovery."

"But he never done yet," the ghost wailed. "I wanta go home. A'want, a'want, a'want..."

"Can someone get him a chair?"

The doctor smiled for the first time. "Of course. I'll update you following surgery."

"Scott Fergusson?"

"I'll find out and send someone to let you know."

"Thank you." Maddox held out his hand like they were making a deal and the doctor shook it.

As she walked back past Andrea and Jimmy, glancing up in acknowledgement of their apparent unabashed eavesdropping, the ghost stopped talking. Stopped walking. Stopped fidgeting. Her gaze sharpened, following every bob and sway of the doctor's exit. Once again, she reminded Andrea of a hound scenting the air. And she was undoubtedly aware of the real world, if only for a moment.

Silent, alert, she darted after the doctor, leaning out around a cart in the hall as if hiding, her long hair swinging, as she peered after her. Then she followed, folding in on herself in a way that made the back of Andrea's neck crawl, until only a thin, unnatural shadow slid along in the doctor's wake, and right through the gap of the surgical doors as they swung shut.

***

"COFFEE?" Andrea said.

Slouched in the plastic waiting room chair beside her, his legs stretched out in front of him, his arms crossed, head pinning his rolled-up jacket between the wall and the top of the chair, Taka didn't open his eyes. "Mocha."

Somehow, he didn't look uncomfortable.

"It's a hospital at three in the morning," she countered.

"Dump some hot chocolate in."

She stared at the side of his face. But then noticed the rise of his cheekbones for like the millionth time since she'd met him as a raw-boned thirteen-year-old.

He caught her watching as he slit his right eye open. "Please."

"Only because you said please. Jimmy?"

No answer. Andrea turned her attention to him, laid out across three seats on her other side, his right hand draped over her jean-clad thigh.

"He's actually sleeping?" Taka asked. "Post-adrenaline—"

"Crash," she said, still watching Jimmy. "Yeah."

Taka sat up, his jacket falling behind him, voice wide awake. "Stay. I'll get the coffee."

She nodded.

He strolled out.

Andrea and Jimmy were the only ones left in the surgical waiting area. His chest rose and fell in even, deep breaths. It had been awkward, navigating their friendship after Christmas, after Taka lit her up with a simple kiss that turned into a rush of hands and need met in minutes, like teenagers, no condom necessary, though the slow burn of muted want for something more sparkled through the both of them through the rest of the late afternoon and dinner with his mom.

Then he'd gone back to Scott, and she'd firmly put Jimmy in the friend zone without much thought and they just . . . fell back into their well-worn roles. There was the occasional look, the slide of his hand along her back or arm, but her need of him was familiar, an old constant she'd grown used to pushing aside. She knew Taka's tells. He loved Scott in the same hopelessly loyal, fierce way he loved his ex-fiancé, Melinda. And Dewey.

And maybe her, though he seemed completely able to bank the fire that had blazed between them, bank it for both of them, cover the burning ember with the details of their lives so that he didn't have to risk losing their friendship to the bloody flames of angst and betrayal that had eventually burned through his relationships with Melinda and Dewey. Knowing the why didn't help. She was still willing to risk it all.

"Them dark haired boys—" the red-haired ghost said.

Andrea's heart jumped hard. She gasped, laying her palm over her chest like that would hold her heart inside her.

"—tried a'burnin' the haint's house one night. He stopped 'em afore they got the second log burnin'."

"And the first?" she said out loud.

"Scorched black but sound," Madeleine said.

Andrea whipped her head around at the logical answer, the possibility the ghost had actually acknowledged her presence, but the ghost was gone. She asked anyway. "Are you Madeleine?"

A cold breeze swirled around her and riffled the pages of the magazines on the tables scattered between the clusters of chairs.

"Is that a yes or a no?"

The breeze died as suddenly as it started. Taka came through the door, two paper cups in his hands. "I made your's a mocha, too."

Jimmy tried to roll over. Andrea laid her hand down on his shoulder and he stilled, his eyes popping open. "Shit," he muttered. "Coffee?"

"Want some?" Taka asked, but the tight lines around Jimmy's eyes and mouth were already slackening. He settled again on his back, his lids dropping closed.

Taka shrugged. He handed Andrea one of the cups. While she blew on it, a nurse bustled onto the waiting area carpet. Andrea straightened expectantly. Taka glanced over at the nurse and then back to Andrea. The nurse walked through him. He shuddered, goosebumps rising on his arms, coffee sloshing from his cup. Andrea grimaced as the nurse emerged and charged onward through the chairs and wall.

"What was that? Tell me some spook didn't walk right through me."

"What did it feel like?"

"No. No, no, no." He held his coffee out and Andrea took it automatically. Lacing his fingers behind his head, he paced to the hallway tile and back, his skin practically rippling. He dropped his arms and shook like a big dog. "Ugghhhhhh. She was a nurse, wasn't she?"

"How do you know?"

"I don't know. I just know. She was, wasn't she?"

"She was. You know she's female, too."

"Yes." He resumed pacing. "Give me a heads up when you see a ghost headed at me, geesh."

"I didn't know."

He dropped back down into his seat and took his coffee back. "We gotta work on that. Have you seen the ghost from the house again?"

"While you were gone."

"Glad I missed her."

Andrea glanced down at Jimmy and back up again. "Do you want to try communicating with her?"

"No. I'd rather wait 'til we have Karie with us." Karie, Waltham-Young's paranormal specialist and now a good friend to both of them. He shuddered again, trying to hide it by sipping out of his coffee, which was a bad idea. He coughed the coffee out his lungs. Andrea thumped her open palm on his back. Jimmy sat straight up, looked around at the empty chairs and then rubbed his face.

"Just us," Andrea said.

"Okay," Jimmy mumbled.

The doctor who'd spoken to them hours earlier came down the hall.

"Thank God," Taka muttered. He stood up.

The doc eyed him but turned to Andrea. "You know Lieutenant Maddox?"

"Major Maddox. Yes."

"Can you contact him for me?"

Jimmy stood, pulling out his badge. "I'm a WVSP major crimes investigator and authorized to speak to you regarding Dewey Sanderson."

The doctor regarded the short hair sticking up in tufts on Jimmy's head, his faded jeans, and the scrub top he'd been given to replace his bloody shirt. She held up her forefinger and dug her phone out of a thigh pocket on her scrubs. She used both thumbs on her screen, then held the phone to her ear. Connected to the state police's dispatch line, she motioned for Jimmy to hold his badge up and read the number off it out loud before saying "yes" several times before hanging up. "Officer Hoyle, could you please step over here?"

"Lieutenant," Jimmy corrected. He didn't go on, though Andrea had heard him also suggest "Trooper" or "Investigator" before, to give people a choice in addressing him. "Officer" drove him crazy the same way Taka said sailors and marines hate being called "soldier".

The doc lowered her voice, but Andrea had no issue hearing her. Jimmy's teammate, Andy Detweiler, came in behind the doc and sat down in the nearest chair, looking washed out and tired.

"Mr. Sanderson is in recovery. As expected, his injuries are non-life-threatening, and he handled the surgery well. You'll be able to speak with him later this afternoon. When his family has been reached, please let us know so we can facilitate his communication with them if he'd like. Your officer is now stationed outside recovery and will accompany him to his room, although he has been cautioned that he's to remain outside."

"Of course," Jimmy said. "Thank you. And the other shooting victim, Scott Fergusson?"

She shook her head. "I believe he's still in surgery. I'll send someone to update you."

"I'd appreciate that."

She nodded, her gaze glancing off Andrea and Taka as she left. Jimmy watched her go down the hall. He swung back around, scruffing his hands through his hair. "I'mma get some of that coffee. I take it you're good?"

"Yeah," Andrea said. "Detweiler looks like he could use some."

"Detweiler?" He turned his head towards the hall and then back to her, brows raised. "When did he show up?"

"Just now." She threw a careless hand wave in Detweiler's direction. "Andy? You want coffee?"

Detweiler lifted his head and nodded yes.

Jimmy's face lost all its color.

"Andrea," Taka said, his voice low.

A heavy sense of dread bloomed in Andrea's chest. No, no, no, no . .
.

But he looked fine. Just tired.

"He's here now?" Jimmy said.

Blood rushed in her ears, distorting his voice.

Staring at Detweiler's confusion while he frowned at Jimmy, Andrea raised both her hands to her open mouth.

2

Taka tugged Andrea into his arms. She pressed her forehead into his chest. The empty chair she'd been talking to mocked him. Jimmy took two steps towards it and stopped. He threw a desperate, wide-eyed look at Taka.

Taka bit his lip, thinking. "Do you know where he is?"

"He was off duty the last two days. Won't be back on until three this afternoon."

"Find him."

Jimmy pulled his phone out. In seconds he was walking to the far side of the room, back turned to them, talking to dispatch. Taka could hear his effort to keep his voice calm.

"Hey," Taka said into Andrea's ear. "Can you talk to him?"

She sniffed and nodded and took a step back. With more than a little reluctance, Taka let her. She'd bottled her shock up fast. She dried the corners of her eyes with her fingers and snuffled up her runny nose before meeting his eyes.

"Find out where he was before he came here."

She glanced over. "He can hear you. He's shrugging. He's watching Jimmy." She went and sat down in the row of chairs facing Taka, looking to her left, towards the hall that funneled in the waiting area.

"Were you at home, Andy? No. Were you at the Coliseum?" She waited, looking expectant at the empty chair. "No."

Taka couldn't stop the hair from rising on his arms. He ran his hand across the back of his neck, trying to quell the shiver that climbed his spine.

"In your car?" Her words hung in the air for a long moment. "Okay, where's your car parked, Andy? He says 'west.'"

"Did he actually say it?"

"Yes, just the one word. West."

West could mean anything. West of wherever he lived, west of town, west of the Coliseum. A game of twenty questions that could go for hours. "Is your phone in it?"

"He's patting his pockets. Andy, it's not here. It's—you're not here." Andrea pressed her lips together and swallowed hard enough that Taka could hear it. "Your phone is with your . . . body. Is your body in your car? Andy. It's okay. It's—he's gone. He just blipped out."

"Dispatch is trying to reach him," Jimmy said, his voice fading at the end like there was no air left in his lungs.

Andrea stood up. "Can you track his phone?"

"If he's late for shift by two hours and doesn't answer his phone."

"I mean, like, Find-a-Friend."

Jimmy grimaced. "I don't want to be tracked off duty, so I've never asked to track anyone in my teams."

Taka couldn't remember if Detweiler wore a ring. "Is he married?"

"Divorced last year." His mouth twisted. "Two kids."

"So they must keep in touch." Andrea said.

"I'll call her."

Poking at his phone, Jimmy again retreated to the other side of the room. Taka couldn't decide if he should stay standing where he was or insist they both sit down? He wouldn't want to be in Detweiler's way if the ghost popped back suddenly. Had he gone looking for his phone? "Is there any chance he's not dead? Y'know, like that movie?"

She narrowed her eyes at him. But she had a habit of always guessing right no matter how vague he was. Maybe he should question that closer.

"The ghosts in the graveyard one?" she finally said. "Zac Efron?"

"Yeah."

"How would I know?"

"You said sometimes they show you their injuries."

"He just looked tired. And he wanted coffee. I don't think he knew he was dead."

"Well," Jimmy said, coming back over. "I just scared the hell out of her and no, she never set anything up like that with him." He tapped his phone against his leg. "Damn it, Detweiler, what were you doing?"

Andrea watched him fidget. "Can you go knock on his door?"

Jimmy's gaze shot to Taka.

Taka held his hands up. "What? I'm here for Scott. I don't think your man on the door is going to let me in to talk to Dewey before you do."

Jimmy grimaced. "Scott's a witness, too."

"Too bad he asked for me then."

Jimmy pressed his lips together, his eyebrows dipping.

The thought came whole, unbidden: Andrea could do worse. But, as always, a frission of cold anxiety crawled through Taka's belly at the thought and he glanced at Andrea, realizing as soon as he did that it was a mistake. She met his eyes, the hurt confusion she thought she'd been hiding from him since Christmas glinting before disappearing beneath her natural compassion.

"It's not like I have any interest in concealing whatever Scott knows, anyway," Taka said to Jimmy, aware of the empty spot at his hip where his badge used to sit. "I want to get whoever did this just as much as you do." He was still a cop, just like he was still a soldier. It's not like that training ever went away.

Jimmy's face hardened to full scowl. "He didn't tell you?"

Andrea laid a hand on Taka's arm. "Jimmy shot him."

For a blind second, Taka could feel Jimmy's throat compressing under his right hand. His Adam's apple bobbed against Taka's palm.

"He pointed his gun at me," Jimmy said.

The sound of his voice shot Taka forward. Jimmy stood his ground.

"Taka," Andrea said.

Counting to six, Taka opened his clenched fists on three. Drew a deep breath in on six. "Okay," he said, although he had to force the word through his tight throat. With four shootings on his tally sheet, he was the last cop who could claim high ground. "Things happen fast out in the field."

"Yes," Jimmy said. "They do. For what it's worth, I'm sorry."

"William Taka?" a woman said from the end of the hall.

Still looking at Jimmy, Taka said, "That's me."

"You can see your partner now."

Andrea caught his hand as he turned away from Jimmy, and he gave hers a tight squeeze. Stepping out in the hallway, he and the nurse maneuvered around a shell-shocked family of seven headed for the waiting area. Taka hoped Detweiler wouldn't cause Andrea any trouble before they could get somewhere more private to try and communicate with him.

Several patients occupied the recovery room in individual areas, some closed off by drapes. Scott's eyes were closed, his face pale but not slack. In the ER, they'd been worried about his broken ribs, spleen, liver, and right lung. Avoiding all the lines to his IV fluids and monitoring equipment and eyeing the tube snaking from under the bandages just below his right ribcage, Taka laid a hand in the middle of Scott's bare chest.

It rose and fell in a steady rhythm. The side of Scott's lip lifted. After a long moment, he cracked his right eye open, then let it fall closed again. His arm slowly rose until his fingers brushed Taka's wrist. Taka shifted to take his hand.

And then the nurse was back. "Sorry, it's a short visit. He's doing fine. You'll receive a text when he's assigned a room. It'll be a while yet, so go home, sleep, eat. It'll be better for him later if you take care of yourself now."

Scott tightened his fingers around Taka's, drawing Taka's attention back to him. Bleary-eyed, Scott squinted at him. "Go," he mouthed.

"Yeah," Taka said. "Okay. Don't go anywhere before I get back."

"Roger-wilco," he mumbled.

"Oh," Taka said, grinning. "Old school following anesthesia. Check."

Scotty tightened his fingers again and let go, sliding back into his twilight sleep.

"We'll take good care of him," the nurse assured Taka as she escorted him out.

He was pretty sure the secure doors hit his butt on the way out.

———

ANDY DETWEILER LIVED south of Charleston, out in Davis Creek. The silent ride out of town gave Andrea too much time to think. Andrea took the deepest breath she could get and let it out slow. "I'm actually creeped out right now because there's not a ghost here chattering away."

Driving with two hands and a grim look, Jimmy stared at the centerline flashing beneath his headlights through the rising fog drifting over Corridor G. Andrea started to say, it'll be okay. But it wouldn't be, would it? There was no good way this could end.

"This is a waste of time," Jimmy said. "He said he was 'west,' right?"

"We don't know what he meant by 'west'. And we have to have a reason to send searchers west, so at least we can say he's not home."

"The simplest explanation would be he's off I-64 west." Jimmy shook his head, his eyes not leaving the road. "Somewhere."

"Maybe we'll discover something that'll give us a starting place to tell searchers to look when he can officially be declared missing." It'd be easier if Charleston PD and the state police knew ghosts existed and that she could talk to them. But she couldn't imagine the attention she'd get if that became public.

"He has two kids, daughters," Jimmy said. "Half the time he misses his weekends because he's working. Mia usually lets him take them when he has a couple of days off, even if it's during the week. He gets them after school, and they spend two nights with him. He likes it better than the weekends. He gets to do homework and dinners and he doesn't fall into the fun dad weekend trap."

Andrea's skin flushed cold. "But he didn't have them the last couple of days."

"Mia said she didn't know he had time off."

"He had other plans, then."

"Or he just wanted a couple of days to himself."

"He had plans that got him killed."

Jimmy choked on his spit and then coughed hard.

"Sorry," she said.

His voice came out strained. "Maybe it's an accident."

"Agreed. Maybe he just ran off the road and no one's spotted the car yet." Maybe.

Dark and lifeless, Detweiler's small, white, wood framed ranch sat on a couple of acres. Two tire ruts dropped off the end of the short concrete drive and curved around to the back of the property. They knocked on the front door and peered through the only uncovered window into the empty living room. Jimmy tried the knob. Locked.

Detweiler didn't make an appearance to wave them off the house or give them a better clue.

Jimmy leaned back into his car and grabbed two small Maglites.

Around the back, they found an old barn and a newer shed in the shadows thrown from a hooded security light. The shed sported windows and a concrete pad out front with several potted plants to either side of the regular door. "Not a workaday shed," Andrea said.

They turned to the barn first.

Although it appeared a bit ramshackle, the doors slid open on well-oiled tracks. They pointed their Maglites inside. An old Ford truck sat midway down the center aisle, leaving room for Detweiler's missing car just past the doors. Jimmy flipped the lights on, banishing the deeper shadows. Neat and clean, obviously a garage.

They fanned out to either side of the fancy shed and peered through the windows. Blinds covered the two windows on Andrea's side. Around back, no rear door, just weedy ground.

"Kitchenette, couch, TV," Jimmy reported as they met again in front. He didn't bother knocking, just tried the knob. It turned in his hand. He pushed the door open without stepping inside. He glanced at Andrea.

She shrugged. It was open, right?

To the right in Jimmy's flashlight beam, the cover to a kid's DVD lay on the floor in front of the TV. An open jug of milk and a cereal box sat on the kitchenette counter next to the sink. Jimmy backed her up a step, held a finger up, and mouthed, "Stay." He drew his gun and swept inside.

It seemed like a long time before he came back to the doorway and waved her in. Two doorways to the left. He pointed at the first one. "Don't touch anything but tell me what you think."

Her light found two sets of bunk beds on the interior walls. Two low dressers under the windows, the drawers open, a child's T-shirt caught on one. The two top bunks were neatly made, but the two bottom bunks were disheveled, covers thrown back, one pillow on the floor beneath. "His daughters sleep out here instead of the house?"

"That would be weird, right?"

"Maybe there's a reason?"

"Like what?"

"I don't know. Maybe he's redoing the house. What's the other room?"

"Bathroom," Jimmy said. "I'm going in the house."

Andrea followed him back through the yard and onto the screened back porch to Detweiler's rear door. He bent over to study the lock. "The bolt's not thrown." Straightening, he reached out and opened the door.

Congealed eggs in a cold pan sat on the stove.

By the coffeepot, a half-full mug.

"He was in a hurry," Andrea said.

"Hang on." Jimmy disappeared into the dark living room. A couple of minutes later, his flashlight beam bobbed back through the room. "Three bedrooms. The girls share one, he uses one as an office."

They both froze at the sound of a passing car turning into the drive. Jimmy crowded against her. "Out, out." He swung the back door shut behind her and they hurried out into the yard.

"Hello," a woman's voice called. "Who's here?"

"It's me, Mia," Jimmy said, waving as they rounded the corner of the house.

Mia wore bright pink scrubs. She held a hand to her chest. "If you're here, you must be really worried."

"Uh, I really need his input on a case. Thought I'd drop in, see if he was sick."

"But he's not here?"

"No."

Mia turned her attention to Andrea. "And you are?"

"Andrea," Jimmy said. "She's an investigator with Waltham-Young."

Mia nodded. "I've always wondered what that place does."

"It's an informational research facility. I'm an archivist. I'm good at looking stuff up that the state police need to know."

Her eyes narrowing, Mia said, "So why are you here?"

"We're both working the case."

Mia opened her mouth again, but Jimmy said, "We really need to locate Andy."

"I don't know," Mia said. "I don't know where he is."

Detweiler stepped out from behind Mia, like he'd been hiding behind her back all along.

Jimmy hooked a thumb over his shoulder. "What's with the shed out back?"

Detweiler walked past them as if they weren't there.

"It's a mother-in-law suite." Mia frowned. "For Airbnb. Maybe he rented it to someone and—"

Before her widening eyes and rising voice could carry her out of control, Jimmy waved his hand in the air. "It's empty, Mia, we checked already." He stepped forward as she wilted and hugged her. "It's okay. I'm sure he's fine."

He sounded amazingly steady.

Andrea peeked back towards the house. Detweiler disappeared around the corner.

"I'm sorry I scared you," Jimmy soothed. "He's going to be pissed at me. Where are the girls?"

"My sister's. I'm on my way to work."

"Go to work. I'll find Andy."

Andrea's skin itched with impatience. The second Mia was out the drive, she spun and ran to the back of the house. No Detweiler. She ran up the porch steps, ripped the screen door open and threw open the back door.

With dawn just breaking, no sun fell into the house yet, but it wasn't as dark as before.

Detweiler was leaning against his kitchen counter, sipping coffee, gazing through the kitchen window.

Jimmy crowded in behind her. "Is it Detweiler?"

"He's drinking coffee. Andy?" She moved closer to him when he didn't respond. "Andy?"

Detweiler straightened and reached for nothing on the counter next to a cluster of liquor bottles and two tumblers. A cell phone materialized in his hand. He lifted it to his ear. "Dewey?" He nodded, set the coffee down, grabbed a pen and scribbled something onto a yellow sticky note pad. "Yeah."

After thumbing the phone off, he ripped the note off, pocketed both, flipped the gas burner on the stove off, grabbed his keys, and rushed out right through Andrea, dragging a cold spot with him. She spun, coming face to face with Jimmy.

"What?" he said

Andrea shook her head and shoved him out of the way. Across the yard, Detweiler went right through the closed shed door. Andrea ran after him and swung the front door open. In the small living room, he stood completely still, his back to her, a small suitcase in one hand, a red duffle slung over the opposite shoulder.

Then he vanished.

"What's happening?" Jimmy asked from behind her.

"It's so weird. It's like what Karie calls an echo. Like he was just a memory. At the hospital, he saw me. But here, it was like he was living in the past. He took a call, packed up whoever was here, and left." She turned to face him. "It was Dewey or something about Dewey."

Jimmy scowled and looked over her shoulder, scanning the small room. "Is Dewey here, too?"

Andrea huffed and herded him out. "The call Andy took was something to do with Dewey."

Back in the kitchen, the grey morning light rising by the minute, she hung over the sticky note pad. "He wrote on this. Can I pick it up?"

"We know he's dead?"

She bit down on the snarky words that wanted to spill out of her. Andy Detweiler was Jimmy's partner, part of his team, and his friend. She turned her head to see him. "I'm sorry, Jimmy."

"Don't touch it. It's one thing to go through open doors in search of a friend, another to move stuff around." He pulled his Maglite from his jacket pocket and turned it on, angling it low over the pad. He adjusted the angle until shadows fell along the impressions in the paper. "You see that?"

"Yeah," Andrea breathed. She took three shots on her phone from different angles. The photos were dark and grainy, but the address clear. *641 Hick.*

3

Jimmy locked the back door on their way out. "Explain how the call Detweiler took was related to Dewey?"

As they walked to the car, Andrea described Detweiler's actions in the kitchen, and how he stood in the shed with his back to her, the suitcase, the red duffle.

Jimmy asked her questions, trying to pull out every detail she could recall, visualizing it as best he could. An echo. A memory playing out. One of Andy Detweiler's memories. One of his last memories? And then it hit him, once again.

Andy was dead.

Andrea was seeing his ghost. What must it be like? Seeing people that others didn't? Not knowing for sure if people were alive or not, if they would see you back or not? If he took her to the farm, would she discover his papaw clomping through the barn still? Dried mud dropping off his worn work boots? Would she be able to talk to him?

She had stopped talking. He stood looking at her for a long moment.

Thinking of his pap, of himself as a child, circled him back to the child's T-shirt caught on the dresser drawer. And the fingerprint Andy Detweiler left on the doorframe of Anna Lansing's house. She'd been murdered and several stray kids who were not her own had gone missing from her house. A house Dewey had entered that fateful evening. And Detweiler had not, not officially anyway. And in the weeks since, Jimmy hadn't gotten any answers from his partner on that one beyond 'Christ, Jimmy, I don't know, I've never been there' and 'I don't know, Jimmy, ask one of the techs, it's not mine.'

"Well, shit," Jimmy said now. "We need to talk to Dewey."

"Are you even allowed to talk to Dewey?"

"No." He was technically on administrative leave. On arrival at the hospital, he'd met with someone who walked him through the after-incident procedure and the ER had assessed his physical and mental health. A trooper had brought him a replacement 9mm since the scene techs collected his. Andrea had arrived to sit with him and there were troopers nearby, so Maddox let him be. Once Scott's statement was collected, Jimmy could probably be back on duty within a week.

But he definitely couldn't talk to Dewey. Whoever took lead on the shooting investigation after the Incident Commander released the scene would do that.

Andrea dialed Taka while Jimmy called the trooper on Dewey's door. Dewey had been moved to a private room but wasn't awake enough to speak with anyone yet.

"We got a partial address, maybe," Andrea said into her phone, "where Detweiler was headed."

She looked at Jimmy across the top of the Impala.

"Hospital," Jimmy said and yanked his door open.

"We're coming back. See you soon."

Jimmy pulled his door shut. Andrea dropped in beside him a second later.

He pulled out of the driveway. Halfway back to Corridor G, Andrea said, "Waze is giving us several possibilities within a few hours' drive."

"Are any of those possible addresses west of the hospital?"

Andrea enlarged the map on her app. "Three." She read the names off and their nearest cross streets. "Any of those Dewey's?"

Of course, she'd already tied the address to Andy's mention of Dewey. He didn't know why he'd thought she wouldn't. "I'll have to run them past Nina. Dewey inherited his dad's property across the state."

Senator Dante Sanderson had been assassinated in October. In the aftermath, Dewey claimed to have discovered that his signature was forged on dozens of documents by the senator or those near him to open multiple shell companies and invest in some dubious business ventures. But those dealings were the basis for the WVSP's continuing criminal interest in Dewey. They were the entire reason Jimmy had spent most of his investigative time over the past two years compiling information on Dewey Sanderson.

The last three months had been a scramble that divided his team's focus between the senator's possible culpability in Dewey's suspected criminal enterprise while maintaining the current operation supporting Scott's undercover work in Dewey's organization. And all the while, keeping an eye on Dewey's legal team as they tried to find a way to prove that Dewey was telling the truth.

"Andy's kids are with Mia," Andrea said, stating the obvious, probably hoping he'd share his own thoughts.

But he couldn't.

Andy could be a dick, but he was solid. A good guy. Jimmy couldn't fathom the possibility he'd traffic kids. On the other hand, Dewey had the connections. And he was still making jokes about owning Taka and Andrea after buying them out of a human auction. Did it matter that he'd helped law enforcement close that case? Had he helped to cover his own tracks? He knew the troopers who had him under surveillance. Could he have planted Andy's fingerprint on that doorframe?

"He wouldn't have rushed an Airbnb renter out like that," Andrea continued. "Or maybe he would have, but that doesn't make much sense. Maybe Dewey has a kid?"

Dewey was gay, but more than one gay man had fathered children along the way. "It'd be a pretty big miss if we hadn't discovered that by now. And why would Andy hide Dewey's kid anyway?" His inner voice, of course, immediately popped up with a dozen different reasons why, most of which involved money or blackmail.

"As a state investigator, why would he be doing anything at all with

Dewey," Andrea said, head down, working her phone with her thumbs, "without your knowledge? But clearly, he did."

Jimmy couldn't argue that point. His stomach churned. Oh, God. How many times had Andy "lost" Dewey under surveillance? More than any other trooper. He'd lost him the night Dewey went to the Lansing house, before she was murdered. Dewey didn't need Scott and Jimmy's friendship to corrupt a state cop if he'd already flipped Andy Detweiler.

A silent mile later, Andrea said, "Maybe he had some reason not to tell you anything yet. Maybe it was a line of investigation he didn't think would pan out or information someone was giving him about Dewey. Maybe whoever was in the shed was just a timing thing. Like he was giving them a ride to the airport or to get a rental car but then he was in a hurry."

"Maybe," Jimmy said. He flipped the impala's visor down against the glint of the rapidly brightening sun off the growing traffic as he waited to turn onto the four-lane. "Or maybe Dewey flipped him. If that address isn't connected to Dewey, it's going to be hard for me to justify anyone questioning Dewey about whether or not he knew Andy Detweiler personally or had any dealings with him beyond knowing he was under surveillance."

"Officially."

Jimmy squeezed the steering wheel hard enough to hurt his knuckles. Because he knew, he knew in his roiling gut, that Dewey had drawn Andy into his sticky web somehow and getting out of this mess, hell, even looking for Andy, was going to be next to impossible without revealing their continuing investigation into Dewey to Andrea and Andrea's ability to his superiors, inviting all the criticism and disbelief that would involve.

Officially or unofficially.

He didn't even know how to proceed at this point and pretend the investigation wasn't hopelessly compromised by the ghost thing and his friendship with Andrea and Scotty's personal relationship with Taka and Taka's endlessly complicated ties to Dewey.

"I'm overwhelmed," he admitted. "Just trying to think it through. How to go about—" He shook his head. "I don't even know how to separate it all in my head anymore. How to do things from here. The first step. Officially or unofficially."

Andrea watched the alternating blocks of steep hillside and strip malls of the G peel by. As they crossed the grey river back into the city, she said, "Archival projects can cover generations of time. Sometimes over wide geographical locations. Thousands of documents. I'm sure you have official timelines. Maybe flow charts. I can start an unofficial timeline including the ghost stuff. Give you a visual reference. Maybe on paper for now. So it's not digital if your investigation is audited."

Another thing to feel guilty about. "Um. I've already been doing that. A green notebook I keep at home." He kept his gaze out the windshield, on the dirty back window of the white Kia in front of him while she studied his profile.

She finally looked away. Settled back into her seat. "Is it detailed?"

Jimmy caught his breath and blew it out again. "Yes. What I've seen. What you've told me."

"What the others have said? Karie? Taka?"

"Yes. And Scott, the little bit he knows. And Bowman." They'd met Lieutenant Commander Luke Bowman in the course of dealing with Aaron, one of the ghosts haunting Louie's pub. He'd just meshed and now he was one of them. Jimmy couldn't imagine stepping away from this . . . gang . . . they'd formed around Andrea and her secret.

"Can I read it?"

It wasn't like he was giving her his journal. The green notebook was mostly straight-up recording. Mostly. He nodded. "I'll grab it next time I'm home. It probably shouldn't stay there anyway. Isn't Karie recording events?"

"Not officially."

"Could I see what she has?"

"I don't think it could hurt your deniability at this point." She was still mad at him, he could tell, but her tone had softened.

"Are you not keeping a journal?"

He didn't think she was going to answer, but then she said, "I only started after the hospital. So Karie and I can cross-reference while we try to find Delphia's grave."

Probably a good idea, since Louie wouldn't be rid of Aaron's ghost until that happened.

"And the visions?"

She nodded. "What I can remember."

"I can't request an official search for Detweiler without cause, but I think I can get away with searching for the address as a friend. Maddox won't tangle me up in red tape on that even if—" He had to stop. If Andrea said Andy Detweiler was dead, Andy Detweiler was dead. "When. Even when forensics goes into his house. It's reasonable that I go looking for him if I need him."

"Will forensics go in if his death is accidental?"

"Considering the circumstances, yes."

"If the address isn't one of Dewey's, how will you connect them?"

He couldn't tell her about the fingerprint. He couldn't tell her they not only still had Dewey under active surveillance, but also under full investigation. "I'll figure something out."

"So, first step?"

"It has to be logical."

"So, we check on our friends, Scott and Taka. And then we go try to find our friend Andy Detweiler. Because we tried to call him to let him know about the attack at Dewey's place, because he's on your team, and needed to be informed of your suspension, but he didn't answer. Now we're worried. That's our first step."

ANDREA LAID a hand on Jimmy's arm as he headed for the parking garage and pointed back towards the hospital. "I see Taka out front."

Jimmy pulled a U-turn to the main entrance. A familiar-looking shaggy-headed blond stood next to him, and the red-headed ghost stood behind him. Taka knocked fists with the guy, who headed back inside. The ghost wavered, her head turning to watch him. Taka yanked the rear passenger-side door open and dropped into the back seat. The ghost flickered and vanished. "They kicked me out until he has a room. That was Dewey's brother-in-law."

Jimmy met her sideways glance. No wonder he looked familiar. The two of them had skulked around his house when Taka disappeared in October.

"And a state investigator showed up," Taka continued. "Tall. Balding. Mark something."

"I know him," Jimmy said. "Mark Compton."

"He handled Tracy's murder," Taka muttered. "I couldn't sit there anymore."

Just the memory of Tracy's burning SUV filled Andrea's nose with the grilled meat odor of his roasting flesh. Bile shot up her throat, but she managed to keep her mouth closed and swallow it back down. Yards away from the SUV, Mark had casually leaned into Jimmy's open window to give him the details of the presumed wreck before anyone knew the victim was CPD Detective Tracy Manners.

"He's going to wait until he can talk to Scott and Dewey," Taka went on. "I asked him about Chet, but he didn't know anything. So, what are we doing about Detweiler? And can we get some real coffee?"

Andrea tilted her head back to see him. "I think you've had enough."

"No, really."

"I gotcha," Jimmy said.

Andrea gave Taka the address fragment and told him about Detweiler's echo. At the diner, they let Jimmy go in to collect coffees.

Andrea turned and hung her head between the seats. "Are you okay?"

"I'm going to need more therapy."

"Seriously."

"I'm totally serious. Jimmy shot Scott and I'm sitting here in his car like that's okay. He's got a chest tube in. His recovery is going to suck. He's got addiction issues. I don't think it's a secret, but I never told you. He's not going to be able to work and I'm already blowing through my savings."

Since CPD let him go, Taka was picking up security work here and there, mostly events and private parties, but hadn't found a full-time job yet. He was too well-known as a trouble magnet. But they also suspected Dewey had put his thumb down here and there, blocking any employment offers since his still stood.

"Scott probably has savings, too. And his family's in Clarksburg, aren't they?"

"They're estranged and he's pretty broke."

"Does he have insurance?"

"I have no idea."

Jimmy tapped on Andrea's window. She whirled around to find his hands full. She rolled the window down and passed the tray of coffees in his hand to Taka, then took two white bags off him. "What's all this?" she asked, but she could already smell the fresh biscuits. Her stomach growled.

"Sausage biscuits and doughnuts."

They demolished the biscuits. Then, with a cinnamon doughnut in hand, Andrea mapped out their route past the three possible addresses west of the hospital and then out onto I-64 West. But, by ten o'clock, out past Barboursville and headed into Huntington, they had to admit they were probably on a wild goose chase, just killing time in hopes it'd be this easy. They'd still look for any sign of Detweiler or his car on the return trip, but they wouldn't hold their breath anymore.

While Jimmy got them turned around, Andrea called Karie. "I'm sorry, am I waking you up?"

"I'm out with the flowers." Karie had planted over two acres of coneflowers as an experimental investment she'd told no one about until a few weeks ago. When Andrea visited last week, the hillside was winter brown, dead stalks with partially harvested seed heads, the rest left for the birds. "What's up?"

"Scotty's in the hospital, at General." Andrea kept talking over Karie's gasp. "Someone attacked Dewey outside the Coliseum and he and Scott and another bodyguard were shot. They're all going to be okay." A man's deep rumble carried across the line. Karie explained what happened, her voice muffled before she came back to Andrea, "Bowman's here."

The commander had become a fast friend in the last few weeks.

"Is Taka okay?" Karie asked

"Not really."

"What can we do?"

"I'm not sure yet. We have another problem. Do you remember me talking about Jimmy's partner? Andy Detweiler?"

"He talked to me when I was in the ER, after Billie Mae."

"He's missing and uh . . ." Andrea turned towards the window, lowering her voice. "His ghost showed up at the hospital. And then we saw what you'd probably call an echo at his house."

Into Karie's continued silence, Andrea continued. "And a new ghost showed up last night before we left the house. She rode with us to the hospital—"

"She what? She traveled with you?"

"Yes. But then she stayed there."

"At the hospital?"

"Yes."

"What about"—her dry throat clicked when she swallowed—"Andy Detweiler, is he still there?"

"I don't know. We're out on I-64, looking for his car, but we're headed back to the hospital."

"I'll meet you there." A rumble. Andrea could guess what Bowman was saying. "We'll meet you there," Karie corrected.

There was nothing on the way back, no skid marks, no glint of a bumper hidden in trees, no recently broken guard rail. Just west of Cross Lanes, a man in ragged clothes that reminded Andrea of photos she'd seen of coal miners in the 1800's trudged along the shoulder. "Is there a man there, coming towards us?"

"No," Jimmy and Taka said at the same time.

When she turned in the seat to watch him as they passed, the wispy shadow of a mule trailed along behind him.

4

Just across the Kanawha, Andrea hit Jimmy's shoulder. "Off, get off here!" Jimmy hit the brakes, threw a wild look over his shoulder and swerved to the right to hit the off-ramp. "Waze just gave me another Hickory address. Hickory Nut Gorge."

Taka leaned forward between the seats. "In Cross Lanes?"

"Technically." She spread her thumb and forefinger on her phone's screen. "It's between Cross Lanes and Poca."

They wound their way north of the river into a rural stretch of country before homes started filtering back into the terraced hollows, backed up against the steep folds of the land. "Here. Right."

A small subdivision of older wood-sided homes opened up around them. They zig-zagged along the parallel roads. Hickory Nut Gorge dropped down a steep hill and back up again, about forty homes lining up along either side.

"Six four one," Andrea said.

Taka pointed to the right. "There, the yellow one."

Jimmy pulled up on the gravel shoulder past the mailbox. He left the engine running. "Safe house?"

Taka grunted. "Makes more sense than the other places we saw."

Too bad Andy Detweiler wasn't standing out front, so they'd know if they were at the right place. Of course, maybe following the address wasn't even what he wanted from them. "What now?"

"I go to the door in this neighborhood, and someone'll be calling the police in two seconds," Taka muttered. He didn't often say anything about living as a POC in West Virginia, but he had a point.

"That's only if they haven't made the car already. They'll know you're with a cop the second I step out."

Andrea turned away from the window to find them both looking at her. "I'm an archivist, not a . . . whatever I am now."

"You interview people all the time," Taka said.

"What am I supposed to be asking? Hey, I found this Post-it note in a house I broke into. Do you know Andy Detweiler? Or maybe Dewey Sanderson?"

Jimmy's mouth turned down and he nodded. "Yeah. I think that could work."

"Seriously?"

"Just say Detweiler sent you," Taka said.

"Or Dewey," Jimmy added.

Were they insane? "Which?"

"When he answered the call," Taka said, "did it sound like he was saying Dewey like a greeting or like he was concerned?"

Andrea shut her open mouth and glared at them. They were serious. She wrenched the car door open and stalked up the driveway to the little curving concrete walk to the small front porch. She stopped and gathered her nerve before she trotted up the steps and knocked on the door. An explosion of yappy barks right behind the door made her jump. She jerked her hand back.

"Who's there," a woman called out over the barking.

"I, um, Andy Detweiler sent me?"

Silence.

"Dewey . . . " she said in a quieter voice and let the name hang in the air, like she might be saying more the lady couldn't hear.

The door swung open halfway. A tiny dachshund dashed out, wiggling and barking, and wound around Andrea's legs. The woman was in her fifties, maybe, and like most women, shorter than Andrea.

Over her head, she could see the red duffle bag Detweiler had slung over his shoulder at the base of the stairs.

"Is Andy okay?" the lady asked over the ecstatic dog's yips.

"I don't know," Andrea said.

"He was supposed to call after he got their mom situated. But I'm so glad you're here. I have a flight, to Seattle, to see my daughter this afternoon." She stepped back to let Andrea in. Yipping in frantic bursts, the dog ran weaving circles around them.

Got their mom situated?

"Don't just stand there, they're ready for you."

"Uh, I just, um . . . Dewey . . . "

"I haven't been able to get him all day. Come in, come in."

Andrea stepped across the threshold and let the woman close the door behind her.

"Simon, stop it," she admonished the dog, who ignored her. "They're in the kitchen, having a snack. They're worried about their mom. Go on through, I'll get their other bag." She ushered Andrea down the hall past the stairs and a living room. Simon followed. "Go on, I'll be right back." She headed up the stairs at a slow climb. Simon bounded past her to the top and barked down at her from the top step with even more enthusiasm.

Andrea eased down the hall to peek into the kitchen. Two girls sat on wooden stools at an island between a kitchen and dining room, their heads bent over coloring books and crayons. Would Detweiler be getting their mom away safe if he was trafficking them?

The older one looked over her shoulder, her eyes wary.

Andrea lifted her hand. "Hi, I'm Andrea. I'm just—what's your name?"

"Harper."

"Hi, Harper."

Upstairs, Simon's barks diminished in volume as he moved away from the stairs.

The little one, maybe four, though it's not like Andrea had much experience guessing kids' ages, piped up, "I'm Sparkles. I'm five."

Harper rolled her eyes. "Her name's Bella." Bella drew back her arm and walloped Harper harder than Andrea would've believed possible before witnessing it. "Ow! That hurt!"

Faster than Andrea could follow, Harper whipped around and grabbed Bella's crayon out of her hand and swiped her coloring book to the floor. Bella wailed, her face beet red, and half-fell, half-slid off the stool to grab the book, crying with her mouth wide open. Simon streaked by, running to Bella at full voice.

"Girls," the woman's voice cracked from behind Andrea. "Enough of that." Andrea moved out of her way as she stormed by. Bella closed her mouth, but the tears were still pouring down her face. She hiccup-sobbed. "Simon, stop it. Get your crayon, Bella." She bustled around the island to the refrigerator and started pulling snack bags out as Bella retrieved her blue crayon from under her stool, Simon wiggling and yipping against her.

"There's apples in one bag and string cheese in the other," the woman said. "This nice lady is going to take you to meet your mom."

"Oh, no, no, there's been a mis—"

"You have the address?"

"No, I—"

"Well, I don't have it. There's safeguards. Didn't Dewey give it to you?"

"He's in the hospital?"

The woman stopped packing cold water bottles into a bag with the snacks. "I don't know. Is he?"

"Yes, he is. He was"—Andrea glanced at the girls and back again—"hurt. He hurt himself. An accident."

"Well, I have to go, you have to take them with you. Maybe you can call him, get the address." She bustled over and shoved the bag at Harper, who took it. Simon leapt up on Harper's legs, barking now at the possibility of food. "Take the coloring books and crayons, Harper, so y'all have something to do." She leaned over and scooped the wriggling, whining dog up in one arm. "You'll be fine. Mr. Andy will take you to your mom as soon as your daddy calms down."

Andrea didn't miss the way both girls shrunk in on themselves when the woman mentioned their dad. "You don't understand, I'm not here to take them anywhere."

"You don't understand." She flapped her free arm, herding them all back into the hallway. "I have a flight." She handed Andrea the small suitcase she'd brought down. "You find out where Dewey wants them, and you take them there. Grab your jackets, Harper." She swung the duffle up. Andrea had to grab it in self-defense. "You wouldn't be here if he didn't trust you."

And then she was moving them to the door and out of it, Andrea stumbling as she walked sideways, nothing coming out of her mouth from the jumbled spill of her thoughts. "Wait!"

The door shut.

The lock turned over.

Simon yapped, his nails scratching on the door for a brief second before he went barking down the hall away from them.

Andrea looked at the girls looking up at her, Harper's brown eyes wide and Bella's face tear streaked. Bella still had the blue crayon clutched in her hand. She sniffed and then rubbed her sleeve across her runny nose.

TAKA HAD no idea how this situation had devolved. Now Andrea was standing outside somebody's plain little ranch with two wild-eyed little girls and three bags.

"What's happening?" Jimmy said, bewildered.

Andrea stepped off the porch and the little girls followed. One was really little, not even five, he'd guess, based on his cousin's kids. The other was maybe eight. Jimmy and Taka got out, leaving their doors standing open, and waited as they approached. The little girls stopped dead about ten feet away, eyeing Taka up.

Andrea lifted her chin at the older girl. "This is Harper."

"I'm Sparkles," the little one said.

"She's Bella," Andrea said. She angled off to the back of the car. "Jimmy, trunk?"

Down the road, a walker's head bobbed over the top of the hill.

The trunk popped up and Andrea stowed the little suitcase and duffle she carried before she slammed the trunk and came back to him. "Let's go," she said to the girls.

The little one climbed into the backseat, but the eight-year-old said, "Where's my mom? Where are you taking us?"

"To your mom," Taka lied.

"Let's go," Andrea said again, glancing back at the house.

Taka met Harper's worried gaze and held it. He still had no idea why they were out here getting in the car, but he did know what to say. "You're safe with us."

It was probably what every human trafficker said to every little girl getting shuttled off to him. Thankfully, Harper didn't argue anymore because he'd have a hard time letting them go back inside if they wanted, since he had no idea if safety existed there.

The walker was halfway down the hill, a big dog straining on the end of its leash after it caught sight of them.

"We got company," Jimmy said, still standing in his open door.

Andrea half-turned to see the dog walker. She lifted a hand. The walker waved back.

Jimmy dropped back into the driver's seat and shut his door.

Andrea hurried the eight-year-old into the back beside her sister. Thankfully, she didn't throw a fit.

Taka leaned towards Andrea. "Are we stealing them?"

"No, but there's a definite misunderstanding and I think we should go. Now."

She got in and he tipped her door shut, lifted his own hand in response to the walker's fixed curiosity and got in the front. He turned sideways, so he could see the girls at Jimmy's back while still watching the road.

They drove in silence out of the little subdivision before Bella pointed at the back of Jimmy's head. "What's his name?"

Sitting next to Harper, Andrea said, "Jimmy." She tapped Taka's shoulder. "And the other one's Taka."

Bella wrinkled her nose. "Taka? That's a weird name."

"That's rude, Bella," Harper said, leaning forward to yell at her sister. "Just shut up. Where's our mom? Where are we going?"

Jimmy caught Andrea's eye in the rearview, but kept his mouth closed.

"Well, that's a secret, isn't it? Until your dad calms down?"

Taka flushed cold at the words. He didn't miss how Harper sat back, clutching the bag the woman gave her harder.

"Tell me the secret," Bella said, her voice bubbling with excitement.

"I can't, it's a secret," Andrea said. "Only Dewey knows it. Have you met Dewey?"

"No," Bella said, shaking her hard so hard her ponytail whipped her face. "Is he a duck?"

"Yes, he is," Taka said over his shoulder. "He's Donald's brother."

Bella held her little hands up, her head tilting. "I didn't know Donald had a brother besides Goofy."

Harper huffed. "Goofy isn't Donald Duck's brother, Bella. He's a dog."

"I don't know about that," Jimmy muttered.

"You don't?" Taka said. "He's a hound."

"I don't know about that," Jimmy said again.

"I've seen this movie," Andrea said. "There's no body though." Taka could hear her wanting to take it back as soon as it came out of her mouth, because there was one, they just hadn't found it yet.

Jimmy said, "What?"

"*Stand By Me.* It's an old movie," Taka said. "Moving on?

Jimmy's jaw clenched. "So, Dewey?"

"Unless you want to, um, call someone more official?" Andrea said. Like Child Protective Services? She stared at him in the rearview, but he wouldn't look at her again.

"Who are you?" Harper demanded.

"We're cops," Taka offered.

"Show me your badge."

He shook his head. "I used to be a cop."

"He still works with the police," Andrea said in that casual, reassuring tone she used to use when she was talking to Billie Mae.

Jimmy levered himself back to pull the badge from his belt. "I'm still a cop."

Taka took it and held it up for Harper to see. The little one, constrained by her seatbelt, reached for it with grabby hands, and Taka let her take it. Their heads bent together as they studied it. Harper looked up. "Is our dad in trouble?"

"No," Jimmy said. At the next stoplight, he scrolled through his phone and then handed it to Taka. Taka held it up, Andy Detweiler on the screen.

"Mister Andy," the little one blurted. "He's with Mommy."

"I think you're getting a little low on gas," Taka said, his tone loaded and then fake, "Oh, look, there's a station right there."

He put the phone back on the dash mount, then made a 'gimme' motion with his fingers at the girls and handed the badge back to Jimmy as he pulled up to the pump.

"Stay," Andrea said. "Let us talk a minute."

"I'm hungry," Bella whined, before both Jimmy and Taka shut their doors.

Andrea got out a second later. "The woman living there thought I was their transport to some address Dewey was providing. She's headed to the airport."

Taka rubbed the back of his neck. Did she need to be intercepted? "Her name?"

"I don't know. She'd been expecting Detweiler to call after he stashed their mother somewhere."

"Damn it," Jimmy spit. "What was he doing? What are *we* doing?"

"She didn't give me a choice, Jimmy. She didn't listen to me. She thinks I'm who Dewey sent. She said to call him for the address."

"We're in Cross Lanes," Taka said. "We can take them to the sheriff's detachment here, get them to pick her up, but we'll have to try and explain our involvement."

Andrea blew her breath out, hands on her hips. "Which means explaining why we're looking for Detweiler and how we got this address."

"I take this to Maddox, bring the girls to HQ, we may never get the next address out of Dewey. And we'll lose whatever advantage we have to find out if he's involved in trafficking. Maybe helping us take out Skinny got rid of his competition."

Jimmy had a burr up his ass about Dewey. Dewey might be manipulative and a bit slippery and most everyone would call him shady. He had been known to facilitate the moves of people he didn't want around him anymore, including those that CPD was most interested in speaking to, but Taka would stake his life on the fact that Dewey wouldn't traffic anyone. He might not stop it, but he wouldn't actively participate. "Whatever this is, it's not trafficking."

"I said, 'if'. And don't forget he paid actual Bitcoin for you and Andrea."

"And I'm glad he did, since I'm here doing God knows what instead of serving a master in only my skin and a spiked collar."

Andrea held her hand up. Jimmy chewed on the inside of his lip but left off. "You can't not take it to Maddox, can you, Jimmy? You thought he'd understand us finding the address?"

Tilting his head back, Jimmy pressed the heels of both hands against his closed eyes. He scruffed his hands back through his hair and locked his fingers together behind his head. "I don't have a choice. I'll just have to convince him that we need answers before Dewey catches wind that anything's wrong."

"So, we take them to HQ?"

"The hospital," Taka said. "Because really, without Detweiler's ghost, for all we know he's dating their mom and since they've both disappeared and the babysitter was in a jam, we agreed to take the kids for her until they're located. We have to be at the hospital to check on Scott and Dewey. End of story."

Jimmy shifted his feet. "She mentioned Dewey."

"So what, Jimmy? Half this town calls Dewey a friend or a landlord. Maybe the mom has some connection to him, so now Detweiler does, too. Call him. Leave a message that we just picked up his date's kids, that we have them whenever he gets out of whatever mess he's in."

"You can do both," Andrea said. "Remember step one? Try to find Andy Detweiler. That led to a babysitter who shoved the kids at us because Andy never brought their mom back. What would any friend do in that situation? Keep the kids and wait for further developments or go ahead and get the cops involved. Since you're the cops, call Andy and leave the message and then call Maddox. Tell him everything."

"Except about the ghost," Jimmy said.

Andrea nodded. "Except about the ghost."

"What about Dewey?"

"Part of the babysitter's story," Taka said. "Go for it."

5

C runching through two packets of peanut butter crackers, the girls were quiet the rest of the ride. After Jimmy got back in the car, Andrea texted him the answers she'd gotten out of them while he talked to Maddox. Their last names, their parents' names, an aunt's name, and the aunt's phone number that their mother had made them memorize. And from Harper, their address, where she went to school.

At a red light, he'd forwarded the info to Maddox and Nina. Bella's eyes were drooping, but every time Jimmy stole a glance in the rearview, Harper remained vigilant, watching their surroundings like she might need to retrace their route.

When they turned off Washington street, Harper sat up, alarmed. "Mom's at the hospital?"

"No," Andrea said, putting an arm around her. "We're just waiting for Mr. Andy to bring her back. He knows we're here with our friends."

"Are they sick?" Bella asked.

"They were hurt in an accident. They're fine, though."

Karie texted Andrea as they parked in the hospital's garage, directing them to the right elevator to reach the critical care floor where both Scott and Dewey had been moved to private rooms. After threading through the hospital maze, they found her and Bowman near the elevators in a small area with chairs and vending machines.

"Littles!" Bowman exclaimed. "Who are you?"

The girls introduced themselves. Bella, once more Sparkles, shanghaied Bowman into coloring with her with no further explanation. Harper attached herself to Andrea. The step-down unit was a large rectangle of patient rooms on the inside and outside walls with two central nursing stations in the middle. Leaving Andrea to fill Karie and Bowman in without upsetting the "littles", Taka headed down one hallway to Scott, while Jimmy followed the room numbers down the other.

He found Mark Compton making small talk with the trooper on Dewey's door. "Still out of it?"

"Yeah. Brother-in-law's sitting with him," Mark said. He nodded to the trooper. "You need a coffee break?"

The trooper gave him a two-finger salute and wandered off.

Mark lowered his voice. "Maddox read me in. You shot your undercover?"

Jimmy shot a glance at Dewey's closed door. "You weren't there."

"I get it, man. The only time I've been shot at is while covering EMS and that guy passed out right after, so I've never even fired my weapon. Things happen fast, right?"

"And in the dark. Maddox is on the way here. I'm worried about Andy Detweiler."

Mark frowned. "Detweiler? Why?"

"I can't find him. You remember Andrea, right? Andrea Kelley?"

"Yeah. I heard you two were seeing each other after all that shit went down at her place."

"It's complicated, but Andrea and I found an address in his kitchen, so we went there only to find out he's off somewhere with a mom and the address was the babysitter of her kids. Only Detweiler never brought her back and the babysitter's headed out of town so now I have them."

"You have her kids?" He craned his neck like they might be hiding behind Jimmy.

Jimmy stuck his thumb back towards the elevators. "Yeah. Andrea's got them. But on top of that, the babysitter acted like she'd been expecting us. And she was all surprised Dewey here hadn't given us the address of wherever they arranged to take the kids until Detweiler shows back up."

"This Dewey?"

Jimmy scratched his head. He really needed a shower. And a nap. "Andrea didn't ask specifically. So maybe not, but she was definitely under the impression that the woman meant Dewey Sanderson, yes. How many other Deweys you know?"

"But Andy wouldn't have any undocumented contact."

"Maybe the mom's a friend of Dewey's or something, who knows?"

"Well," Mark said. "Dewey should know."

"Exactly my point."

***

SPRAWLED on the floor with Bella, Bowman cajoled Harper into joining them. Karie sank down onto a chair by the hall, pulling Andrea down beside her. After a few minutes of his stealing and hiding crayons and asking for non-existent colors, the girls settled into their own discussion of what color unicorns really were and why fairies' wings should be different shades of green. Bowman turned his head enough to give Karie a slight nod, his eyebrows lifted.

"You look tired. Are either of the—" Karie glanced out to the hall, listening for a moment, and then whispered, "ghosts here?"

"No."

Andrea didn't realize how alert Bowman had remained until his tension eased. He sat up and propped himself against the chair between them and the girls without leaving the floor. The girls paused mid-chatter to assess and then carried on. The elevator dinged, drawing Andrea's attention. The doors whooshed open, and Captain Maddox stepped out. His gaze swept over all of them and then locked on her. "These the kids?"

"Yes."

"Lieutenant Hoyle here?"

"Yes, he went to Dewey Sanderson's room just now."

It didn't seem Maddox's face could harden anymore until it did. He stalked off.

"That didn't seem good," Karie said.

Andrea pressed her lips together. "Jimmy was off duty. He was leaving the Coliseum when the shooting started and shot Scott before he recognized him. He's been suspended until he's cleared."

"So, he can't talk to Dewey," Bowman said.

Andrea shook her head. "And we need to. That echo, it was like a replay of Andy Detweiler's morning. He said Dewey's name when he answered his phone before he—" Men's voices rose from the hall to Dewey's room, indistinct, coming back their way before they stopped. Their low rumble continued, a female voice answering some question while a single set of squeaky footsteps came on down the hall.

Dewey's brother-in-law appeared, head down, lost in thought. The red-headed ghost trailed after him. After a cursory glance in their direction, he pushed the button on the elevator.

The ghost drifted closer to Andrea. "That slip of a girl from Copper Ridge, what's she sayin' now 'boot that haint down homestead way and that spotted hound sniffin' the breeze?"

Andrea stood up. "Excuse me," she said to Dewey's brother-in-law. "I'm Andrea, Taka's friend. How's Dewey?"

"Still groggy." He ran a hand back through his shaggy bangs, shoving them out of his eyes. "I always told him this would happen one day."

"Because he runs a club?"

"Because he wholesales guns. Guns kill people."

Bowman shifted.

Dewey's brother-in-law swung his head to eye him. "Ex-military? Gonna tell me people shoot people with guns, the guns are innocent? Don't. Think about a world where guns don't exist at all, in any form, no pistols, no rifles, no cannons, no missiles. Where people have to talk to each other when they're angry over whatever."

"There'd just be some other type of weapon to strike with," Bowman said, keeping his voice soft. "Tyrants will always try to grab power using whatever means available. Swords. Arrows. Sieges. Hot oil. Catapults."

The blond man snorted and shook his head. "You types will never give peace a chance."

Bowman shrugged. "Serve and defend. My types play defense. I'm actually on your team."

"Sure, man."

The elevator opened and he stepped in.

Andrea strode over and placed her hand against the side of the door. "Does he know who shot him?"

"If he does, he didn't say. He's still out of it. Keeps talking about a homestead. I got the docs to deny the police request until tomorrow."

"A homestead?" she said as the ghost said, "That crossvine a'grows so thick down there."

"I don't know. Probably land his family owns. Near Richwood." He lifted his head and met her eyes. "You two decide against buying that property next door to me?"

Andrea willed the blush flushing her cheeks away. "I thought you looked familiar."

"Uh-huh."

She let go of the door. It took five seconds too long to close as they stared at each other.

"What was that all about?" Karie said.

Andrea tucked her hair behind her ears as she turned back to her. "He's Dewey's brother-in-law. Jimmy and I did a walk-by on some of Dewey's properties last year and ran into him."

"Ah," Bowman said.

"The red-headed ghost keeps talking about a homestead."

"The crossvine grows thick down there," Bella sang out, still coloring.

Andrea stared at her. "They do. The place is haunted."

"Lovely," Karie said.

Bella lifted her crayon and looked up at them. "What's crossvine anyway?"

HANDS IN HIS POCKETS, Taka watched Scotty sleep through the sliding glass doors to his room. Jimmy walked down from the nurse's station to stand next to him.

Taka tilted his head towards the big man Jimmy had left down the hall, talking into a cell phone. "Maddox?"

"Yep."

"Locate the aunt?"

"Nina did. She also pulled every paper Detweiler's handled recently and found my written reprimand for not answering his phone while off duty. Maddox keeps prying at me about what makes this time different. I told him my gut, which was backed up by Detweiler being a no-show at the babysitter's. But at least he's pulled out the stops now and sidestepped protocol."

"Good."

"Dewey's asking for you."

Taka's stomach looped over. "Me?"

"Mark can't stop you seeing him. Dewey's the victim here. We have to wait for medical clearance and his cooperation to collect his official statement. So yeah, he's asking for you. You can get the info we need."

"Chet and Scott are going to be out awhile. He's been wanting me onboard his security team. That's what he's going to want to talk about."

"So maybe you talk to him about that. Among other things. Maybe then you come talk to us."

"And by 'us', you mean as an informant to the WVSP."

Jimmy shrugged. "CPD's just as interested in him as we are."

"One, I don't work for CPD anymore. Two, CPD doesn't spend money chasing Dewey's rep down anymore. They'd only get involved these days if someone actually accused him of something or they caught him red-handed. I thought the state was on the same page."

Jimmy shrugged again.

Scotty's chest rose and fell in deep, even breaths. His face was turned away, but his left hand was relaxed, palm up, fingers splayed open.

"I can stay here until you're done," Jimmy offered.

Taka sighed. "He's fine. I'll go talk to Dewey. You do whatever you need to do next."

"What I need next is a stiff drink."

Taka laughed. "I wish." Despite what he'd said, he was grateful Jimmy just waved him off, remaining in front of Scott's door as Taka walked towards Maddox. The man's back was turned to him, his voice an intermittent rumble.

Taka turned between the nurse's stations and across the hall to Dewey's room. An empty chair sat right outside the sliding door, beyond which lay an alcove with a counter, sink, and computer station, and then curtains pulled across an angled rod for privacy. Compton was kicked back in a spare wheelchair on the opposite wall, phone balanced on his thigh, one corded earbud in his off ear, the other dangling on his chest. Taka raised an eyebrow and with a resigned look, Compton lifted his hand in a 'go on in' gesture.

Taka slid the door open, closed it, crossed the alcove in a single stride and brushed past the curtain. He scanned the monitors, the lines running to Dewey's chest, fluids into an IV taped to his wrist, before settling on the purple bruise staining his left cheek. Above his left ear, the thick mop of his blond hair was shaved away from half his head, with a patch of taped gauze hiding the damage. His left leg was propped up, thigh heavily wrapped, the thin bed sheet swagged over his hip.

"Damn," Taka said. "Did you survive a femoral artery tear?"

"Down to seven lives," Dewey croaked. He opened his bleary blue eyes and pointed at his head. "It'd just grown all the way back in from last time."

"Another bullet?"

"Naw. Cut it on something when my leg went out from under me." It was strange to hear a mountain drawl leaking out from under Dewey's usual, carefully curated accent.

"You remember what happened?"

He blinked, his eyes losing focus. "Every second."

"Know who it was?"

"Not a clue."

"Okay."

Frowning, Dewey raised his right hand a couple of inches, wiggling his index finger at Taka. "That face, my friend, does not match that okay."

"Andy Detweiler."

Dewey's eyelids drooped closed. Both his eyebrows climbed his forehead in his effort to open them again. "Uh, yeah. One of the state guys."

"Dewey," Taka said, stretching the name out in a long sigh.

"What, William?"

"He's gone, missing along with a woman whose kids were left with a babysitter who said you'd have the address of the place they were to be moved to next."

The drugs kept Dewey from hiding his reaction for once. His gaze wandered from Taka's face to the curtain to the wall below the TV throwing shifting light into the room with the sound off. Wincing, he rolled his head away from Taka on the pillow to stare up at the ceiling. His lips moved but Taka couldn't hear him.

He stepped closer. "Water?"

Dewey cleared his throat. "No. My papaw had this abandoned place. The family just called it the homestead. I haven't been there since I was a little kid. Five? Six, maybe? But now I can't stop thinking about it. These red flowers covered the front porch, crossvine, they were called." He shifted, trying to get more comfortable. His face crunched up before falling again, like he couldn't sustain the effort.

"What's going on, Dewey?"

"You gonna come work for me?"

"You trafficking those kids?"

"You insulting me now?"

Taka hung his head. The spotted linoleum floor was probably supposed to be a warm cream color but just looked dingy. When he looked up again, Dewey was watching him.

"You've spent a long time," Dewey said, "trying to forget how well you know me."

"Because I can't forget how you lied to me."

"I never—"

Taka spun on his heel.

"William." Even hushed, the command in Dewey's tone froze Taka in place. Anger whiplashed from his gut into his chest. He hated that instinctual reaction. Before he could force himself forward, Dewey continued. "I never lied to you. I never promised anything to you. I never made you promise anything to me. I never will. You may find my tastes not to your liking." He paused, and then added, "Sometimes," a hint of amusement warming his voice before fading again. "You may find some of my business relationships selfish. You may question some of my methods. But there's a reason nothing's ever stuck through the courts and it's not just because I pay my lawyers and accountants an awful lot of money."

"Did you disappear Detweiler?"

The hum of the machines filled the silence. Taka finally strode forward. He brushed the curtain aside, rattling the pole.

"I would if he asked me to," Dewey said.

Taka pulled on the slider.

"If he asked."

Startled at the speed of Taka's exit, Compton jumped up, the wheelchair sliding sideways. Taka didn't bother to shut the door.

"Taka," Jimmy said, his voice sharp.

He was at the nurses' station with Maddox. Taka stalked over to join them.

"Do I need to check if you killed him?" Compton said from behind him as he crossed the hall to the open door.

Taka rolled his eyes.

Maddox nodded at Compton and waved him on.

"He's fine," Taka grumbled.

"What'd he say?"

"That I was insulting him."

"Worth a shot," Maddox said, rotating his wrist to check his watch. "I've got a hold on the homeowner when she goes through security at the airport. The aunt came back clean, should be here in a few minutes to take custody. She lives here in Charleston. She's the mom's sister. Says she has no idea what's happening or where her sister and her husband are. She claims no knowledge of Sanderson or Detweiler or why her sister's in contact with them. But she made no bones about sharing the fact that her sister's husband is an abusive bastard. She hasn't seen the kids in a couple of years."

Did you disappear Detweiler?

"When'd she last see her sister?" Jimmy asked.

I would if he asked.

"Met her at a drive-through about a year ago."

Taka couldn't quite grasp what his brain was trying to connect. He stared at Dewey's door, only half-listening.

"She wanted out," Maddox continued. "But was too scared to make a run for it."

If he asked.

Had she asked Dewey to disappear her? Or had Detweiler asked him to disappear her? Or to disappear both of them? Had it gotten him killed?

"You said Detweiler has kids?" he asked Jimmy.

"Yeah, why?"

"He wouldn't run off with a married woman with an abusive husband?"

Jimmy opened his mouth, then closed it again as he actually gave the question some thought. After a moment he shook his head, his tone confident. "No. He wouldn't leave his kids behind." His voice cracked a little on the last word.

"You got eyes on the husband yet?" Taka said, to draw Maddox's attention, willing Jimmy to snap to and pull his grief back.

"No," Maddox said. "Not at work or home. We have ABPs out on all three of them, hubby's truck, and Detweiler's car."

"She doesn't have a car?"

"No. Stay at home mom, home schools."

"Why is it always homeschoolers?" Compton kibitzed.

"Can it, Mark," Jimmy said. "I was homeschooled 'til high school."

Taka eyed him. "Really?"

"Yeah. Not all homeschooling parents are religious zealots or maladjusted preppers."

"You're so . . . normal," Compton said.

Jimmy grimaced. "You're prejudiced because of your exposure through law enforcement. I'm from the majority pool of non-criminally active homeschool families. I'm socially well-adjusted and went Magna Cum Laude from UC on scholarship. Education."

Compton lifted his hands, palms out. "Sensitive much?"

Maddox lifted the silent cell phone in his hand to his ear. "Maddox. Yeah." He punched at the phone and then said, "They're coming up now."

They left Compton on Dewey's door, arriving at the elevator as it dinged and disgorged a tall, bony woman in a flower print jacket and jeans. High cheekbones gave her the same angular face Harper would age into and the same mousy hair pulled up in a messy bun. Two troopers stepped out behind her.

"Ms. Farley, I'm Captain Maddox. I'm sorry to be meeting you under these confusing circumstances."

Harper came flying around the corner from the waiting area, Andrea and Karie right behind her. "Aunt Janice," she cried and rushed into the woman's arms.

Bella peered out from between Andrea and Karie's legs and then, tears spilling down her cheeks, backed away into Bowman, who knelt, and when she put her arms around his neck, picked her up, patting her back. He murmured in her ear.

"Bella baby," Aunt Janice said. "It's okay. I'm here, sweetie. Auntie Janice. Remember me?"

Bella shook her head against Bowman's shoulder. "I want my mom," she sobbed.

"I know, sweetie, she'll be back soon. We have to let all these nice policemen get back to work, right? We'll go get some ice cream and then you can take a nap at my house. And then I'm sure she'll be back, okay?"

"We'll go down with you, all right?" Bowman said. Bella tightened her arms but nodded against his neck.

"Sure, we can," Karie said, her voice bright. "We'll bring all your stuff, so you're all set at your aunt's." She scooped up the coloring books, while Harper darted between them to gather the crayons. Andrea grabbed the duffle, and Taka took it from her so she could get the little suitcase. Karie grabbed jackets. Taka had done a lot of babysitting for his cousins' kids, but it struck him again how much stuff kids required.

"Deems," Maddox said to one of the troopers. "I want a car on the house, got it?"

"Yes, sir."

"Redding, back on Sanderson's door. Hoyle, I need a minute with you alone."

Jimmy met Taka's glance and then looked away. The pit of Taka's stomach yawned. After they loaded up in the elevator, Jimmy and Maddox stood there in the hall, shoulder to shoulder, hands in their pockets, until the doors closed.

6

In the parking garage, a cool pleasure after the overheated hospital, it didn't take long to see the girls off. The floor vibrated as the aunt pulled away, the fresh stink of exhaust filling Taka's nose. Deems followed in a cruiser with the lights off.

Still waving at their taillights as they descended the ramp, Bowman said, "I need, I don't know, a briefing. Or lunch. Maybe both if you're so inclined." He let his hand fall. "Do we need to keep looking for Detweiler?"

Andrea wasn't looking at any of them, she was staring at the spot the cruiser had pulled out of.

"Andrea?" Taka said.

"He's trying to show me something." She squinted at the spot. "But I can't tell what."

Focusing on the same spot, Taka thought about Detweiler. He didn't know him well, but he could conjure the man's frame and features.

Andrea covered her ears. "West," she said, the word bursting from her.

Karie touched Taka's arm and he looked at her. They'd been working on this with Aaron at Louie's now and then. Taka seemed to amplify a ghost's presence for Andrea. If he was aware of where the ghost stood or really focused on what Andrea was doing when she was in contact, communication was sharper, the ghost more defined, and in the case of Aaron, if Andrea let him touch her, able to share visions. They hadn't gone so far as to try that with any other ghost, but they had been working on dialing Taka up or down like a volume control.

"Shhh," Andrea said.

Taka let his gaze fall to the stained concrete and tried to soften his focus. His neck muscles tightened. He'd spent years honing his attention to danger and now he was having to pull his situational awareness and senses back, trust Andrea would have his back if they needed to move fast.

"He was shot. In the head. Are you in your car, Andy?" Lowering her hands, she said, "You were shot in your car. West of the hospital? No? I-64 West? No. West. He's pointing." She looked right, past Taka, and pointed. "There."

"That's north," Bowman said.

"Is he trying to say more, Andrea?" Karie asked.

"No."

"Do you want to try touching him?"

Andrea shuddered. "No. He's gone."

Taka immediately moved, pulling her into his arms. She hugged him back, hiding her face against his chest. "We were up most of the night."

He gave Karie and Bowman the short version. When he started in on his non-conversation with Dewey, Andrea rotated away from him, wiping her face, and settled under his arm.

"When we came downstairs," Karie asked, "where'd the redheaded ghost go?"

Andrea looked to Karie's left. "She's still with us. Hey!" Andrea stepped away from Taka and clapped her hands. "Hey! Madeleine!" She slid her hand up and down as if in front of someone blind.

Taka bounced his fist against his mouth. Despite months of exposure, despite picking up an actual ghost child in his arms, it still creeped him out to see Andrea interacting with nothing he could see. How many of the mentally ill experiencing hallucinations were instead experiencing some aspect of someone else's life after death? Even if it were only one percent, those people were living on drugs that would never help them. Just the thought freaked him out.

Karie looked fascinated, but Bowman stayed stock still, eyes wider than when she'd been addressing Andy.

"Are you Madeleine? I hear you. Winslow Creek, red crossvine, and the slip of a girl from Copper Ridge, but"—she raised her voice, enunciating each word—"are you Madeleine?"

"She's still talking?" Karie said.

"On and on."

"She's not louder now that Taka knows exactly where she is?"

"No, she's the same no matter where he is."

"Crossvine?" Taka said.

"Red crossvine. At the homestead," Andrea said.

"The haunted homestead," Karie added.

"There's a 'haint' there," Andrea clarified.

"Dewey mentioned his grandfather's place called the homestead, and crossvine on the porch there."

Andrea lit up. "Really? His brother-in-law told us he thought maybe the homestead was family property near Richwood."

"Winslow Creek's near Richwood," Bowman said, crossing his arms. "I was there. It's unincorporated, backs up to Monongahela National Forest."

Karie tipped her face up to look at him, shoving her own bobbed red hair back behind her ear. "What were you doing out there?"

"Looking for my sister."

Becky. Andrea had told him she was dead, but Taka was pretty sure that wouldn't stop Bowman from looking for her, or the man, Donny, who'd been her handler while she was being trafficked. "Why Winslow Creek?"

Bowman looked away, throat working as he swallowed hard before he could speak. "Uh, not Winslow Creek specifically. I went through there, to somewhere else. It was a dead end."

Not ready to share. He hadn't asked for their help in the weeks they'd known him. Andrea had dredged up the bare facts of his sister's disappearance from a couple of images that had come to her when she touched him in some way they hadn't tried to sort yet, and an internet search on his name combined with Becky's. They didn't have time for it right now, but . . . "Crossed circumstances," Taka said.

Andrea and Karie both groaned. Maybe he'd been a little over enthusiastic about the sketchy theory Andrea had formed and he had latched onto, but making connections was how his brain worked. An older couple with a teenage boy in a cast came through the door to the stairwell, letting it bang behind them. They glanced over but headed in the other direction.

"Let's get back to that later, okay?" Taka said. "You think this ghost is related to Dewey, Andrea?"

"Yes," she said, shooting a glare at the empty space beside Karie. Her face changed, her eyes going distant. "She's telling a different story now, about 'sanging' again, whatever that is."

"Picking ginseng," Karie said. "It's an old Appalachian expression."

"Her name *is* Madeleine," she said in a dreamy tone. She listened for a few more seconds before she snapped back to the present. "And now we're back to Winslow Creek."

A wave of tired hit him. Taka straightened from his slump, and stretched his arms up, his backbone cracking in a series of small snaps. "I need to stay awhile with Scott."

"I'm your ride," Andrea reminded him.

"You've been up all night," Karie said to Andrea. "If you want to leave your keys with Taka, we can take you home. Bowman?"

"Yeah."

"Will you go with me to Waltham-Young? Get some equipment to see if we can help with Madeleine, or even Detweiler if he comes back?"

Bowman ducked his head. "Sure, anything I can do."

Taka remembered being surprised that Dewey knew Bowman before any of the rest of them. "I'll try to pry some info out of Dewey about the homestead, give you a place to start." While he was prying, he'd try and get info out of Dewey on Bowman, too.

Andrea thumbed the carabiner holding her keys to her beltloop and handed them over. "You'll let me know if Jimmy hears anything about Detweiler?"

Taka nodded and caught her hand when she would've pulled it

away, but his voice stuck in his throat. Dewey and Scott were upstairs. Detweiler dead. Letting her go felt reckless.

She leaned up and kissed his cheek. "It's okay," she said. "Make sure he's all right."

MADELEINE TRAILED TAKA BACK INSIDE.

Silence.

Andrea didn't realize how uptight she'd been until she wasn't. Like Aaron and Billie Mae, Madeleine spoke on a loop, but her loop was more mindless and constant. Except that somewhere behind it, the ghost was absorbing the living world and reacting. Even her physical motions were different than theirs or the boy in Louie's. She stayed visible for longer, she drifted, she faded to shadow. Except for following, she seemed more like Detweiler's echo, not trying to gain Andrea's attention physically or reacting to her response.

On the road in Karie's Kia, Andrea shivered.

"You cold?" Karie asked. "Bowman, is my hoodie back there?"

"This thing's huge," Bowman said, passing a voluminous orange hoodie forward.

"I won it at a conference. Ghost trivia."

"Of course, you did," he said. "If you'd told me eight weeks ago, I'd be in a car with a paranormal investigator and a person who legitimately talks to ghosts, I'd have—"

Andrea tugged the hoodie on, then burrowed into it.

"You'd have what," Karie said, turning onto the highway.

"I'd have probably hit you."

Bowman eight weeks ago was rail thin and hollow eyed. He'd put on ten pounds since then. And although he still had his port for some sort of sepsis he'd suffered, he'd not had to have any more infusions of antibiotics or steroids. He'd told Andrea she'd given him hope for his sister and enough peace of mind that he could sleep a few hours at a time, but he still had deep shadows beneath his eyes.

She was tired but wired and he'd said something about lunch. The biscuits and doughnuts weren't going to get her much further. "I need a burger," she said. "Like a real steak burger, not fast food."

"You know Cowboy's on Westridge?" Karie said.

Andrea leaned back in her seat. "Haven't been out there yet."

"They do black and bleu?" Bowman said. "I haven't had one of those in forever."

Karie smiled at him in the rearview. "They do everything. And onion rings."

Something in her tone made Andrea really look at her. Then she glanced back at Bowman, who noticed her noticing. The corner of his mouth lifted, and he gave her a one shoulder shrug.

"Yeah," Karie said.

Andrea grinned. "Onion rings all around then."

Karie zipped past Andrea's exit and headed north on I-77 where 77 and I-79 split. Westridge had been carved out between 77 and the old end of Sugar Creek. All the articles she'd seen said they were going for the feel of South Hills, with its mix of new and old homes anchored by shopping. In the meantime, there wasn't much to see, and Andrea found herself once again watching for skid marks, new breaks in the guardrails, damaged trees, while Bowman asked Karie a dozen different questions about ways to capture Madeleine's voice, although so far, she'd been unsuccessful recording Aaron beyond a barely distinguishable word or two.

Off the exit, Westridge was still mostly raw earth and half-built mini mansions. Light traffic headed to the new shopping area, the gas station, Cowboy's.

"West," Andy Detweiler said in her ear.

A screeching half-scream shriek tore out of her.

Karie swerved. Bowman's head thunked against his window. Karie swerved back, another driver already hitting the horn. Andrea clapped her hands over her mouth. Her ears rang and her throat burned.

"What," Karie yelled.

"Keep going," Andrea gasped. "West."

Past another new subdivision going in, Westridge Road dropped from a four lane to a two lane through unbroken woods, its new pavement spooling around a downward ridge to its connection with

Sugar Creek. Just over the top of a steep rise, Andy Detweiler stood in the road.

"What is it?" Bowman said, his voice low and urgent.

Karie stepped on the brakes. "Andrea?"

Andrea turned away from her window, her heart in her throat and tears already falling now that the moment had arrived. A car passed them in the opposite direction, slowing down in response to Karie slowing so abruptly. Andrea swiped at her cheeks. "Keep going, keep going."

When Sugar Creek Baptist came into view, she said, "Pull in here."

Karie wheeled around in the parking lot and stopped. "What's here?"

"Nothing. Andy was standing on the road back there."

"Rocky. Steep drop off from the shoulder," Bowman said. "No guard rail. No immediate trees. We should go check."

Andrea shook her head, her throat closed tight.

One hand on either front seat, Bowman leaned into her space. "If the woman's still with him, she might still be alive. We need to go back, right now."

"There's too much traffic. If we stop, we'll draw too much attention."

Karie reached over and took Andrea's hand. "Andrea, he's right."

A wild, out of control, swirling lifted Andrea's voice right out of her chest. "We have no reason to be here. Where are we supposedly going that we just happened to spot a wreck no one's seen in hours and oh, it happens to be our friend? You think Pete Tamarin's going to let that slide after arresting me a few weeks ago? You think the state police won't question it after *we* were the ones who brought down a whole trafficking ring?

"I killed Oliver Fitch! I shot him in my kitchen. Karie almost died! No one's going to be like, before October this chick is *nowhere*, a *nobody*, and *now* she's discovering dead bodies and catching bad guys left and right? And you guys, you're all on their radar now, too! None of us can be here. We have to go. We'll call in an anonymous tip."

"Andrea," Karie said, tone a rebuke.

"Look," Bowman said. "We don't even know for sure that's where the car—"

Andrea turned in her seat to glare at him. "Andy Detweiler is standing there. That's where his car is. He's been shot in the head. He's dead. We'll call it in. Not from our cells."

Karie squeezed her hand. "But Andrea, weren't y'all looking for him this morning?"

"Yes, but we had that address. If we'd found him along the route, that'd be different. This is . . . random. So random! And it's Detweiler. Jimmy's getting overwhelmed trying to sort what he can say to his team and what he can't and how to explain"—she waved her free hand around—"this kind of stuff."

Bowman let go of the seats and sat back. Barely audible from the radio, Dave Matthews implored the gravedigger to make his grave shallow so he could feel the rain. Andy wasn't ever going to feel rain again. Karie reached out and turned it off. A man came down the church steps with a potted plant in one hand and half a bag of potting soil in the other. His blank gaze bounced off them. He walked to the back of the church and disappeared around the corner.

"If she was with him, we have to make sure she doesn't need help," Bowman said. "We'll go back. Drop me off and keep driving. Park at the shopping center. Note the mileage. I'll call you so you can go in somewhere and make the call either way."

Andrea was afraid she wouldn't remember where exactly and that Detweiler would no longer be there, but he was, looking resigned. "He's there, at the curve, at the top of the hill."

There were no other cars in sight.

Karie pulled to the shoulder ahead of the spot. Up close, tire tracks scored the dry clay. The lip of the drop off was uneven, crumbled away in chunks. Bowman slipped out of the car. Detweiler blipped away. Bowman prowled to the edge and stepped off, one hand steadying himself on the torn ground before they lost sight of him. Karie gunned the engine and pulled away.

Two and half miles, ten cars going the opposite direction, three cars up their tail, before they got to the shopping center. Not thirty seconds after parking, Karie's phone lit up. She thumbed it open. "Hey. Yeah.

Okay. We'll be back in a few." She ended the call. "She's with him. Both shot."

"Okay."

"I'll go call in a tip and then we'll go get him."

After responding deputies found ID, there'd be a huge response. She and Jimmy would have to give statements because they'd been at the house, picked up the kids. The babysitter wouldn't make it to her daughter's. "I guess I shouldn't call Taka or Jimmy."

"We can tell them later," Karie said. "After."

Waiting in the car, Andrea watched Karie enter a busy hair salon. After a short explanation, the receptionist handed her a cordless phone. A few minutes later they were on their way to collect Bowman and get out of there before the deputies showed up.

***

MADDOX AND COMPTON stood on either side of Scotty's raised bed. He looked a little less grey. Maybe. In the hall, Taka fished a water out of the café bag he carried, cracked the cap, and drank half in one go.

Jimmy wandered up from between the nurses' stations. "Looks better."

Taka handed him a protein bar, then stripped the wrapper from his own. "I can't believe you shot him," he said and took a giant bite.

Jimmy finished chewing and swallowed. "Yeah. Water?"

"I don't know if you deserve it."

Jimmy started to say something but then closed his mouth and started again. "It was dark. But I knew it was him as soon as I pulled the trigger. I wish I could take it back."

"He knew what he was getting into when he signed on," Taka said and stuffed the rest of the bar in his mouth. He rummaged in the bag again, handed a water over, and finished drinking his own. "He pointed a gun at a police officer and got himself shot."

"Uh, I don't know if I'm happy you got there already after wanting to kill me this morning, or if I'm scared."

It was true. Point a gun at an officer during a live fire situation and nine times out of ten that officer was going to shoot you. Or try to, anyway. Taka knew it was true. But his heart still wanted blood. "Maybe say you're sorry again."

"I am. I'm truly sorry that Scott was defending himself and I reacted before fully assessing the scene."

"Maybe you should've coached me in my shooting investigation."

"At least that guy actually fired on you. Scotty pulled his shot, or this would've been an even sorrier situation."

"I guess he can't sue you since he was pointing a smoking gun at you."

"No."

Turning his shoulder away from Scott, Maddox answered his phone.

Watching Maddox, Taka said, "Dewey better come through for him."

Compton lowered the notebook he'd been scribbling in. Both his and Scotty's focus shifted to Maddox. When Maddox lifted his head to look at Jimmy, Taka knew. "They found Detweiler."

"You talk to Dewey again, please pass on what you can," Jimmy said as Maddox and Compton made a hasty exit. "You want to formalize a relationship with us, let me know."

"It's not good news, Hoyle," Maddox said. "I'm sorry."

Jimmy clamped his lips tight. Taka said, "What happened?"

"Car wreck off Westridge."

Taka was tired enough, he had to work not to react. Westridge was exactly where Detweiler had pointed to in the garage.

"Suspicious death. Kids' mom was with him. She's dead, too."

Although he'd expected as much, it still made him flush cold. Poor kids.

"Ride with me," Maddox said to Jimmy, and it wasn't a request. And to Taka, "He talk to you about your help with Dewey?"

"Yes."

"Think about it." He stuck his hand out and Taka shook it. Compton and Jimmy did the same and then they headed for the elevators. The coiled dread in Taka's chest didn't go with them. He took a deep breath and blew it out through his mouth like he'd been taught, but that didn't help either.

When he glanced up, Scott was watching him through the glass slider. Taka held his finger up. He called Andrea, never taking his eyes off Scott. "They found Detweiler off Westridge. The mom was with him."

"I know," Andrea said. "We found him."

"What?" Taka turned and paced down the hall, lowering his voice. "Are you there now?"

"No. We called in an anonymous tip." Her voice broke on the last word. She caught her breath. "I was too scared to be the one finding another body."

"I get that," he soothed. "You home?"

"We're at Waltham-Young. Karie's getting us some equipment for the house."

"Ghost stuff."

"Yeah. Scott doing okay?"

"The docs were in with him, then BCI. I haven't seen him yet."

"You'll come to the house later?"

"Yeah." They hung up and Taka walked back down the hall.

Scott's eyes were closed.

His chest rose and fell evenly.

Taka breathed along with him for a full minute, but still the tension in his chest pressed on his heart. As quietly as he could, he made his way inside and leaned down to kiss him. Scott captured the back of his neck, his hand rough and warm, and held him close a few seconds longer, his breath ghosting across Taka's skin. Taka's anxiety only increased. "What's wrong?"

7

Scott shook his head and let Taka go. "I'm going to need extended care. But as long as I make myself available for interviews, I can go home."

"You can come to mine."

Scott held his gaze.

When the penny dropped, it physically hurt. "You mean you're going home to Clarksburg."

"My parents moved to Raleigh a while back."

Taka pulled back, resting his forearms on the raised siderails of the bed. "Raleigh's only, what? Five, six hours?"

Finally, Scott looked away. "It might as well be Mars. My parents are aware of but not tolerant of my lifestyle."

"They don't like that you're gay."

"Asking them to accept a boyfriend would be hard enough, but—"

"I'm not white."

"Or Christian."

"I'm not not Christian."

"They think agnostics are atheists."

"So," Taka said. "Is this a 'this is going to be difficult' talk, or a 'this is on hold' talk, or a 'I'm breaking up with you' talk? 'Cause I could carry us a little while and it's not like I'm working much. We can give up both our places and move to my mom's because you could be an actual Martian and she wouldn't care what we get up to as long as you're nice to the dogs."

"Oh," Scott said. And for the first time since Taka had known him, tears welled in his eyes. He sniffed and plucked at the sheet over his waist. Taka took his hand and threaded their fingers together. "That's— I didn't expect that. This was a 'I have a long recovery and you're in love with Andrea' speech."

Dropping his head, Taka closed his eyes, the dread that had been eating at him finally falling away. "I love Andrea but I'm not in—"

"Tak. Being afraid doesn't mean it's not true."

Taka knuckled his own tears away with his free hand.

"I know you love me. But you're in love with her. Like, love for the rest of your life love." Scott laughed, a half-sob slipping out with it. "And don't you dare say she doesn't love you back. She and I are both besotted with you."

Taka lifted his head. "Besotted?"

"Hopelessly besotted." He grabbed a shallow breath. "Damn that hurts. This"—he lifted their hands—"hurts. I gotta go, Tak."

"I don't want you to."

"Let me ask you this. We can let our apartments go. You aren't working much here. Come with me to Raleigh. We'll rent a house. You'll get a job. We'll win my parents over."

Incongruously, it wasn't Andrea he thought of first. It was Chuck, Andrea's fiancé who died on a snowy road in Germany. They'd been at Taka's aunt's house. A fall bonfire. The kids were sacked out inside already, Andrea and Taka's date were on the porch, digging in coolers for more of the right kind of beer, Taka's cousins were playing drunk cornhole. So it was just Chuck and him camped out at the fire. Chuck had leaned in and opened his hand, revealing a ring box. He flipped it open to show Taka the small solitaire diamond mounted on a simple gold band.

"What do you think?" he said, and Taka remembered exactly what he'd thought.

That he was too late. That he'd wasted his opportunity and now it was gone. He'd clapped Chuck on the shoulder. Chuck popped the question a few minutes later, and Taka kept his mouth shut when Andrea glanced over at him first.

"Yeah," Scott sighed. "That's what I thought. Could you bring me what's at your place? My dad can pack my apartment up later."

Still holding Scott's hand, Taka roughly rubbed his cheeks dry. "Sure." He leaned in again, grateful that Scott not only let him, but kissed him back. "Before I go, that call Maddox took. Andrea saw Andy Detweiler's ghost this morning. He was involved with Dewey. Did you know him?"

"They asked me the same thing, but no, never saw him, except at the bar sometimes. He came in with Jimmy once. Never saw Dewey talk to him."

So, Dewey knew Detweiler as a state cop, but hadn't shared that knowledge with a member of his security team? Or Scotty thought it privileged info.

"You know," Scott continued, "it wouldn't be the end of the world, Taka, if you went to work for him. Health insurance, 401K."

"Maybe. I'll leave your bag at the nurse's station later."

"Yeah. Okay."

When Taka tried to pull away though, Scott hung onto his hand, tugged him back. Taka kissed him one last time and left.

At HQ, Maddox sent Compton back to work on the shooting. "My office," he said to Jimmy.

His assistant held up a thick stack of messages and reports as they walked by, which Maddox snatched without a word. He closed the door hard behind Jimmy, stalked to his desk, and pulled two shot glasses and a large mason jar from the lower drawer.

"Moonshine?"

"White Lightning." He poured one shot and held the jar up, brows raised.

"By all means," Jimmy said, and Maddox poured another.

Jimmy held his shot uncertainly.

"I got nothing to say," Maddox said.

They both drank.

"That damn fingerprint. Professional Standards hasn't said boo." Maddox snorted and slammed his glass down. He recapped the moonshine and put it away. "Dillon said they were still going through the logs we sent, getting their duckies in a row. Too late to question Detweiler now. At least it's not on us. Dillon's sending an investigator from Pro Standards and Greg Stack from CPD to go through the entire Sanderson file. An investigator from District Three is taking lead on Detweiler's case. I'll call North Carolina about returning Fergusson to them. That's gonna cost us. Check in and see if he pushed Taka at Dewey. Go tell your team what's happening. Go see Detweiler's ex. Then go get some sleep, you're going to need it."

With no privacy anywhere, Jimmy stole into the restroom to call Scott. Empty. He leaned against the back wall and tried not to think about how tired he was while the phone rang.

"Yeah," Scott said, voice quiet.

"You make the suggestion?"

"Yeah. I did my fucking job."

"And your faultless service will be reflected in our grateful recognition to the state of North Carolina for loaning you to us."

Silence. Then, "You know Dewey's not good for him."

Jimmy sighed and dropped his officialdom. "I know. He tell you about Andrea and Detweiler?"

"Yeah. I hope she can help."

"I'm sorry, Scott, for the bullet. For everything."

"Don't let him get in too deep, yeah?"

Jimmy laughed. "Right. Stop William Taka from jumping into trouble with both feet."

"God, Jimmy," Scott breathed. "I don't know if I can do this."

"You don't have a choice. Neither of us have a choice."

"There's always another choice."

"Did he offer you one?"

After a long minute, Scott said, "Yeah, but . . ."

"There was always going to be a 'but,' Scott. You're going home. You're going to recover. And you're going to be a legend."

Scott huffed out a soft breath. "Don't have anything else to do, so might as well, right?"

"Right."

"See 'ya, Jimmy."

"God, I hope not. Take care."

In the tiny team room, Bill spun his chair away from his computer station as soon as Jimmy walked in. Nina stood at one of the three whiteboards, charting the basics of a timeline. She'd already taped up photos to another board of Detweiler, Dewey Sanderson, and a woman Jimmy didn't know.

"Hey, boss," Bill said.

Nina turned. "Hey, boss," she echoed. "Mathers is on scene. You know Andy was executed?"

Jimmy nodded. Whether he was killed by the shot or shot after he died, either way he was dead just like Andrea had said. He stood where he'd stopped just inside the room, hands in his pants pockets. "Who's that?"

"Stacy Carruthers Owens. She was with Andy when he wrecked. Also executed. Housewife. Homeschooled the kids. Sister is Janice Carruthers Farley. She was the one approved by Child Protective Services for pick up."

"I met her. You found the babysitter?"

"Carol Smock. She's being detained by airport security until Ronnie Horton at CPD can send someone over for us."

Bill snagged another photo from the printer and held it out. A man. Pale, forties, beer gut.

"Gavin Owens," Nina said, taking the photo from Bill. "Stacy's husband. Probable suicide. Shot to the head. Discovered about six this morning in his car in the parking lot of St. Mark's. Priors for domestic violence. No convictions. No connection to Dewey yet. Or Andy for that matter."

"I'm still running background and searches," Bill offered. "How's Scotty?"

"He'll recover. He's out."

Nina's eyes widened. "He tapped out?"

"Came down from above."

"They pulling the plug?"

"Just our undercover. For now." He circled his index finger at their efforts so far. "Gather as much info as you can. We'll hand it over to the lead coming in from District Three. Pro Standards and Greg Stack are going to put eyes on every report we have on Dewey. We'll be giving them recorded interviews and full access."

"I'll compile it all, boss," Bill said. "And hard copy the spreadsheets so they know where to find everything."

"Thanks, Bill. Nina, can you have the night shift relieve the trooper on Dewey's room at the hospital? One of them can go assist Mathers, too."

"Sure, boss. Can I have a word?"

"Of course."

She taped up Owens's photo and then walked him all the way out to the parking lot before she felt comfortable. "What about that fingerprint?"

"I took it to Maddox after Andy blew me off."

Nina melted, a hand on her chest. "Oh, thank God. I love you, but I'm not willing to give up my career for you."

"I'd never ask you to. Pro Standards got our request weeks ago. It's their problem now, but it's killing me. What the hell was Andy doing there?" The rage he'd been containing boiled up like a geyser. "He was working with Dewey behind our backs, that's what. And what'd they do with those kids? Without names, they don't have families to fight for them, so no one's looking for them anymore!"

"We'll look for them."

"And if he compromised Scott, no wonder Scott couldn't get anything on Dewey."

"You're saying maybe Dewey keeping Scott at arm's length wasn't just caution until Dewey got to know him better."

Jimmy threw his hands up. "Maybe. I don't know. I thought I knew Andy. I thought—"

"You could trust him with your life."

"Yeah. Now I don't know what to think. Two years of research and six odd months of active investigation and surveillance are gone. Wasted time. And I shot a goddamn undercover on top of it all." He spun on his heel and slapped the hood of his car with both hands. "He trusted *me* with his life . . . goddamn it!" He raised his hands and slammed his fists back down, denting the pop metal. "Fuck!" He shook his hands out. "I changed his goddamn life forever, Nina. I gotta go."

"We got your back here, Jimmy. Go."

ANDREA STARTLED AWAKE. Taka sat on the edge of the bed, still wearing the inside-out T-shirt he'd pulled on the night before. "Is he still okay?"

"As okay as he was this morning. He's going to Raleigh. His parents are there."

"To recover?"

"He broke up with me."

As confused as she'd been since Christmas, Andrea knew his heart was broken. He loved Scott. And she loved them together. While she couldn't quite reconcile what she wanted with Taka, she had found she didn't mind sharing her space with the both of them, if that made Taka happy and kept him in her life. That couple of months when he wasn't around after Billie Mae, that had been harder.

She sat up and hugged him. "I'm so sorry, Taka."

He laid his cheek on her head. "Me, too."

Something thumped downstairs. The murmur of Bowman's voice.

"I think I woke them up."

A voice in the doorway said, "Those girls, I told them now, you watch out for them dark haired boys. Them bones don't lie . . ."

"Oh, God," Andrea said, burying her face against Taka's arm. "You brought her back with you. I thought she was attached to Dewey."

Bowman's voice floated up, "Did you see it? Here . . . run it back."

Karie's voice, though Andrea couldn't tell what she was saying, with the ghost rambling on.

"She came down—no, there."

"Shhh, inside voice," Karie hushed.

"I'm awake," Andrea yelled down. Madeleine paused to look at her. She was remarkably solid and remarkably familiar. The eyes, the line of her nose, the curve of her bottom lip. "She's related to Dewey. He looks more like her than either of his parents."

"Ever-body knows why the crossvine a'grows so thick down there—"

"On the homestead," Andrea said along with her.

Madeleine closed her mouth, looking at Andrea expectantly.

"Because there's love and there's fate," Andrea ventured. "And then there's Robie Dawkins and that slip of a girl from Copper Ridge. I don't—"

Taka wrapped his arm loosely around her shoulders, his other hand coming up to hold onto her forearm, but he stayed relaxed.

Madeleine drifted closer. The effort cost her substance. "The red crossvine a'grows so thick down there, on the homestead."

"I don't know why," Andrea whispered.

"Ever-body know why," Madeleine said. She leaned in. Andrea held still as Madeleine's cheek brushed hers. The word burst on Andrea's eardrum, like cold fog, like distant thunder, and retreated like a wave, leaving the warning of a coming storm behind. "Blood."

Andrea ducked away, crashing into Taka's chest. Taka scooped his other arm under her legs and stood up, carrying her right into the dissipating billow of Madeleine's dress.

Cold water and a boot on her chest.

Her lungs fill—

—running through a meadow, the hip-high seed heads slapping against her open palms, laughter in her ears, blue sky above—

Falling. Wind knocked out as she hits a hard dirt floor, stinging warmth against her neck. Her hand comes away bloody.

. . . and then Karie calling her name, Taka still holding her. She coughed. "My neck."

But her hands came away clean. All the lights blazed in the living room. Karie sat beside Taka. Bowman hovered, his brows pinched together.

"Blood," she whispered. "Blood's what makes the crossvine grow so thick at Dewey's homestead."

"Dried blood fixes nitrogen in soil," Karie said. "It's an additive to increase nitrogen levels and acidify the soil when planting in the same bed year after year to keep the new plants strong."

Listening to all the words, Andrea felt like her brain was broken. "I think she means fresh blood."

Karie considered, tipping her head side to side. "Well, it's water soluble, so you usually spray it on as a liquid."

Bowman's mouth dropped open. He frowned. "I can't believe you just said that. What am I doing here?"

"You're the one who woke me up to see the ghost," Karie bit back.

"I don't know how you fell asleep."

Taka pushed Andrea up to sit next to him. "You were out at the kitchen table when I came in, Bowman. You snore."

"I . . . I do not!"

"You do," Karie said.

Bowman looked wild-eyed at her and then at Andrea and Taka. Like it wasn't obvious they'd become a thing. "Okay," he sputtered. "Well, I still saw her."

"Wait," Andrea said. "You saw Madeleine?"

"On the recording. I was playing it back and there she was, standing in the hall. Well, not 'there she was', but there was a shadow, which, you know, I thought was a shadow until it, kinda, *slid* up the stairs."

"And when was this?" Taka asked.

Bowman checked his watch and then frowned. "Fifteen minutes in, so right after Andrea went upstairs three hours ago?"

"She's been in my bedroom that whole time?" Andrea leaned forward to get a breath. "She didn't—I didn't see her. I didn't hear her! She's a motor mouth so how is that even possible?"

Karie pointed between Taka and Andrea. "Have you heard her when you haven't been together?"

"At the hospital, but—"

"Taka was still there," Karie finished. "Somewhere."

"My throat was cut," Andrea said, rubbing her neck. "Or her throat was cut, I guess. I was lying on a dirt floor in a log cabin, I'd been, she'd been, knocked down. Her wind got knocked out of her and then her throat was cut."

"It was Madeleine?" Karie said.

Andrea shook her head, unsure now. "Aaron gave me other people. Maybe this was the same. Maybe she just connected with a memory, but it was real. A woman died there at the homestead and her blood fed the red crossvine growing on it and everyone around there knew it."

"We need to find out who Madeleine is," Karie said.

Andrea agreed. "And who she is to Dewey."

"And where this freaking homestead is," Bowman said.

Taka held his hands up. "But first I need coffee. And whiskey. And a sandwich. And then I don't care. Y'all can go to town on research while I sleep."

"Scotty's going to Raleigh, to his parents," Andrea said.

Bowman broke the silence first. "Dude. I'm so sorry."

"He's leaving?" Karie said.

"He's not much good to BCI in his condition," Bowman reasoned.

Taka stiffened.

"BCI?" Andrea said. "Like, the state police? Jimmy's division?"

"Dewey said he was cooperating with the BCI investigation into the death of his father," Bowman clarified, frowning again. "He let them plant Scott in his operation. I mean, Dewey said you guys knew, but . . ." He looked to Taka. "He's undercover, right?"

"Not very, if you know about it."

Andrea hadn't been so confused in a long time. "Scott's undercover?"

Bowman crossed his arms over his chest. "I got a high-level intro to Dewey when I came to town. He helped me narrow down my investigation and I helped him untangle a couple of legal knots he'd gotten himself into. I was out of line saying anything about it, even though he's out. I just . . . with the ghosts, and Jimmy and you are cops, and Dewey . . ." He glanced at Karie, then his gaze darted back to Taka. "I've gotten much too comfortable here. I should go."

"Don't go, Luke," Karie said, standing up.

Taka stood, too. "It's okay," he said. "I was just surprised you knew."

"I didn't know," Andrea said. She was having trouble wrapping her head around it, though it made sense. Dewey wouldn't want to scare away his customers or connections or whatever he had that kept him so in the loop by having a known cop at his side. But having him there meant Dewey was safer while the feds figured out who killed his dad.

But that meant—she drew both hands against her aching chest. "But Jimmy shot him. They aren't just old friends. Jimmy shot another cop?"

"I don't think they knew each other bef—you know what, I should shut up now. And go. I should definitely go." He grabbed his jacket off the pile of them in the living room chair closest to the foyer.

Taka followed him. "What kind of high-level intro did you get, Bowman?"

Bowman met Taka's eyes, but his whole demeanor had changed. This man was the one with the flat eyes who'd sat next to her in the car after helping Dewey buy them from the Conlons. "The government kind." He spared a tight smile for Karie. "I'll call you."

She tucked her hair behind her ear. "Please."

"Taka," Andrea said, when he started to follow Bowman to the door.

Taka stopped, back and shoulders tight.

The icy night rushed in as Bowman let himself out.

After the door snicked closed, Andrea said, "When did you find out Scott's a cop?"

"Just now," Taka said.

"Oh, Taka," Karie whispered.

8

Taka wore off the coffee and sandwich Andrea had forced on him before letting him leave her place on the heavy bag hanging in his condo. When he sat down on his bed to strip the wraps off his hands, he made the mistake of letting his back hit the bed. Sometime later, in the dark, he fumbled for his phone in the sheets beside him. Six forty-five.

At least his six hours had been dreamless.

Groaning at the stiffness in his back, he stood up and stretched, then dropped for get-his-blood-moving push-ups. He started the shower, then did everything else he needed to before he hyped himself up by blowing his breath out hard several times and got in.

By seven-oh-five, he was back in the Yukon and at seven-twenty, pushing his way through the diner's double doors. It took him a hot minute in the bustling restaurant, but he'd guessed right. Jimmy sat in a booth in the back corner. It was a good location for this conversation.

He stalked past the hostess as she greeted the couple in front of him. Her smile didn't falter as she thrust one of the menus she held at him without a glance. He took it.

Jimmy continued to butter his toast when Taka slid onto the bench opposite him and slapped the menu down.

"The omelets are good," he said.

"I'm not hungry."

A waitress with a coffee pot in her hand materialized from nowhere at his left elbow. "Coffee, hon?" She didn't wait, just poured coffee into the empty mug at his place setting. "What can I get you?"

"He'll have the three-cheese omelet," Jimmy said. "Stack of blueberry pancakes and bacon. Could you add sausage to my order?"

"Sure, hon," she said and breezed away.

"I'm not paying for it."

Jimmy bit into his toast and talked around the mouthful. "This has become a business meeting. I'll expense it."

"I'm not going to work for you. I'm not going to work for Dewey. I'll work for who I want, when I want."

"You're hangry." He finished off his toast and started buttering the second piece.

"What's his name?"

"Who's name?"

"Your undercover from North Carolina."

Jimmy looked up at him, his expression unreadable, but his eyes calculating.

"Dewey says he's cooperating with BCI in his dad's murder investigation. He says you planted Scott with him."

"There *is* an interagency task force investigating the senator's murder, and I *am* BCI's liaison, but no, Dewey is not a part of that investigation, and Scott's just a friend from back home in Clarksburg. Dewey's winding you up."

"This info came from an independent source."

"If that source is just repeating what Dewey told them, then it's just Dewey spinning his webs. You said it yesterday, until he makes a big enough mistake, none of us are putting any more money down the Dewey Sanderson rabbit hole. He's strictly a witness to the senator's assassination. That's the only cooperation anyone's asking of him."

The waitress sashayed up, both arms loaded. She set down the huge omelet, bacon, and pancakes in front of Taka, more pancakes, scrambled eggs, cheese grits, and sausage for Jimmy. Taka stared down at all the food in front of him. His stomach growled. Jimmy shoved the creamer his way. "You aren't running an active investigation on Dewey," he said, pouring creamer in his coffee.

"Not until now. Those little girls yesterday might be his mistake. The problem is nothing happened to them because we intervened."

Taka inhaled a piece of bacon and chopped his fork into the omelet. "You say that like it's a bad thing. He could still be a family friend. Maybe she asked him to help her leave her husband. Compton interviewing him today?"

"Here you go, sweeties," the waitress chimed, popping up again with no warning. She dropped butter and syrup, topped off their coffees, and sailed away.

Jimmy stirred salt and pepper into his grits. "You think any more about working with us? It might go a ways towards applying for a full-time job."

"CPD let me resign, they aren't going to recommend me for a state job. Pass the syrup."

"I don't know," Jimmy said, pouring the syrup over his own pancakes before handing it over. "The state can absorb more liability and you have useful experience."

"I don't wanna work for the state, anyway. I'm done."

"Mall security?"

"Not that done. I have contacts in private security."

Jimmy hummed and stuffed his mouth with pancake. Taka did the same.

Chasing a bit of yolk with a forkful of pancake, Jimmy said, "Charleston's not that big. You'll be an events bouncer or traveling all the time, bodyguarding all over the state." He pointed the fork at Taka. "That is, if Dewey doesn't scare them off."

"Andrea told you." He polished off most of his stack before he spoke again. "Scott's leaving. Though you already know that, too."

Jimmy held his coffee up. "News to me."

"Sure."

"Seriously. I haven't spoken with him. And Maddox didn't say anything. But for what it's worth, I'm sorry. You going to do long distance?"

Taka pushed his nearly empty plates away. "No."

"Well, then I really am sorry."

He wrapped his hands around his mug and watched Jimmy clean his plate. The waitress zipped in. Taka covered his mug with his hand. She refilled Jimmy's coffee and cleared their plates and dropped the check. Jimmy sat back with his mug and studied him.

Taka didn't know Jimmy's tells. He was either a very good liar, which made him a very good cop, or telling the truth about Scott. Taka's long knowledge of Dewey was tipping him to the liar side of the scale. "Why aren't you with Andrea?"

"We're friends."

"You'd like to be more."

Jimmy gave him that crooked smile that reminded Taka of Andrea's confession that she liked his lips. "She's in love with someone else. He's stupid for her, but because he's stupid, he can't see it."

Taka grimaced, glancing down at his chest to see if there was an actual pointed spear sticking out of it, and drank the rest of his coffee. "I've gotta go."

"Go. Ask Andrea to text me if she sees Detweiler—" He cleared his throat. "Uh, if she sees him around. If he tells her anything else."

"I'm sorry for your loss," Taka said and meant it. Tracy Manners was only four months in the rearview.

Jimmy nodded. Taka slid out and left him contemplating the coffee in the bottom of his mug.

By virtue of spending half the night logging into every genealogy site Waltham-Young had access to, by eight-thirty in the morning, Andrea had a good handle on Dewey's family tree.

No Madeleine, she texted to Karie. *Direct or as a sibling to direct ancestors.*

She'd traced the senator's side back to England and Scotland and stopped in the mid-1600s, though when she clicked through on some of the names, she found some enterprising soul had taken some of the lines back to the 1100s. She'd had to curb her curiosity more than once after coming across genealogy related rants demanding payment or reparations for the various shortcomings of the senator's American ancestors. She'd made a note about unpaid debt on a mule that she knew she'd never get back to, but couldn't resist wondering if an intern, maybe Megan, would be able to use it as inspiration for a cultural project.

Dewey's mother's side was a dead-end. They'd immigrated too late for the time period Andrea thought Madeleine was from and never lived or died anywhere but Wilmington, or Charlotte or Charleston, apparently. And they'd been in Charleston a long time. Much of the senator's family, on the other hand, lived and died in and around Nicholas County long before it became Nicholas County, long before Richwood boomed with oil and coal.

Winslow Creek didn't exist as a township, but southeast of Richwood, she found a tiny tributary of the Cherry River called Winslow Creek and references to the community of Winslow Creek in several hunting forums, in Greenbrier County. Google Earth revealed hints and the occasional curve of what she suspected were unpaved roads under thick tree cover with only a sparse field here and there that must mean livestock and a way to get to them. There was no street view tracking. She'd have to talk to Bowman.

She stretched and got up to make a snack, walking around the camera set up to capture the kitchen, office, hall, living room doorways, also getting the front door and edge of the stairway, where Bowman saw the shadow ascend. Slathering peanut butter on toast, she wondered if Madeleine was related to Dewey at all. She seemed drawn to him and his brother-in-law, but she'd followed Taka, too, and returned to Andrea. Probably as her only chance to communicate after not getting anywhere with Dewey beyond his restless dreams. Scary thought, though, ghosts whispering in people's ears at night. She shivered.

"Are you here now?" she asked out loud, half-hoping Madeleine might show herself in answer, half-hoping she wouldn't. Having an adult ghost in the house creeped her out more than Billie Mae did. Andrea refreshed her tea and carried her toast to the table. The light on the recorder was still burning.

She settled back and munched through half her toast, washed it down with tea and said, "Are you blood related to Dewey Sanderson?" After a moment, she said, "Are you related to him through marriage?"

She finished off her toast before asking, "Was the homestead with the red crossvine owned by Dewey's father's family?" And just for good measure, "Was it owned by his mother's family?"

A rapping directly behind her made her jump up, spinning around to see what was there. No one. From the corner of her eye, she caught her tea sloshing over onto the recorder. She grabbed the teacup in one hand and the recorder in the other and shook the liquid off. By the sink, she turned it off, ripped paper towels from the roll, and dried it. The light still burned.

She thumbed the power button again, a toggle switch, but it was definitely off. Maybe it took a second? The light died. She put her cup in the sink and took the recorder back to the table. The light came back on. "Are you here now?"

Her heart lurched at the rapid knocking on the kitchen doorframe. A cop's knock.

"Andy?"

Nothing.

"One knock for yes. Two for no."

Nothing.

"Are you Andy Detweiler?"

Two knocks.

"Madeleine?"

Two knocks.

Before she could stop herself, "Oliver Fitch?"

Two knocks. Thank God.

"Do I know you?"

Two knocks.

"Do you know Madeleine?"

She gasped. A stinging line traversed her throat. She slapped her hand on top of it and warmth ran down her neck onto her chest, but there was nothing there. "Who are you?"

Rapping thundered from throughout the house. Dropping to her knees, Andrea covered her head.

Silence.

The light dropping through the kitchen window onto the floor brightened like a cloud releasing its hold upon the sun. The air seemed easier to breathe. Cleaner. She lifted her arms, one at a time, but nothing happened. On the table, the light on the recorder was out.

Hands shaking, she turned it back on and rewound it. After a couple of tries she landed on "crossvine." She ran it back some more. The rustlings of her reviewing her genealogy notes. Then her, asking *"Are you here now?"* Her voice moving closer. Eating, drinking. Her questions with no response, then *"Was it owned by his mother's family?"* The furious rapping that made her spill her tea sounded even louder on the recording. A break as the recorder shut off and came back on.

"Are you here now?" The cop's knock.

"Andy?"

"No." The voice was a man's. The word clipped, but clear.

Nothing more until, *"Who are you?"*

"The trapper."

And he laughed as the rapping boomed through the speakers and the recording cut off.

OFF THE ELEVATOR, Taka hesitated, but then walked down the hall to Scott's room. A nurse and two people in blue uniforms were inside. Scott had already been disconnected from all his monitoring and transferred to a gurney. The duffle bag Taka'd brought last night nestled between his lower legs along with a medical box of some sort. One paramedic held an IV bag.

Taka stood to one side of the slider for the time it took them all to agree they were set, sign various papers on each other's clipboards, and get moving. The paramedic at Scott's feet eyed Taka as he came through the door.

Scotty gave him a pained smile. "They gave me something for the ride, but it hasn't kicked in yet."

The paramedics didn't seem inclined to stop, so Taka walked alongside.

"Long bus ride to Raleigh."

"This guy's flying to Charlotte," the medic at his head said.

"Charlotte?"

"Trauma unit," Scott mumbled. He grimaced at the bump into the elevator. "Before the rehab in Raleigh will take me. My mom's meeting me there."

"Will you text me? Let me know you got there okay?"

Scott nodded, his face tightening, lips turning down, and held up his cell phone.

Forcing the words out of his tight throat, Taka said, "Take care."

The doors slid closed.

Taka bowed his head and let himself feel the separation for a few seconds. Then he squashed it down, put on his game face, and went down the hall to find the truth. Mark Compton stood outside with Sheryl and Karl, the Charleston Police Department detectives assigned to the kids missing from Anna Lansing's house. If CPD hadn't already known Dewey was there at Anna's house before she was killed, the state had certainly let them know now.

"Man!" Karl said, holding out his hand and leaning in for a half-hug when Taka took it. "How you doing? Where you working?"

"Nowhere much."

"What you doing here? Never mind"—he patted Compton on the shoulder—"Matt here—"

"Mark," Compton said.

"—Mark told me you were in on finding those kids."

"We just relieved the babysitter."

"Yeah, but probably saved them from sexual depredations. CPD was all wrong firing you."

"I resigned."

"We'll get Dewey Sanderson yet, for these two, and the Lansing case, if he was involved."

Dewey claimed he'd never seen the kids at Anna Lansing's. "Karl. How many uppers have you taken today?"

"None." He pulled a baggie with three different colored pills out of his pocket. "You need something? Take the stress down a level?"

Compton blanched.

Taka took the baggie. "Sure. I'll take the lot. Pay you next week?"

"Sure, man." He rolled his eyes. "Like you're ever gonna pay me for those."

Sliding the pills in his jacket pocket, Taka said, "Just take it down a notch, yeah? You're scaring poor Matt—"

"Mark," Compton said.

"Mark." Taka grinned despite his anger at Karl popping speed already this morning. He was still good at his job, but he wasn't going to last long enough to rank up out of field work and get his twenty years in if he kept using. "Karl's a good detective, Compton. We're just kidding, right, Karl?"

"Course. Except about Dewey. Man's a menace."

"Totally," Taka said. "Sheryl."

"Taka."

Beyond the slider, the curtain in Dewey's room was pulled. "Somebody with him?"

"His lawyer," Sheryl said.

"Saw y'all coming?"

Compton shook his head. "Wanted his lawyer before he'd even give his victim statement about the shooting. Haven't had a chance to ask about the kids yet, or how he's involved." He lifted his chin at Karl and Sheryl. "He doesn't even know these two are here."

"Why are you here?" Taka asked, directing his question to Sheryl.

"That information's related to an active investigation, Taka. Why are you here?"

"The state asked me to stay friendly with Dewey. Pass on what I find out."

Her expression remained neutral. "You planning on doing that?"

"Course he is," Karl said. He slapped Taka on the shoulder. "Once a cop, always a cop."

At least until they lost sight of the line between cop and criminal and plenty did.

Sheryl continued to stare him down. Taka shrugged. "If I can."

Karl rolled his eyes again. "He will."

But it was clear Sheryl understood the lack of commitment in that answer.

Compton side-eyed him, mouth tight.

There was no way they would let him in to talk to Dewey before they got their shot. He stepped between them and slid the door open, calling out, "Knock, knock, housekeeping."

"Hey," Compton barked, and stuck an arm out, but Taka was by him already, yanking the curtain back six inches. He recognized silver fox Ryan Merritt from court, though he'd never met him in person. His client list was somewhat wealthier than the offenders Taka was usually in court to testify against.

"William," Dewey said, and Taka brushed past the curtain. "We were just about to let the wolves in. You here to accept your position as my head of security?"

A sharp woman's voice from the hallway, not Sheryl's.

"No, Dewey, just seeing if you lived through the night," he managed before a protective nurse swept in and clonked the slider shut.

Dewey placed his hand over his heart. "I knew you cared."

Taka couldn't get the next retort off his tongue before the nurse snapped, "This is a critical care unit, gentleman. Mr. Sanderson isn't in need of social calls." She hustled over to check the bandages around Dewey's thigh and placed two fingers briefly under the back of his knee, while scanning the heart monitor by his bed. "You have fifteen minutes, Mr. Sanderson, before I must insist you rest." She felt his bare foot and checked the pressure cuff on his other leg. "Now," she said, meeting Dewey's slightly amused gaze. "Who absolutely needs to be here?"

"Sorry, Taka, I might have to hire her instead. Can you send the cop in?"

"CPD or state?"

Dewey's eyebrows lifted. The nurse brushed back past Taka to the computer station by the door and started tapping at the keyboard.

"Who's handling the shooting?" Merritt said.

"State it is, then."

Merritt's lips pursed as he tilted his head. "And what part does CPD have?"

"I don't know," Taka lied.

"Time's ticking," the nurse said, opening the door.

Taka strode out. "You're up, Compton."

"Watch yourself, Taka," he said, knocking Taka's shoulder with his as he bulled past him.

"Same." Pulling the baggie out, Taka tossed it at Sheryl. She caught it with both hands against her belly. "If you don't take them to Horton, I suggest you flush those."

Karl glared at him. "Not cool, Taka."

Taka rounded on him. "You're a good detective, Karl. You've still got your job. Your benefits, a small pension. Clean your shit up before you get tagged or someone dies. Make sure it isn't your partner here." He pointed a finger at Sheryl. "You don't have to put up with this shit."

She stared back at him, wide-eyed.

What a waste of time his morning had been so far. Taka turned on his heel and left.

9

The light knock on the mud room door jolted Andrea from her Greenbrier County tax deed search. She waited for more, but Karie called out her name instead. She got up and let her in, glad to see Bowman with her.

"We brought brunch," Karie said. "Chicken and waffles?"

"You're going to want to hear this recording," Andrea said. She paused, waiting to see if there was any reaction to that, but the sunlight still poured in and nothing disturbed the Sunday morning peace that had settled in while she searched for any references to trappers in the area of what was now Greenbrier County—plenty, but none that seemed relevant—and the Sanderson property—nada.

"From last night?"

"This morning."

They set their bags down and Bowman set himself to making a pot of coffee. Karie checked the cameras as Andrea pushed her notes and laptop back and rewound the recorder again. She hit play.

Bowman, pot full of water in his hand, spun around at the man's voice replying *"No."*

"Who are you?"

"The trapper."

Andrea pushed stop.

"The trapper?" Karie said.

"That's what I heard."

"Me, too," Bowman said, his tone full of awe. "That's creepy as hell."

"What's creepy as hell?" Taka said from the mud room door.

They all jumped. Karie squeaked.

"Did you just squeak?" Bowman said, and the three of them laughed.

"Run it back," Karie said.

Taka had come all the way in. He stripped his jacket off and dropped it on the back of a chair, then braced his hands on it. The shadows under his eyes made him look exhausted. "What are we listening to?"

"A ghost," Andrea said. She hit play.

"Are you here now?" The cop's knock.

"Andy?"

"No."

"Who are you?"

"The trapper."

This time Andrea let it run.

The trapper laughed as the rapping boomed through the speakers at the last and the recording cut off.

"What was that knocking?" Bowman asked.

"The trapper," Andrea said.

"But what was he knocking on?" Karie said. "That was loud."

"Every door frame in the house."

Taka pulled the chair out and plopped down on it. "I need coffee."

"Play it again," Karie said.

Bowman turned back around, poured the forgotten water into the coffee maker, slapped the lid down, and hit 'brew'.

They listened three more times, Andrea running it back further the third time.

"Was it owned by his mother's family?" followed by the furious original rapping after her first set of questions.

"Enough," Taka said. "What'd y'all bring?"

The tension from the night before remained, but Taka put Bowman to work laying the chicken tenders they'd brought on an oven sheet to warm them, a method which Bowman heartily approved of, and pulled Andrea's ancient waffle maker out. Andrea ran through the very minor, mostly negative findings of her search for Madeleine, Winslow Creek, and her plan to search property deeds.

While she talked, Karie had been swapping out SD cards and checking batteries, but now she said, "Was it owned by his mother's family? The homestead?"

"No," Andrea said absently. "His mother's family wasn't in the area. And none of her family surnames owned property anywhere close."

"What if we just drive out there?" Karie said.

"Where?" Taka said.

"To Winslow Creek," she clarified. "Or as close as we can get?"

"It's like two hours from here," Bowman said, propped up against the counter near the oven. "I don't know how far you'd get just knocking on doors. It's more like a location than a town."

"Or even a township," Andrea said. "It's unincorporated."

"But there's definitely a pocket of civilization strung out between a couple of historic hunting camps, maybe three miles apart?" Bowman said. "There's a Winslow Creek general store and a restaurant or two. A bakery. A small meat processor. A church."

"If there's a church, it might as well be a town." Taka opened the waffle iron ahead of the "done" beep to reveal a perfectly cooked waffle. "You hear of a place called Copper Ridge?"

"No."

Taka forked the waffle out onto a plate. "Where'd you go, when you went through Winslow Creek?" He picked up Andrea's large measuring cup and poured more batter into the iron in a spiral from inside to out.

Bowman covered the first waffle with a warmed plate. Andrea made a mental note to remember that trick. "Someplace even smaller. Stone's Hollow. It was a dead end."

Although he'd become a fixture at the occasional dinner gathering and they spoke easily, he had never brought his sister up after that first meeting, never asked Andrea if she had more info or could get more. She'd asked Karie once if she'd referred him to Miss Ava, the medium who helped her with Aaron. She said she'd offered to put him in touch, but he declined. Andrea realized now that they had never physically touched again since that day she'd met him. If Madeleine was connected to Dewey, would she get anything more about her if she touched Dewey?

"I need to collect a story out at Strange Creek," Karie said. "If we plan to go to Winslow Creek after that, I can fold it into that project. We can stay overnight. Camp, or get an Airbnb or something."

Andrea smiled. "Bobby Waltham would say camp."

Karie laughed. "Yes, he would, but it's pretty cold. I don't know how much gear I can gather."

"I still need to talk to Dewey," Taka said. "Andrea and I can figure out some way to see if he knows anything about Winslow Creek or where the homestead is. And if he's ever heard of a Madeleine in his family. Then y'all can make a plan."

They settled in then, Taka and Bowman working to get breakfast on the table while Karie sorted and put digital files on flash drives and reset the SD cards and cameras. Andrea set the table around Karie.

"You heard from Jimmy?" Taka asked, handing off the waffles to her.

"He texted that he'd call tonight. I can't imagine his day today. Andy's brother is coming in from Virginia. Did you hear anymore from Scott?"

"Headed to a Charlotte trauma unit before Raleigh rehab."

Andrea slid a quick glance at Bowman, but he turned away to grab the coffee pot.

***

TAKA FINISHED WIPING off the counter while Andrea put soap in the dishwasher and turned it on. She turned and leaned against the counter, her arms crossed.

"You didn't eat much," she said.

"Saw Karl and Sheryl at the hospital," he said, skipping over his breakfast with Jimmy. He flipped the damp dishtowel over his shoulder and mirrored her position. "Karl was so high. I hope Sheryl busts him."

"Were they there about the kids from Anna Lansing's?"

"They wouldn't tell me. Maybe they're working Harper and Bella, too. See what Dewey's role was if he had one."

"I'm really curious if he'll know the name Madeleine."

Taka tilted his head. "I'm really curious if he'll remember mentioning the homestead at all. He never talks about his childhood."

"When do you want to go?"

"Depends on how he's doing. What are your plans?"

"Shower and research."

"Madeleine gone?"

"She'll probably show up as soon as I get in the shower. What are you going to do?"

"Clean my guns." In case I need to shoot someone for lying about Scott.

But Andrea always knew what he was thinking. "You can't shoot Jimmy."

"I can dream about it, though."

10

While Andrea showered and Taka cleaned all the guns he carried in his Yukon, plus hers, Dewey had been stepped down to general care. Though he still had protection on his door and a private room, being on a different floor made visiting easier. "You brought back up, I see," he said to Taka, while looking at Andrea.

He didn't know the half of it. Out on I-64, Madeleine's sudden appearance in the backseat had scared Andrea silly. And when Andrea swerved into the next lane, scared Taka. She wandered past Andrea to Dewey's bedside and stood near the head of his bed, dress and red hair fluttering against that strong spectral breeze she carried with her.

"Them bones don't lie," she said.

Andrea tuned her out as she rambled on.

Taka squared himself up. "You need me as head of security. I need answers."

"Squirrelly. I give you answers, you walk. I'll trade you a month's work for every answer."

Andrea held up her hand.

Dewey grinned. "Yes?"

"You can't use routine questions against him. Like while he negotiates this deal with you."

"I can't get a month for answering 'yes' to his, 'are you being serious'?"

"No," Andrea said.

Taka rolled his eyes and said, "I'd never doubt your seriousness when it comes to getting what you want."

"Them dark haired boys get what they want," Madeleine said, and Andrea could swear the ghost was looking right at her.

Dewey's hand was lying on his chest. He tapped his fingers twice against his heart. "I'm touched, William, you do know me."

"Eight hours for every answer. I say when we're done with that part of the 'Dewey Wants' show."

"A week per answer. Full pay, three times your CPD salary. Benefits if you commit for at least six months after serving your time."

"No."

"The answers are very good. You want them or not?"

"There's other ways to get answers, Taka," Andrea said. She wasn't sure exactly what he wanted to ask, but Jimmy would eventually sort the question of Dewey's involvement with Andy Detweiler and the kids or Andy would show up and she'd shake off her heebies and try to connect with him like she had with Aaron. Just the thought snaked a slow roll of cold down her spine and she could feel the slap of the grass against her open palms from her brief brush through Madeleine, who had fallen into crooning something that sounded like a hymn as she ran the wispy trails of her fingers over Dewey's head.

"Why'd you tell Commander Bowman that Scott's BCI?"

That was not the question she'd been expecting Taka to ask. Dewey relaxed, settling deeper into the pillows propping him up with a smug smile. Madeleine relaxed, too, falling silent as she petted Dewey's hair. "Because it suited my purposes."

"You told him I knew so he'd feel comfortable sharing."

Dewey shrugged. "Is that a question?"

"What's his real—"

"Wait!" Andrea shouted. Luckily, Taka stopped talking. "Who is 'he'?"

Taka mulled over her interruption and then nodded, the corners of his lips lifting slightly. "Thank you. What's Scott Fergusson's real name?"

Oh. She hadn't thought about that, so caught up in her own little mystery. He seemed like such a Scott, but it wouldn't be his real name, of course.

Dewey sighed. "That I couldn't ascertain."

Taka's gaze fell to the tile floor while he thought. Then, "Jimmy says Scott doesn't work for BCI, that you're just winding me up."

Dewey rolled his hand forward in the air. "Question?"

Taka considered for a moment. "Do you have proof he works for BCI?"

"No." Dewey grinned.

"Detweiler confirmed he does. Did."

Dewey waited.

"Did Detweiler confirm?"

"No, Detweiler did not. I didn't ask him. And Scott still is," Dewey said. "Different state, probably North Carolina, possibly Georgia."

"I checked his cover."

"I sent Trevor to Clarksburg High. Hoyle graduated eleventh in his class. Fergusson's a ghost." He looked over at Andrea. "I get two weeks for those freebies?"

"One."

Taka shot her a glare. Madeleine started in on the ghost that spent its time a'sanging, digging for ginseng.

"Sorry," she said, but she wasn't. To Dewey, she said, "You could've asked Detweiler that question?"

Looking like the Cheshire Cat, he agreed. "Anytime. But I didn't want him to have to choose between loyalty to BCI or to me. We had a close working relationship."

"The kids?"

Dewey wagged his finger at her and then pointed at Taka.

Crossing his arms across his chest, Taka settled into a wide legged stance. "The kids?"

Dewey pulled his fingers back in a gimme more gesture.

"Did Detweiler or Stacy Owens ask for your help?"

Nodding with his mouth turned down like he was impressed, Dewey said, "Stacy Owens."

"Did you ask Detweiler to help?"

"I did. We had an agreement."

"Why help her?"

"Why not help her?"

"So, what, you're a secret do-gooder now? What were you supposed to get for helping her?"

What would he get out of helping her? The kids? A lien on some future service? Why would Detweiler put his career on the line, heck, seeing his own kids if he got caught, to help Dewey what, traffic women and kids from one bad situation to another?

"That's two questions."

Detweiler walked into the room out of thin air. He didn't seem to notice Madeleine.

"Did you take those kids from—" Andrea blurted but stopped herself.

Taka didn't hesitate. "Anna Lansing's?"

Detweiler shook his head.

"I did not," Dewey confirmed.

Taka scrummed deep in his throat.

"But you helped them," Andrea said.

Detweiler nodded.

So who actually took the kids from the house?

"Is that a question?"

Taka's voice hardened although he didn't shift his resigned stance. "Did you help disappear those kids, Dewey?"

"Yes, William, I did."

"Are they safe from—" He thought for a second. Andrea noticed Dewey's expression sharpen as he watched him form his question. "Are they in better hands than the Conlons' and living lives safe from harm that'll lead to productive, independent adulthood?"

"Why, yes, William, they are."

Detweiler agreed.

"What's in it for you?" Taka asked again.

Dewey sighed.

"No," Andrea said. "What was in it for Detweiler?"

"Giving kids a better life than he had."

So she needed to research Andy's personal life, specifically his childhood. She almost asked how him old he was but caught the question on her tongue. Did Detweiler go to Dewey about the kids, or the other way around?

Taka had been lost in thought but drew her attention when he lifted his head again. "Detweiler didn't know those kids were at Anna Lansing's, until you did. What did you know about him that made you think you could recruit him?"

"His father killed his mother in front of him, then died in prison. Trooper Detweiler came of age while still in the foster system."

The Conlons scooped kids up when their lives went wrong, before they entered into the complexities of the foster system. But when found by CPD or BCI or the FBI, the ones without family would end up with either good foster families or bad ones.

Andrea glanced over at Detweiler.

He nodded.

Dewey truly took knowledge is power to heart. If he knew so much about Detweiler before he approached him, how much did he know about Jimmy? Or her? Did he already know about her ghost issue?

Considering Dewey, she said, "Now I have lots of questions."

In the corner of her eye, Detweiler blipped out.

"Me, too," Taka rumbled. "But I'm done."

Madeleine said, "Tucker says he's done a'shuckin', but shuckin' ain't never done . . ."

"Good," Dewey said. "Because I'm done giving answers. I count thirteen weeks, but I'll make it three months from today. Get Chet to bring you up to speed and then tell him I'm giving him a month's paid leave."

"Can I ask a completely random question"—she waved her hand in a circle between them—"not related to all this?"

"Maybe," Dewey said.

"Your brother-in-law mentioned you were rambling on about your grandfather's homestead. Out near Richwood."

Dewey hesitated, something she'd rarely seen him do. Usually, he took a calculated pause. "And your question?"

"Homesteads are an interest of mine, the ones established before West Virginia became a state that are still owned within the original family. I'm mapping them."

"I don't own it."

"But someone in the family does?"

Again, he hesitated, but he didn't shut her down. "It's a sore subject."

"May I ask where it's located?"

"Somewhere near Richwood. It was already falling in on itself twenty years ago."

"He said you mentioned the crossvine on the porch there."

"Did I?"

Madeleine nodded and Taka rolled his eyes. "The crossvine a'grows thick down there," Madeleine said as Taka said, "Yeah."

"And talked about someone named Madeleine."

He smiled, shaking his head. "Must've been quite the dream."

"Would your sister or mom know where it was?"

"My sister," Madeleine sighed and wafted away.

"No. They're not about tramping around in the woods." He cast a long look at Taka. "Your Taka is the best woodsman I've tramped around with. Sometimes I miss those days."

"There will be no tramping around the next three months, I can guarantee you that," Taka said.

Dewey's sharp gaze slid to Andrea and then back to Taka. "I think we all know that, William." He brushed the air with both hands. "Shoo. Y'all are bothering me. Answer your phone when I call."

Taka faked a yawn. "Or what, you'll fire me?"

"William Taka does nothing halfway, not after he's committed." Again, a glance at Andrea and back. "Except the one thing. Now go, get out."

Andrea opened her mouth to say something, she didn't know what, but Dewey folded his hands over his belly and shut his eyes. Taka was already halfway out of the room. She caught up to him when he turned on his heel in the hallway to address the trooper on the door. "I'm

Dewey's new Sanderson Security chief. He's requested you contact me prior to any changes in the situation here. That means if any law enforcement comes knocking, any visitor requests entry, protection is taken off his door—"

"I call you, sir. Got it."

"You call me before anyone but authorized medical personnel enters his room. You do not go in and ask him. You call me."

"Yes, sir."

They exchanged numbers through a text and Taka ushered her on down the hall with a hand at her back. After the doors closed on the otherwise empty elevator, he said, "That didn't go like I thought it would."

"Do you think Scott was really with BCI?"

"I don't know."

"Jimmy would have to know right?"

"He says Scott's not with them."

"Dewey's lying?"

Taka blew his breath out. "No. He's never lied to me. He avoids or omits or complicates, but he's not an outright liar."

The doors re-opened on the same floor. Andrea punched the 'close doors' button with a knuckle and Taka tapped the Ground floor button three times, like that would speed their exit up. The elevator lurched into motion.

"I feel like I've done nothing but lie the last few months," Andrea said. "Did you hear me spouting off in there about homestead mapping? Did you ask Scott straight up?"

Taka leaned back against the side wall, hands in his jacket pockets. "At the start of all this, I questioned his 'copness'. I don't know any more what's true and what's a lie."

"And you asked Jimmy."

"I did. I still don't know. I mean, I get it. If he's undercover, they have to protect him. But I met him at Dewey's. Starting up with me? Not just leaning into a friendship for information, but—" He shook his head, jerked his hand out to press on the outside corners of his eyes.

"That part's real," Andrea said.

"And Jimmy?"

"Maybe that's why we stalled."

"Yeah."

"He never pushed for more, but maybe if you'd shut the door on the possibility of us, I'd have been more attracted to him."

He shoved his hand back in his pocket and met her gaze. "I tried."

"I know."

"And I don't regret kicking it wide open when closing it didn't work."

"But . . ."

The elevator clunked and the doors slid open.

A young woman with a girl at her side and a toddler in a stroller waited for them to step out. Her gaze bounced between them. "Why don't you just, y'know, I'll wait for the next one."

"No, we're—"

"I insist," she said. "I've been there. You guys finish"—she circled her finger at them—"whatever this is."

The doors slid closed. After a second, Andrea reached out and knuckled the button for the top floor. When the elevator ground into action, she said, "But?"

"There is no 'but'. I don't regret it. I love him in a different way. I never trusted him, not fully, but I still—" He tilted his head back, squeezed his eyes shut. "God, he gets me. He gets us, you and me." He looked back at her, into her. "He gets how much I love you. He gets how much that scares me. But you? You don't because you're fearless. How many times have you offered me everything and how many times have I turned you down? I'm a coward, Andrea." He drew a tight breath and huffed it out, gaze darting around the box trapping them in this moment. "Pure and simple."

Andrea couldn't move. "Just don't shut that door right now."

He laughed and rubbed his face and then linked his fingers on top of his head. "We're a pair. I'm too afraid to love you the way you deserve, and you love me so much you'll let me get away with it."

Her brain unfroze and she blurted, "If you love something, let it go. If it comes back to you, it was yours all along, if it doesn't, it never was."

"Well, I've returned several times now, so are you going to keep me this time?"

"Are you going to let me?"

The elevator slowed and clunked. Taka dropped his hands.

"Let's—can we put this on hold for now?" She grabbed one of his hands and squeezed it as the doors opened. "This whole afternoon has been—"

"Unexpected?"

"I just need to process." She pivoted to lean against the wall beside him, shoulder to shoulder.

"I never even got to ask about Bowman. He's another big question mark."

"And how."

A nurse pushing a wheelchair carrying an older man approached and Taka flattened his free hand against the door to hold it. Andrea forced a smile. The hunched-over man peered up at them over the oxygen tube looped over his ears and running under his nose.

"Sir," Taka said.

The man lifted a hand as the nurse swung the chair around to face the closing doors.

They rode back down in silence, Taka's hand warming Andrea's, as she tried to catch and pin her fluttering thoughts down until she could get back to each one later.

11

Later that night, Andrea sipped from her Malbec, contemplating their empty spaghetti plates. "I think that was a new level of excellence."

"Thanks," Taka said.

She'd spent the early evening on her laptop in the living room, hockey on in the background. Taka'd kept mostly to the kitchen, wandering in now and then to check the score or watch a re-play. Using both hands, he slowly spun his wineglass where it sat on the kitchen table.

"So, it seemed like Dewey gave us a lot of information, but it wasn't actually," Andrea ventured.

"Dewey's good at that."

"One, Scott's law enforcement," she said, and started counting out each point on her fingers. "Two, Dewey helps people that need out of bad situations into better ones. Three, Detweiler was working with him. Four, they moved those trafficked kids missing from Anna Lansing's house."

Taka waggled his head. "Do we believe Scotty wasn't aware they did that? Do we believe he didn't know Dewey had recruited Detweiler?"

"Depends on if Dewey isolates his contacts from each other." She took another sip of wine. "He sent Trevor to Clarksburg, so does Chet know Scotty's a cop? About the kids? Heck, does Chet know Bowman?"

"I'll shake Chet down. What did Jimmy say?"

"I left him two messages to call me."

Reaching over, Taka took her plate and stacked it on his. "I think Dewey knows more about the homestead than he's willing to admit. How important do you think it is that we get more info from him?"

"It's important in regards to getting rid of Madeleine, but I'm sure I can figure that out without Dewey."

"You mean without telling Dewey there's a ghost around who's sweet on him."

"Exactly."

He carried the dishes to the sink but before he started the water, his phone vibrated on the counter. He scooped it up. "Scott."

"Can you just straight up ask him again?"

Taka stared at the phone.

"Taka?"

"I don't think I'd believe anything he told me right now."

"So why ask him anything?"

He nodded. "Exactly."

Did she trust Jimmy to give her a straight answer now? "You think Dewey's telling you the truth."

Still looking at his phone, he said, "I do."

"Do you trust him?"

He laughed and slapped the phone down. "No. Dewey only serves himself, for his own purposes. If he's helping anyone, it'll be because of something he wants. Or needs."

"Appreciation? Gratefulness? The knowledge he's creating a safer place for someone who needs it?"

Taka flipped on the water and started in on the dishes. "Before therapy, I'd have said no, Dewey would be after more. A favor owed, avoiding consequences of his actions, paying off someone who could damage his reputation, maybe his business, but now? Maybe. If, and that's a big if, he's trying to, in his roundabout way help people live a better life, it's satisfying some psychological need he has."

"Redemption?"

"I've never heard Dewey express regret, so maybe more like spite."

"Or revenge."

He half-turned, hands soapy. "How would helping kids or women and kids disappear like he disappears people inconvenient to him be revenge? What for?"

"Jimmy said that, when you were kidnapped. That Dewey sends people away. That they're unwilling to talk."

"That's revenge."

"So how's spite different than revenge?"

"It's mean. Petty. Revenge is calculated. It's purposeful."

She tilted her head to one side and then the other, considering. "Which sounds more like Dewey?"

He rinsed the sauce pot and put it aside. "Dewey had an intact family and a privileged childhood. He hated his dad, but it wasn't because of abuse. He recruited Andy, who was abused, to help him, so he had to have a reason, but no one would be hurt by him taking those kids except for any family who might still be looking for them."

"So not spite or revenge," Andrea agreed. "Misguided altruism?"

"Ego? Thinking only he could provide a better life for them?"

"Maybe he asked them?"

"Asked who?"

"The kids?"

"Asked them what?"

"About their families. Maybe that's who they're with? If they had any. If they wanted to go to them."

He rinsed the glass in his hand, shut off the water, and put it in the washer before turning around. "Seriously, Andrea? Where are you going with this?"

She looked at her laptop, the open transcript Karie had sent her of the exchange between her and the trapper. The knocking had started after she asked if Dewey's mom's family owned the homestead. But his mother's family had never been anywhere near Richwood or Winslow's Creek. "I don't know. Some almost-thought I can't think right now."

"It doesn't matter anyway. We have nothing to take to CPD, or even Jimmy. Dewey might tell me, us, the truth, but he's definitely not going to talk to them. I need to keep Dewey safe from whoever took a shot at him—"

"And I need to sort Madeleine. Are you staying?"

He shook his head. "I'm meeting Chet at Dewey's warehouse on Kirkby. I'll just go home from there."

"I'll let you know what Jimmy says when he calls. Do you want me to ask about Scott?"

"No."

"Do you want me to keep our conversation with Dewey between us?"

"No. I'm paying for the information with my agreement to work for Dewey. And if he commits criminal acts, I'll report him. Share away."

He gave her a quick hug, gathered his things, and left.

Andrea eyed the kitchen, wondering if Madeleine was with her. If the trapper was lurking. She'd gotten relatively used to seeing ghosts, but the thought that they might be around when she wasn't seeing them creeped her right out. Stop it, she chastised herself. It was no different than before Billie Mae, when she was as unaware as most people of the ghosts among them.

"If anyone's here, knock twice," she said out loud.

Nothing.

Not as reassuring as she had thought.

She closed her email and went to work finding out what she could about Landon "Andy" Rutherford Detweiler. He maintained a low profile. She discovered a couple of awards, the announcement of his engagement to Mia, some baseball stats from his sophomore year of high school, and the media coverage of his mother's murder. No social media account.

She searched for the two historic hunting camps along Winslow's Creek, or "meat camps" as Bowman called them. Once she had their locations, she pulled up a map and postal code info to get addresses in the area. Plugging the addresses into the tax deed records for Greenbrier County gave her several properties bearing the surname Sanderson. Four looked rough on Google Earth, with only hints of current structures. The others were houses that looked to be occupied the last time Google shot them, but a couple had large acreage that might conceal a tumbled down house.

She narrowed down the list to five addresses based on the fact they were all estates being paid by Sanderson heirs of various names. It was a start. Next would be a state and county land records search and then tapping a favor from a Waltham-Young related realtor, but if Dewey's ancestors were anything like him, their property ownership might have been layered in business names and false fronts.

She sighed and tapped her cell phone where it sat on the kitchen table.

Past midnight.

No missed texts.

No call from Jimmy.

———

AT A QUARTER past noon on Monday, Andrea came back from the research room with her hands full and found the screen of her cell phone, which she'd left behind, filled with texts from Taka.

You take lunch?

Should I bring lunch?

Dewey's being discharged early tomorrow. Don't know how my days will go then.

Helllllooo

Panera's?

I'm getting Panera's anyway.

Are you in a meeting?

In the lot.

Coming up.

Her landline rang.

"Your dark-haired boy is here," Marji said.

What was it Madeleine said? *Them dark-haired boys get what they want.* She almost told Marji not to let him up, but said, "Thanks, Marji," instead.

She sat down and rearranged her finds into discrete stacks for a small municipal project due at the end of the month.

"Hey," Taka mumbled from the door. He held up the Panera's bag and a single bottle of cream soda.

"Yes, please," she said. "I left my phone on my desk, sorry."

He plopped down in the chair she'd left in the back corner for him. "S'okay, I'm interrupting your day."

She spun her chair around to face him. "Dewey's getting out?"

"As long as he walks twice today without bleeding. And Ronnie Horton called right before the state cops pulled his protection. Pending ballistics, the husband of the woman who was with Detweiler was the shooter."

Andrea straightened up. "Oh. That seems like an obvious possibility now that you've said it. Are they leaving him alone about the kids?"

"No." He held the bag still on his lap, making no move to open it. "Detweiler's fingerprint was found at Anna Lansing's house. In the kids' bedroom and on the back door frame. BCI also has Dewey at the house that night on a surveillance report. With the babysitter also connecting them, there's a whole lotta agencies who are taking an interest."

So Detweiler *was* there when the kids were moved. "I know it's irrelevant at this point, but I don't get when they moved the kids. Dewey talked to Anna Lansing before Linda Conlon killed her. How'd they get the kids before she did?"

"Anna knew she was in trouble. She asked Dewey to get them out of the life."

"And Detweiler's fingerprint is on the back door, so Detweiler took them out the back while Dewey was still there?"

"The surveillance report was through an undercover out front who never saw the kids."

Damn. Almost certainly that meant Scott really was undercover then. And that Detweiler knew he was there. "I'm sorry, Taka."

"You talk to Jimmy?"

"No. He texted that he couldn't talk, and he'd call when he could." Taking in his defeated posture, she frowned at him "I take it you told Horton that Dewey moved the kids?"

"No."

"What else is wrong, besides Scott?"

"Chet gave me names and locations."

Everything came to a brief standstill. She could hear the faint tick of the wall clock hanging in the hall. She closed her mouth.

"He made me memorize the list, then burn it."

"So there's no concrete evidence."

"Digital or paper."

"But they have Dewey at the house, and you'd be considered an expert witness. Way more believable than, say, a cellmate confession, and prosecutors use them all the time, right?"

He dug into the bag and handed her napkins and her wrapped sandwich.

She took it. His hands were cold. "Did Chet say something else?"

He took his own sandwich out. "He asked me to check on the kids myself, before I spill. He asked me to consider the fact that Detweiler was willing to risk everything instead of sending the state in."

They unwrapped matching turkey and tomato on sourdough sandwiches. "I approve," Andrea said. "Keeping to the basics. Do you think Dewey knows Chet told you?"

"Chet wouldn't have told me unless Dewey asked him to."

They ate, passing the single bottle of cream soda he'd bought between them.

A shadow fell across the light from the door.

"Cozy," Karie said. "Tomorrow for Winslow Creek?"

Andrea swung her chair around to her desk and checked her calendar. "I can do that."

"You coming with, Taka?"

"Taka," Andrea said since Taka was still chewing, "is going to be holding off the cops at Dewey's tomorrow."

"Or throwing him to the wolves," he rumbled.

TAKA WROTE the list down from memory. A shell company shuttled money to the last company on the list, Brighter Day, which Chet only knew as the point of contact if the families needed help with the kids. Andrea gave him her personal laptop and space at her work counter while she worked at her desk, sorting paperwork, and tapping away on her desktop keyboard.

He liked being here with her in her office. The conversation and security walkthrough with Chet had lasted til midnight, then he'd turned Chet loose for the next month and gone home to the emptiness of his apartment. It was no emptier than when Scott stayed at his own place, but it felt like it been scraped clean and filled with echoes.

This morning, he'd opened up the four main properties—Dewey's house, the Coliseum, and the two warehouses located in Charleston— with Chet's keys and security codes and double-checked every security system. Then he'd gone through the personals on each employee and called Dewey's personal assistant and each of his three managers to update them and make sure they were on top of the week and would update each employee under them personally.

He tapped in "Brighter Day, adoptions" and found references to the company as a network of resources for guardians needing legal guidance. The website was simply a landing page with a photo of a kid running down a hill and contact information. Using only free internet White Pages and social media links through two different search engines, he easily located contact info for five of the names Chet had given him.

He went out into the hall so he wouldn't disturb Andrea and left a message on his first two calls, to numbers in Ohio and New York. Someone answered at the third number, in Morganton, West Virginia. "I'm William Ta—" At the last second, he thought better of using his last name. "—Tallson, Brighter Day's head of security. I'm calling to follow up with Jessica Polk regarding Arial Summit's welfare?"

"Arial's doing great. Loves her school. We got her a dog."

"How are you handling her legal and medical needs?"

"Uh, I'm not sure what you mean? You said you're with Brighter Day, right?"

"Yes."

"So, you know about the lawyer, right?"

"Yes," Taka said, thinking fast. "Of course, I meant how are you all handling the process? I know it takes time."

"Oh, sure, Ms. Gallagher is real nice. She's explained everything, how we have to wait six months to establish third-party guardianship, but we got Ariel's birth certificate, so that helps, and she's on our health insurance now. She's seeing my friend, who's a therapist, too. What that poor child went through, man, oh, man."

"Has she mentioned her family?"

"No, except about her mom. We did a sort of memorial service for her, since we don't know where she's buried, or if she was, since that awful friend of hers sent Ariel away right after she watched her mom die. Drugs are a scourge on our society, I tell you. She don't have nobody else, she says. She's so much happier than when she arrived, I can tell you that much! And we love her, she's just the prettiest little thing ever."

"I'm glad it's going well. Contact Ms. Gallagher if anything changes."

"Got her number in speed dial."

"Awesome. Thanks for talking to me."

"Thank you! Bye now."

Taka thumbed his phone closed and stood looking out at the meditation garden. School, therapist, dog. His mind whirled without latching onto anything. Third-party guardianship. He wandered back into Andrea's office and looked that up. Over time, they could claim the kid by showing that they were responsible for her care and the cost of that care without the little girl ever going into the foster system. Basically, they'd taken over the custodial care of an abandoned child and formed a bond with her.

He leaned back in his chair. His aunt had informally adopted two of his cousins' friends when they had de facto moved into the house and never left. She never had a formal arrangement with their families, who were mostly absent, in prison, or gone away elsewhere. She signed permission slips and took them to doctor appointments. Was this the same thing? Kinda?

"Okay," Andrea said, swinging her chair around. "What's got steam rolling off your brain?"

"Third-party guardianship."

"Is that how they're doing it?"

"Keeps them out of the foster system. I don't know how he found the families."

"He's Dewey."

"True. I'm trying to decide if I need to know all the details."

"If you hand the info over to CPD, they can find out the details. Regardless of good intentions, Dewey and Detweiler basically kidnapped those kids."

"Or rescued them."

"Last night you said he kept them from their families, who might be looking for them. Detweiler should have taken them straight to BCI or CPD."

Maybe. Taka had no experience with the foster system. Detweiler obviously had strong feelings about it.

"You're scrumming," Andrea said. "Does that mean you're going to defend him?"

He pushed back up to his feet. "I'm going to make a few more calls, because last night *you* said maybe they asked the kids about their families."

"How'd you find out? About the fingerprint? That seems like it'd be privileged information."

"I may have overheard a thing or two."

"And have a friend or two. You know what you're going to end up being, right?"

"What?"

"A private investigator."

"I hate private investigators. I'm not going to be one."

"You say that now . . ."

"And mean it." Never. Security was work he could get behind. Cheating spouses and missing persons weren't for him.

12

Jimmy signed off on the statement he'd given Pro Standards. The assigned investigator, a short, slight, weasel of a woman picked it up and slid it into the top folder of the stack on the table in front of her. "Do you know when they'll clear Trooper Detweiler's house? His wife wants to collect some of his daughters' belongings?"

The woman lifted the stack with both hands and tapped it to even out the folders. "As we told her, we'll let her know when she can have access."

He sighed.

She slid the stack into her leather laptop bag on the table before she looked at him again. "Has Captain Maddox explained the limitations being imposed on your activities until our investigation has been completed?"

No field work. The Lieutenant from District Three would be taking lead on the Sanderson investigation for the foreseeable future. Jimmy was to collect his assignments from and make his reports directly to him. His other cases were being farmed out as well. He'd spent the last two days bringing everyone up to speed. "Yes, ma'am."

Pulling her closed laptop closer and lifting the top, she gave him a tight-lipped smile. "You're dismissed."

Hands in his pockets and head down, Jimmy made his way back to the Sanderson team's room. District Three's Lieutenant Chapman noticed him in the doorway first. "Buck up, Hoyle. Pro Standards won't find anything on you, right?"

"No."

"And they're leaving you with us because you know more than anyone in the state about Dewey Sanderson, so it's not all down the drain."

Accurate, but not much of a comfort since his co-lead had crossed the line, then died. He shrugged.

"You're to help Nina with whatever she needs and keep communicating with former Detective William Taka. Encourage Dewey's new security head to feed us insider info as he finds it or maybe"—he faked a punch to Jimmy's shoulder across the three feet of space between them—"just hang out at your girlfriend's and continue to make friendly chit-chat with her bestie."

Now didn't seem to be the time to correct Chapman that his relationship with Andrea was no longer romantic-leaning and possibly not even a friendship after Taka's hostile approach at the diner. Especially if Scott backtracked on his commitment to his job and the shove he'd given Taka towards Dewey.

"Get us what you can," Chapman said and spun away, striding over to Bill, who shot Jimmy a bleak expression and then huddled up with Chapman in front of his outsized computer screen.

Nina waved him over. She held out a folder. "Background on Stacy and Gavin Owens. Compton asked me to ask you to interview the kids since they know you."

"I'm not supposed to be in the field."

"I cleared it with Chapman. He said anything I needed help with, and I need help on this. There'll be a social worker at the aunt's house at nine-thirty tomorrow morning to monitor your conversation."

"Yeah, okay. Can you print me some photos to take?'

"Just make me a list, Boss."

"Better whisper when you say that," Jimmy chided her.

She laughed. Chapman, who couldn't have missed the conversation, looked up and gave him a two-finger salute.

Jimmy went back down the hall and into the bullpen, which was quiet although most of its desks were occupied. Before he reached his desk, Compton rolled his chair over and placed a thin sheaf of folders on Jimmy's blotter. He rolled away before Jimmy arrived, turning his back on him as he went back to his computer.

Jimmy rifled through the folders. Interviews. With Mia, Dewey, the babysitter, and the kids' aunt. Huh.

Compton stole a glance over his shoulder and Jimmy nodded at him.

TAKA SLID BACK inside Andrea's office from his hall pacing as he spoke quietly into his phone. "Thank you. Call your lawyer if you need anything. He can get in touch with us." He stood still for a second, one hand in his jeans pocket, other holding his phone against his chest. "You were right."

She looked up from packing her files into her backpack. "About?"

"I managed to get four more families on the phone. Two of them are relatives of the kids. One was a close family friend. I couldn't find a way to ask the fourth."

"So they consulted the kids."

"Looks like."

"But—"

"But it still feels like something I should report to CPD."

"Are Sheryl and . . ." Andrea snapped her fingers three times.

"Karl," Taka supplied.

She pointed at him. "Karl still—"

"Yeah. But without names—"

"They're at a dead end."

"They came to talk to Dewey yesterday."

"So, still at a dead end."

"They'd have to interview the kids to find out they were at Anna Lansing's."

Taka nodded. "It sounds like the families got different stories from Brighter Day."

"Stories they believe to be true."

"Stories based in truth, so it'd be hard to connect the kids to Anna Lansing."

"Pretty easy to tell a traumatized kid they were in a different town than they thought or the person they were with had a different name than they were told."

Gaze roaming the various photos, notes, bills, and mementos on Andrea's corkboard wall, Taka said, "Any kid, really. I'm sure CPD has the kids' prints from all over the house."

"Good point. It's not like you have to decide today. The kids don't seem to be in distress, right?"

Taka shrugged. "I don't know. Only talked to one. But he seemed . . . settled."

"Done with the laptop? Louie's?"

He helped her shut down and pack up.

They wandered down the hall and the central staircase, various colleagues from random offices joining their exit. Fairy lights twinkled across the high ceiling of the lobby. The setting sun threw red light across every surface, mottling all the art on display in weird and breathtaking ways. Taka stopped on the middle-landing and soaked in the light. "This place really is something else," he muttered as Andrea's co-workers flowed around them.

Andrea loved working here. "It really is."

Karie halted on Taka's other side.

"Louie's?" he said.

"I'm meeting Bowman."

"Bowman's fine," Taka said. "Dewey orchestrated that."

"Dewey's a dick," Karie said.

"Bet you can't say that ten times. Wait, I've said it a million times already."

Karie held out her fist and Taka bumped it, opening his fingers and he fisted his other hand and Andrea bumped it.

"You're blocking traffic," Randy complained, running into them on purpose. "What are you looking at?"

"The light," Andrea said.

Randy threw both his arms open wide. "Magnificent!" he yelled, the high ceiling carrying his voice.

Laughter, a shouted, "Ooo-rah," and a couple of "Hallelujahs" filled the space.

———

At Louie's, Andrea and Taka went to the bar to greet Louie and request a table. A few minutes later, they met Daisy at the hostess stand. Jimmy came through the door, swinging his head as he looked for them. Andrea raised her hand. Daisy grabbed another menu and took them into the back, to a six-top.

As Daisy distributed the menus around the table, Andrea gave Jimmy a hard hug. His arms wrapped right around her, and he held on tight for a long moment. She could practically feel his emotional exhaustion.

"Who's coming?" Jimmy asked, letting go of her, and adding, towards Taka, "We okay?"

"Karie and Bowman," Andrea said as Taka said, "Yeah."

Andrea and Taka pulled chairs out against the wall.

Jimmy sat down opposite them. "Scott make it to Charlotte okay?"

"Yeah."

It took Andrea a second to read Taka's tone as the same as a teenager saying, "duh."

Jimmy ignored it. "You took the job with Dewey?"

"Three months."

Jimmy nodded.

Playing with his menu, Taka said, "Dewey sent Trevor to Clarksburg."

"That's where Scotty and I met. High school."

"Scotty's a ghost there."

Jimmy shrugged. "He graduated same as I did." He rubbed his fingertips across a wrinkle in the tablecloth. "Well, not same as. You might say Scotty fell to the lower end of the scale in high school. We weren't the best of friends."

"Stoners still have records."

"I don't know what to tell you, Taka. Shit happens, even to high school records."

"Your parents live here, now," Andrea said. Karie waved from the doorway. Andrea waved back.

"The farm, which y'all have yet to come see, was my papaw's," Jimmy said, turning to see Karie and Bowman as they threaded their way to their back corner. "They moved back while I was in college. Hey."

"Hey," Karie said, pulling the chair out beside him.

Bowman stuck his hand out and Jimmy shook it. "So sorry, dude, losing a partner's hard."

"Thanks, Luke."

Bowman sat down on Karie's other side, his glance taking in Andrea and Taka both.

"Andrea and I are going to Winslow Creek tomorrow," Karie said to Jimmy. "When's the funeral?"

He cleared his throat. "Memorial service Saturday. They wanted to give Mia's family time to fly in. I'm attending the cremation with his brother and Mia later this week after he's released by the ME."

Andrea wondered if an honor guard would be allowed, considering the investigation into Detweiler's involvement with Dewey. But she knew more than she should about all that, so she kept her mouth shut.

On the same page though, Karie said, "Will he get full honors?"

"No, because he died off-duty. But the honor guard will be at the service and there'll be a police escort for his brother and kids if he and Mia want it."

Movement towards their table caught Andrea's eye. Faded and see-through, Detweiler drifted to a stop near Jimmy. Their waiter pivoted from the next table over and brushed through him to ask about their drink orders. By the time he walked away, Detweiler was just a wisp. He turned the suggestion of his head to study the far end of the table. Andrea looked, too.

Louie's resident ghost, Aaron, stood there in bar apron and boots, watching Detweiler. "Sad," he said.

Detweiler strengthened in appearance, his details building up until he was recognizable again.

"Someone here?" Jimmy asked.

Menu in his hands, Bowman's brows raised, and he sat back in his chair as Andrea became the focus of everyone's attention.

"Aaron," she said. "And Detweiler."

"Can you ask him if cremation's okay?" Jimmy blurted.

"He's nodding. He's laying his hand on your shoulder."

Jimmy tried not to look but failed. "Why was he helping her?"

"Dewey asked him to," Taka said.

"Why was he working with Dewey? Why was he in Anna Lansing's house?"

Andrea didn't dare look at Taka, but she laid her hand on top of his. He turned it and closed his fist over her fingers. "He's shaking his head," she said. "He can't tell me that much."

"Can you—"

"He's gone, Jimmy."

"Ninety-two," Aaron said. Andrea looked over at him.

"What?" Jimmy said, following her gaze.

"Ninety-two," Aaron boomed.

Andrea dropped Taka's hand to cover her ears.

"Sorry," he said, looking away from Aaron and then closing his eyes.

Aaron smiled and rolled his eyes and disappeared.

"Oh my god," Andrea said and slapped Taka's shoulder.

His eyes popped open. "I said I was sorry."

"No, Aaron rolled his eyes at me."

Karie laughed. "He did not!"

"He did. Thanks to Taka."

"Did he say something?" Jimmy almost shouted, and they all sobered. "About Andy?"

"I don't know," Andrea said. "He said, 'Ninety-two.' Does that mean anything to you?"

Jimmy's eyes lost their focus as he thought. "No."

"Birth year?" Bowman asked.

"Eighties baby."

"Something will come to you when you least expect it," Karie said.

"At least he's good with the cremation," Andrea added.

Bowman set his menu down. "I'm having the bison steak frites."

"Me, too," Jimmy said.

The blond waiter they all called "Aight", who worked the bar, was headed their way. "Drinks are here," Andrea said.

"Just in time," Taka muttered.

13

Once they were past the city limits the next morning, Karie settled back in the passenger seat of Andrea's FX, a paper map on her knees. "So, Madeleine make any more appearances?"

"At three a.m., I was literally dreaming about crossvine growing across the walls in my bedroom, and I wake up to Madeleine singing some lullaby about a baby being left behind by a mother picking blueberries. I remembered a line about a curlew crying so I looked that up, and it's an old Scots song about fairies stealing untended babies."

"Lots of Scots-Irish in the Appalachians."

"Blaeberries, not blueberries."

"Oh!" Karie turned, tucking one leg up under her so she could face Andrea. "Blaeberries are bilberries. They're like blueberries, but European. Though they do grow wild here. Do you think she's Scots?"

"Her accent is . . . mountain folk?"

"Appalachian? What they used to call 'hillbilly,' in a not nice way, in Philly."

"Different, because she's from I don't know when exactly, but similar."

They rehashed Madeleine's appearance and vocabulary, then moved on to her possible connections to Dewey. Karie mused about how likely it was that siblings that grew to adulthood might still be missed in the genealogy. "Whoever records it can only go on what they're told, right? Maybe great-uncle Johnny doesn't know grandpa had a third sister because she never came up? It's not like many people ask their relatives to list out all their siblings at one time. And for the few dedicated amateur genealogists, if a kid isn't listed on the census, how would they know to go looking for birth records?"

"It's a miracle we found Aaron."

"Being sold made him more findable in the end than Madeleine might be."

"I haven't made much progress yet finding Delphia's grave," Andrea said.

"It's kinda cool having him around though. Translating for Detweiler like he did for Lucy Garcia if Jimmy can figure out what 'ninety-two' means. That's just—it's incredible."

"Could Madeleine be an indentured servant?"

"Does anything she's said seemed related to indentured servitude?"

Andrea shook her head. "Anyway. Are we going to Strange Creek about the legend of William Strange?"

William Strange was a camp cook lost on the first day of a surveying mission in the late 1700s east of Fort Lee, the future site of Charleston. Following his back trail through the thick forest, the surveyors found he'd wandered miles away from the pre-ordained location he was to meet them. At some point, he tied his safely recovered horse and cooking supplies to a bush to locate the spot without baggage. Zigzagging across heavily wooded slopes, they found where he had slept for the night, but several miles on, his trail was lost. Some unknown years later, bones were found at the base of a large beech tree on Turkey Creek. William Strange's name and final message were carved into the tree. Turkey Creek became Strange Creek.

Unfortunately, no one actually knew where the beech tree stood or had ever re-discovered it anywhere along the length of the creek. The town of Strange Creek itself sat on the banks of the Elk River, though near Strange Creek.

"I never heard the story in Philly, but everybody in central West Virginia seems to know about him. His bones and his rifle have been found at least three times, but no one's mentioned any related paranormal phenomenon, so no."

"So, you're collecting a story but not doing an investigation?"

"Correct. It's a residence near the town cemetery and there's been two private investigations already. One was amateur, with no data, just a sensationalized online story about the visit. The other, though, contained some interesting data. The homeowner's eighty-two, living alone. The sort of video collection I'm doing today will help me decide if I should launch a full investigation. And it'll get distributed to anyone working a historical, cultural, generational, or linguistic project who might find elder testimony useful. I'll ask for all sorts of historical data points."

"Background info."

"Correct. Turn right up ahead."

THE HOUSE HAD BEEN BUILT in 1903 and remained in the family. Two ancient elm trees that had yet to succumb to Dutch Elm disease flanked the house. They were gorgeous and set up an expectation of a highly maintained interior that wasn't disappointed. Andrea loved the wide front porch, with its collection of fish baskets and fly-rods hanging neatly on hooks alongside several sizes of waders. The open beams carried into the house. An impeccable great room shone with muted colors and polished wood floors distressed by years of wear.

Karie impressed Andrea with her adroit and thoughtful questions. When their host wandered off to fetch more tea, Andrea leaned over, voice low. "You could give Detective Pete a run for his money in interrogation skills."

"I'm interviewing," Karie protested.

"No, you're interrogating. It's fascinating."

"Wait till you hear the details of the haunting."

Twenty minutes later, Karie finally asked their host to describe the events that triggered Karie's interest. The old homeowner cleared his throat. "It comes from the cemetery. Night or day."

"How do you know?" Karie asked.

"Sometimes it drags in the smell of fresh-turned earth."

Only after an older woman came quietly into the room from the kitchen did Andrea recognize the soft whap of a screen door she'd heard a moment before. The woman nodded to her and settled on the chair nearest the room's entrance. The homeowner glanced over and back to Karie, sitting next to the tripod and video camera she'd set up.

"Not all the time?"

"Sometimes it's the scent of late bloomin' magnolias, wet with early morning dew. There's three or four there in the cemetery, in a row near the river. Sometimes it's just a whiff of rain, or maybe the spring house that usta straddle tha creek branch right across the driveway there. It's been gone . . . twenty year back, more than that now."

The woman leaned Andrea's way, "Twenty-four," she said, low.

Karie asked, "Is it just the scents that make you think it originates from the cemetery?"

"No, but I can't be clearer'n than that. It's like I can feel it comin', like it's pushin' the air along ahead of it as it makes its way here'n to my bedroom."

"How do you know it's in your bedroom?"

"It turns the lights off if'n they're on and on if'n they're off. Like to get my attention."

The old woman snorted.

Andrea couldn't help but give her a good hard look then. She was younger than the man, maybe by twenty years or more. A skunk stripe of dark hair split her braided grey down the middle. She'd twisted the long braid up into a bun. She wore a heavy dress, old-fashioned woolen leggings that looked warmer than Andrea's, and sturdy work boots with a fold of wool sock showing at the ankle. Her mittens were fingerless, her fingers swollen with age and knobby joints. Working hands.

"Then what happens?"

"It fla-foots."

"And what do you mean by that?"

"The dance."

"Could you explain?"

The woman stood and, stepping away from the chair, moved her feet like she might be dancing, shuffle-stepping to one side and then the other, than turning into a little circle, boots tapping.

"It's like cloggin', only close to the ground, light steps. You can flafoot alone, just letting the music bring a rhythm to your feet."

"And what's clogging?"

"It's like tap dancin', only louder and like a line dance with a group of people. It's . . . joyous."

"And flatfooting's not?"

The woman flowed across the floor, her rhythm soft and quicksilver. It sounded to Andrea like the burble of a stream.

"Can be. But it's moodier."

The woman picked up the pace and now her steps were like whitewater, tumbling over rocks and drowned trees. She slowed and circled, an eddy pool, the flash of fish in the deep hollows.

The old man cocked his head. "Do ya hear it?"

Andrea's breath caught and as she drew it in sharp, the smell of rain gusting across a fresh mown field filled her nose. "Oh," she said.

Karie turned her face towards her, questioning.

"I smell rain coming." Sun dropped through the window between them. Clear, hard winter light. "Summer rain."

The woman's steps now mimicked the patter of rain against glass, a tin roof, building, building, to steady downpour before softening, fading away. The woman, the ghost, stopped.

"Did 'ya hear it?" the old man asked.

"We did," Karie said.

The old man sank, relief loosening the tight wrinkles of his face. "They didn't get anything, y'know, those investigators. Set up their recordings and their cam-e-ras and spent the night."

"They did though," Karie said.

"Just the house," he said. "It's old. The wind howled while they were here. A jar fell in the pantry, but that's nothing that bothers me. An old ghost cat been spookin' round the place a hundred years now."

He stopped to listen again.

The old woman shuffle stepped, flat footing while she hummed a little lullaby of a tune that Andrea had to strain to hear.

"Fairies," he said. "My mam sung all the old songs."

Andrea leaned forward. "Fairies?"

He sung in a rough, quivery voice, the woman flat footing along, her mouth moving, though Andrea couldn't hear her.

"O woman, washing beside the river,
Hush-a-by baby, babe not mine,
My woeful wail, do you pity never?
Hush-a-by baby, babe not mine,
A year ago, I was snatched forever,
Hush-a-by baby, babe not mine,
From my home to the hill where hawthorns quiver,
Hush-a-by baby, babe not mine,
Shoheen sho, ulolo,
Shoheen sho, strange baby O!
Shoheen sho, ulolo,
You're not my own sweet baby O!"

The woman continued dancing although the man stopped singing. He cleared his throat. "It's about a woman tellin' her husband how to rescue her from the fairies keepin' her as a nursemaid. If he don't free her within the year, she becomes Queen of the fairies and lives in fairylan' evermore."

"Do you think this haunting could be fairy folk?" Karie asked.

The woman stopped to laugh, muted and faint, struggling to catch her breath and then pealing off again. Andrea grinned and then laughed, too, Karie frowning over at her. After a minute, the old man wheezed into a kind of choking laugh, coughed, and then laughed a little looser.

Karie looked between them. When they quieted, she said, "So not a fairy then?"

Both the man and woman lit off again, taking Andrea with them. When they finally quieted, the old man and Andrea wiping their eyes, the old woman said, "Teel the ol fool I feel in over yander." She faded a little with every word. "I'm scattered cross the river beed. Them bons he need be in tha book."

"You don't think that sound could be the house as well? Maybe the refrigerator?"

"It'd be a very musical motor wheeze then," the old man said as the transparent ghost turned to Andrea, a whisper of sound escaping her lips.

"What?" Andrea said, reaching out to touch her, but nothing happened.

"It'd be strange," the man said. "For the icebox to fla-foot a song now, wouldn't it?"

The old woman disappeared, leaving a single word in the hush of Andrea's eardrum. "Fairies."

"Fairies," Andrea said. "Of course."

Karie screwed her face up. "What?"

"I don't really believe in 'em," the old man said.

"Do you have a fairytale book?" Andrea said. "Maybe one you read to your kids growing up?"

"Shore. Just there." He pointed to the double bookcase filling the wall beside the front door. "My Manda used to read it to 'em, and the gran'kids, too, fore she lef' me. Keep mean'n to send it to the oldest in Chicago, for the great-gran'kids."

Andrea crossed the room. "I think she'd rather you have it."

"Was Manda your wife?" Karie asked.

"Amanda, yes."

Andrea scanned the books. Bibles, herbals, recipes, science fiction, mysteries, and there, tucked in between Charlotte's Web and Black Beauty, a worn book of Celtic fairytales. Literally stories of fairies. Andrea opened it and riffled the pages. About three-quarters back, there were folded sheets of paper stuck in three different places. Old HH bonds from the early 1980s and 1990s, EE bonds from the same time, and two I-bonds issued in 2000, all for hefty amounts. She didn't know much about bonds, but knew they represented money the old homeowner could probably use to maintain his independence. Andrea closed the book, replaced it on the shelf, and handed the bonds to the old man.

He stared down at them. "I don't have my reading glasses on."

"They're bonds."

"Bonds?"

"Savings bonds."

"You found the bonds?"

"In the book on fairytales."

"I thought she took them with her when she lef' me."

The scent of magnolias filled the room and the power failed. Andrea shook her head. Storm rain, cut grass, fresh-turned earth. Karie spun, looking around the room. The old man stood from his recliner.

Andrea said, "She didn't leave you. The magnolias grow at the cemetery? On the river?"

"Yes," the old man stuttered.

"We should go over there."

"We should?" Karie said.

Andrea looked at the uncertainty on the old man's face. "We should."

They put their jackets on and Karie dug in her equipment bag, coming up with a black camera with a short lens. "Do you mind if I keep documenting?"

Both the old man and Andrea shook their heads.

On the way out, Andrea snagged the waders closest to the door. The old man's back straightened and his steps firmed as they walked across his yard and down the road a little ways. As they crested the hill, the cemetery and the huge magnolias along Strange Creek lay before them. Karie lifted her camera and took a photo.

The old man stepped onto the grass along the road verge and walked on a diagonal into the park of the cemetery before threading his way between stones and ground plaques to the first of the magnolias. A humming, the fairy song, filled Andrea's ear.

It strengthened as she walked down the row of magnolias to the third one, then stopped. Andrea turned to the creek, studying the shoreline, the ripple of the cold, grey water, the sun glinting off the strong current as it flowed past. The wispy shape of the old woman formed about five yards out on the wide bend.

"Allow me," the old man said. Andrea turned her head to find him squared up beside her. His rheumy eyes were soft, his chapped lips pressed hard together. "I thought she lef' me. Brandon Stoat lef' town the same day she went gone and she was always sweet on him."

A strong scent of apple pie swirled on the cold breeze. Karie's camera shutter clicked.

"She was always tryin' to wheedle his mama's apple pie recipe out of him." He took the waders from her hand.

"Why would she be here, on the river?"

"It was hot, mid-July." He walked to the creek bank while he talked, where it dropped to the water, forming a natural shelf. "She might've walked down the creek. She liked to sit in the springhouse sometimes, though it was fallin' apart even then." He sat and pulled the waders on.

Karie came up beside her and took a picture of the old man sitting on the bank, the creek tumbling past him.

The wisp sank into the water.

A brilliant light rose, blinding Andrea. She raised her hand in defense.

Karie's camera clicked, but she was still focused on the old man as he waded out, head down as he scanned the creek. The shutter clicked again.

"She's passed," Andrea said to Karie, then called out, "Bear right."

The old man didn't look back, just bore right. He stopped, and then kicked at the creek bed. He took two more steps, bent, and lifted a long bone, creek water streaming from it.

14

Jimmy eyed Sparkles aka Bella and she eyed him right back. She looked cranky and in need of a nap, but Harper's eyes bore dark circles under them, and her eyes and nose were red and swollen. The girls sat side by side on a comfortable-looking couch. The social worker sat on a hard back dining room chair in the home's front hall, trying her best to be present but unobtrusive. Jimmy appreciated the failing effort.

"Did you know that our mom and dad," Harper croaked. "That they were—"

"No. We were looking for my friend. They were together."

"Mr. Andy," Bella said. She glanced over at Harper, staring at her hands in her lap, and then met Jimmy's gaze. "He's an angel now, too."

Jimmy couldn't do it. Biting the inside of his lip, he dropped his head.

"I'm sorry," Bella said.

Shit. His eyes filled and he had to sniff to keep his nose from running. Fifteen years in and he'd never lost it in an interview before. Even with the wife of the guy who drove his car into the Kanawha to drown his kids. She'd clutched the youngest's bedraggled stuffed lion, recovered from the river, in her arms through their every interaction.

Bella hopped down and laid a hand on his.

"Mr. Andy was really nice," Harper offered.

"Bella," the social worker said.

She must've motioned Bella back. The little girl backed up and parked herself on the edge of the couch. Jimmy sucked it up, thumbed the tears from his eyes. "How well did you know Mr. Andy?"

Bella lifted her hands, palms up. Harper shrugged a shoulder. Kids. Right.

"Did you meet him before you stayed at his house?"

"Yes," Harper said. "And a few days later, Mom took us to his house."

Bella wiggled, bouncing on her seat. "We stayed in a funny little house behind his house!"

Jimmy smiled at her. "How many nights did you stay?"

"Two," Harper said. "And then Mom and Mr. Andy took us to that lady's house."

"Miss Carla," Bella added. Her face fell. "I miss Simon."

"Simon?"

"He's Miss Carla's funny little dog." Her eyes widened. "He didn't go to heaven, too, did he?"

Harper shook her head at Jimmy. "No, Bella, Simon's at Miss Carla's, you don't know anything."

Frowning, Bella crossed her arms. "You don't, either."

"More than you."

"You both know just what you should," Jimmy said. "Did your dad meet Mr. Andy when you did?"

They both shook their heads.

"Mommy told us not to talk about him," Harper said. "So we could surprise Daddy."

"Surprise him how?"

"With a surprise trip. We packed after he left for work, so he wouldn't know."

"Do you know how your mom met Mr. Andy?"

Bella bounced.

"No," Harper said.

Jimmy opened the folder he had on his lap. Bella craned her neck to see what he was doing. He pulled out the phot of Detweiler. "That's Mr. Andy," she said.

He slid it to the bottom of the pile, Dewey now on top. He was in his own front yard, caught looking straight into the long-distance lens with a flat stare. "Do you know this guy?"

"No," they said together, then Bella laughed.

"Jinx," she yelled.

"Bella," the social worker said.

Jimmy swapped the photos.

"That's Greg," Harper said. "He works for my dad."

And owned the gun he used to kill Detweiler and the girls' mom, and then himself. Greg had fallen all over himself and then broke down during his interview. He was on suicide watch in Memorial's locked ward. The question was, how'd Dad find out where Mom went and who she was with, and that Dewey was involved?

"Do you know the names of your mom's best friends?"

"Lizzie," Bella said. "I miss Lizzie." She kicked the carpet. "Can we go stay with her?"

"No, Bella," Harper said, her voice sharp. "You might not know Aunt Janice, but I do! I'm staying here."

Bella burst into tears. "I want to go home," she wailed.

Footsteps ran down the hall as the social worker stood up, and Janice came around the corner from the hall. "Come here, Bella," she said, and despite her apparent resistance, Bella ran into her arms.

Janice picked her up. "We'll just go to the kitchen. Are you all right, Harper?"

Harper nodded but her voice quavered, and tears streaked her cheeks. "I'm fine."

Janice retreated, but the social worker came and sat down on the couch, a cushion away from Harper.

"I'm fine," Harper said again, and wiped her tears from her cheeks. "Did Mr. Andy hurt my mom and dad?"

"No," Jimmy said, unable to keep the surprise out of his voice. "No, sweetie, has no one told you what happened?"

"I don't think—" the social worker said, alarmed.

Jimmy understood, right then, what a favor his papaw did him. Growing up, he could always count on blunt truth from the old man. When he wanted real answers, he always went to his papaw. "You dad hurt your mom and Mr. Andy. He shot them with a gun. And then he shot himself."

Head down, Harper twisted her fingers together, but she didn't cry. "My dad wasn't the best," she said to her lap. "He was mean to my mom."

"But he was still your dad, and you still loved him."

She sniffed and wiped her cheeks again.

The social worker got up and came back with a handful of tissues. After Harper blew her nose, she finally looked up again. "Lizzie is mom's friend. They go to book club on Wednesday night. Dad doesn't like her to go anywhere alone. That's the only time we aren't with her."

"Lizzie's last name?"

"Roberts. If you talk to her, can you tell Perla that Aunt Janice is going to get me a cell phone so I can call her?"

"Perla?"

"Lizzie's her mom. She already has a phone, for emergencies. Can you get me her number? She lives the next street over from us."

"I will," Jimmy promised. He might have to take somebody with him to go further into the field, but he'd get that number back to Harper if it was the last thing he ever did.

"Oak Bend Circle, that's where they live. In the grey house with the red door. They have a rope swing."

"If Perla's home when I go, I'll call your Aunt Janice so you can talk to her, okay?"

Harper nodded, tearing up all over again.

THROUGH DUCK and on the way to Sutton on twisty County Road 40, a Braxton County sheriff's car passed by going the other way, lights spinning, but no sirens. Whether or not the driver was headed to

Strange Creek, Andrea was relieved to be on the way to Summersville where they'd cut east on another small road to Richwood. Still. "You think he'll be okay?"

Karie didn't look away from the road. "His friend Sam seemed capable."

Not really an answer. "Are you mad at me for not wanting to stay?"

"No, I'm worried that you're going to get outed before you're ready. It was a bad idea to bring you along now that you seem more..."

When she didn't continue after a minute, Andrea said, "More what?"

"Visible?"

"To the ghosts, you mean?"

"Yes."

"I don't know. I haven't seen any random ghosts on the road today or at work the last few weeks."

"Except violin guy."

"Yeah, except him, and only the once. I don't think I've seen an increasing number of them after that initial surge before Christmas."

"You think maybe your awareness has peaked?"

Andrea laughed. "I have no freaking idea. I hope so."

"Still, I shouldn't have put you in that position today."

"You said real hauntings are few and far between."

"That was up until I met you."

"I'm just saying, you didn't expect there to be an actual ghost involved, right?"

Karie relaxed, her whole body dropping two inches. "I really didn't."

They drove in silence for another ten minutes, before Karie directed her onto the left-hand fork of another county road with a long string of numbers instead of a name. She studied her phone and then dropped it onto her paper map. "Good thing we weren't depending on cell service."

"Do you think he'll give them my name?" Andrea asked.

"Mr. Charles? I only gave him your first name and I doubt he'll remember it. I gave him my card to give the deputies. The video camera was focused on him, so there's only your voice and hand recorded.

Bobby Waltham will back me up on protecting you as an unnamed resource. With an official paranormal investigator onboard and the length of time since she died, after they establish the bones are his wife's, they'll let it lie. I'm dying to know what we got on the video, if anything, but these roads are too curvy to look at it."

"You took a lot of photos by the river."

"I'm hoping I got orbs."

"Spirit orbs? I've seen pics online. I wish I'd taken photos of Billie Mae."

"I wish I'd asked you to."

"It's overwhelming."

"It is."

They settled into the ride.

Andrea wondered the whole way to Richwood if the old man, Mr. Charles, was okay. If the deputies and his friend Sam believed him. And how Amanda felt disappearing into the light.

———

Taka sounded tired. "Where are you?"

"The Cherry River Falls Lodge?"

"You don't sound sure that's where you are."

"It used to be something else. It's old but clean." Andrea let her gaze wander from her laptop to the large picture window that framed the river and allowed the insistent rush of the white water to fill the room with white noise. "Lots of wood paneling. I think we're the only guests."

"February probably isn't the strongest of the four seasons for them."

"They said they'll be packed with skiers over President's Day. It's an hour to Snowshoe."

"Nice. You have a plan for tomorrow?"

"Drive around?"

"I'm not used to you sounding so Valley Girl."

"There's a flashback. How long has it been since anyone said 'Valley Girl'?"

"Seventh grade?"

"Got you?" She crowed, letting her voice rise and drawing out the inflection. Their whole class had spent a week talking Valley Girl after Donna's mom put the old movie on at a sleepover.

"So you did?" Taka teased. "Wanta go to the mall tomorrow?"

"Maybe? The mall of the trees?"

"Maybe Madeleine will be there?"

"Duh?"

Taka laughed, loud and deep, and Andrea's heart swelled with it. When he caught his breath, he said, "Whatevs."

She dropped her voice back to its normal tone. "Do you know what flat-footing is?"

"Only that's it's kinda like clogging."

And then she told him all about the dancing ghost, the bonds in the fairytale book, and the bones in Strange Creek.

TAKA THUMBED HIS PHONE CLOSED. He leaned back in the desk chair in Dewey's office at Kirkby Road. The one locked file drawer bothered him. He'd spent most of the day re-running background checks on all of Dewey's employees and meeting with the two warehouse managers. And the security team, eight in total, six men and two women.

Four of them were adequately trained. Two needed to move on to jobs that better suited them. He'd spend tomorrow working out a training schedule. One of the managers was going to help him with interviewing and hiring replacements over the next few weeks. He wanted to put the wait staff at the Coliseum through a safety course. And learn the warehouse protocols for customer safety and shipping security. The warehouses weren't open to the public, but that didn't stop people from dropping by.

He eyed the wet bar, then got up and helped himself to ice and three fingers of Bushmill's before settling back at the desk to sip it and think about the call he'd just made. He'd called the private cell number he'd dug up on CEO Caroline Masters at Brighter Day. Since Dewey'd have him hung and quartered if he approached her directly, he introduced himself as Dan, an associate of Dewey Sanderson's interested in donating an estate inheritance. He had tread carefully, asking open ended questions. She'd spoken to him in a confident, soft southern lisp.

She graduated summa cum laude with a law degree and passed the bar six years ago. She met Dewey while acting as a congressional aide to Senator Sanderson and they'd stayed in contact. When she left the corporate law office she burned out on, Dewey rang asking if she had any interest in non-profit work and Brighter Day was born.

It turned out Brighter Day did not place kids.

Families with kids who weren't legally theirs learned about Brighter Day through the ads she ran and the websites who listed it as a resource. Some learned about Brighter Day through Child Protective Services or social workers after families asked how they could become legal guardians. But either way, families contacted her directly. The kids were already in their possession for one reason or another. If they were prepared to fight for them, Caroline would open her network of lawyers, therapists, and financial support.

As far as Taka could tell, Dewey wasn't involved in the non-profit beyond charitable funding. But they didn't place kids. And while Detweiler might have helped, Taka had no doubt it was Dewey who disappeared them and arranged the cover stories the families gave Brighter Day. Taka spun his glass and then opened his phone and thumbed Dewey's name. It only rang once.

"Yes," Dewey said.

"What you doin'?"

"Lying on my couch." The words seemed to take a lot of effort on his part.

"You already took your ten p.m. pills?"

"Yeah."

Good timing. "I'm enjoying your Bushmill."

"Good. Somebody should be," Dewey said, rousing a little.

"Why shouldn't I go to Fields or Tamarin about the kids at Anna Lansing's?"

"What kids?"

"Dewey."

"Seriously, Taka. They don't know who they are, no real names. The only images they got are two young girls from the back with someone who may or may not be Anna, a bunch of dead-end fingerprints and empty bunk beds at her house, a housewife across the street and an absent-minded carpool mom who saw a couple of kids they can't describe, and a school full of staff who didn't notice anything of note. Shit, there's not even any definitive images of those kids from security cameras at the school."

"Detweiler get that info for you?"

"Yeah."

"Why get involved?"

"I told you. Anna asked me to get the kids out of the life and I did."

"But why?"

"I can't be a nice guy, William?"

"It's not self-serving."

"Ouch. I'm hanging up now."

"Andrea sees ghosts."

Silence, then rustling. Dewey huffed into the phone. "Okay. I'm awake now. I must've fallen asleep while we were talking."

"She fell last spring. Hit her head. Started seeing a little girl in her house."

"The one that her crappy neighbor killed."

"Yes."

"I don't believe in ghosts."

"You don't have to. Listen, there's a ghost who's pretty attached to you right now."

"Hanging up."

"Wait. Her name's Madeleine. She's the reason you were thinking about the homestead. She keeps telling Andrea about the red crossvine growing there." Into Dewey's continued silence, Taka said, "Andrea can't find Madeleine in your family tree. But when she asked if she was related to your mother's side of the family, Madeleine, or somebody, started knocking on every door frame in Andrea's house."

"Put the whiskey down and get Sean to drive you home."

"Dewey."

"Good night, William," Dewey said, voice clear and tight, and hung up.

Taka sipped his whiskey.

Dewey used a letter opener. It sat at the front of the desk, above his leather blotter. Nice deer bone blade mounted on a sanded piece of antler. Taka weighed it in his hand and checked the tip.

Then he jimmied the locked drawer open.

15

The morning sun filtered through the bare trees to either side of the narrow, winding two-lane south of Richwood, creating a flickering light along the south fork of the Cherry River through the FX's windshield. Andrea blocked it with her open hand. Karie dug in the small backpack at her feet and came up with a pair of sunglasses.

"Thank you, I'm about going blind here."

Just then the woods gave way to a sweeping valley to their left, pastures sparkling with dew.

Karie waved her hand at the landscape. "Gorgeous."

A couple of turns off Johnstown Road brought them to a T-intersection. They could go either way and pass through one of the former meat camps that served the community who worked along Winslow's Creek. Two of the five addresses Andrea wanted to visit would take them right. The other three left. "Pick a direction."

"No ghosts pointing the way?"

"We could only wish."

"Right."

Farther into the hills east. A mile on, they came over the top of a hill and as they curved down, the road joined Winslow Creek and ran alongside it. Shallow and wide, the creek's white water riffled over river stone. In summer, Andrea could imagine the line of cars snaking along the scenic route, but it was desolate today. Another mile, and snow sat along the roadsides. More roads started to diverge from their route, peeling up through the bare woods. A small cluster of brown cabins huddled on a sloping hillside across the creek.

Then around a curve sat the tiny town that had grown from the eastern meat camp, cars parked neatly along the curbs. An insurance agent, a small indie grocery store, a grill, a lawyer, a coffee shop.

"Small," Karie said. "We go left here."

"Here" was the end of the block and the town. Small houses with front porches and cars parked in the yard. She bumped across an old steel and wooden bridge over the creek. Karie directed their winding path three more miles into rural country hillside with breathtaking peekaboo views as they climbed higher.

The last road was a paved one lane, no painted lane markers. With no GPS service, Karie was back on the paper map before she pointed at a dirt road to the left. "There."

A barking dog ran out from a rundown wooden home on the right, a blue tarp tacked to the roof. He followed them a hundred yards, snapping at the tires of the FX before stopping in the middle of the road.

They saw no other houses before the road dead-ended at a gravel driveway that ran up through a palisade of planted maples. A red Chevy pick-up sat in front of the two-story white plank house sheltered by old, massive oaks. No wonder the house hadn't been visible on Google Earth.

A man stood on the front porch as if waiting for them. Andrea pulled in next to the truck. He came down the steps to greet them. Andrea turned the car off and opened her door.

"Ain't got time right now," the man called out. He was maybe six-foot, mid-thirties blond. Not unattractive.

"Excuse me?"

"No time for whatever guvment stuff you're here about today. I'm going to town."

Karie got out first. "We're with Waltham-Young."

"That library place in Charleston?"

"You know it."

"My cousin took me to a wine tasting art thing there a few years back."

Andrea shut her door. "I'm Andrea Kelley. This is Karie Wilson. We do actually need a few minutes of your time."

"Is that library guvment funded?"

"No, sir," Karie said and shut her door, too.

"Come on up, then." He waved them to the porch swing as they trotted up the steps and took one of the two other chairs for himself. "I ain't never checked any books out, so I know you ain't here about late fees."

"We're not that kind of library, Mister . . ." Andrea let the word hang.

The man sat back, looking between them. "Who are you here to see, exactly?"

"Lee Sanderson."

His chin drew up and he nodded. "Why?"

"Well," Andrea said. "I have a professional interest in mapping property held over generations by the same family. We're trying to locate property that Dewey Sanderson said his grandfather owned. He hasn't been to it in years and couldn't direct us to its location."

"But we know it's on or near Winslow Creek," Karie added.

The man scratched his cheek. "Dewey."

His tone was puzzled, but neutral.

"Are you Lee Sanderson?"

"My uncle. But he's been gone ten years."

"So you know Dewey?"

"One o'my cousins. H'aint seen him in—" He looked up, gaze traveling the porch ceiling. "Lordy, a coon's age."

Andrea glanced at Karie, their eyes meeting. Whoever he was, he was a poor liar. And whatever 'gone' meant, the house was still in Lee's name. Maybe that's why he had no time for government stuff. She leaned forward, planting her feet to stop the slow sway of the swing, canting it sideways, since only Karie's tiptoes touched the ground. "Do you know where the Sanderson-owned properties are located?"

"Sure."

"Any referred to within the family as the homestead?"

He frowned and shook his head. "No."

"Any that have or used to have a home with a front porch covered in crossvine?"

He thought for a second. "Them orange trumpet flowers? No. My aunt had some on a, what you call it, a garden arch? Like a trellis. For my cousin's wedding." His voice was deeper, more confident.

She'd bet anything this is what truth from him sounded like. "Could you point us at the properties you know about? Even the ones no longer owned by the family?"

"I could."

"Maybe you have the addresses?"

"Dewey know you're here?"

"Yes," Andrea said firmly although she couldn't remember now if Taka had told Dewey she was interested enough to hunt the property down.

"His papaw was my great-uncle. I know a couple he owned, that good enough?"

Karie held her phone up. "Shoot."

He only had one street number but gave them directions on finding two more.

Karie's thumbs flew over her screen.

"All near Winslow Creek?" Andrea asked.

"Close enough for guvment work."

In this case, the postal service?

"Anymore?" Karie said.

"Properties? Probably. Sandersons have owned a lot of land around here, one time or another."

"Maybe you could ask the family?" Andrea said. "Or get street names for us?"

"Maybe."

"Do you know if your great-uncle lived on any of the other family properties? Or called any of them his?"

"He lived here in this house for a while before he got married. After my great-aunt died, he moved back from Charleston and lived out on the Falls Branch Road property. It was his sister's place. I never knew her, but I been out to see him there before he died."

"Ever heard of an ancestor named Madeleine?"

"Can't say that I have."

"Thank you," Andrea said, pushing up from the swing. With the automatic manners that marked his Southern upbringing, he stood as she did. She held out her hand and he took it in a gentle half-shake. "And your name?"

"Beau. Beau Sanderson."

"Can I call you in a few days? See if you came up with anything else?"

"You can call," he said, drawing out the word call. And implying she could call but he might not answer.

BACK IN THE CAR, Andrea waved at Beau, still standing on his front porch. He lifted his hand. "So do you think he knows where we're talking about?"

Karie waved, too. "Maybe?"

She three-point turned and drove back along the long drive to the dirt road. She watched for Beau's truck behind them, but they made the paved one lane without a sign of him. "Two of the addresses are others we were going to check out."

"So you want to go to the third one first."

Andrea grinned. "How do you know me so well?"

Karie laughed. "It's been an intense friendship in a short amount of time."

"And how. I know I'm one of *those* friends."

"Don't get me wrong, meeting you has literally changed my life, but in a good way, Andrea. I love Waltham-Young, but I didn't have more than say-hi-in-the-hallway and go-for-a-quick-drink friends here in Charleston. The job is everything I wanted. It's fascinating. I meet people like Mr. Charles yesterday, who have stories I want to hear, who are living history that people years from now will be watching on video I shot to learn about life today and how we got here.

"But I was lonely. And now I have you and Taka, and Jimmy, and Luke, and I'm closer to all of you already than anyone I've met since high school. I've never really had friends like you guys that I can text whenever, that I can freely talk to, and you don't shut me down or call me a morbid freak. I can swing by and crash dinner without an invitation. Heck, I could move and not speak to you for ten years and I think you'd still pick me up at the airport if I called."

"Oddly specific, but fly your freak flag high, as the Buffy fandom used to say, and of course. You could call from Patagonia, and I'd come pick you up." She pulled up at the one-lane's intersection with the marked county road. No Beau yet. Andrea reached out and laid her hand over Karie's. "I can't think of anyone that could've helped me like you have the last few months. Maybe my friend Lauren, but she's in Texas. I don't know what I would've done without you. I'm so glad you're here. And I think we'd have been friends anyway, once our paths crossed."

"But ghosts," Karie said, squeezing Andrea's hand. "Ten timesed our getting to know you period."

Andrea laughed and took her hand back. "So where are we going?"

WALKING across the middle of a through street in a sprawling terraced subdivision to meet him, Jimmy took in Taka's black winter windbreaker with Sanderson Security stamped large in yellow on the left arm and breast. "Nice jacket."

"Found a bunch in a storage locker."

What business could Taka possibly have in the little suburb of Big Chimney? "What are you doing here?"

"I could say the same."

Jimmy held a hand out as Nina joined them. "You know Nina, right?"

"We've never actually met." He stuck his hand out. "I'm William Taka."

"You're big, is what you are," Nina exclaimed, shaking his hand, which engulfed hers despite the fact she wasn't a small woman. "Nice to meet you. Never seen Dewey's guys labeled before."

"You will for the next three months."

Jimmy opened his mouth to make a bet that would only be until Dewey recovered enough to rein Taka back in, but then thought better of it. Instead, he said, "So?"

"Following a lead," Taka offered, which told Jimmy exactly nothing.

"And he's careful," Nina added, nodding in approval.

"On the kids?"

Taka considered for a second. "Yes."

"Harper and Bella?" Jimmy clarified.

Taka shrugged. "Maybe. I don't know yet."

He let the sudden lightning jab of jealousy that Andrea preferred taciturn and stubborn burn through him and away. "This job's not going to do you any favors."

"Why are *you* here?" Taka shot back.

"To follow up on a lead," Jimmy said, as Nina said, "Looking for background on our investigation."

Taka's brows rose as he looked between them. "Aren't you on suspension?"

Nina crossed her arms over her chest. "He's on limited duty, on my watch. We're collecting background information for our investigators."

"Harper and Bella?"

Give a little, get a little. Jimmy sighed. He was supposed to be bringing Taka over anyway and Nina knew it. "Yeah."

Taka pointed across the street, behind Jimmy and Nina. "Doing due diligence on one of Dewey's existing projects."

Jimmy looked down and then away, down the quiet street. Not a soul in sight. "I think you're either in the pool or not, Taka. Dewey's not going to let you just stick your feet in."

"And the state will?"

Jimmy was aware of Nina being still, analyzing the addition of their postures as they stood in the street, Taka's tone, the data she'd been crunching on Dewey for two years, the dry facts of Jimmy plus Taka plus Andrea plus the bullets that tended to fly when they were all in the same location.

He turned his head and met Taka's eyes. "We'll take what we can get."

Taka made a burr of a sound down in his throat that Jimmy couldn't describe, but Nina smiled. "He's on to your shit, boss," she said. And then to Taka, "But seriously, it's not like we have any leverage. We'll take whatever you can give us."

She dropped her smile. "But we'll also prosecute you to the fullest extent of the law if you cross any lines, even grey ones, so watch where you place those massive boots while you're doing Dewey's business."

"I am not," Taka said, just as seriously, "and will not, be doing Dewey's business. I'm the concrete block, for the next three months, between Dewey and those who would do him, or his businesses, or the people those businesses serve, physical harm. So, while your colleagues are shooting each other"—rolling his eyes, Jimmy let his head drop back, and stared up into the cloudy, cold, and endless sky—"I'll be making sure they don't accidentally shoot Dewey while he's recovering from the shooter they didn't stop."

The word "colleagues" clicked in Jimmy's head. Again, Taka met his eyes when he reengaged. "Let it go, Taka, Scott doesn't work for us."

Nina's face changed when she got it and Jimmy saw Taka seeing the calculation cross her features before she said, "You're talking about Scott Fergusson. He works for Dewey."

Aiming his words at Jimmy while staring down Nina, Taka said, "I'm sure she knows more about me than my own mother does, but she shouldn't be in the field, Jimmy."

Nina sneered. Jimmy didn't think he'd ever seen her look so impressively badass.

"She's a tech, Taka. All we're doing is collecting follow-up for the team looking at Andy's activities."

"Follow your lead, I'll follow mine."

"I know you'll do the right thing, you always do."

"Thank you." Taka stepped to the side and headed past them to the house.

"Wait," Nina said.

Taka stopped.

"You're going to Lizzie Johnson's house?"

Taka turned on his heel. "Yes?"

"We made an appointment with her," Jimmy said.

"Great. Then she'll be home."

"So this visit *is* related to Harper and Bella," Nina said.

Taka shrugged and spun back around.

If he was so unsure if his "due diligence" was related to Harper and Bella, why was he here? Nina glanced over at him, questioning. "Let's find out," Jimmy said.

VERY AWARE OF Jimmy and Nina at his back, Taka knocked on the door.

Lizzie Johnson proved to be a gracious Hispanic blonde with full lips and a full heart. Although a wariness passed over her face when she first took him in, she lumped Taka's presence in with Jimmy and Nina without further explanation. She sat them at her kitchen island with coffee and homemade shortbread cookies but remained standing across from them.

Unwilling to be the first to ask a question, Taka stirred milk and sugar into his coffee and waited to see who would shift the meeting past the silence of everyone knowing Lizzie Johnson had lost her friends to murder-suicide. Surprising him, Lizzie laid it on the floor first.

"I'm not one to pretend I don't know what's going on." She shifted her attention to Taka. "Obviously, you're here because they"—she tilted her head at Jimmy and Nina—"know Mr. Sanderson was helping Stacy escape."

Taka avoided looking at Jimmy. She was talking to him, so he'd have to override his own instincts to let Jimmy take lead since he couldn't ask her what he'd come to ask. "Yes. How did Stacy Owens and Dewey Sanderson know each other?"

"Have you asked Mr. Sanderson?"

"Yes," Jimmy said before Taka could respond. "We'd like to hear it from you. May I record?"

She scrutinized each of their faces, coming back to Taka before she nodded. Jimmy set his phone on the counter and noted the setting, time, who was present, and repeated Taka's question before she spoke again. "They don't. Didn't. Know each other, I mean."

Taka took a sip of his coffee. No one said anything. He set the mug down. "So who made the connection for her?"

"You did."

Taka straightened. "I did?"

"Well, I don't know if you did, but Sanderson Security did."

Elbows planted on the counter, Nina leaned forward with her mug in both hands. "And how did that happen?"

"We go to book club with Rebecca Barr. It's the only time Gavin . . . do I need to . . . you know who Gavin is. Owens, Stacy's husband. He doesn't—didn't—like Stacy to leave the house without him, even to get groceries. She had a car, for emergencies, but she never drove it. The only time he let her go anywhere without him was on Wednesday evenings when we went to book club. It was the only time she got to herself."

Taka nodded. "Rebecca Barr?"

"Her nephew works at Pinch Sports and Gun. Y'know, in Pinch?"

Taka had briefly dated a girl from Pinch. He knew it only had two stoplights.

"I was born in Pinch," Nina said, and took a big gulp of her coffee when they all looked at her.

"Pinch Sports and Gun," Jimmy said, making notes in his small notepad.

"Book club was, well, we do read books and talk about them, but we also do other things sometimes. We went to buy Stacy a gun. Just in case."

"Just in case," Taka echoed.

"Gavin's meaner than he used to be. Was meaner. But we didn't buy one anyway. Stacy started crying and we tried to explain to the nephew and his boss came over and then they called the owner and next thing we knew, someone from Sanderson Security was on the phone, making a plan to help Stacy leave Gavin." She looked again to Taka to take some of the pressure off. "But you know all this, right?"

Taka tried to look reassuring. "We're just confirming the details. In your own words. Did you catch a name?"

"No, except Andy Detweiler. I didn't know his name until I saw it in the paper. They gave Stacy a codeword so she'd know she could go with him. He came and picked them up from here."

"Here from your house?"

"Yes."

Jimmy lifted his pen. "Stacy, Harper, and Bella Owens?"

"Yes."

Taka lifted his coffee and then noticed the tears filling her eyes. He set it down as he slid his other hand across the island. She took it.

"I'm sorry," she said.

"Don't be," Nina said, her words soft. "She was your friend."

Lizzie's breath hitched before she caught it. She let it out slow. "It was my fault."

"Why do you think that?" Taka asked.

"Gavin and his asshat friend came here, first thing, when he realized. I told him she was gone, that he shouldn't try to go after her because Sanderson Security was protecting her." She blinked hard. "It just popped out."

"It wasn't you," Jimmy said. "They were killed before Mr. Owens went after Mr. Sanderson. Ms. Owens called her husband from a gas station. It's likely Sergeant Detweiler didn't know she turned her phone back on and left it on after the call."

Lizzie dropped. Taka shoved his coffee mug to the side and lunged over the counter, but she hadn't fallen. She'd jerked the lowest drawer in the island open and was fumbling inside it.

"It's gone," she cried out and then sat down, boneless, finally letting the tears come.

Taka scrambled back. He and Jimmy rounded the ends of the island at the same time. "Why, why did she take it? He told her to leave it here," she sobbed, pissed and grief-stricken.

It was Nina who slid down onto the floor to place an arm around Lizzie's shoulders.

Taka's own heart hurt listening to Lizzie's heart break.

Movement in the doorway had Taka standing. Three kids crowded the entry to the kitchen. They spilled in. "Is Aunt Lizzie okay?" the oldest, a tween white girl with long dark hair asked.

Taka met them halfway into the room, saw her recognize the name on his jacket. "Yeah, she's sad about her friend. Why don't we—"

The middle kid, a blonde girl about Harper's age, the spitting image of her mother, darted around him. "Mommy!"

Lizzie's sobs choked off. Taka studied the tween, noting her blue eyes, and the youngest kid, a sturdy boy, maybe five or six, tousled blond with dark eyes and brown skin.

"I'm okay," Lizzie croaked. "I'm okay, sweetie. Go back to the playroom with Sadie and Mateo."

Confirmation then, of the name he knew. The tween in front of him. Sadie.

"Hey, uh," Jimmy said. "Are you Perla?"

Taka turned, catching the little girl's shy nod. Lizzie Johnson and Nina stood up, Lizzie wiping the tears from her face.

Jimmy pulled out his phone, found a number, and called it. "Hey, it's Jimmy Hoyle. I'm at Lizzie Johnson's. I have someone here who would like to talk to Harper."

"Harper," Perla exclaimed and reached up with both hands.

Then Lizzie was crying again, but silently, watching Perla's face all lit up, tears streaming over her cheeks and dripping from her chin.

Jimmy let Perla take his phone. "Harper," she said again, excited when her friend must've answered. "It's me. Where are you?" Holding the phone to her ear with both hands, she came back around Taka.

Sadie reached out and took her wrist. "We'll just—"

Taka followed them out of the kitchen into the foyer. Sadie gave him an uncertain glance. "Is Aunt Lizzie really okay?"

"She is. Can I ask you something?"

"Y'all go on up," she said to the younger kids.

When they were halfway up the stairs, Mateo jumping up each stair with both feet, Perla still listening intently to Harper on the other end of Jimmy's phone, Sadie turned back to him. "Yes?"

"Is there somewhere you'd rather be?"

Her gaze dropped to the Sanderson Security name on his chest. "No. I'm safe here."

"Who is she?"

"My mom's best friend."

"And where's your mom?"

She lifted her gaze to stare at him. "You're new."

"Chet was shot."

She nodded. "I know. And Mr. Andy's dead." Mr. Andy. Ten to one, then, that Lizzie lied about not knowing his name before now.

"So, is there somewhere else you'd rather be?"

"Aunt Lizzie said I could stay here forever if I wanted to."

"Do you want to?"

"Yes."

"Okay then."

"I don't have to leave?"

"No. Just checking on you." He patted his pocket, only then remembering he no longer had his CPD business cards. "You got a phone?"

She pulled it out of the back pocket of her torn jeans and handed it to him. He put his name, Sanderson Security, and his cell number into her phone, then showed it to her. "Taka. Call me if you ever need help or to be moved. I don't care if it's a month from now or when you're thirty. Or where you might be. Got it?"

"Yes."

He watched her go up the stairs and then turned.

Jimmy stood in the kitchen doorway. "What was that all about?"

Eyeing Lizzie and Nina talking with their heads together at the island, Taka said, "Later."

Then he hightailed it out of the house, already calculating the best route to Pinch.

16

T all grass nearly hid the faded "No Trespassing" sign hanging from a chain bolted to the tops of two rotten fence posts on either side of the old drive. Andrea nosed the FX in at an angle, so the tail end was off Falls Branch Road and shut the engine off.

Karie craned her neck, trying to see down the tire-rutted path. "Are we going in?"

"If anyone asks, Beau Sanderson gave us the directions."

"Hope they ask before they shoot."

They got out and surveyed the narrow lane.

"I hope all the snakes are hibernating."

Andrea patted her Sig239, hidden on her hip. "Just in case."

They ducked under the chain. Karie took the lead, zigzagging across the ruts from less icy slick spot to shallower mudpuddle and back again. A ten-minute walk in, the drive opened to an overgrown clearing. Two massive oaks towered over a fallen in wood frame house, saplings springing up through the windows. The remains of a barn lay to the left. A rusty green tractor with an old hay harrow still attached and missing half its tines stood waiting in the yard for a Sanderson farmer who never returned. A row of demolished and picked apart cars and a bubble-curved pick-up truck from, possibly, the fifties, hosted what Andrea suspected to be a bramble of blackberry bushes.

"I didn't think about the season," Karie said.

"In my dream, they had leaves like ferns, like bleeding hearts." Andrea's grandmother had favored the delicate bleeding hearts, fussing over them every spring when they came up under her shade trees.

"I think crossvine is mostly evergreen. It has big leaves with a central stem."

They made their way through the grass, stalky bushes, and around the clumps of junk and weedy trees to the tumbled-down porch. The roof lay crooked across the base and steps. Rhododendron bushes thrust through the moldering wood. Bare vines ran wild over all of it, winter-dead. Fingered brown leaves lay in heaps. There were no desiccated flowers or ghosts of last summer's blooms, but a pair of dirty bare feet took faint shape.

High-waters, suspenders over a grey and white striped shirt. A transparent teenage boy with slicked back hair held a more vibrant tree branch with green leaves in his hand. He looked up into the closest oak tree, showing Andrea his crushed skull, then disappeared. Andrea followed his cue. He sat on a phantom limb, maybe fifteen feet high, reading. He flung his head up as if he'd heard something. He scrambled up. His foot slipped. Andrea's belly curdled in horror, a scream climbing into her throat. He faded before hitting the ground but his book hit, right in front of her, dust puffing up around it, before it too disappeared. Her breath escaped in a hard yelp.

Karie spun, grabbing her arm. "Andrea!"

Andrea grabbed onto Karie, gulping down the need to yell that rushed into her mouth in hard, shallow breaths, the frantic calls for help that he no longer needed.

"What's happening?"

"Ghost," she spit out. "Fell. Years ago."

"From the tree?"

"Yes. He was reading."

"What was he reading?"

Andrea closed her eyes, almost able to see the cover again, but not quite. She shook her head. "I don't know."

"It was a stupid question. Is he still here?"

"No."

"There's nothing green here along the porch. This isn't the right place."

Andrea looked back at the collapsed porch, the abandoned barn, the ramble of nature re-claiming what was once hers and would soon be hers again. A cool breeze lifted her hair. Clouds had overtaken the weak sun and dropped the temperature during the few minutes they'd stood in the yard. She zipped her open coat closed.

"What are you thinking?"

Andrea searched the ruins. "That there's nothing I can do for him."

"I'll look at the property's history. See if there's any connected stories."

"Okay."

They retreated down the path towards the FX, Andrea's back crawling the entire walk.

"Let's remember to ask Dewey, or maybe Beau," Karie said, glancing back over her shoulder. "Maybe there's a family story."

Once they were on the road again, Andrea tried to take a deep breath and failed, her chest tight. "He didn't feel like the boy at Louie's. I've never been anxious about that boy. My stomach's flipping."

"One ghost at a time is my motto. Maybe you should adopt it?"

"They always show up in multiples!"

"I mean, focus on one at a time. You have Madeleine and the trapper, already."

"And they're probably connected."

"Your turn is coming up on the right. So, we're focusing on Madeleine first and we might cross the path of the trapper while we do that."

Andrea's chest finally gave and let her get a good breath. "Right. House with the red crossvine."

A twisty twenty-minute drive later, Andrea sat at the end of a short gravel drive, the FX's engine idling. The house was decidedly occupied, in great condition, but lacked a front porch altogether. "What if the homestead's been demolished and a new house built on the property?"

Still peering through the windshield, Karie leaned even further forward. "Not something I'd considered. How long have the Sandersons' owned it?"

Andrea twisted around to pull her backpack from the rear seat and rifled through it. She handed a green file to Karie and dropped her pack back onto the rear seat.

Karie flipped through the research. "1887."

"We could pull permits, I guess. See what renovations have taken place over the years."

"If permits were pulled."

"Yeah, I imagine that not all Sandersons could be bothered, but we might get lucky. Next address?"

The third home wasn't far, on Cusper Road. Again, a contemporary, updated house on land held by a Sanderson family relative since at least 1864. Nothing seemed familiar to Andrea from her dream of a porch draped and overflowing with red crossvine flowers, but that may have been a stress dream rather than Madeleine whispering in her ear. The thought brought with it the lullaby of baby-stealing fairies Madeleine had been crooning when she woke.

They drove back toward the location of the west camp to check the other addresses. They spoke to a renter at an address with acreage who walked them down to the creek and said there were no home remnants on the land. None of it looked familiar to Andrea. At the last home, a young mother answered the door. The senator was a cousin by some connection, but she didn't know Dewey and she'd only maybe heard the senator's dad's name in passing. She didn't know of any family property called the homestead.

"Guess the day's a bust," Karie said. "Should we find lunch?"

"Let's head back to Winslow Creek. Maybe someone can point us at a historian in the area."

CAMP GRILL WAS LIGHTER and brighter inside than Andrea expected. The unique take on color-block walls was a combo of natural wood panels and cream-colored drywall. Dozens of black-framed photos filled the walls, creating a chaotic geometry. A long counter with bolted down stools fronted the open kitchen and booths lined the two plate glass windows. The place was about half-full. She headed for the counter and Karie followed.

They perused the menu and ordered. While they waited, they watched the flat grill cook work. When he noticed, he asked where they were from. "Charleston," Karie answered.

"Actually," Andrea said, "we're here doing historical research on local properties."

"Oh, yeah? Like which ones?"

"Any properties related to the Sanderson family, so Sanderson, Handley, Swain, Buckley, Gill?"

A male customer two stools over from Karie said, "Swains had a place out Cusper Road."

The one they'd been to last. "Thank you. Do you maybe know of a Sanderson property with an abandoned house on it? We were told about one with a gabled front porch with a load of red crossvine growing on it but no location."

The cook's mouth turned down as he thought. "That those orange trumpet flowers with the yellow crosses inside?"

"Yes, but red and red."

"Nope," the cook said, and the customer shook his head.

"Well," Karie said. "I'm only here for the ghost stories."

"We got plenty of those," the cook said.

The customer lifted his soda like he was toasting the cook. "Amen!"

Karie parked her elbows on the counter. "Give me an example."

"A friend from Pennsylvania went camping about twenty miles from here, north, in the heart of the Cranberry."

The only time Andrea had been to the Cranberry Wilderness, a huge slice of the western part of the Monongahela Forest, was a trip with her parents when she was in elementary school. She shivered. Karie side-eyed her, but the cook grinned.

"You know the Cranberry?"

"The museum. My mom made my brother and I stand by the bear cut-outs. I was eight." And to Karie's confused frown, "They're life-sized."

"Those bear cut-outs are scary," the customer said. The cook fist-bumped him.

She'd been terrified. At once, she'd viscerally understood a bear could eat her, any bear, no problem. "The bears are standing on their hind legs," she explained to Karie. "The grizzly is taller than the polar bear and the polar bear is like three times the size of the black bear. And the black bear was twice as tall as me."

Karie thought for a second. "But there aren't grizzlies here, are there?"

"No, but black bears are big enough, thank you."

"Can't you yell at a black bear and scare it away?"

"No," the customer said. "You have to wave your arms."

The cook pointed at him. "And talk low. Don't scream or run away. That'll make 'em come after you."

Karie cocked her head. "Have either of you ever actually seen a wild bear?"

"Sure," the cook said as the customer smiled and shook his head. "From my car. Saw one eating blackberries on the side of the road."

"One crossed my front porch," the waitress said. She set their waters and Karie's Sprite down in front of them. "Went to eat the neighbor's trash. Was you gonna tell her about the Cranberry guy?"

"Yeah. Hang on." The cook flipped the burgers he had lined up on the grill and pulled the fry basket, reaching for the salt.

"Y'know," the waitress said, lifting the glass dome covering a cherry pie, wielding a spatula in her other hand. "Bob Montpelier talks about that Shawnee brave he saw crossing the road one night."

"And my neighbor," the customer said, "swore he and his whole boy scout group heard a battle taking place all around them in the fog when he was a kid at Droop Mountain. But there was nobody there."

A fresh basket of frozen fries hissed in the hot oil next to the grill and the cook turned back around, wiping his hands on his spotless white apron. "So, this guy I know took his family hiking in the Cranberry. It's like the Bermuda Triangle out there. People disappear all the time. He didn't believe it though, just figured people get lost, inexperienced hikers, you know." He turned back to the burgers, dropping buns on the grill to toast, but raised his voice. "It rained for two days. The kids were cranky. When they get back to camp the second evening, his wife bailed. He had the week off and wanted to stay. They pack the tent and kids' stuff, he strings up his hammock and mummy bag, and he walked them two miles to the car. His wife is gonna come get him two days later.

"He's heard coyotes out there before, but while he's walking back to camp, he hears a howl like he'd never heard before. Scared the piss out of him, but a few minutes later, the coyotes started yipping, so that's all it was, a big yote. But all the way to camp, he keeps hearing the woods rustle around him and he feels like he's being watched. That night that same howl rips him right out of a dead sleep. Sounds like it's right under him. And something stinks, a strong, gamey smell. Then something bumps him from below. It's snuffling and snorting at his hammock.

"You talk about bears—he thought one was gonna eat him. Anyway, he lays there scared shitless till dawn, then decides he was dreaming, and drops outta his hammock, straight into mud. His ground cover and boots were gone. The bag of food he hung was gone. The ashes from his fire were scattered. He heads down the trail a ways to find his stuff and finds footprints headed into his camp. Human. Barefoot. A dozen different sizes. And handprints, too, like they was walking like the kid in the jungle book. He was so freaked out, he just flat-out ran like he had hellhounds chasing him, in his socks, the two miles to the trail head parking lot.

"There's this guy just arriving who took pity on him and drove him to the ranger station where he called his wife to come get him. That was ten, fifteen years back, and he's never been camping since, not even in his backyard, and let me tell you, his kids bug him to death about it."

Andrea couldn't help but think about Adam Ward, abducted from his backyard tent by her neighbor, Susan Pepper. Karie met her eyes and Andrea knew she'd had the same thought. She picked up her water, her throat dry.

"Do you think he'd talk to me?" Karie asked.

The cook set their burgers down in front of them. "He don't go spreading that story around."

"Bob'll talk to you," the waitress said, coming back from delivering the pie to a booth. "He has a little woodshop up the road. I can give you directions."

"I can give you my neighbor's number," the customer added, and towards the cook, "Hey, you think that's what happened to that couple disappeared a few months ago? Got abducted by a cult?"

"Those wildcrafters?" The cook stood there a second with his hands on his hips. "Maybe, if they were in the Cranberry."

Wildcrafting. Andrea knew the term because slaves had often practiced the collection of wild edibles on the plantations to supplement their diets, sometimes domesticating plants they brought back for planting in the vegetable plots near their cabins or cook sheds. Now she wondered if Louie ever bought some of his menu items off wildcrafters.

The waitress refilled Karie's soda. "Or poaching."

"Thanks," Karie said, as the waitress started gathering more glasses, shoveling ice into them.

"Someone disappeared?" Andrea asked, shaking ketchup on her hot fries.

The cook nodded. "A married couple." He snatched up a flat metal blade on a straight wooden handle and started scraping the oil and food bits off the grill.

The customer leaned closer to Karie like he was telling a secret. "Lived up on Bruffey Creek in a cabin they built. They did a fair job of it. They were trying to scrape together a living from YouTube."

Loading the drinks on a tray, the waitress snorted softly.

"Maybe a bear ate them," the cook mused. "Or Bigfoot."

Andrea bit into her burger, surprised at the flavor that burst on her tongue. Holding her hand over her full mouth, she said, "This is really good!"

Freezing with his blade in the air, the cook dropped his mouth open and looked at her over his shoulder, taking pretend offense, then laughed. "Of course, it is! Not much to do around here in the winter but perfect my recipes."

"Well, this is a pretty perfect burger."

He bowed. "Thank you, ma'dam."

She circled a fry in the air. "Is there anyone around here who acts as a town historian maybe?"

"Not anymore," the customer said. "But Ruth Tyson at the pawn shop is older than God."

"And has his memory," the cook quipped, and they exchanged another fist bump.

Karie swallowed the bite of burger she'd been chewing. "There's a pawn shop here?"

"Technically it's an antique shop," the waitress said, sailing by with a trayful of used dishes.

"But she's the unofficial loan officer and resale queen for our little part of the world," the cook clarified. "Not that she ever sells anything she knows somebody's partial to."

The customer pulled a stray order pad from next to a canister of sugar on the counter, wrote his neighbor's info on it, triple-lined "Shawnee ghost" at the top, and slid it over to Karie.

"Thank you," she said.

"You're welcome. Be sure to call him, he's a great storyteller." He dropped a ten on the counter and shoved off as well, leaving Karie and Andrea to devour their lunch alone.

When they'd finished, the waitress swept back by, refilled their waters, and gave them directions.

Karie tucked the notes she'd collected in her jeans pocket as they left the grill. "Sorry," she said. "I'm sure you're sick of all things ghost."

Andrea waved her hand in the air. "They didn't know anything about the properties and it's your job. If this takes as long as Aaron's case, we'll both need an excuse to be over here more."

"Did you just say *case*?"

Andrea thought back to what she'd just said. "I guess I did. But that's what they are, right? We solved Billie Mae's murder, and Lucy Garcia's." She pointed across the street at the pawn shop. "There it is."

"Do you think Madeleine was murdered?"

Did she think that?

Karie stepped off the curb between two parked cars, looking both ways along the nearly deserted road before jaywalking. Andrea followed her. The only traffic in sight turned right before reaching them.

"Billie Mae was murdered," Karie said when Andrea caught up. "So was Bruten Wilder. Aaron appeared after his cousin's murdered remains and his murdered murderer were dug up. He was murdered by the Union, it just took years for him to die. Lucy was murdered. Andy—"

Andrea stopped on the sidewalk in front of the bay window off the pawn shop. Karie had a point. On the other hand, "I've seen other ghosts."

"But all the ones who have come to you in some significant way—"

"—have been murdered." Madeleine hadn't shown her an injury, but not every murder method left a mark on the outside. "I'll have to think about that."

17

Taka let his Sanderson Security jacket introduce him. The girl manning the counter was happy to fetch the manager for him. The manager, a lanky twenty-something with brown hair, a barely-there blond goatee, and a nametag proclaiming him "Nick," moved Taka off into a small office tucked in beside the four-lane indoor range. It was well-insulated. The shots being fired came through the walls as muffled booms. A large, tinted window allowed him to see the full-range and the matching window on the other side of the firing stalls where a safety officer stood in his own office watching an instructor work with a student.

"I guess I know why you're here," Nick said, lifting a stack of files from a foldout chair in front of a cluttered desk. He carried the stack around the desk with him and sat down with it on his lap before he looked at Taka again.

Taka remained standing. "Why is that?"

Wariness narrowed Nick's blue eyes and kept his mouth shut.

Taka bit the inside of his lower lip, caught himself, and stopped, but tilted his head, letting Nick see his determination to wait him out.

"That lady whose husband shot her. She came here."

Taka waited.

Nick's eyes slowly widened as his eyebrows crept up. "She didn't come here?" He paused and then said, with abrupt decision. "She didn't come here. She was never here."

Taka shook his head and sat. Nick deflated.

"Somebody's coming here. Probably state troopers, but maybe a CPD detective or county sheriff." Taka flapped a loose hand at the kid. "Doesn't matter."

"I won't tell them."

"Wrong answer."

"But . . ." Nick said.

Taka waited but the kid just frowned at him.

"Tell them," Taka said. "It's not illegal to help a domestic abuse victim leave their partner."

"Really? Bill said to call him if I ever had a situation like hers, but he made it sound hush-hush. Said not to talk about it."

Taka relaxed and sat back. "Why do you think that is?"

Nick's gaze dropped to the desk, his frown easing away as he thought.

A shot in the range boomed and Taka counted unconsciously as the firing went on.

Four shots.

Silence.

"Safety," Nick said and lifted his head to meet Taka's gaze. "A lot of women come in but a lot of the time they have guys with them. The majority of our customers are men. If we plastered the place with offers to help or made a big deal about it, some of our customers wouldn't care for that. We'd be less likely to be able to help a woman in trouble."

"You're smart. That's good."

"We probably don't help as many as we could though. Just three in the two years since I started here."

"You're a gun shop. You do what you can for a woman like Stacy Owens. Maybe throw some profits at a shelter. Tell the cops you helped, give them all the details, give them names. But ask them not to make your name or store name public so you don't become a target. Tell them keeping a gun range safe is hard enough without a random abuser taking offense that his partner might get help here."

"Plus, I read that a lot of women go back."

Taka thought about Stacy Owens calling her husband from a concrete gas station bathroom while Detweiler filled the tank, about how she left her phone on when she came back and climbed into the car. Did she think he'd treat her better if he were jealous? Expect him to be nicer so she wouldn't leave him? Think she could change him with an ultimatum? "Some do," he finally said. "Some don't. Sometimes the people who help them pay a steep price. You should know that."

"There's not much help around here. I'd do it again."

Taka stood up and pulled his phone from his jacket pocket. "I wrote a couple of other numbers down for you." He opened his Notes app to the screen he'd worked on in the parking lot before he came in and held his phone out. Underwhelming was an overstatement. There were two numbers. The YWCA Resolve program in Charleston and the statewide coalition against domestic violence that referred victims to local groups. In Pinch, that would take anyone seeking help straight back to Resolve. He'd talk to his aunt later. Her church connections might lead to more under the radar help.

Nick pulled out his own cell and took a photo of the two numbers. "So are y'all not gonna help anymore?"

"We're in flux. Call us. We'll either help or try to make a connection for you. Or transport at least."

"Thanks," Nick said, holding out his hand. "You are?"

Taka shook his hand and let go. "Short term. Just doing some policy and procedure clean-up."

Nick withdrew his hand, suddenly awkward. "Oh."

"It's all good. I work directly for Mr. Sanderson. You can call the same number as before."

"And I can tell the cops everything."

"Absolutely."

"Okay."

Nick walked him out.

Taka hadn't shut his truck door yet when his phone rang.

Jimmy.

TAKA'S CELL went to voicemail twice before he finally picked it up, the bastard. "What are they going to tell me when I get there?"

"Where?" Taka said like he didn't have a clue what Jimmy was talking about.

"Whoever's talking at Pinch Sports and Gun, and don't tell me that's not where you went."

"Manager's a kid named Nick. He's got nothing to hide."

Words pooled on Jimmy's tongue, but Nina shifted next to him, and he remembered he wasn't alone. He discarded the first three replies he wanted to make.

"You still there?"

"Yeah," Jimmy spit. "You're tainting this investigation."

"I'm Dewey's head of security. Pinch Sports and Gun is his client. I have every right to check in on a client affected by a tragedy related to the sale of a gun we supplied."

"Did Gavin Owens purchase his gun there?"

"I left that one for you."

"You're on speakerphone," Nina said, leaning forward like she could get closer to Taka that way. "And I'm recording this conversation."

"Nice timing," Taka drawled.

"The gun Gavin Owens used was purchased in Charleston three years ago," she said. "This is the first we've heard of Pinch Sports and Gun being involved. Their involvement might also pertain to CPD's trafficking inquiry related to Detweiler, so you both need to butt out at this—is that you coming up on the Sunoco?"

Jimmy squinted down the opposite side of the four-lane. A big, black Yukon coming fast towards them. Damn if it wasn't. "Pull in," he growled.

Taka's phone cut off.

Jimmy sped up, but the Yukon was slowing. Taka shot him the bird as he turned in.

Jimmy waited in the median for another car to pass and then trundled in after him. Taka pulled his truck over to the dirt shoulder where the station had several U-Haul trailers and trucks parked.

Jimmy blocked him in.

They met at Taka's back bumper.

"I told him to tell whoever came asking the truth," Taka said, leaning against the tailgate. "All they were doing was helping her leave her situation. Safely, I might add."

"She could have called police. She could have driven the kids into Charleston with her."

Taka swung his head, surveying their surroundings, drawing Jimmy's own attention to it. The station, trees, a flapping, wind-tattered American flag on a wooden pole, an abandoned lot next door with overgrown weeds and a tumbled-down outbuilding, two rusting cars, and more trees. "You love a man you don't trust. You have two small children. You get a small window of time once a week to work your courage up. Someone offers to do the hard work of where to go and when for you."

"So, you take it," Nina said. "I get that but going to buy a gun just in case—"

Taka shook his head. "You don't get it. You're a strong woman. You're independent. You have skills and an education. You wouldn't have given Gavin Owens more than twenty seconds of your time before you doused his gaslight with your beer."

Nina sighed, her breath a streaming white puff. "You'd be surprised to meet younger me. Okay, Stacy had no social media accounts. He probably monitored her phone. She had no ability to research resources."

"And they didn't sell her a gun. They got her help."

Jimmy shoved his hands in his jacket and hunched his shoulders against the dropping temperature. "From Dewey?"

"From Chet, anyway," Taka said. "And Detweiler."

"How much involvement," Jimmy ventured, "do you think Dewey actually had?"

Taka shrugged. "The babysitter knew his name."

"He called Detweiler and gave him her address," Jimmy said.

Nina scuffed at the frozen ground with the heel of her boot. She looked sideways at Jimmy. "That call came from a burner."

Jimmy's brain stuttered, giving him Andrea giving him the blow by blow, "*he said, 'Dewey?'*" And her uncertainty if that meant Det was talking to Dewey or about Dewey. A semi passing by on the road washed more cold air over them.

After a long second, she said, "I like the bad guys to wear big 'ol black hats."

Taka lifted his head, his gaze shooting to her, and then he laughed, hard and quick. "Grey doesn't suit Dewey's coloring."

Nina grinned. "Too blond. Way too white."

Before Jimmy could think of anything to add, she said "I can give you Stacy's situation, but what's with the white girl calling Lizzie her aunt?"

Taka sobered, his eyes sharp. "Apparently Dewey's been trying to lighten his hat for a while. And has a hate on for the courts and CPS."

"So going to Pinch Sports and Gun," she said, "wasn't random on Lizzie's part."

Taka waggled his hand. "I doubt it?"

"We're back to CPD and Anna Lansing's kids, aren't we?" Jimmy asked.

Nina nudged his arm with her elbow. "You're the one who was worried no one would keep looking for them."

"You know where they went?" Nina asked Taka.

He nodded. "But Lizzie's girl isn't one of them."

"I'm just a tech," she said. "But my integrity means everything to me. My hat is snow white and it's staying that way."

Taka's gaze wandered to the gas pumps and the man in a brown jacket watching them over the top of his pick-up truck's bed while he pumped his gas. "Who's your liaison?"

Jimmy's nose was running, and his cheeks stung with the slap of the wind. He straightened, ready to get back in the car, go to Pinch. "Horton."

"Ask him to come see me at Kirkby," Taka said, still leaning on his truck. "Tell him not to send Karl."

Jimmy opened his door. "I guess you're not on speaking terms?"

Yanking her own door open, Nina dropped into the passenger seat, flashing an open hand at Taka, and slammed her door shut.

Taka looked away. The fluttering and torn flag snapped on its lines. "Dewey knows I'll always be a cop."

"And he wasn't afraid to hire you."

Their eyes met.

"Exactly," Taka said.

Which meant Dewey also hadn't been worried that Scott would discover enough to charge him with anything. On the other hand, he hadn't given Scott full access or let him in on Detweiler's activities. The only thing Scott had gotten them was the Beretta 92.

Jimmy could've hit himself.

The Beretta.

It had come back as a match to a decades-old homicide.

Is that what Aaron had meant by 'ninety-two'?

Why would Detweiler want him to focus on the Beretta?

"What?" Taka said, standing all the way up.

"Just had a thought." Jimmy pushed his thumb at the open car door, hoping Taka got the hint. "About the number ninety-two. At Louie's."

"Okay."

"Okay," Jimmy said and climbed into the Impala.

Taka relaxed again and didn't look inclined to leave, so Jimmy reversed into a three-point turn and left him slouching there with his hands in his jeans pockets and a thoughtful look on his face.

"WHO'S THERE?" Mrs. Tyson called out when the bell on her door rang. The store was large and packed with huge sideboards, chests, wardrobes, headboards, and trunks. Slanted stacks of doors leaned against the front wall, alongside a collection of andirons and carved fireplace mantles.

"No one you know," Andrea said. "We were sent over by the staff at the grill."

Seated near a pot belly stove in one of four rockers, she waved them over. "I don't see well, but I know my inventory. Come tell me what you're looking for."

"I'm Andrea and this is my friend, Karie. We're researching the history on a couple of properties in the area and were told you doubled as the town historian."

Mrs. Tyson laughed. "I've heard that old joke about me. Ninety-eight is nowhere close to God's age and my memory is only good because my friend Tess really was the town historian."

Was. Andrea sat down next to Mrs. Tyson. "Was as in she's not anymore?"

"Not since she passed three years ago."

"We're sorry for your loss," Karie said, claiming the rocker on Mrs. Tyson's other side.

"She's with her family and I'll see her before too long." Mrs. Tyson reached out and patted Karie's arm. "But thank you. Now what can I help you girls with?"

"We're trying to locate a property related to the Sanderson family. We're just getting started but came to see a few we found." Andrea recited the road names and told her about their brief meeting with Beau Sanderson.

Mrs. Tyson having nodded at the mention of each property, smiled at the mention of Beau. "He's always been a secretive one. Sanging will make you that way."

Madeleine's voice rang in Andrea's head, *that one's a wraith and ain't it been seed a'sangin' in the holler, diggin' and pickin' like it was still a'this world.*

Karie stopped rocking. "Does he deal in ginseng?"

"That Sanderson branch was digging ginseng before I was born. Harvesting, buying, selling. Beau farms it now, too, but the wild men are still worth the most."

"Wild men?" Andrea asked.

"The most valuable roots are shaped like people," Karie said. "Upright with two legs, two arms, a head the plant springs from."

"Twisty people pulled from the ground by their hair," Mrs. Tyson said. "When I was little, I could hear them screaming." Since having her worldview turned upside down in the past few months, Andrea didn't doubt her matter-of-fact statement. "I was out on Falls Branch to meet the senator's man after his dad died. What kind of shape is the house in now?"

"Falling in," Andrea said. "But the two sentinel oaks on either side of the porch are still healthy and the barn is standing. There's some rusted out cars and an antique truck."

"No, with the oaks and that old truck, that's the old Bennett place. The Sandersons owned the property across from them."

"Beau meant on the right instead of on the left?" Karie said.

"We'll have to ride back out there."

Still rocking, contemplating, Mrs. Tyson stared into the fire, but Andrea knew she wasn't seeing it. "Their only son fell from one of those oaks when he was fourteen. Broke his neck. Mr. Bennett was maybe my age when he passed? I don't even know, thirty years ago? His daughter lived there for some time before she passed. The granddaughter ran off. Maybe the state owns it now. Tess probably had a lot of records you might could use. Deeds, for sure. Birth and death records she copied from old journals and family bibles and church registries. Lots the county mightn't have. Old newsletters and announcements. When the little town paper folded up the second time, Dr. Bob, he was Annette Graves' son, gave her all the archives and microfiche. People gave her papers and letters their families had and she wrote down lots of stories told to her about the old days and the meat camps and how the first settlers got here. I miss her. She livened the place up."

Karie paused her chair again, like she couldn't talk unless she was still. "Where'd her records end up?"

"Do you know that library in Charleston?"

"The State Archives are at WVU's library."

"No, the big one on the river, with two names?"

"Waltham-Young," Andrea said.

"That's it," Mrs. Tyson said. "She willed it all to them."

"We work at Waltham-Young," Karie told her while Andrea's mind raced, cataloguing where she might find those records filed, wondering if they'd been digitized yet.

"Well, there you go. Tess Albright."

"None of the properties we saw today were the one we're most interested in from talking to Dewey Sanderson," Andrea said, getting them back on track. "He said it was owned by his grandfather, had been in the family for generations, and that he'd been there as a boy. He called it 'the homestead'. Maybe it's been sold and re-developed, or completely abandoned, but none of properties were what he described."

"And how was that?"

"Off the road, like the Bennett place," Andrea said, the real or imagined dream of it coming back to her in a rush. *Running up through a steep meadow in a dress, the hip-high seed heads slapping against her open palms, laughter in her ears, blue sky above . . .* more details. Maybe Madeleine had touched her while she was sleeping. "A gabled front porch, absolutely covered in red crossvine flowers, thick vines wrapped around the posts, almost making it a private escape. A single story, not big." Andrea closed her eyes, trying to capture the surrounding, *grasping at the hip-high grass, the pebbled slap of the seed heads against her palms, her bare thighs . . .* "A sloped grassy meadow out the back, past the house, cupped like a hand, the deepest part of the palm a pond."

"That's not the place on Falls Branch. Red crossvine. Let me think now," Mrs. Tyson said.

The fire popped and hissed in the stove. They all rocked in a slow discordant rhythm. The store was filled with the kind of solid wood pieces that would withstand centuries of wear and charming baskets filled with doorknobs and sink faucets, and over in the far corner, a stack of oriental carpets laid flat. It occurred to Andrea that everything she could see from her vantage point could be put to practical use. There were no books or toy soldiers or other kinds of knick-knacks. Mrs. Tyson's antique store specialized in salvage. No wonder the people at the grill sent them here.

"I've never seen red crossvine, I don't think. But I feel like I've heard of a place where the crossvine grows wild like nothing you've ever seen before. There's a cemetery lost out there. I'm almost certain Tess would have a note about it somewhere in her papers."

"Have you ever heard of Copper Ridge?"

"Only from the song."

"What song?"

"Oh, Lordy, it's been nearly all my life since I heard it. Mamaw used to sing it to me. Something about a Dawkins boy and a girl from Copper Ridge who broke his heart."

A wild swirl of discovery gripped Andrea, squeezing her breath out.

"She read his future and sealed his fate."

Andrea gasped, sharing a wide-eyed look with Karie.

Mrs. Tyson stilled. "Are you all right, darling?"

"Do you think that story might be in your friend's papers, too?"

She nodded. "We talked about it once, a long while ago. So maybe, if she ever found it."

"We can't thank you enough," Karie said.

"Maybe it was John," Mrs. Tyson said. Her tone was soft, she was still thinking. "You walk down to the Baptist church there on the corner. There's a little churchyard there. Ask for John. He caretakes the place. You ask him about where he keeps looking for that family cemetery he can't find. Ask if there's a place out that way with crossvine growing on it."

18

The Baptist Church was a small wooden frame building with a graveyard filling a two-block area around the back and down the side street. Andrea and Karie climbed the stone steps and pulled the doors open. The familiar scent of old wood laced with floral notes and some earthy incense enveloped them. The church was spare, plain wooden frames on the clear, tall, double-hung windows lining both sides, simple pews, where a single parishioner sat in the third row, and a solid altar. A single, albeit large, crucifix hung by itself on the back wall. The sad-eyed Jesus stared down at an older white man unloading glass vases from a cardboard box behind the altar.

"Excuse me," Karie said, "Mrs. Tyson sent us to speak with John?"

"I'm John." He dusted his hands and came to meet them.

After shaking hands, Andrea explained the situation and described the property. "Mrs. Tyson said she thought you mentioned a property with an unusual amount of crossvine on it while searching for a lost cemetery?"

He looked up, tapping his chin with his fingers.

A rustling in the pew drew Andrea's attention. When she looked, though, the woman was gone. Not in the aisle or leaving, just gone. A draft of cold air blew in, but the doors remained closed. John shivered, turning his gaze across the roof.

"I've got to find that draft," he said, absently.

Andrea didn't think that was going to be possible.

"Oh, that's where it was, it's coming back to me. It's been a couple of years ago, I can't believe she remembered it. I was hot and headed in the direction of a feeder branch to Winslow Creek that I knew about to cool off and found a thicket of crossvine."

"Do you remember about where you were?" Andrea said.

"I was crossing the old Wright homestead—"

Andrea's heart jumped and sped up.

"Homestead?" Karie said.

"That's how its named on the map I have. What'd I say?"

"John," Andrea said, trying to calm the excitement of discovery that made her grab Karie's arm. "Can we get a copy of that map?"

"Sure. If I remember correctly, I got it from an old county survey journal."

"Is there a house on the property?" Karie asked.

"I don't know. I was just crossing through."

Karie, still holding onto Andrea's hand on her arm, turned to her, "Are the Wrights related to the Sandersons?"

"Not that I saw, but I can keep looking, I didn't dig that deep."

"They aren't," John said.

"You know that?" Andrea said, her enthusiasm dimming.

"I'm a Sanderson cousin by way of the Gill branch. I've done a lot of the genealogy myself. That's why I'm looking for a family cemetery that no one knows where it is anymore. No Wrights in the Sanderson tree."

Karie and Andrea let go of each other, Karie asking, "You know Beau?"

John made a funny face. "I do. I don't like to admit it."

"Why not?"

"He's law adjacent if you know what I mean."

"Enough said." Lots of property had been homesteaded in this area over the past three centuries. Still, the crossvine thicket and knowing where it grew might help them narrow their search. The shadowy parishioner reappeared in the third-row pew. She turned the shaded eyes and nose and mouth of her face to Andrea, lifting a barely-there finger to her lips in the universal sign for silence. Andrea didn't know if she meant to hush the three of them or for Andrea to keep the secret of her presence from John. She could get them out of the woman's way, though. She glanced at her watch. "Would it be possible to copy that map today? We might have time to do some recon before we have to head back to Charleston."

"Sure," John said, ushering them back to the front of the church. "There's a copy machine in the office and you can take a photo of my master map if you want. I've marked significant landmarks on each of my searches, though I didn't consider a heap of crossvine as one of them. It'll maybe help you get your bearings."

Andrea glanced back. The woman in the third row remained, once again at peace.

John turned right just before the double doors, taking them down a short hallway into a long narrow reception room and then into a wider office with two desks with computer monitors and keyboards, a mini fridge, a printer, and a couple of metal filing cabinets. A dark-haired woman in her mid-twenties sat at one of the desks, tapping on the keyboard. She lifted a hand in greeting, unfazed at their entry.

John snatched up a packed-full camo backpack leaning against the fridge, lifted the top and extracted a three-ring notebook. He laid it on the second desk and beckoned them forward. He flipped the clear sleeves holding notated maps of all different types and in varying conditions. Each sleeve had a sticker with a map coordinate on it and a sticky note containing references like last names, and landscape features —"sleeping dog rock," "old woman tree". It gave Andrea all sorts of thinky-thoughts on organizing some of her more awkward papers and Karie said, "I should do maps like this for my coneflower fields."

John kept flipping pages, scanning each, looking for the right one. "You have different varieties?"

"I do."

He tapped the sticker on the next sleeve. "Someone brilliant," he said, throwing his words across the small space to the young woman, "suggested it." Six pages later, Andrea spotted the "Wright homestead" reference. Below it was "crossvine house". "Oh, I did reference it!"

"Why'd you say 'crossvine house'?

"I've never seen a thicket that big, the vines must've brought down a couple of trees over the years, or . . ." His eyebrows shot up.

"Covered a house," Andrea said, a glimmer of hope returning even if the Wrights weren't related to Dewey.

He nodded. "It was big enough. Oh! And the flowers were red. I remember now. That's pretty unusual. Only red crossvine I've seen out there."

Her heart tripped again. Hopefully Madeleine wasn't being metaphorical because of her ideas about blood and how thick the crossvine grew.

He fished the map out. It was a taped together seven-page copy of an old survey map with "Wright Homestead" written in an old-fashioned hand to the side. A hundred and ten acres. Iron spikes at the several corners of the awkwardly shaped property bounded by the north fork of Winslow Creek and the feeder creek, three landmark size trees, and a ridgeline. "I don't dare un-tape it."

He carefully folded it, copying it out in sections. After he finished, Andrea waved at the desk. "May I?"

"Sure." He moved the keyboard and they spread the map out.

No buildings were indicated on it. The county would also have plat maps that included the property, but plats didn't usually include buildings. She'd have to see if the county had recorded deeds on the property. Maybe Dewey's grandfather or another relative had acquired the property at some point.

John traced a wavy line on the western edge. "This is the north fork. The crossvine was here"—he tapped on the interior of the map—"on the far side of a field off Charter Woods Road and along the tree line. I entered the property here," he said, running his finger to the western line. "From a deer trail I was following." He tapped again, this time on the eastern boundary. "I seem to recall maybe there was an opening here with an overgrown drive, off the road, but I was just crossing the property, it's not one I was searching per se."

"You're looking for a cemetery?" Andrea said.

He straightened and rubbed his chin. "I am."

The woman swung her chair around. "It's a family quest."

"One I'm beginning to think is quixotic at best," John said, his tone rueful.

Andrea glanced over to see Karie glancing at her with a small smile. During some over-dinner conversation involving a reference to Don Quixote, Taka and Scott had taken to repeating "Quixotic!" at the end of every sentence anyone else uttered, laughing themselves silly until the whole group had joined in and Louie had sent Daisy and Aight to quieten them with unordered desserts.

"How long have you been looking?" Karie said.

"Five years or thereabouts. Here, let me show you the master map."

He replaced the survey and plucked a thick map from the back of the notebook. A regional topographical map of southeastern West Virginia, John had painstakingly hand-drawn in the properties he was searching across four counties. He pointed at a tiny property near his handwritten "Winslow Creek". "This is the Wright homestead. The red Xs to the north and west were original to Sanderson relatives."

"So those might be the properties we're interested in," Andrea said. "If Dewey Sanderson's granddad ever owned them."

John shook his head. "No, ma'am. Dewey's Sanderson grandad was Ezekiel. Now this property across the north fork is still owned by Ezekiel's uncle's descendants, but this property to the west, across the feeder branch, the Sandersons sold that in 1910."

"Have you come across the name Madeleine in the Sanderson family tree?"

"No, ma'am, don't recall ever seeing that name. I think that'd stand out among the Sallies and Janes and Abigails."

Karie picked up the stack of photocopies John had made. "Charter Woods Road?"

"Do the Wrights still own it?" Andrea asked.

"As far as I know."

She snapped a photo of the master map. "Thank you for your time, John."

"Thanks," Karie echoed. "You've never heard of a place called Copper Ridge, have you?"

"No."

The woman swung around again. "I have. It's from a song, but my grandma always said it's really about a girl from Copper Holler over near Slaty Fork. There used to be a community there, but it's been gone a long time." She held out a church business card. "I wrote my cell number on the back. My hobby is abandoned places photography. If you find that crossvine and it really is covering a house, will you call me?"

Andrea took the card. "Absolutely. Have you been out to Copper Holler?"

"No, but I want to."

Andrea pulled her small wallet from her jacket pocket and fished out a business card of her own. "If there's anything left whenever you do, will you call me?"

Her eyes widened as she took in the Waltham-Young logo. "Sure thing."

John showed them back out and waved them down the steps.

A pick-up truck rattled by.

They crossed the street and walked back along the shops to Andrea's FX.

"It's probably a fluke," Andrea said.

"It's the Appalachians. Crossvine's common here."

"It's not Sanderson property. Sounds like John would know if Dewey's grandad ever owned it."

Karie stopped at the passenger door of the FX. "If Copper Ridge is from a song, what's Madeleine trying to say?"

Thinking about Madeleine stroking Dewey's head, Andrea unlocked the car, checked traffic, and stepped off the curb. "I couldn't find any folklore connected to blood and red flowered crossvine. It's a snipe hunt."

"Still, John said it's the only red crossvine he's seen in five years."

"I'm beginning to think Dewey isn't a Sanderson at all."

Karie laughed. "Have you seen how much he and the senator look alike?" She sobered. "Looked alike. Dewey looks just like his dad."

But his eyes looked like Madeleine's. She had to be related to him through one side or the other. Chewing on her lip, Andrea looked at Karie across the top of the car, which made her think of talking to Jimmy over the top of the Impala and Detweiler and the resulting mess

Taka had stepped in with Dewey and the kids. And husbands who thought their wives had left them and fairies stealing babies and some girl from Copper Ridge who broke a boy's heart. Nothing about murder. Which part had brought Madeleine to her? If she figured that out, Madeleine might be the ghost to disprove Karie's theory about murdered ghosts.

Karie held up the copied sections of the map. "What do you think?"

"I think we should find out how far Charter Woods Road is from here."

TAKA WATCHED six or eight vehicles pull into the Sunoco, letting his thoughts spin, before he got cold enough to get back in the Yukon. The information he'd learned in the last couple of days changed nothing. And changed everything. This Dewey wasn't the man he knew. Or thought he knew. And yet, he was.

Dewey had always had a knack for mysteriousness. He always skirted the truth with honesty. He never showed his full hand. He always had a personal motivation for any generosity he offered, always expected something in return. Could it be that occasionally that return was simply a feeling of self-worth? That he didn't always expect some favor or future duty in return? Would he ever go to each of these kids or women or men, for that matter, he helped into new lives to help him in some dark future purpose?

Taka couldn't see that he'd obligate kids or battered women, no matter what he always thought he'd known about Dewey. All he really knew was the perspective Dewey presented him. He was like a damn gemstone, something multi-faceted and shiny on one side, shadowed and burnt on the other. Taka had never considered him unknowable, but maybe everyone was unknowable in one aspect or another. He thought of himself as transparent, but Andrea probably wouldn't like the Taka he'd been in the military. He'd never share his undercover mindset. He had secrets he'd never tell her. Did she?

Of course, she did. It was stupid to think he knew her every aspect, who she'd been with Chuck, how she really . . . His mind blanked, giving him a different Andrea at work and another who saw ghosts. He knew she wavered between confident and scared of what might come next, but really, he couldn't fathom how she steeled herself in the face of it all. He knew he hadn't, probably never would. And it might surprise her how much stronger she was than him.

Scott, too. How much strength had it taken Scott to keep his mouth shut? To encourage Taka to go to work for Dewey? How stupid did Jimmy think Taka was? That wasn't fair though, Jimmy didn't know the things Taka had lied about and the people he'd lied to in the course of pursuing justice. And what for, now that his career had been cut short?

Now Detweiler. Taka had hardly known the man, but a Dewey-enabler seemed far from the trooper he appeared to be. And not just to him. Jimmy was driving on two wheels, trying to stay out of the ditch right now, trying to mesh his friend Andy and partner Detweiler with this man who worked with Dewey to transport kids away from law enforcement instead of to them.

And talk about ditches, Luke Bowman had swerved into a deep one, falling for Dewey's ploy to pass Scott's truth onto to Taka and revealing more than he intended in the process. How the fuck did Dewey do that? And what was the rest of Bowman's story? How did he and Dewey fit together?

Taka pulled his cell phone out. Nothing from Andrea. Nothing from Dewey. Nothing yet from Ronnie Horton, but Taka knew once Jimmy made Taka's request to meet him at Kirkby, Horton would contact him directly. He hovered his thumb over Bowman's contact info. There may not be anyone else he could mine right now for a different perspective while he reeled from his week of personal discovery, but Luke Bowman stood front and center, covered in a layer of mud ready for scraping.

And some of that mud was Dewey's.

He laid his thumb down, chose call, and listened to Bowman's phone ring. It went to voicemail, to Bowman's now familiar voice, dredging up the memory of the skeleton he'd been when he'd opened the door to Taka's knock in Clay less than three months ago. It's like everyone had changed when Taka wasn't looking.

Not "you've reached Lieutenant Commander Bowman" or

"Commander Luke Bowman" or even "Luke Bowman". Nope, the commander's voicemail said, "If you called for a good reason, leave a message. If not, please don't." Please. If Taka didn't know better, he'd think Bowman was a southerner. Taka was calling for a good reason, but his voice wouldn't come.

He cleared his throat.

"It's Taka. Call me."

He hung up and called Chet.

"Taka," Chet said.

"Chet." Thanks to Sadie, he already knew the kids knew Chet and Mr. Andy, but . . . "Do those families, the ones who have the kids, know you?"

"No."

"Did they know Detweiler?"

"No."

Okay, not what Taka expected. He'd thought Lizzie was lying about not knowing Detweiler. "Who's their contact?"

"Brighter Day. You need the number again?"

"How did Dewey set up their cover stories?"

"Cover stories?"

"How the kids got to them. How the families got the kids."

"Ain't no cover stories."

Counting to five, Taka tilted his head back. There was a small stain on the Yukon's headliner in the shape of Tennessee. He closed his eyes. "How'd the kids get to the families they're living with?"

"We took them to other towns and the kids called 'em to come get them. Some got dropped off on doorsteps."

"Three are with families who are strangers to them."

"Hired intermediaries to make friends with the family, abandon them there." He said the word, 'intermediaries' very carefully.

Taka's eyes popped open. A semi came around the corner from the back of the station, the headlights blinding him. He scrunched his eyes tight and then blinked hard. "How'd Dewey know they'd keep them?"

"How would I know that?"

Taka took a deep breath. From the start, he'd gotten way more information than he thought he would. Although disbelieving of the lengths Dewey went to on the one hand—hiring intermediaries? He probably wouldn't risk them to anyone sketch who might just sell them again, so personal security, ex-cops, or military for hire. Bowman came to mind again. On the other hand, Taka was impressed by how clean Dewey made the transition for the kids.

No cover stories.

They could tell their own truth.

Interesting.

19

Twenty-five minutes of winding, rough travel on mostly gravel roads brought Andrea and Karie up the north fork of Winslow Creek to an area skirting the Cranberry Wilderness. There was little traffic, far fewer obvious driveways, and they were separated by long stretches of forest and rambling uphill fields guarded by old-barbed wire fences. Charter Woods Road was marked, but with spotty cell service, they crept along, looking for the survey landmarks on the road: a massive white oak and a possible overgrown drive before the road crossed a short, flat bridge over the feeder creek.

"There's a big oak," Karie said, pointing to the left.

They rolled past. A couple of hundred yards later, a well-established muddy drive, slushy with ice, appeared.

Andrea hummed.

"Yeah," Karie said.

Another two hundred yards, though, took them around a curve in the road and an unobstructed view of a bridge over a creek. "What do you think?"

"I say we take a peek. If the crossvine's not there—"

"It's either gone or we're at the wrong place."

Andrea drove over the bridge, so they weren't U turning on a blind curve. She jiggy-jogged through a multi-point reversal on the narrow road with its deep ditches and drove back over the bridge just as a red truck appeared in her rearview. No "No Trespassing" signs were posted on the barbed wire along the road, though that meant little if there was someone on the property who cared. Nearing the tree-lined driveway, she slowed way down to feel her way into the turn on the icy mud.

The red truck had barreled around the curve and was closing the gap between them fast. Watching the mirror, she tapped her lights, to make sure he saw her. Big and blond, he slowed and lifted a hand. She eased into the drive, again glancing in the rearview as the truck swung wide and went on by, the driver looking right at her.

"Is that Beau Sanderson?"

Craning around in her seat, Karie tried to catch a glimpse. "It's a red Chevy truck. Did it look like him?"

Andrea shook her head. "I don't know. Not enough input for government work."

Karie laughed. "We need everyone in Winslow Creek to paint their cars and houses and acreage with their name and relationship to the Sandersons." She blocked words out in the air with both hands. "Cousin. Customer. Friend. Ex. Previously Owned By. None."

The FX handled the muddy track easily. They drove into a big rolling field with no house or out-building. Andrea stopped. The tire ruts, less muddy out of the woods, continued through the field in a wide curve and back into the far tree line.

John had entered the field from the left. Although she couldn't spot the deer trail hidden in the winter-bare woods, Andrea started looking from that side, over the drive, to the right as far as she could see. She eased down the driveway to give them more of a view to the right. Nothing.

They were almost across the field when Karie threw her hand up. "There!"

And there it was. A grown over mound surrounded by knee-high, winter-brown grass, vine-choked trees at its back. *Grasping at the hip-high grass, the pebbled slap of the seed heads against her palms* . . . "This isn't it," Andrea said. "There's a meadow in back and a pond."

Karie frowned at her then looked back out the window. "Maybe the front faces the woods? The field could be the meadow?"

"Maybe."

"Should we see if there's a house or someone around?"

In answer, Andrea drove them through the tree line. The driveway became a muddy puddle as it wound around and between two huge trees before ending in a parking area in front of an old two-story A-frame with a shallow front deck. No vehicles in front and no lights on in the gloom of the tree shadowed clearing.

Peering through the windshield, Karie said, "You can't leave a business card, can you?"

"I just gave my last one away."

"I don't want to leave one with my title on it. Wait, I think—" She dug her wallet out of her shoulder bag and fished through it, then held up a bright blue business card with a brilliant yellow cone flower on it.

"That'll work," Andrea crowed.

"Should I write a note about the crossvine?"

"I guess you could say someone told you about the color?"

"That'll probably spark a bunch of questions later."

"Yeah," Andrea said, wondering if John had permission to cross property lines in his search. "Maybe just the card. We can figure out the rest later if we have to."

Karie jumped out, cold air rushing in, and leaving her door open, ran up the steps to the deck and knocked on the door. Andrea tapped the steering wheel. She'd hunted down lots of different kinds of information, knocked on stranger's doors to confirm provenance or ask about the history of whatever nearby property she was researching, or about restoration they'd performed to further her knowledge or to learn about resources she could make use of in her job.

But she'd never tried searching for a property like this, by a description and physical search. John had been hunting down his family cemetery by the same method and had been at it five years. How long might it take her to find Madeleine's cabin like this? Aaron was still waiting for her to find Delphia's grave. Her fingers hurt. She loosened her grip on the wheel. Was Madeleine going to be chattering at her for the next ten years?

Karie spun and headed back. Nobody home. Walk across the field or not? She couldn't imagine driving away.

"Ready?" Karie said, sliding into her seat.

"Are you okay with trespassing?"

"In this case? Yes."

She turned around and drove back into the field before pulling just off the drive and parking. If the owner came back, they'd be able to see both the car and Andrea and Karie inspecting the crossvine thicket. No surprises.

When they got out, Karie put another of her cards under the windshield.

"Good idea," Andrea said, zipping up her jacket against the stiff wind.

They kept their heads down and hands in their pockets as they headed for the crossvine thicket. Taka would disapprove of their lack of readiness to counteract a fall or an attack, but it felt like the temperature was dropping by the minute. Coming over the last little hill, Andrea surveyed the field behind the house. Definitely not the right location. The depth of her disappointment surprised her.

"This isn't it," she said, but the wind snatched her words away. Karie, twenty feet ahead, didn't turn.

Did she really think she could just bust out here and locate the place by driving around to a few properties she'd found online? She'd only looked in Greenbrier County, but Nicholas, Pocahontas, and Webster might all be considered "close" to Winslow Creek. And if the Sanderson clan bought in or homesteaded before any of these counties existed, she still had a lot of research to plow through.

She went the other way around the thicket from Karie. Some of the vines were as thick as her wrist with smaller vines threading through the larger and forming a dense mat. Small buds lined the vines beneath the mix of green and brown leaves, biding their time until warmer weather came in March and April.

They met around the far end.

"This isn't it," Andrea said.

"It's wide enough to be a small cabin. And look," Karie said, pointing at the top of the side Andrea had come from, the side facing the field. "It's higher on that side."

She was right. They walked back that way, Andrea paying attention this time to the details, letting her gaze wander the entire face. "It drops off from the middle."

"Like a gable," Karie said.

"Like a gable," Andrea breathed.

They waded closer through the thick, dead grass. Andrea was glad they both wore boots. Her toe hit something solid with a thunk. "Wait."

They felt it out. A wide step. They pulled the long weeds back until they could see weathered grey wood. Another step up and a third and once their eyes adjusted, the porch foundation peeking from between the wall of cross vine. Andrea stepped up on the second step.

"Careful," Karie said.

"Hey, is there somebody there?" A man's voice. Weak, desperate, and coming from inside the vines. "Help me! Please!"

AT LOOSE ENDS and not sure where he wanted to be, Taka went to Louie's.

Daisy opened the door to him an hour before opening. "Need a drink?"

"Yeah."

She went behind the bar herself, scooped some ice into a glass, and splashed a generous pour of Jack Daniels over it. She replaced the bottle and set the whiskey in front of him. "This here is life-figuring out juice. Don't waste it."

"No, ma'am."

Aight backed through the kitchen's saloon doors with a crate of clean bar glasses, steam still rising off them. "Hey, man."

Taka lifted a hand. And found a metal jack parked against his glass.

He held it up.

Daisy smiled at him and took the jack. She tossed it into a half-filled jar of them sitting next to the vodkas on the back bar and went back to her work at the hostess stand. Aight finished placing the glasses and took the crate back into the kitchen, only to re-appear a minute later with a board of sliced bread, a couple of small wedges of cheese, a few slices of salami, and assorted olives. "Boss says eat that and then come back and earn it."

Taka's heart squeezed. "Thanks, man."

Aight held both hands up. "All Louie. I love that man."

"Me, too."

He also knew Louie wouldn't appreciate him horking it down. He watched Aight prepare the bar and savored each small bite as he sipped his whiskey. Feeling remarkably re-centered and finally warm all the way through his bones, he took the board and glass into the kitchen. The wonderful wafts of aroma that had been present in the bar filled his nose.

"Feeling better?" Louie said from across the kitchen where he was working something in a pot with both hands.

"What is that?"

On his way over to Louie, Jesus took the board and glass from him. Taka peered into the massive stock pot where Louie was tearing apart chunks of tender meat with two forks. "Smells divine."

"Venison stew," Louie said. "Been on a few hours, the meat's falling apart."

"What can I do?"

"Roll up your sleeves and wash your hands."

Taka spent the next forty-five minutes not thinking. Instead, he cut cabbage and tomatoes, peeled and rinsed potatoes, and basted duck breasts while they slow fried in a massive wok for Louie's classic shredded duck salad. Then, with appetizer orders coming into the kitchen, Jesus pointed at two small crusty French loaves and a bowl of whipped butter sitting on the prep station. "You go now. Sit at bar." He made shooing motions with both hands, already turning back to his work.

The sous chef grinned as he passed by and said, "Thanks for the help, Taka."

"Anytime," Taka said and realized he meant it.

He almost spun back around when he saw Bowman sitting at the bar, a beer in front of him already. No wonder he'd been shoved out of the kitchen with two loaves of bread. The bartender, a woman named Sue, lifted her brows at him. "Sam Adams. Please."

Bowman grinned over his shoulder at him. "I saw your truck so I knew you must be here somewhere."

"You sure Dewey isn't tracking my phone?"

Bowman shut his mouth and shrugged. "I wouldn't know, man."

"I don't believe that for a second." He set the bread down, Sue slid his beer in front of him, and Aight flipped three small plates onto the bar in front of them like it was a dance they had practiced. Aight poured oil and vinegar in overlapping circles on the third plate and moved on.

Bowman broke a loaf in half for his plate, tore a chunk off, and plunged it into the oil and vinegar. "You called me."

Taka followed suit and they ate half the bread before he said, "I thought you'd just call me back."

Bowman set his beer down and scratched his cheek. He half-turned in his chair like he was gonna get up and lifted his thumb towards Daisy. "You want, I can go over there and call you?"

Taka rolled his eyes. They ate the rest of the bread and sipped their beers in companionable silence. Finally, Taka cleared his throat. "You do Dewey favors, or does he pay you?"

"Why?"

"I need you to do something for Dewey, so I need to know how you guys work."

"Go ask Dewey."

"Dewey isn't going to like it."

Bowman side-eyed him and then took a big swig of his beer while he thought. He set it down and wiped his upper lip with his thumb. "Dewey doesn't like a lot of things. Never seemed to stop you before."

So, Bowman had done some research. Well, Taka had done some on Bowman, too. Or tried. All he found was top of the folder stuff. SEAL. Rank promotions, commendations. He couldn't even find out if Bowman was retired or not. Considering the port at his collarbone, maybe he was on medical leave. Considering his sister Becky's disappearance, maybe hardship leave. Maybe he transferred to the Naval Reserve and was spending his two years deferment from deployment hunting for his sister. "You ever find those kids who were with Anna Lansing?"

"No. What was Andy Detweiler doing at her house?"

Taka frowned.

"Jimmy asked—" He glanced around but the stools to either side of them were empty and no one was standing nearby. "Detweiler, at dinner the other night. Andrea said he couldn't answer."

Yeah. Watching Sue make a martini, Taka spun his beer glass. Bowman's patience as they waited each other out forcibly reminded Taka that SEALs were trained in interrogation. A little differently than he had been, but Bowman might work best on the the tried and true give-a-little-get-a-little approach. "Dewey recruited Andy Detweiler to help him move Anna's kids."

Bowman's face made an amazing transformation into granite. His whole body hardened in a second flat.

"He got them out of the life, like she asked him to."

Bowman didn't relax, but he didn't explode into a tornado headed at Dewey, either. He lifted his beer, smoothly for a guy imitating a tripwire, and drained it. Taka raised his hand in a shot glass gesture at Aight and he hustled over, magicked two shot glasses from under the bar onto the counter, and Sue turned from the Manhattans she was making and slapped the Tattersall into Aight's palm like a true medical professional. He filled the glasses and waited, bottle still raised.

Taka edged one into Bowman's range and drank the other, slapping the empty glass down on the bar. Bowman's gaze shifted to the glass. He picked his up and shot it down. Aight refilled both glasses, handed the bottle back to Sue, refilled Bowman's beer, and headed for the kitchen.

"Okay," Bowman said. "You know where they are?"

"I do. They're with families working with a lawyer who handles third-party adoption."

He clinked his second shot against Taka's where it still sat on the bar and they both drank. Bowman nodded to himself, slowly loosening.

"You're going to know where they are, too."

"How's that?"

"I need someone I trust to go get DNA on each of them."

Bowman considered the foam in his beer. "You don't want Dewey to know?"

"Not yet."

"Handing law enforcement a bunch of swabs isn't going to convince them these are the same kids."

"That's why a CPD detective's going to go with you. Photos, prints, and swabs. CPD can use the photos to confirm ID with the schools they went to here and the neighbors, the carpool drivers."

"And the swabs will clear them from missing persons reports."

"Yes."

"It might actually help their adoptions."

Taka shrugged. "I don't know. Seems like it might?"

"You don't think Dewey would go along with it?"

"I think he'd rather they not be located. He doesn't want anyone looking to closely at what he does. I'm thinking he doesn't want CPS deciding the families need to be fully investigated and inspected before placement can be considered. Or removing them to foster homes until that process is complete."

"That doesn't worry you, too?"

Aight came down the bar with bowls and more bread. Taka's stomach rumbled. Maybe they should order soon—Aight set the bowls of steaming stew and paper-wrapped bread in front of them. "For us?"

"Courtesy of Louie."

The man himself came through the swinging doors, a tray of small plates on a tray. Aight set linen-wrapped silverware down by the bowls. Louie distributed the plates to three bar tables and then came over to pat Taka's shoulder while addressing Bowman. "Hello, Commander, good to see you this evening."

"Hey, Louie!" Bowman shook his licked-clean spoon at the bowl. "I wouldn't miss this stew for anything. This is killer."

"Good to hear that, sir. You boys need anything, you just holler."

"Yes, sir," Taka said. "Thank you."

Louie patted him again and left, making small talk all down the bar.

After he'd assuaged his initial ravenous hunger, Taka broke his bread and buttered a huge chunk of it.

Between bites, Bowman said, "So?"

"So, what?"

"You aren't worried about the cops resorting to CPS first and asking questions later?"

"The lawyer's sharp and the kids aren't wanted. No one's looking for them but us."

"You're saying no one cares."

Taka dunked his bread in the stew. "Cops are human, but CPD doesn't even know yet how many kids they're looking for, only how many different clear prints they got. They may or may not have turned in trace for DNA. I'm betting not, because it'd cost too much. If they did, it'll be bumped a dozen times for higher-priority cases, and it might be years before it's completed. I want to offer them a way to close this case. I give them proof these are the kids missing from Anna Lansing's and they're safe and the courts are addressing the situation and they can bow out."

"And they'll back off Dewey again."

"Human trafficking isn't the right question to be asking about Dewey."

Bowman gave him a long look, obviously questioning Taka's wording and trying to decide what to ask. In the end, though, he just went back to eating.

"Thank you for not reminding me he bought me." In more ways than one.

"I know the Conlons. He saved your life."

Taka's phone vibrated on the bar. He turned it over to a missed call from Ronnie Horton and a text from Andrea. Bowman frowned and dug his own phone out. Taka thumbed Andrea's text open.

20

"You heard that, right?" Karie said.

"You heard it?"

"A guy saying, 'help me'? Yeah."

"Thank God!" Andrea slapped her hand against the crossvines, but it didn't make much noise. "Sir? Sir! Are you trapped?" But stupid question, he must be right?

"Are you being held by someone?" Karie asked.

Andrea looked over her shoulder, her hand straying to her hip holster for reassurance. She hadn't thought of that. "Sir?"

"My wife, my wife," the man said, barely a whisper.

Karie came up next to her and scrabbled along the vines, tearing handfuls of green and brown leaves away, revealing a thick crosshatch of new and old vines.

Trying to rip the smaller vines away from the larger ones, Andrea said, "Are you hurt, sir? What's your name?"

Karie dropped to her knees to look at the base of the vines. "They're so thick. We need an axe or something."

"Flynn." Again, just a brush of sound, barely there.

"Okay, Flynn. We're going to try to get you out of there."

"Flynn?" Karie said. "I couldn't hear him. Ask him again if he's being held here."

"Flynn, do we need to worry about someone coming back?"

Nothing.

"Flynn?"

Karie stood back up. "There's a breeze, right?"

There was a slight puff of moving air hitting Andrea's face. "Yes. This must be the front porch. The vine's running up and over the roof. It can't be that thick here."

"I'll get a stick if I can find one, maybe we can pry the vines apart."

"I have a lug wrench in the car if you can't."

"Be right back." She carefully stepped down into the grass again. "I'll yell if I see someone coming."

Andrea leaned out. "I can see the top of the car. I'll keep checking, too."

If Flynn and maybe his wife got in, it couldn't have been that long ago, so they must've found another way in. "Flynn! Flynn, can you tell me if someone's keeping you here?"

She'd lost the swish of Karie moving through the grass in the breeze. "Flynn? How'd you get in, Flynn?" Now that the first flush of adrenaline had dropped, she saw how impossible it would be for Flynn to have entered from this spot. Crossvine couldn't trap him here, it had to be a person. "Are you locked in, Flynn? Flynn!"

Had he fainted?

She felt her way down the steps and again went back around the house the opposite way from Karie. Now that she had the shape of it, she could see the small cabin's angular lines. Like many rural cabins built in the eighteenth and nineteenth centuries, it must be a story and a half. Eight feet tall on the fireplace wall and maybe twelvish on the tall side, where heat would rise into a sleeping loft. The windows were small and located high on the outer walls, not for the view, but to catch summer night breezes while being easy to cover during the winter.

Beneath the weak, late afternoon sun and rampant growth of vines, something shimmered. The panes of old, waved glass were somehow intact. Around the back, again, the growth was undisturbed. Andrea located the back steps, a stack of flat stones and ripped away enough leaves and newer growth to find the back doorknob. It was cold to her touch, ice-cold iron. It rattled as she jiggled it. To her surprise, it gave with a rusty feel to the joints and turned.

She pushed the door open a few inches. Nothing impeded its opening. A musty, breath of colder-than-the-outside air wafted over her. "Flynn? Flynn, are you there?" No one answered. Andrea shifted on the stairs, torn between absurd relief and fear for the man.

"Here," Karie said behind her, and Andrea startled, her heart thumping hard.

Karie brandished a thick fallen limb, maybe three feet long, the wood stripped where she'd torn off a couple of branches.

"You scared me," Andrea said as Karie said, "Sorry, what are you doing?"

"The back door was unlocked."

"There's no way anyone's been through these vines in like . . ."

"Years, right?" Andrea finished for her. "This isn't months of growth, it's years."

"And if they pushed their way in—"

"They could push their way out."

Andrea pulled her keychain from her front jeans pocket and twisted the mini-tactical flashlight head. A brilliant beam of light shot out. She pressed her hand back through the vine. Karie came up beside her. Like two kids pressing their faces to a backyard fence, they followed the path of the light through the inky dark of the cabin's interior. They couldn't see it all, but there was still furniture, a split leather couch, a rag rug in front of the open fireplace, a pot still hung on the crane arm that would swing it over the fire. Beyond that, a tub sink with an old-fashioned pump handle. A solid round table and four chairs sat behind the couch. Glasses and a stack of plates and bowls sat on a sideboard filling the bit of wall between two doors below the loft. Andrea could just make out the edge of the corner stairs. Shredded curtains. Cobwebs and dust.

"It's like, early seventies?"

Dewey came to his granddad's place as a kid in what must've been the late eighties. But this was the Wright homestead. She pushed that stray thought aside. "Flynn?"

"Flynn?" Karie called, louder.

"He was inside the house, right?"

"Sounded like it."

"Flynn? Flynn, are you there?"

They straightened up. Andrea turned off her flashlight. "Maybe he, like, crawled underneath? For shelter?"

They went back around the front. The older plants climbed the porch beams, the younger plants grew near them, glomming on one and two and three feet up. Plenty of room here at ground level for animals or a person to take cover beneath the house. Andrea squatted and shone the powerful light between the porch beams.

"Flynn?"

A whine drifted out of the darkness at the back. Andrea ran the light across the space, seeing only the stacked stone pillars holding up the floor joists. Beside her, Karie shuffled left, her hair swinging as she tilted her head. "To the right."

Andrea reversed the sweep of the light. Animal eyes flashed red, and the whine drifted to them again. "Sounds like a dog."

"I don't know," Karie said. "Whatever it is, it's big and lying down."

Andrea held out her hand. "Hey, pup, c'mon."

The animal crept forward on its belly.

"C'mon, pup, you're okay, c'mon."

The dog, and it was a dog, Andrea could see now, whined, wriggling forward, and wagging its tail.

"Oh," Karie said. "Poor thing. C'mon, baby, c'mon."

Near skeletal, the dog was all long face and ears and back. And scared. When it neared them, it stretched its neck and head out, tongue licking the air just beyond their fingertips, crying piteously. Andrea handed the flashlight to Karie and wiggled between the vines to crawl under the porch. Crying still, the dog lay over on his side, stretching out his front legs to paw at her.

"It's a bloodhound," Andrea said, rubbing the dog's head and ears. "It's okay, pup, you're okay. Pass me the light?"

Karie gave her the light then stood for a second. When she crouched back down, she said, "We're still alone. Except for Flynn, wherever he is."

"What if he's passed out in the house?"

"I don't know how he could be. How would've he have gotten in without it being obvious?"

The dog appeared okay except for some oval scabs across her lower ribs and flank. "It's a girl. She's okay, starving, and some scrapes that are healing." She shined the light across the crawlspace. "Nothing else under here but a pile of boards."

"Maybe Flynn can hear you better under there?"

"Flynn?" Andrea called out. Then she leaned her head back and really yelled up at the floorboards, "Flynn? Flynn are you there?" A long moment later as she listened hard for any sound above her, a breathy 'yes' echoed in her ear. All the hairs stood up on her neck and her skin prickled with goosebumps. A cold breath of air kissed her cheeks. She scrambled back. The dog rolled up on her chest and let loose two booming barks, then lifted her face and howled.

Karie lunged under the crawl space to grab Andrea's jacket and pull her out. "What? What?"

"Flynn," Andrea rasped. "Flynn's dead."

"But I heard him."

"What'd you hear?"

"Same as you, 'Help me.'"

"I heard him ask if anybody was there and then he said, help me. He mentioned his wife. Gave me his name."

"So I heard a disembodied voice? That's rare."

The dog went back to whining. She army-crawled to Andrea, where she lay half in Karie's lap, both of them sprawled on the ground just outside the crawl space. The dog had a weathered leather collar on. Andrea's fingers slid over it as the dog scrabbled out from between the vines, but she couldn't grasp it.

The big, dirt-crusted dog bolted into the tall grass, then fell. She staggered up while Andrea and Karie climbed to their feet, then totter-trotted away. Andrea looked at Karie, who shrugged. They followed the dog. She headed in the direction of Winslow Creek across the field.

Andrea was a little worried about the footing in the tall grass, but the ground was fairly firm, and not too uneven. The creek was wide but shallow. The dog didn't cross it. She lapped for several minutes, long enough for Andrea and Karie to catch up to her, but she skittered away when Andrea reached for her collar again.

She headed along the creek away from Charter Woods Road and the bridge crossing, towards the same tree line that traversed the field. The sun broke through the cloud cover, low above the horizon. Andrea yanked her phone out.

"What time is it?" Karie said.

"Quarter til five." They had maybe an hour and fifteen minutes before full dark. No signal out here. "Hey, pup! Pup, come! C'mon!"

Andrea turned back the way they came, slapping her thigh. Karie followed her lead. They walked a few steps back, calling to the dog. But the dog didn't come. She stopped when they kept retreating and sat down, her hips and back legs jutting through her skin at grotesque angles. After a moment of watching them leave her, she pointed her nose up and howled, a long, deep, mournful bay.

She had a beautiful voice. Andrea stopped.

"This is so sad," Karie said. "Who would abandon her like this?"

The dog got up, snuffled along the ground, and disappeared into the trees.

"God," Andrea said.

Karie broke into a trot. "Come on."

In the woods, they found the dog again waiting on them before she leaped up and moved deeper into the gloom. Ten minutes later, they broke cover near where the feeder stream babbled into Winslow Creek. Hundreds of starlings in the trees chittered and warbled. A crow on their side of the stream cawed and fluttered his wings.

The dog splashed across. Under the shade of an oak ten yards from the stream, a magnificent male bloodhound bounced up at the sight of her, running out to meet her. The dog, their dog, wagged her tail and stopped to say hi, but when the male snuffled at her ears, his head went right through hers and she jumped away from him.

Andrea froze.

Losing his solidity, he gave chase, but she was too weak to go far and turned back towards him. She lowered her front end in play-with-me mode, but then her hind end sunk until she was laying down. She panted, her sides heaving. He circled her and lay down facing her, head on his paws. Andrea could see the sparse, stalky weeds he should have compressed sticking up through him.

Karie had splashed on through the creek and up the shallow bank. With their always startling synchronicity, the flock of chatty starlings lifted from the trees and ground as one and wheeled away, leaving the crow cursing them from his tree. Andrea's blood rushed through her, deafening her to the crow, and she plunged into the creek. Her breath stuttered in her chest at the shock of the cold water spilling over the top of her short boots, soaking her socks and feet.

Karie crouched and petted their dog. By the time Andrea reached her, she'd stripped her belt from her jeans and threaded it through the dog's collar. The ghost of her companion stood, mouth open and tongue hanging out between his large teeth, looking at Andrea with expectation.

Karie frowned up at her. "What are you looking at?"

"There's another dog here. He's a bloodhound, too. Gorgeous."

Karie laid a hand on their dog's bony back, as if to reassure herself she was flesh and blood, still living. "I have a bad feeling about this."

"And how," Andrea said.

The companion turned. Their dog jumped up, pulling Karie to her knees. "Whoa, girl."

The dog whined, straining against Karie's hold on the belt. Her companion walked past the oak, away from the stream. Andrea followed, Karie and their dog behind her. Only a few feet past the oak, Andrea saw the companion's skull on its side, among a scatter of bones half hidden under leaf mold. Not far away, an ochre half-dome of bone rose above the ground, a shoulder blade resting at an angle across it.

"Is that—?" Karie stage whispered.

Andrea walked around the half-dome to see the other side.

A human skull.

"Yes."

The companion lay down among the bones.

His anxious gaze traveled from Andrea to the rambling holly bush surrounding the trunk of a young maple. She crouched down. The empty stare of a second human skull bore through her. When she glanced back at the companion, Madeleine sat beside him, stroking his head, but watching Andrea.

The companion sighed.

Madeleine's dress and red hair lifted.

A gusty breeze rattled the holly's limbs, and a handful of brown leaves drifted down.

And then they were gone.

Beside Karie, their living dog's long howl stilled the small rustlings around them and silenced the crow.

———

"AND THE HITS just keep on coming," Taka muttered.

"That Andrea?" Bowman said. "Karie says they found human remains. They're waiting on the sheriff's office."

"She told you they found the same yesterday, right?"

"What'd they find twice?" Jimmy said from behind him.

"Bones," Taka said, aware he sounded sour.

"Madeleine's, do you think?" Bowman simply sounded intrigued.

"Is that the chatty ghost's name?" Jimmy had the grace to look around too late, but the noise level had built to comfortable to talk, but too loud for private conversations to be easily overheard.

"Yeah."

"Why you upset?"

"Andrea doesn't want to call attention to herself but finding remains two days in a row isn't exactly keeping a low profile."

"She was really scared to report finding Andy," Bowman added. "That's why we did it anonymously."

Jimmy lifted his hand at Aight. "Tamarin tossing her in a cell made an impression even if it was just for show."

"I told her that's probably what he was doing," Taka said. "Did you?"

"No. Maybe we should make Tamarin tell her."

"Naw. He really gave us the side-eye after everything else went down. Now that I'm gone and working for Dewey—"

Aight grabbed the Tattersall on the way over, but Jimmy stuck his hand between Taka and Bowman to cover their shot glasses. "Could you make me a sandwich to go? Tell Louie anything he wants to give me is fine. And bring these guys their check."

Bowman lifted his brows. "Where we going?"

Aight hustled away.

"Not you so much as Taka." He straightened up, directing his next words to Taka. "Ronnie Horton said you didn't answer. He told me to find you."

Taka glanced over at Bowman. "You in?"

Bowman nodded. He picked up his beer.

"I won't ask," Jimmy said. "You still want to meet him at Kirkby?"

Meeting Horton by himself at Kirkby was one thing, but with Bowman and Jimmy along, it'd take longer, and if word got back to Dewey before the plan was in motion, he'd be scrapping for a knockdown drag out fight with Taka that he wasn't ready for. "Andrea's. Ask him to bring Fields."

"Fields?"

"Please."

When Taka didn't say more, Jimmy said, "Andrea going to be there?"

"She and Karie are still out near Winslow Creek."

"Madeleine's bones, right," Jimmy said. He turned and threaded back to the door to make his call outside.

"He didn't know they were going out there?"

"He's been busy."

Bowman once again made the wiser choice. "Fields. He with CPD?"

Taka took the check Aight handed him. It only totaled the beer and two shots. "Horton, too. He's liaising with the state."

They put their cards on their checks. Bowman finished his beer. Taka eyed the remainder of his and drank half his water in one go. Aight came back with Jimmy's sandwich and Taka added his check to his share. What was Jimmy doing out there? Working out a whole surveillance plan for Andrea's?

Five minutes later, they found Jimmy still on the phone outside. Taka pushed his sandwich bag into his chest. "You owe me," he mouthed and kept walking. The crowd was middling for a cold

Wednesday night. The bakery next to Louie's was selling huge cupcakes from a sidewalk cart. Live music and wide swaths of light spilled out of the art gallery, its doors open to the cooler air as patrons gathered in clumps with drinks in their hands.

Jimmy fell into step with them. "Yeah, Sparkles, I'll tell him. Thanks. Okay, tell your aunt I said bye. Okay, bye." He thumbed the call closed and said to Bowman, "Bella says thank you for coloring with her."

Bowman's face lit up like someone had just given him a Lamborghini. "The littlest little? Why were you talking to her?"

"I, uh, kinda made plans with her aunt for dinner, but—"

Bowman's expressive brows drew down as he connected dots. It made Taka appreciate the effort he must put into his poker face, because despite his easy show of emotion, Luke Bowman's stony stillness when he put it on was impressive.

"Sorry," Taka said.

"It wasn't a big deal. Just to give her a breather."

"Getting two kids dumped on you would definitely be an adjustment," Bowman said. "She's not married?"

"No."

"She got help dealing with her sister's arrangements?"

"Her mom and younger brother and his family live here."

They'd crossed the street to the Huntington Bank parking garage and up the first flight of stairs. Taka pulled the door open.

"Nuh-uh. You're not driving," Jimmy said.

"It was two shots, half a beer, and a lot of stew, I'm fine."

"Nope," Jimmy said.

"I had more," Bowman said. He pointed to his port. "I wasn't planning to drive anyway."

"Both of you with me. I'll bring you back in the morning."

Taka let go of the door and held his hands up. "Whatever." And the truth was, he was tired. He needed a good workout and a shower and a full night's sleep. Two out of three at Andrea's would be fine.

Once they were in the dark quiet of Jimmy's Impala and headed out, he texted Andrea. *Bowman and I going to yours for night, okay?*

Her answer came right away. *K. Depty just arrived. No signal at the propty. Don't know when I can call you.*

Are the bones Madeleine's?

No.

Another text bubble popped up right away with three dots as Andrea composed. In the front passenger seat, Bowman was also texting.

It wasn't even Sanderson propty, Andrea sent back. *I don't know how its connected. Gotta go.*

Then why were they even there? And who had they found? But he only texted, *Stay safe.*

She texted back a thumbs up emoji and a heart.

Great.

"Karie said they found a cabin covered in red crossvine," Bowman said. "And a dog led them to the bones."

"More than I got," Taka said. "The property they were, probably, trespassing on isn't even a Sanderson holding."

Jimmy caught his gaze in the rearview. "Hey, they're fine."

"They don't even have signal out there."

Jimmy looked back at the road. "Andrea can protect herself. You taught her how."

"And they're with Greenbrier County deputies," Bowman added. "They're waiting for animal control to come get the dog and take it to a vet. Apparently, it's been on its own for a while." He held up his phone so Taka could see the pic Karie sent him.

An absolutely huge and emaciated dog lay across the back seat of the FX, its head in Andrea's lap as she sat with the doors open. Thinking of the mouse she'd seen at Waltham-Young, he said, "At least it wasn't a ghost dog."

Bowman laughed. "There was one of those, too."

Taka shook his head. "Send me that pic."

His phone lit up a second later. He studied the dog. And the girl. His girl. She always had been. He'd just always been too afraid to let her. He just wanted her here and safe. Actually, he wanted her here and safe and in his arms. An Andrea hug and reassurance that he was making the right decision about the kids would go a long way right now. For a moment, he let himself think about the impulse he'd had to kiss her in the elevator. He should've kissed her.

"My folks always have room for another dog on the farm," Jimmy said. "If no one claims it."

He'd known as soon as he kissed her for cover in December, there in the parking garage they'd just left, that he wouldn't ever leave her again. That he'd either prove his cowardice by keeping her at arm's length to preserve their friendship or finally find his courage and give her the love she deserved and hadn't found yet. He hadn't expected Scott to see through him.

"I'll tell them," Bowman said, thumbs flying.

And, forced to admit he'd never leave her, he hadn't expected this . . . fall . . . for her. He thought he'd already loved her fully, deeply, just not physically. But just looking at her, the long straight plane of her nose, the angle of her cheek, the shadowed curve of her lips, her long hair pulled loosely back, draping over her shoulder onto the dog as she stroked it, he fell a little more.

"Andrea already told them she's keeping it," Bowman said. "They're headed back to take the deputies to the bones now."

"Good," Taka said and closed his phone.

21

J ust before six a.m., Jimmy dropped the Columbian Taka favored by
the spoonful into Andrea's coffee maker. The choice to meet at
Andrea's had been a good one. While Jimmy planned only on
playing the part of facilitator, Ronnie Horton not only asked him to
stay and witness, but also had him record the meeting.

Pacing the kitchen, Horton had time to process Taka's revelation of
the purpose behind Dewey's meeting with Anna Lansing while Andy
Detweiler snuck the kids out of her house through the back. Taka
explained that as Dewey's head of security, he had already hired Luke
Bowman as a neutral contractor to collect neglected evidence to protect
his employer against any future claims of wrongdoing related to his
employer's charitable work. He invited Horton to allow Fields to
accompany Bowman as a witness to assuage future concerns CPD, the
WVSP, or the FBI might have concerning his employer's charitable work
providing abuse victims with safe haven.

To Jimmy's surprise, Horton accepted Taka's explanation and
invitation. He also agreed to keep Karl and Sheryl in the dark until they
were needed to verify the info and run missing child checks to make sure
no family was searching for their missing kid. Taka seemed sure that
wouldn't be the case. Since Linda Conlon had chosen her victims well,

Jimmy figured he was right. He filled the coffee pot with water and poured it into the maker, flipped the lid down, and hit the brew switch.

What Taka didn't ask, and Horton hadn't promised, was not to run it all by the DA before closing the case if the info checked out. But Horton did agree with Taka that trying to prove Dewey was doing anything criminal by removing kids from an unsafe situation might be a hard swing and a waste of taxpayer money. He kept any thoughts he had on a possible charge of bribing a state officer to himself, which Jimmy appreciated.

God, if Detweiler had taken money from Dewey, Jimmy really *would* start questioning his instincts. How had he not known Andy had been compromised? Seen it? Heard it in Andy's protests that anyone could lose a suspect in traffic, that he needed down time away from his phone?

Jimmy set out three mugs and pulled a carton of milk from the fridge. He could've gone home, but after Horton and Fields left, he finally ate his sandwich while Taka and Bowman finished off Andrea's ice cream. They'd caught him up on Andrea's latest ghosts, including the flat-footing grandmother. By then they'd finished her half-full Jamison's and were talking Valley Girl. Taka made no bones about taking Andrea's room and Bowman had claimed the couch, so Jimmy slept in the guest room, trying not to think about Taka's depiction of being creeped out by Billie Mae while sleeping there, or Bowman's description of Madeleine's shadow slipping up the staircase.

He hadn't slept well.

Stealing a notepad and pen from Andrea's pile by her cookbooks, he started a list of what they needed to replace. Taka padded in, pulled the coffee before it was finished, and filled two of the mugs. The pot hissed and steamed when he stuck it back on the warmer. He doctored his and slid Jimmy's in front of him black.

"Thanks, man. Bowman?"

"Snoring."

They sipped.

Taka added sourdough bread to Andrea's list.

"So," Taka said. "The ninety-two?"

"How good of friends are we?"

"State stuff?"

"Yeah."

Taka met his eyes. "I'll keep pretending Scott's not law enforcement and that you never told me anything related to the number ninety-two."

The words of denial were right there but Jimmy couldn't bring himself to lie anymore about Scott. "An asset gave us a Beretta 92 from Dewey's collection. The casing was a possible match to one found at the scene of the senator's assassination."

"The senator had a Beretta 92. Did he fire it in self-defense?"

"It wasn't a match. But it did come back as a match to a murder from the 1980s."

"Why would Andy want you to look at that? They're sure Gavin Owens shot him, right?"

"Yes. Bullet match for Gavin's gun. And yesterday morning they matched a bullet lodged up against Gavin's pelvis as mine."

"So you hit him. Why the Beretta then?"

Jimmy kicked back in his chair and sipped his coffee. "Only reference to ninety-two I can think of."

"Did you pull the old murder case?"

"No. We noted it and had the asset replace the gun before Dewey missed it."

"Can you still pull it?"

"I don't know. Probably not without a lot of questions. I'll ask Nina to. Can you figure out a way to ask Dewey how his dad ended up with it?"

"I can try. Bowman's up."

They listened to him close the half-bath door and turn the fan on before he started retching.

"He looks better," Jimmy said.

"Still gotta suck to be him right now." He got up and gathered eggs and ham and cheese.

Jimmy added all three to the list. Bowman came in looking pale and sat down. Taka poured milk and coffee in the third mug and handed it to Jimmy who shoved it over in Bowman's direction.

They all lifted their heads at the growl of Andrea's FX pulling in. Taka pulled down two more mugs and Jimmy was glad he'd made a full pot. The mud room door swung open. Andrea smiled wide when she saw the three of them. "Luke's here," she called back to Karie.

"Oh, good! I was worried."

"And Madeleine, yay," Andrea said, with faint sarcasm. "She's talking about the fair-haired boys being a nickel for every dark-haired dime down Jackson way."

"Is the trapper here, too?" Karie asked.

Jimmy tensed, waiting to see if they'd all hear the physical rapping Taka and Bowman had told him about, but Andrea shook her head. "I don't think so. It felt weird when he was here, kinda dark and heavy."

"Where's Jackson?" Taka asked.

"It's abandoned," Bowman said. "It was a community that flooded out on Cherry Creek over a century ago between the western Winslow Creek meat camp and Richwood."

"What he said," Andrea said, making a beeline for the coffee. Taka turned, holding out their mugs. Andrea took a long swallow, then immediately pitched in. She flipped the oven on and dug a bag of English muffins out of the freezer.

Karie hugged Bowman from behind, then flopped down beside him and added English muffins to the list. Bowman looked a little better after getting half his coffee down, but Karie said, "You look terrible. Are you okay?"

Bowman rubbed his face with both hands. "I, uh, drank a little more than I have in a long time. My anti-b's didn't agree with my decision."

Karie's brows shot up and she looked at Jimmy. He put his hands up in self-defense and then got up to set the table.

Taka poured a dozen beaten eggs thinned with milk into heated pans for two large omelets. "They take a guess on the remains?"

Andrea finished breaking the muffins apart and shoved the baking sheet she'd put them on in the oven. "They did, based on the dog. She had a collar with her name and a phone number that matched the number of a couple that went missing a few months ago. Flynn and Rachel Iverson."

She handed butter and jam to Jimmy.

"But we already knew Flynn's name," Karie said, taking the butter and jam Jimmy passed to her.

"Let me guess," Bowman said.

"I heard a disembodied voice!" Karie said before he could. "First time!"

Jimmy handed her five plates. "How can that be so exciting? You've seen an actual ghost."

"Yeah," she said, setting the plates out. "But this is the first time I ever heard a disembodied voice!"

Taka flipped the eggs with a spatula. "And that's exciting?"

"Damn straight."

Taka grinned at Andrea and flipped the second omelet. She spread a huge handful of shredded cheese on the first. "You heard more than she did?" he asked her.

"Damn straight."

"So what'd that have to do with Madeleine?" Jimmy said, passing silverware to Karie.

"Haven't the foggiest," Karie said.

"But show them the photo of Flynn," Andrea said, dropping cheese on the second omelet.

Karie picked up her phone and scrolled through it. She held it out to Bowman. He squinted at it and then his eyes widened. Jimmy leaned over the table to see, Karie turning the phone to show him.

It took a second because Flynn wasn't blond, but then it clicked. "Well, shit. Does Dewey have a brother we don't know about?" Before the words were all the way out, he was remembering the fake birth certificate.

"No," Taka said and came over to look, spatula in hand.

The fake certificate they only knew about because of Andy's insistence on checking Dewey's mom's DNA.

Jimmy watched Taka cattywampus to see his reaction. A deep frown. He didn't know.

Why had Andy latched onto that? He'd been obsessed.

"You know," Taka said, "what's been bothering me?"

Jimmy shot a look at Andrea. She glanced over her shoulder at them but was trying to get ham on the omelets and from the look in her eyes he wondered if she was listening to Madeleine.

"What?" Bowman said.

Taka noticed Andrea still dropping ham and returned to the omelets, flipping the eggs over on themselves and squashing them down with the spatula before he spoke again. "That knocking, from the trapper or whatever." He flipped both omelets over again and turned the stove off while they waited for the other half of his sentence. He turned around to face them. "It came in response to Andrea asking if the homestead was owned by his mother's family."

"But it wasn't," Karie said. "Andrea checked."

"His mother's family never owned anything in West Virginia except in Kanawha County," Andrea said. "And not as long ago as I'm guessing Madeleine's from. But—"

Jimmy hoped his face was as blank as he was trying to make it.

Bowman's gaze slid over and met his for a moment.

Jimmy shrugged and Bowman looked away, back to Andrea.

The inspection made him wonder all over again just who Bowman was and if his sister's disappearance was all that had brought him here.

"You say it first," Taka said.

Andrea narrowed her eyes at him, her lips pressing together. She drew in a deep breath and said, "Maybe Dewey's mom isn't his biological mother."

Taka brandished the spatula. "Exactly what I was thinking."

At least Jimmy could rest securely knowing he'd not compromised his legal knowledge, even if it felt like he was once again being dishonest with people he'd become closer to in the last few months than most of his work mates.

And, with a fresh burst of remorse, he wished Scott was here with them. Though, really, he and Scott had inserted themselves and lied to all of them and interfered with Andrea and Taka's dynamic and if he cared so much about them, why the fuck was he still here? Not only here, but still lying to them?

Across the table, Karie snapped her fingers. "Earth to Jimmy, Jimmy come in."

"Yeah," he said. Because Taka might actually stand a chance of finding out why Dewey's birth certificate was fake. And why Andy cared. And yeah, give the investigation more room to run, 'cause Jimmy was that guy, the one who only lived to work.

Andrea stood beside him, holding out a plate with a perfectly toasted English muffin and a wedge of omelet on it. "Here, go sit down. I'll get you more coffee."

Studying him, Bowman shoved the chair closest to Jimmy out with his foot.

"Yeah. It's just been a long few days," he said, sitting down, feeling like shit, but unable to stop himself. "I've gotta change and meet Mia and Andy's brother at the crematorium."

"That's rough, man," Bowman said.

Jimmy nodded and dug into his food, conscious of the sympathetic silence as they all let that thought lie.

"Okay," Taka said as he and Andrea sat down with their own plates. "Tell us what happened."

"For a while there," Andrea said, "I felt really stupid to think we could just go out there and drive around looking."

Stuffing his feelings down deep in his gut, Jimmy shoved a big bite of omelet in his mouth and listened up. Because not only did meeting Andrea make him want more out of life than work for the first time in his career, meeting Andrea had completely blown up his worldview. And ghosts were fascinating.

"One," Taka said. "Recon is valuable."

Taka had done military recon overseas, but Jimmy couldn't remember if Taka had ever told him that or he'd read it in a file.

"Two," Taka continued. "I can't tell you how many hours at CPD, first as a patrolman and then as a detective, I spent cruising streets just looking for people or cars."

Jimmy pointed at Taka with his fork. "At least half. It's ridiculous how many times that's our only option."

"Start at the beginning," Bowman said.

And taking turns, Andrea and Karie laid out everything in detail.

THE THING about being a state investigator? Jimmy always had a fresh suit in the car. Andrea had a meeting at nine, but she waited to see him off. They all did. Taka and Bowman gave him hugs, Karie stood on her tiptoes and kissed him on the cheek. "We're here for you. But if you need us there with you, just call."

Andrea kissed him on the other cheek and straightened his tie before giving up and hugging him. He hugged her back, a little longer than he should have maybe, but he really, really didn't want to go witness Detweiler's literal bodily end. It was hard enough knowing he'd never hear one of his really bad jokes again or argue about the finer points of a case, or watch his smile widen when he talked to his kids on the phone. It was hard enough accepting he might never know Andy's motivation in crossing the line to work with a criminal suspect, let alone exposing an undercover, and getting mixed up in a domestic dispute that cost him his life.

He drove over to the Embassy Suites, somehow, because he couldn't recall anything about the drive. Andy's brother, Leon, was a soft-around-the-middle cyber network salesman, his dark hair greying at the temples. He stood out under the portico with his hands in his suit pockets. Jimmy pulled up beside him and he yanked the passenger door open and dropped inside. They didn't speak.

The ride wasn't long. Jimmy parked in the side lot of a family-run funeral home with a long history of serving law enforcement in Charleston. He turned off the Impala's engine but didn't make any move to get out. They were early. Mia's car wasn't there yet. "How'd your meeting with the investigative team go yesterday?"

"It helps that they already know who killed him. They told me the killer offed himself, but you had shot him, too. I'm okay with that. Thank you for getting him."

"I didn't know, when I shot him, that Andy was already gone."

"I don't care," Leon said, tone vehement. "You shot him defending others. He might have killed them, too, otherwise."

Jimmy nodded.

Leon sighed and looked out the windshield at the beautiful brick building that hosted the leftover bodies of the people who had once inhabited them. The small crematorium was just visible, a separate arched entryway attached to the main business by a covered walkway. "You know," he said. "Andy and I aren't really brothers."

"I do know that. But you were brothers in every way that counted. That's why he listed you as next of kin."

"We were in foster care together. Four homes over the years where we ended up spending time together again. By the last one, we'd figured out pre-paid phones and always managed to beg, borrow, or steal enough to stay in contact. In high school we met up a lot, stayed away from our fosters as long as we could get away with until we aged out. We roomed together off and on after that."

"How'd you end up in foster care?"

"My mom and dad were addicts. Meth, crack, heroin. They didn't care what they used if it got them through the next few hours. They made the mistake of selling me to an undercover officer when I was five. It wasn't all bad being in foster care. The families I was with were better than being in the group homes. I never hit the golden ticket, but at least we had a lot more freedom. But Andy had a bad turn with a foster dad when he was like, ten, and he never settled in anywhere after that. Hated every second."

"You know about his parents?"

"Yeah. His old man killed his ma. Got life. You know he saw it, right?"

"Saw what?"

"He was sitting right next to his ma when she was shot. Said he could never get rid of the feeling of warm blood on his face, like it was a scar you couldn't see. He still did that funny thing when he was reading or whatever, right?"

"You mean rubbing his finger under his eye and up over his temple?"

"Yeah. When he was a kid, he sometimes rubbed that line raw."

"Drove me crazy some nights when we worked late. Especially on surveillance."

Leon slid his gaze over and met Jimmy's eyes. "Trying to wipe the blood away."

"Jesus Christ."

Leon went back to staring at the building. "Hey. Will you check for me?"

"Check what?"

"That it's really him. In the box." He rubbed his palms over his knees. "Y'know, before they flame him up."

Jimmy's stomach rolled. Andy had been shot in the head. They last thing he wanted to do was look at him. But Leon was pale. A bead of sweat rolled out of his hairline and down his cheek before he swiped it away.

"I just gotta know, you know, that it's really him."

"Of course," Jimmy said. "I'll make sure."

22

On the way to work, Andrea called Megan, the shared intern she snagged at the start of the year for her exclusive use. Although she'd been scared that the cost of her arrest in December might be her job, Bobby Waltham had preferred to focus on the fact that one of his employees had stopped not one, but three murderers using Waltham-Young resources and the great publicity that gave the institution. Although he still wasn't clear on the details, he had basically told her to keep up the good work. As long as she kept her paying clients happy, he'd give her freedom of time and resources for as long as he could. They'd meet and re-evaluate annually.

Andrea didn't intend to take advantage. With intern Megan's help, she'd try to earn her keep, and Megan's, in the kinds of projects that she'd ended up specializing in over the past decade. But it didn't look like her problem with ghosts was going to simply resolve itself, so not taking Bobby Waltham at his word wasn't going to be an option. On the fifth ring, Megan answered, out of breath.

"I'm headed in," Andrea said.

"Your nine o'clock," Megan huffed.

"Yes. Are you okay?"

"I couldn't get my phone to answer your call. I'm down in the warehouse."

"Did you find—"

"I did!" Megan exclaimed. "The collection hasn't been digitized, but there's two UC students who just started interning this semester and I got it assigned to them. They can start on Thursday, so I'm just trying to assess what might be there and who might be interested."

"You're fantastic."

"Well, you might not think so when you see the piles I've made in the warehouse," Megan said, then laughed.

"I don't care. Just find me anything related to that song, or the names I gave you. I'll help you assess after my nine o'clock. Anything else I should know?"

"I left a stack of messages on your desk. That cute contractor, Lincoln, has a question for you about the kitchen at Ivystone."

Andrea grinned. Lincoln was a hands-on twenty-eight-year-old general contractor with a passion for historical restoration who was working on two of Andrea's commercial projects, Berrylane and Ivystone. Megan had only met him once, but after stalking him on social media and discovering he was single, she'd decided she needed to bump into him again. "Maybe I'll find a reason for him to come to Charleston, or for you to go out on one of the plantations."

Megan squeed a little like the fangirl she was, but reined it in. She cleared her throat. "I'd love the opportunity to speak with him again."

"Uh-huh," Andrea said, letting her amusement bleed through.

"He's just so darn cute," Megan said. "And employed."

Andrea did laugh, then. "So important."

"So, so important," Megan echoed.

Andrea's phone dinged with another incoming call from the same area code as the deputies from Winslow Creek. "I'll come down as soon as I'm free."

"See you," Megan said and hung up.

Andrea thought she'd missed the call, but then a man's voice boomed "Hello?" through her speakers.

"Yes? This is Andrea Kelley."

"Miss Kelley, this is Ted Goddard, Greenbrier County Sheriff."

"Good morning, Sheriff."

"I just thought I'd call and introduce myself. My investigators had a look-see at your background, and it seems you've found yourself standing in bodies more than once in the last few months."

Andrea flushed cold, but then immediately hot, her cheeks burning. She made the right turn onto Kanawha Boulevard that would take her down to Waltham-Young.

He grunted at her silence. "They reported to me that your friend, Karie Wilson, left a business card on Roger Wright's front door. That the two of you then saw the dog in bad shape and followed it. Now, considering the circumstances, and the fact the land isn't posted, we didn't take issue with you being there yesterday, or under a structure on that land when the dog retreated initially, or with your being armed with a firearm while trespassing on the property and under the structure. But considering your background, I wanted you to know that we spoke to Mr. Wright, and he's asked us to trespass you both from the property. Do you know what that means?"

"Um." Andrea wasn't sure she'd heard everything he said as her pulse was beating in her ears, but she did catch that she'd been trespassed. "Are you warning me not to trespass onto the property again?"

"That's correct. If you trespass onto Mr. Wright's Charter Woods Road acreage again, you will be prosecuted and if convicted, appropriately fined. I'll be speaking with Karie Wilson to inform her as well."

The cabin with the red crossvine wasn't on Sanderson property, but if the vine grew there, it might also grow in the surrounding area. Might there be a similar place on the property next door or across the stream owned by Sanderson ancestors?

"Miss Kelley, do you understand?"

"Yes." She hit her blinker and turned right into the Shoney's parking lot and into the nearest spot. "Honestly, we were looking for an old Sanderson family home where red crossvine grows. We heard there was crossvine on the property, so we left the card. But then we saw the dog."

"There's crossvine growing all over these hills."

"Not red crossvine. That's rare."

"If you say so, Miss Kelley. I'd say it's rare for civilian folks to find one body in a lifetime, let alone three or be involved catching a murderer or killing a home invader, but you've done all those things in less than half a year, so what do I know?"

His tone wasn't particularly harsh or scolding but Andrea flinched from it all the same. He didn't even know about Andy Detweiler or the bones of the flat-footing grandma in Strange Creek. "It's not like I've been trying to do those things. They just happened."

"Like finding the dog of a couple seven months missing and it led you right to their bones."

"She did. We couldn't catch her." A thought occurred to her, and her voice strengthened with it. "Didn't Roger Wright ever see her out there?"

The sheriff sighed. Based on nothing but TV images, she thought about him removing a worn felt cowboy hat and swiping his forehead with the sleeve of his button-down. "He did. Shot at it. Vet said she removed a dozen pellets of birdshot from around its hip. We been reporting those dogs were with the Iversons for months and he never goddamn said a thing. Said it was just one old bloodhound, not two, so he didn't think anything about it. Didn't want her poaching rabbits and squirrels from his stew pot."

"Will I still be able to keep her?"

"Rachel Iverson has a sister. If she doesn't want her, it's fine with me. You'll owe the vet bill and whatever animal control requires."

"Will you let the vet know I still want her?"

"I'll double-check she has your contact info. Look, you understand you can't just be wandering around out there? You're likely to get hit by birdshot, too."

"Yes, sir. Do you think Roger Wright would still talk to us about the crossvine?"

"Don't see much hope for that. He was pretty hot under the collar. Practically a recluse out there and not particularly stable. Don't go bothering him, okay?"

"Yes, sir. Do you know how the Iversons died?"

"Not yet." His voice hardened again. "And let me be clear. We don't need any help finding out."

"Of course not."

"The deputies informed you we may need to speak with you again?"

"Yes, sir. Do you—"

Before she could finish asking if he knew if Roger Wright was related to Flynn Iverson, he said, "Okay then. Thanks for your time, Miss Kelley," and cut the call without waiting for her reply.

It took Taka a hot minute to remember seeing the white Clay County Public Works truck in December and telling himself he was being overly paranoid, but here it was again. Dent in the left quarter panel and all. Two cars down from his Yukon in the Huntington Bank garage.

"You guys good?" Karie said as he and Bowman swung their doors open.

"Yeah," he and Bowman said at the same time and then looked at each other.

Karie just laughed. "You two are cut from the same cloth."

"Thanks for the ride," Taka said and got out. Seeing Bowman lean towards Karie in his peripheral vision, he shut the door to give them a moment.

Bowman was grinning when he got out. They stood together and waved Karie off before heading to their cars. Only Bowman didn't go far. He unlocked the Clay County truck. "That's yours?"

"No," Bowman deadpanned. "It's Clay County's."

"Why are you driving it?"

"You'd have to ask my boss that."

"You work for Clay County?"

"Yeah, part-time."

Nothing came into Taka's head. "Really?"

Bowman laughed. "Yeah."

"They gave you a truck for part-time work?"

"My hours are weird."

Clearly, he wasn't going to offer information. But he didn't seem averse to answering questions either. On impulse, Taka said, "I was just going home to make calls to the families and set up your appointments. It'll go faster if we split the list."

"Sure."

"Let's see if Louie'll give us coffee, then."

They locked their trucks back up and walked down the stairs and across the street. Louie wasn't there, but Jesus let them in, and the sous chef made a second pot of coffee. Taka pulled the printed list of families he'd made from the inside pocket of his jacket and tore the paper halfway down the page. Five families for him, four for Bowman. Two days to travel and meet with all of them.

Bowman tapped his pen on his half. "You know this might end your friendship with Dewey all together, right?"

"We're not friends."

Bowman lifted his brows. "Frenemies?"

Taka rolled his eyes.

"Seriously, man."

"I don't know what we are. Stuck with each other, I guess."

"Well, whatever you want to call it, this might end it."

If Dewey never talked to him again, that'd be fine. "So be it." His stomach rolled a little. He picked his coffee up and took a big gulp.

They worked out a script and the schedule. Bowman and Fields would drive a rough, wavy loop, the northernmost and fourth stop a family in Ithaca, New York.

Then Taka called Caroline at Brighter Day first to heads up her. He put her on speaker so Bowman could listen.

He gave her his real name. He said he was working with the West Virginia State Police's Bureau of Criminal Investigation. He gave her Hoyle and Maddox's names as references.

"It's come to our attention that several of your clients have kids in their possession who went missing from a home in Charleston, West Virginia, late last year." He gave her the basic details and then the names of the kids.

"So, these nine kids all came from the same location?" She sounded confused.

"They did. Their placements are solid, I think. I've run thorough background checks on every associated name. And their backstories are ninety percent true."

"We do discreet checks as well when families come to us. No red flags were raised. We can't always fully trace a child, there's usually gaps because if they've been abandoned, they've usually stayed in a lot of different places. Some aren't old enough to give us much to go on. We do check with missing child databases."

"I'm sure you do a good job."

"But all nine are from the same place? I've got all their files up now. The youngest is eight. And my assistant confirmed their last known schools—Oh."

"What?"

"All of them were out of school for varying amounts of time before their current placement. Their previous known schools confirmed ages though. And she traced all but three known biological parents to death certificates or prison records. The families helped or provided documenta—Y'know? I don't want to know. Are you recording this conversation?"

"No."

"Then I don't want to know. We followed industry standard procedure, and the kids are doing well in their placements. You do what you have to do, we'll facilitate identity checks if you need our help with scheduling those. I'll send a notification to the parents that we've been contacted by law enforcement, and they should cooperate."

Taka was fairly confident that she was unaware Dewey played any role in placing the kids with the families before having them contact her. 'Intermediaries' and no cover stories had him thinking not even the families knew Dewey had been involved. "That's fine. Thank you."

If he got a call from Dewey in a few minutes, he'd know he was wrong.

23

Andrea closed her Zoom screen when her meeting ended and pressed the heels of her hands against her burning eyes. She and Karie grabbed a room at the SureStay in Summersville after the deputies released them from the scene, but four hours sleep and two coffees might not get her far today. She ran through her messages and called Lincoln, making notes on the info he needed. Megan could definitely handle the research, so maybe Andrea really could help her strike a spark there.

Between the Wright cabin, Madeleine's appearance, and seeing the photo of Flynn Iverson, she was dying to look for Madeleine. If she was part of Dewey's biological mother's family and the homestead Dewey had been to belonged to that family, Madeleine had to be hiding in the genealogy of the families connected to the Winslow Creek area. The Wright family would be up first. But helping Megan assess Tess Albright's papers, records, and recorded history of the community along Winslow Creek would be a more useful to Waltham-Young as a whole.

She grabbed a new bag of trail mix from the drawer she'd thrown it in last week, slipped her water bottle into her backpack and headed downstairs. She found her office neighbor, Eddie Alvarez, on the main staircase, going up to his office with a stack of vinyl records in his hand. "Andrea, where you been?"

"Out on a property search near the Cranberry."

He tapped the records with his thumb. "I got an original '80s pop classic in here you might like."

She laughed. "I think you might have me confused with my mom."

"Then next time you've got a minute, I'll fire up some vintage Nelly Furtado for you."

"There you go, maybe some early Eminem or Outkast, too."

"No Doubt."

"Coldplay."

"Maroon Five?"

"Whoa, whoa, whoa," Andrea said, holding her hand up.

"Oh, you're good. Let me know now."

"I will," she said, and they went in their opposite directions.

The DAR ladies who lunch were just gathering in the main reception area for their meeting. They were dressed up, mostly older woman, their hair done just so—or wearing very good wigs. A white-haired woman entering through the automatic door in her wheelchair reminded Andrea of Mrs. Tyson and her purpose in going down to the warehouse. She whirled around.

"Eddie!"

Her voice echoed through the great hall, and everyone below fell silent. Eddie turned near the top of the stairs. Andrea held her finger up. "Hang on!" Looking back down at the ladies and Marji, at the reception desk, who'd stood to see what the trouble was, she called down, "Sorry, nothing's wrong!"

She beat it back up the stairs, Eddie meandering back down to meet her. "Hey. Sorry. You ever hear of a song about a Dawkins boy and a girl from Copper Ridge? It might be from here. Not *here* here, in Charleston, but about a real West Virginia girl from Copper Hollow near Slaty Fork."

"Like a folk song maybe?"

"Maybe."

"Not ringing a bell, but I can do some research."

"I might be able to give you some lyrics, if I'm lucky."

"That'd be helpful."

"Thank you."

"You're welcome."

"Okay," she pointed back down the stairs.

He grinned at her. "See 'ya."

"See 'ya!" She trotted down to the lobby and straight to the front desk.

"I'm sorry, again," she said to Marji and the ladies close enough to hear.

"No worries," Marji said. "What can I do you for?"

"Megan and I are working on intake for the Albright collection in the warehouse today. Could you reserve a fourth-floor conference room for me starting Friday?"

Marji switched chairs and tapped on a keyboard. "How long you need it for?"

"Two weeks will do. I'll need two scanners and three computers."

"Done. Room 406. Need me to notify maintenance?"

"No, I don't know when we'll be ready. Megan can do it."

"Okay, doll, that it?"

"Hey, Doll," Donny says. He shakes the Tupperware at her. She used to put meatloaf in one just like that. She's just drunk enough that she can let herself say her daughter's name. Elsa.

Marji called everyone 'doll', always had, and had addressed Andrea that way a hundred times since Christmas. When would the little jump of her nervous system wear off at hearing it? When would it stop instantly tossing her into Becky's memories, remind her of the stricken look on Luke Bowman's face when she said Elsa's name, when she told him about his sister and Donny?

"That's it," Andrea said, trying to be bright.

But Marji frowned. "Are you sure?"

Andrea shoved down the memory, caught her enthusiasm for what she might find in Tess Albright's collection by the tail and hauled it back inside her. "I am. I just remembered something totally unrelated. Thank you for everything you do for us eggheads."

"You're welcome, doll. I love my job."

"I'm off," Andrea said and turned tail. She ducked into the corridor that would take her to the interior warehouse doors. After several minutes of brisk walking and several nods at various staff as she passed them, she swiped her keycard and entered the back of the warehouse.

She walked past the chain linked bays to the front. All the outer garage doors were closed against the cold. There was no security guard at the big front desk. She texted Megan for her location and walked down the rows. The youngest of the security guards, whose name she didn't know, popped out of the end of an aisle, waved at her, pointed down another, and disappeared again. A couple of whistled notes floated back to her, but she couldn't place the song.

Megan saw her just as she came even with the bay. "Hi! Somebody boxed these, I think, after Ms. Albright died." There were maybe eighty large cartons at the back of the bay, with six at the front, labeled in sharpie for several different departments. Megan sat in the center of a semi-circle of stacked manila folders. She had on bright pink wireless earbuds.

"The content's pretty mixed," she continued. "But everything's in folders that are mostly labeled in some way, either subject or series of years." She flopped a hand at the back. "Those five boxes in the back right corner marked OH are transcripts of oral histories and stories. I haven't found anything related to crossvine, although I came across a whole box of crop and gardening histories along the lines of 'Ms. Simmons grows three kinds of apple trees and a variety of cut flowers she provides to the local church and shut-ins', with a list of all the flowers she grew. Or 'Tom H. has thirty acres of flood bottom in red dent corn and another eighty acres of higher ground devoted to winter wheat and rye.'"

For the first time, she looked up at Andrea. "I'll bet any reference to the song you're looking for will be in the oral histories, though this lady was organized! She might have folders on music somewhere in all this stuff."

Andrea took in the number of boxes again and the folders surrounding Megan and the can of Red Bull and the small blue cooler sitting by her thigh. "How much caffeine have you had?"

"Way, way, too much. Speaking of, I need a restroom break."

"Go ahead. I'll take a peek at what you've got going on here."

Andrea rummaged through the department boxes first, then scanned the folders on the floor. She moved a few boxes around the pile in the back, reading the Sharpie labels. Megan was back by the time she'd lugged the five boxes of oral histories to the front and made her own little workspace. When she opened the boxes, the must of decades old paper floated up.

Megan produced a second clipboard from her tote with several pages of lined inventory forms, ready for filling out. These would follow each page of Ms. Albright's legacy through its Waltham-Young journey and, in the end, be digitized and filed themselves as reference material and location guide for the originals and all duplicated formats.

She glanced at her watch. She could spend two hours getting back to basics. She silenced her phone. Megan, presumably, went back to listening to whatever she was listening to. Andrea had never had the ability to listen to something else while sorting research. Her head was too full of the voices of the past and what they had to say and where she might slot that knowledge for future use.

This was the heart of her job, and she loved it.

NONE of them felt like lunch after witnessing the start of Detweiler's cremation process. Leon wanted to see Andy's girls, so Mia took him home with her. Jimmy sat in his car in the crematorium's parking lot and watched the thin rise of white smoke from the cremator's chimney.

He leaned forward and rested his head on the steering wheel.

The directory just inside the door had listed the private family viewing for Stacy Owens at two this afternoon. Like Detweiler's was supposed to be, "viewing" meant a private goodbye and seeing the start of the cremation, not pulling the funeral director aside and insisting on an actual look at the body. He didn't think Leon had noticed the directory. It made him wonder who was handling Gavin Owens.

He should probably head in and see if the team needed him.

But he didn't want to.

He should call Taka and see if he needed help setting up the identification schedule, but Taka would contact Horton or Fields if he had an issue.

He considered going home and kicking around the farm. Maybe ride out with his dad on the gator to check fence line. There was always something down that needed repair.

Instead, he heaved a sigh and started his car. When he lifted his head, his gaze went right back to the chimney. The smoke had dissipated. The air above the chimney shimmered with heat. He wheeled out of the lot, drove two blocks down to the river and made a right. Past City Hall and Haddad Park, he told himself to just head to HQ across the river.

But that wasn't what he wanted.

At Waltham-Young, the soaring lobby was quiet and filled with natural light. There were a couple of staffers on the grand staircase and another crossing the lobby's polished floor, her heels clicking. Two women manned the reception desk. Jimmy recognized Marji. He spoken to her before. The other woman smiled and moved to greet him.

Jimmy automatically went to flash his badge and stopped himself. There was nothing official about this visit. He stuck his hands in his trouser pockets. "I'm Jimmy Hoyle. Here to see Andrea Kelley. She isn't expecting me."

"I'll call her office."

"Hang on," Marji said. "I think she's still down in the warehouse." She clicked away on a console four times bigger than a standard computer keyboard.

Jimmy's phone vibrated. He ignored it.

"Yep, she hasn't swiped into the hall and none of the outside doors have opened." She poked around a bit more, watching the security screens over her head.

"There they are," she said and pushed her chair back. "I'll walk him over to her."

"You don't want to call her cell phone?" the other woman asked.

"Signal's spotty down there." Marji levered one of several walkie-talkies out of its charger base. "Yell if you need me."

"Will do," the woman said and turned her attention to a trio just pushing their way through the big entry doors.

Marji joined him, handing over a visitor's badge. "Officer Hoyle."

He clipped it to the zipper edge of his jacket. "Good memory."

She tapped her temple with the walkie's antenna. "It's a little bit of a walk."

She didn't try to engage him in conversation or offer him tour facts about the art or details of the modern building, for which he was grateful. The silence was companiable. They passed through a hallway lined with solid doors and down a short flight of stairs, then another hall with glass-fronted offices like Andrea's, only smaller. Every intersection hosted discreetly placed cameras near the ceiling and motion sensors tucked into the corners. All the staffers walking the opposite way greeted Marji by name.

It was a good thing he wasn't up to anything criminal, he'd never get away with it.

Finally, she stepped into a short dead end and swiped them through a solid door marked "Warehouse 3: LL-RR". The space was cavernous and sectioned off with chain-link pens filled with all sorts of things from boxes to a huge neon sign shaped like a flamingo and even one stuffed with different types of wicker air-balloon baskets stacked atop one another. Some of the pens were large with metal rack shelving in part of them and some were sectioned off together behind gates with key card entries.

"I had no idea," he said.

Marji chuckled. "Half our staffers have no idea."

She confidently walked him past the numbered spaces as his head swiveled, taking everything in, until his eye caught Andrea, her hair pulled up in a sloppy bun, sitting in a smaller pen on the ground. A jumble of several boxes with their flaps all open were arranged in front of her, with stacks of paper all around her. A girl in a grey WV State Yellowjackets hoodie and bright pink earbuds sat at the back of the space on a flattened box with an open box at her elbow. Her stacks of paper were laid out in a neat semi-circle in front of her and she was writing on a clipboard. She spotted them first and said something to Andrea.

Andrea's eyes widened when she saw him but then she smiled.

His insides unclenched.

"This okay?" Marji asked, waving her hand up and down in front of him.

"Yes," Andrea said.

Marji lifted her walkie and keyed it twice. "Headed back to station, need anything?"

Static crackled and then the woman at the front desk said, "Ten-four, I'm good."

"You'll see him out?" Marji said to Andrea.

"No problem," Andrea said.

Marji smiled as she turned towards him and patted his arm on her way by. She had solid boots on, and her firm steps clumped away and faded as Andrea waved him into their workspace.

"Jimmy, Megan," Andrea said. "Megan, Jimmy."

"Hi," Megan said, sketching a wave.

Jimmy nodded and lifted his hand.

Andrea patted the ground.

Jimmy glanced back at Megan, but she was already digging in her box again.

He walked over and sat, cross-legged. Since it was chilly enough that he was glad he still had his jacket on, the concrete was warmer than he expected.

Reading his face, Andrea said, "Radiant heating. The whole place is climate-controlled."

He nodded.

"Don't want to talk about it?"

He shook his head.

She held up a crumpled half-bag of trail mix.

He shook his head.

"Want to help me look for any mention of red crossvine, or any crossvine, really, or a trapper, or a song that mentions Copper Ridge or maybe Copper Hollow? Or a Madeleine, spelled however." Her gaze wandered off, some thought striking her. "And maybe any references to fairies."

"Will it help you?"

"Yes. I've been doing it the proper way, checking each page, and logging it with a one-line summary. But Megan can teach the new interns how to do that and they'll have the logged pages I've already done as an example. With you here, I have an excuse to just rifle through, and with two of us, it'll go a lot faster."

"You had me at 'yes'."

She gave him a smile for that and leaned over and kissed his cheek.

He glanced back at Megan, but she was absorbed, bopping her head to whatever music she had going. "You know he loves you, right?"

Andrea looked down. "It's never been enough before."

God, why couldn't he have been the one she wanted? "Scott asked him to go with him. Taka said no."

She lifted her head, her eyes meeting his.

"Something changed, in December. Between the two of you. I could see it. Scott could see it. After that vision you had. After he took you to the hospital." Jimmy saw her eyes shift, before she looked back at him, which told him he was right.

She surprised him by not shying away from it. "He kissed me, for cover, when we overheard Conlon's guys talking in the garage and one of them almost caught us."

"Why would that change things?"

"We'd never kissed before."

If somebody had waltzed in and swung a two by four at him, he couldn't have lifted an arm in defense. "Really? In all the years you've known each other, sleeping in the same bed, living out of each other's pockets, never?"

She shrugged and then let her shoulders drop hard. "No?"

"You guys are like chocolate and wine, cheese and grits, bacon and eggs, and never?"

"Are you sure you're not hungry?"

An autopsy technician had washed Andy's face and hair. Mia had brought his best suit. But as there was no official viewing, the damage to his head remained untouched. "Leon asked me to check. Make sure . . ."

"That it was Andy?"

"I may never be hungry again."

She took his hand. "I'm sorry, Jimmy."

"Can we just"—he squeezed her hand—"sort?"

"Yes," she said, injecting some force into the word. She reached into the closest box and gave him a folder containing a three-inch pile of differently sized and colored pages. Some were copies, some typewritten, some hand-written.

He turned his head again, taking in the boxes. "This is gonna take a while."

"Months, probably. Just skim. Try not to get caught up, 'cause it's all interesting."

And it was, but he doubted he found it as interesting or engaging as Andrea probably did. His fourth thick stack contained the story of a murder, though, decades after the deed as told by an older male resident of a little hollow west of Winslow Creek. He recounted the speculation running wild through the community and piqued Jimmy's interest. He set the three pages aside and Andrea looked over.

"Story about a homicide. I want to read the full thing later."

She suppressed a grin and held up the sheet in her hand. "Ghost story. Caterwauling white lady that was probably a big cat heard through a lot of alcohol."

"I could use a lot of alcohol."

Megan jumped up. "Andrea!"

Jimmy startled, having almost forgotten she was there.

Megan held up five stuffed manila folders. "Music stuff. Events, bands, singers, songs. There's another five folders in the bottom of this box."

"Awesome," Andrea said, and stiffly climbed to her feet. She stuck her phone in her back pocket. She bent over and grabbed her backpack. "My butt's numb and I have project research to do, so I'm going to take those to go."

Jimmy set the rest of his unfinished stack back in the box it came from, grabbed the trail mix, and levered himself up. North of thirty was apparently too old for sitting on concrete floors for hours whether they were warmed or not.

"This stuff looks pretty clean, Megan," Andrea said, taking the trail mix from him and stuffing it in her pack. "Have you seen anything that worries you?

"No. A dried wing or two and a dead fly."

Andrea slung her pack over her shoulders. "We have Room 406 for two weeks. If you ask maintenance to move everything into the freezer, they can probably have it done and to the room Friday morning. You and the interns you found can work half-days so you can sub out to other teams. Sound good?"

"Perfect." She rummaged in her tote bag and slid the folders in a huge Ziploc bag with "quarantine" written at the top and gave them to Andrea. "I'll get this stuff packed away properly and go put in a request," she said, retrieving the second set of five, bagging them, and handing them over to Jimmy.

"Freezer?" he asked Andrea as they walked back out to the main aisle.

"We have four walk-in freezers. Cold freezers, well below zero. Maintenance will sample the collection, decide what needs doing, and freeze everything for an appropriate length of time. They'll call me if I'm way off."

"But why?"

"Oh! Silverfish, firebrats, beetles, roaches, booklice, bedbugs. The cold'll kill anything living in the collection."

Jimmy shuddered. "Bedbugs?"

"Oh, yeah. Everything goes through inspection and decontamination if needed before permanent storage."

Jimmy looked down at his folders. "Is that why Megan bagged these?"

"I doubt they're an issue, but I'll do a thorough inspection when I open them. If they're clean, they don't have to go through the whole rigamarole. What are you going to do now?"

Extreme heat to extreme cold in three hours. Might as well go where he was used to the temperature. "Work." Maybe Nina would have something on the homicide connected to the Beretta. Maybe Maddox would give him an idea of how much longer he'd be on the sidelines.

They saw no one else in the warehouse.

It kinda creeped Jimmy out.

But he was fine until Andrea nodded and said, "Hey," turning all the way around as they passed the security desk. "What were you whistling earlier?"

She walked backwards, grinning. "That's it! Wait, I know it . . . Jolene! Dolly Parton. Right? See 'ya!"

She flipped back around and kept walking next to him. "Love that song, don't you?"

Jimmy glanced back over his shoulder at the vacant desk.

"He can really whistle."

The warehouse was silent except their footsteps.

He couldn't even hear Megan rustling around anymore. "Uh, yeah. Great song."

"Well, there goes the rest of my day," Andrea said.

"What do you mean?"

"Madeleine's here. Yep, you're just another fair-haired boy, though you're more precious than the dark-haired boys. Or maybe it's the other way around?"

They pushed out through the same door they entered through.

Jimmy's cell vibrated in his pocket, and he pulled it out. Text messages scrolled up his screen as they downloaded. Nina, his mom, Maddox, Taka, Nina again. Maddox and Nina on missed calls.

Andrea held her phone up and shook it at him. "Geesh, disappear for a couple of hours and the world blows up. Taka asking if I've seen you. Him again, something about Bowman. Two of my co-workers, my friend Lauren."

"Work, Taka, my mom." Jimmy turned his screen off and stuffed the phone back in his pocket.

When they emerged back out into Waltham-Young's lobby, Taka had his elbows planted on the reception desk's high counter, talking to Marji.

24

M arji pointed and Taka pivoted, one elbow still on the desk, and gave them a wave.

"Hey," Andrea said, when they got closer. "What you doing here?"

"Then Tucker says to me, them green beans need a'pickin' now," Madeleine said.

"Nina called, looking for Jimmy," Taka said, lifting his chin at the man. "As you can imagine, the WVSP is a bit on edge right now when their investigators don't answer their phones after a couple of hours." He looked at Andrea. "And you weren't answering either."

"They's gone a'sangin' down on Winslow crick."

Eying Madeleine, she shrugged. "I'm at work."

He smiled at her. "I know," he said, glancing over his shoulder and sharing a conspiratorial smirk with Marji before turning back to her. "That's why I'm here."

How his smile could still warm her up like that after all these years, Andrea didn't know. She presented Jimmy like she was Vanna White. "And door number two is . . . Jimmy."

"Ever-body knows that 'bandoned homestead's got haints that'll scare the skin right off'n yourn . . ."

That 'bandoned homestead's got haints

"I know," Taka said. "I called the dogs off, thanks to Marji."

Andrea's brain gave her the Iverson's dogs, one dead, one live, greeting each other.

Marji laughed and shook her head and went back to her console.

Jimmy shifted. He was reading his phone, thumb on the screen. He looked up when he noticed their attention on him. He held up his phone. "I guess I gotta go."

Taka's amused glance caught her eye again. "Probably a good idea," he said, as Madeleine said, "I wanta go home. Tomorrow is what Tucker always sez, tomorrow, Madeleine, I'll be a'taking yous home."

Jimmy had locked back onto his screen again.

Taka straightened. "Everything okay?"

Jimmy finally met his eyes. "There might be a hitch with Gavin Owens. Make sure Dewey lays low awhile longer."

"Ever-body knows why them crossvines a'grow so thick down there at the homestead."

Blood. Andrea shivered.

Taka frowned. "I have security at the house."

"Good. And I might need that Beretta, on the up and up, if there's a way for you to get it."

"I'll ask him for it."

"Scorched black but sound," Madeleine said.

Jimmy pressed his lips tight and then dropped his chin, gaze going to his shoes, before he looked back up. "Right." Andrea wondered what that was about. The fact that he couldn't just ask Dewey for a gun he wanted? He passed his armful of folders over to her. "Thank you. I needed some silence."

She could use some silence from Madeleine. "I've always got work for you if you want it."

They watched him leave through the big double doors and trot down the entry stairs.

"There's love and then there's fate and then there's Robie Dawkins and that slip of a girl from Copper Ridge."

Andrea rolled her eyes. Every time she started to grasp for something more logical to Madeleine's repetitions than just random echoes, she'd throw a verbal curveball. Whatever.

Taka turned to her. "You got topographical maps here somewhere?"

"Yeah?"

"Bowman had a thought."

He took one of the bags of folders from her and they went upstairs to her office, Madeleine trailing them. Thank God she'd stopped talking. "Why does Jimmy need a Beretta?"

"Remember Aaron saying ninety-two at the table?"

And Aaron rolling his eyes? "Yes."

"Dewey has a Beretta 92 from his dad that ballistics matched to a murder from the eighties."

"How does Dewey still have the gun then?"

"An asset," Taka said, making air quotes with one hand. "Took it from Dewey's collection and returned it after testing."

Andrea side-eyed him, but let it go. Obviously, he thought "asset" meant Scott, but thoughts weren't facts. Chet could be BCI for all they knew. They turned into her office and Andrea noticed they'd lost Madeleine on the way.

She plopped the folders on her desk and collapsed on her chair although she'd been sitting all morning.

"You need a nap," Taka said, laying the bag he was carrying down gently beside the first.

She rubbed her eyes. "I need Dewey to tell us if Karie and I were at the right place. It kinda matches, but . . ."

Running up through a steep meadow, the hip-high seed heads slapping against her open palms, her bare thighs, laughter in her ears, blue sky . . .

Her innate understanding of—"I thought there'd be a meadow out back." Eyes closed, she held out one hand, fingers curling up. "Sloped." She tapped the deepest part of her palm. "The lowest point a pond."

Her eyes flew open, gaze shooting to Taka's face as she sat straight up. "Abandoned. Madeleine said the homestead was already abandoned during her lifetime. And haunted. And maybe partially burnt but still standing. The cabin Karie and I were at had furnishings in it from the seventies."

Taka had his patient face on.

"What?"

"It won't help with the cabin, but the topographical maps, if we can locate any of the area, might help us find your slope and low point for a pond. They'd have to be fairly detailed."

Andrea woke her iMac up and did a quick search. "Drones are being used to do very detailed maps." She spun her chair around and dug under her work counter for her latest Waltham-Young Directory.

She opened it on her desk and ran her finger down the project pages as she flipped. Say what you want about easy to update digital directories, Andrea loved the printed versions. She picked up her landline and dialed Toby Richardson's extension. "Hi, Toby, this is Andrea Kelley in Historic Preservation."

"Really?" He was young. And a little breathless.

"Yeah."

"Oh, my God! You and that Civil War historian, you solved that murder!"

"We did."

"And then his wife turned out to have all that info on your preservation project? And you're getting to work on those mystery burials with that famous forensic anthropologist in Charlotte? That's so fantastic!

Andrea widened her eyes at Taka and made the universal "talking" motion with her hand.

"You know," Toby continued. "Combining drone mapping with ground-penetrating radar is a great way to locate unknown burials. Shit, I'll shut up now. Excuse my French, I just can't believe I'm talking to you."

"It's nice to talk to you, too, Toby."

"I don't know why you'd want to, though."

"We all work here for a reason, right? We're good at what we do."

"Oh, uh, yeah? I mean, yes, not to toot my own horn, oh, geesh, I sound like my dad now."

"You're fine, Toby," Andrea said, trying not to laugh out loud.

She had to bite her cheek, though, at Taka's half-concerned, half-quizzical face. When she flapped her hand at him to get him to stop, he hissed, "What's so funny?"

She spun her chair away from him. "Not to toot your own horn but you're a pretty good drone operator?"

"I am, but my skill's really in laser mapping technology. I've got three patents pending for Waltham-Young."

"Just the man I need."

"Me?"

"I have a client here. Can I put you on speaker?"

"Sure."

Andrea turned and punched the button as Taka said, "Thank you," and parked one ass cheek on her desk.

She gathered her thoughts for a second. "The project directory says you've been working on innovative agricultural land use by identifying acreage in the Appalachians appropriate for intensive small crop or livestock use."

"Yes." Toby said. "I've been working with Navi Kanan. He does all the soil testing and botanical mapping."

"Botanical mapping?"

Taka mouthed, "Botanical mapping" and nodded to himself.

"Yes. He maps the flora on designated parcels, so we don't damage native or endangered species when making forage and land use recommendations. He also does field tests to ascertain best practices. We pull the economics guys in, too. Like guys in general, you know, gals, too, to give clients profit projections based on best use."

"You don't happen to have topographically mapped along Winslow Creek, have you?"

"Uh, remind me where that is."

"It's a tributary of the Cherry River, just south of the Cranberry Wilderness in Greenbrier County."

"The Cranberry! Yes, we did a lot of preliminary mapping out that way. It's prime territory for small acreage intensive farming. Do you have coordinates of the area you're looking for?"

"No, but I can email them to you in a few minutes. Do you detail landmarks?"

"We do a multi-layered map, so yes."

"Would a small pond be marked?"

"We do a thermal layer that should capture a cooler spot that can indicate water. And video."

Andrea couldn't make her mouth work for a hot second. "How old?"

"Last winter."

"I'll send you coordinates."

"No problem. I hope we have the right area for you."

"Can you ask Navi if he's ever come across red crossvine out there?"

"He's here." Rustling and Toby talking, his voice muffled. Another voice questioning, then, "No. Not red. We've seen all sorts of other weird things, though. Over the east Monongahela a couple years ago, we sent data to a cryptozoologist."

"What was it?"

"Well, don't laugh, but it looked like a group of hairy humanoids? It was weird. And we never heard back from the zoologist." He sounded embarrassed now. "Probably just a cult. Or weird shadows. Anyway, shoot me those coordinates and I'll see if we have anything for you."

He had Andrea thinking about a multitude of different size hand and footprints under a camping hammock. "Will do. Thank you!"

She hung up.

"What's a group of Bigfoots called? Bigfeet?" Taka said.

"Yeah. That took a turn I didn't expect. And now a story that Karie and I heard makes more sense. If I give you addresses, can you sort coordinates for me?"

"Sure."

She pulled her notebook from her backpack, flipped to the pages she'd been using for notes and handed it to him. "Maybe give us a big rectangular area along both sides of the creek that includes all these addresses?"

He went to work, and she settled in on a preservation home project in East End that was due within the month. But she couldn't stop hearing Madeleine's voice in her head. Abandoned and burnt. *Then Tucker says to me, go on up to Leah Beth's and fetch her girls up in the holler.*

"I never saw a Tucker or a Leah Beth either."

"What?" Taka said absently.

"Nothing." She was missing something. She pulled one of her desktop sticky note pads over and wrote *Tucker, Leah Beth/Wright/Prop*

Deeds on neighbors /Record Madeleine loop. But her thoughts kept circling.

When Taka announced he was done, she said, "Me, too. I am so tired."

He studied her face. "Can I drive you home? Then I need to go see Dewey."

"Yeah."

She emailed the coordinates to Toby, shut down her computer, slapped the sticky in her notebook, stuffed it and her laptop in her backpack, handed Taka the stack of folders and they went out in the hall. Staring out the window, Andrea stopped. Sometime in the last few days, the daffodils and paperwhites in the garden below had bloomed all along the spiral walkway.

"What?" Taka said, stopping on her heels.

"The flowers." Andrea lifted a hand over her aching heart. Her mother had planted bulbs in all their beds around the house. She craved the first color coming up before the last frost, shining yellows and whites through the grey foggy morning and rainy February days.

The daffodils bloomed the day before she died.

Every year, it was a hit the first time she saw them. She wished her mom had seen this garden from this window.

"I'm so glad I work here," she said.

"She'd have been proud."

Andrea turned around and kissed him and pulled back right away.

His full lips turned up at one corner.

She read the description once of a smile tucked in the corner of a man's mouth and it was just exactly this smile.

"Thank you," she said.

He leaned forward and she kissed him again, lingering just a second longer, the folders pressed between them.

Then they went down the stairs and through the lobby, walking too close together, jostling arms and shoulders every few steps, and trying not to look at each other.

"BLACK SHEEP BURRITO?"

Andrea's stomach rumbled.

"I guess that's a yes. Order for us?"

Andrea found the number and called. When she hung up, she said, "Fifteen minutes."

Taka turned the Yukon away from the river on Court Street and hung a right on Quarrier. He ran into Black Sheep a few minutes later and handed the bag to her. "I'm hungry. Let's just eat," she said.

After doling out the food and setting the nachos between them, Andrea ate half her curry burrito before she said, "I might want to go with you to see Dewey."

He stopped chewing, his face falling still before he caught himself and resumed.

"What was that?"

He swallowed and looked over at her. "What?"

"That look."

His gaze dropped to the nachos. His bottom lip pulled sideways when he bit on it.

"What'd you do, Taka?"

"I kinda told him about Madeleine."

Her stomach dropped. The burrito inside rolled over. She set down the half left in her hand. "Kinda?"

"I told him you see ghosts. I told him he has one that's pretty attached to him and her name is Madeleine."

"What was his reaction?"

"He hung up on me."

"Well, now I have to go, don't I?"

"No, you don't," Taka said. He dropped what was left of his burrito in the wrapper and folded it up.

"Taka. The Greenbrier County sheriff called me this morning to trespass me off that property. I don't care, it's not even the right one, but he knew all about Susan Pepper and Oliver Fitch and Lucy Garcia and Parker. I'd probably be in cuffs already if they knew I found Andy, and Karie's going to get connected to that woman in Strange Creek, but at least that's a different county."

"It was all over the news, one of his deputies probably just googled you."

"Jimmy said he's starting to have a more difficult time remembering where info he's acting on is coming from. And explaining it. The more people we tell, the harder it's going to be to hide it."

Taka's lower jaw shifted forward. His gaze went over her shoulder, probably watching another car pull in beside him. But then he frowned. "It's the commander."

25

B owman tapped his keys on the passenger window.

When she turned towards him, Andrea's heart leapt at his nearness.

Taka opened her window from his side.

Bowman braced himself in the window on his forearms. "Karie just texted me. They found her car on camera at both the church and the shopping center. She's following Fields over to CPD."

"Why not WVSP?"

"He specifically told her she's not a suspect."

"Because they already know Gavin Owens killed them," Andrea said. "Except—"

"Jimmy said there was a hitch." Taka said. "They know there were more people in Karie's car."

"Between the cameras and any traffic cams," Bowman said, "They might know I was out of the car."

"But we weren't there until hours after the murder."

Taka un-scrunched the takeout bag and packed away his burrito wrapper and the barely touched nachos. He held the bag out for Andrea's burrito, but she shook her head. He closed the top of the bag in his fist. "It'd probably be best to confront this head on."

"Go to CPD," Andrea said, anxiety spiking through her. "I can't believe we were just talking about this." She tugged at her coat. Bowman reached in and helped her get it off. "Literally, we were just talking about this. Taka told Dewey."

Bowman shot a glance past her at Taka. The bag crinkled behind her.

"The Greenbrier Sheriff called her this morning," Taka said.

Andrea did turn her head then to glare at him.

"Well, shit," Bowman said. "Will this jeopardize Fields and I going to test the kids?"

Andrea whipped her head back around. "Test the kids?"

"I was going to tell you while we ate," Taka said, bringing her head back around. "Fields and Bowman are going to take two days, go collect DNA and photos on the kids from Anna Lansing's."

"Good," she said. Crossing her arms, she looked straight out the windshield. "One less thing to lie about. Tamarin's going to be all over me."

"He's not a part of it."

Her heart continued to pound. "Let's just go."

"Get in," Taka said to Bowman.

Andrea patted the jacket in her lap and found her phone in the pocket. It was a miracle Corporal Mendel hadn't told anyone yet anyway. He'd found out back in October and stayed mum through the whole December debacle.

Bowman grabbed a Yeti, a jacket, and a leather knapsack from his truck and slid into the back and shut the door. "You gonna eat those nachos?"

Taka handed him the takeout bag, then backed out of the space by the time Andrea found Sweet Joe Babbington in her contacts. The lawyer wasn't in. She left a message. "You have a lawyer, Luke?"

Bowman finished crunching on the nacho in his mouth then talked around it. "I'm good."

Andrea shook her head but decided arguing wouldn't matter. Although her belly was rolling, she was still hungry. She pulled her burrito out from under her jacket and unwrapped it. She caught Taka side-eyeing her. She took a big bite. He was the one who gave the nachos away.

He picked his water up and drained it.

CPD was only minutes away, but she'd destroyed the rest of her burrito and finished her water by the time Taka parked on the third floor of the garage. All she wanted to do was go home, shower, and read through Tess Albright's music folders until she fell asleep. But no, she was probably going to tell Pete Tamarin she saw dead people and get locked up again with that freaking scary ghost that yelled at her last time.

Without looking at Taka, she unbuckled her belt, unthreaded her holster, and handed her gun over. Bowman kept his mouth shut.

"We're waiting on Sweet Joe, right?"

"Yes. His paralegal said she'd text him. He's at the courthouse doing filings."

Taka got out and Bowman followed suit. Andrea took a couple of deep breaths, but it didn't really help. Taka opened the back to stow her gun in his safe.

"You carrying?"

Bowman muttered something. Rustling as he did whatever he had to do to get to whatever he had on him. She'd never noticed him carrying.

"Ankle?" Taka asked.

Bowman blew his breath out hard enough for Andrea to hear him, said something else.

"And the knife," Taka said. "You got a pocketknife, too?"

More rustling.

Bowman really had two guns, a knife, and pocketknife on him and she never had a clue?

The clunk of the safe closing.

She slipped her card holder out of the front pocket of her backpack and stuffed it in her jeans pocket. Her phone rang in her hand. Sweet Joe. "Hey. I need to talk with CPD about finding a body."

"Another one?"

"Yeah. I'll explain it to you, but I need to tell you something else, too. Are you available now?"

"I'm at the courthouse."

"I'm in the garage at City Hall."

"I'll meet you inside in a few minutes."

She didn't bother to put her coat on, just took it with her.

Taka closed the back and set the alarm.

She walked ahead of them down the stairs and across the drive and back up the city hall stairs, but Taka's arm shot out past her and pulled the door open for her. "Thank you," she muttered.

"You're welcome."

They went through the doors and nodded at security sitting nearby, but Andrea didn't see Sweet Joe right away. She stopped to one side of the grand three-story staircase.

Taka wrapped his arms around her from behind. "I'm sorry," he said.

"I'm just scared."

"I know."

She patted his arm, turning towards him and the open lobby. He let her go.

Bowman had his blank face on.

"Tell them the truth," Andrea said.

"You mean," he said, "about you seeing Andy out there?"

"Yes. And if Tamarin or Ronnie or Fields asks you, Taka, go ahead and tell them."

Taka looked up at the high, elaborately plastered ceiling, making her take notice once again of the beauty surrounding them. Clusters of people were gathered on or walking across the sweep of the marble flooring and talking together on the stairs. With Taka right beside her, she didn't dare look at any of them too closely, afraid she wouldn't know if they were real or not.

And then there was Joe, lumbering across the hall, smiling at people as they moved out his way simply because he was big and tall. A former University of Kentucky lineman in lawyer's clothes, she'd learned he was unassuming, with a sharp mind.

"Come talk to me," he said.

They walked over to one of a series of shallow alcoves along the wall. They were decorative but served well for a private conversation. She told him about the shooting at the Coliseum, and then about Detweiler's act of kindness and how it got him killed.

"We insisted on looking for him before WVSP was overly concerned because we already knew he was dead."

Sweet Joe glanced up, thinking, then he said, "I don't want you to tell me if you were in anyway involved in his murder."

"No, I wasn't."

"How'd you know he was dead?"

Bile rose in her throat. She swallowed it down.

"It can't be that bad," he said, with his trademark gentle smile.

"I see dead people."

He laughed. Softly. "My niece does that line better."

"It's a little different when it's real." She held his gaze and after a few seconds, his demeanor changed.

"You're serious."

"I am."

"You saw Anna Lansing after she passed? She told you Linda Conlon killed her?"

"No. Another ghost . . ." It was Aaron who had drawn her attention to Anna outside Louie's and then inconsistencies in the stories she was being told and the research she was doing. "No. Most of the time they don't actually very communicate well."

"Maybe then, it isn't something others need to know."

"Except, sometimes when they do communicate well, it gives me information I have no other way to know."

"Is that the case here?"

"When you see someone's ghost, you know they're dead, even if no one else does."

"Makes sense."

"Andy Detweiler's car wasn't visible from the road. We knew where it was because Andy was standing out on the road. Then Bowman"—she pointed back at Taka and the commander, who were trying to pretend they weren't watching—"went down and checked the car, to make sure the woman that Andy was with didn't need medical help."

"He have a lawyer?"

"He says he's good."

"Hmm."

"Will you please tell them you're Karie's lawyer and ask to see her?"

"Is her last name Wilson?"

"Yes."

"She called before you did." Comprehension lit his face up and made his smile a little more wry than he usually allowed. "She's the paranormal specialist at Waltham-Young. The puzzle's coming together."

"I want it out in the open. I don't care if they don't believe me. They know I've been hiding something. This is it. They can take it or leave it."

"You're sure? It'll be as complicated this way as the other, just in different ways."

"I'm sure."

He picked up the large, worn leather briefcase he'd set down against his leg. "Let's go."

When they reached Taka and Bowman again, she repeated, "Tell them the truth."

"We're going with that?" Bowman said.

"We are," Sweet Joe said.

When they got upstairs, Taka asked for Fields.

Bowman and Andrea sat in the narrow little chairs along the wall, while Sweet Joe and Taka stood in the way of everyone needing to get by. Bowman watched everyone around them with a steady intensity that Andrea found slightly unnerving. When Fields came around the corner ten minutes later, Bowman stood up, but Andrea froze.

"I was in Karie's car that day," Bowman said.

Fields held his hand up to stop him. "Do you mind talking in a room?"

"No."

Andrea heard the "sir" there, but Bowman had withheld it. She wondered if Fields could tell.

"Andrea?" Fields said. "You mind talking to us since you're here?"

She looked up. "That's why I'm here with my lawyer."

Fields nodded at Joe. "Mr. Babbington."

"Ms. Wilson is also my client, and I'd like a private word with her."

"We just had a couple of questions. She agreed to talk with us. You three come on back. You mind waiting downstairs, Taka?"

Taka shook his head but stayed in the hall until they turned the corner.

Fields opened a door and nodded at Bowman. "In here, Commander. Need water or coffee?"

"Coffee with creamer, please."

"You got it." He left the door open. They turned down yet another short hall before he opened a door for Andrea. It looked like the last interrogation room she'd been in. Two chairs in front of a beat-up table with a chair on the far side. "Other side if you don't mind. Water? Coffee?"

She shook her head.

The disheveled man standing in the corner held up his index finger, but Fields didn't see him. He stuck his hands back in his pockets and kicked at the thread bare carpet with the toe of his black boot.

Sweet Joe gave Andrea a reassuring wink.

Fields left the door open.

It didn't help.

JIMMY STOOD in the back of the team room, hands in his pockets, watching eight traffic cam recordings on four split-screens in front of Bill and Nina. Two additional techs from District Three were crammed into the middle of the room with their own monitors and towers and paperwork.

His burner phone vibrated. His mom or Andrea, he figured, but it was from the new burner he'd given Taka a couple of weeks ago when they dumped the old ones from December.

Call me.

He slid it back into his pocket.

The phone tree had activated. Taka would want to know if Andrea was next. And yes, she was, because the cameras showed a woman riding shotgun in Karie's car. And a man in the rear seat, there when they arrived in Westridge, gone when Karie made the 911 call about

Detweiler, back again when they left Westridge altogether. It was all they'd done.

They drove straight down Westridge to where it became Sugar Creek and then back again. They hadn't wandered, searching. As far as everyone in this room was concerned, they had prior knowledge of the crash site. It certainly wasn't visible from the road. And first responders noted more than one set of footprints around the car because they hadn't expected to see any, let only multiples.

Mark Compton had remembered Andrea and Karie being at the hospital with a man. Maddox confirmed. The cameras in the garage worked. Bowman had been identified by facial recognition before Jimmy confirmed his name.

"There," Nina said. "Screen three." She ran it back. Still two men in Gavin Owens car. One of the new techs marked the camera on a map taped to a white board with a red X, the camera's unique code, and a time stamp.

A new camera flickered up on screens three and four.

The question now? Was the same man in Karie's car the one who accompanied Gavin Owen on his psychopathic killing spree? He'd know where the bodies were. "Two," Jimmy said.

"Running back," Bill said.

The tech marked the map.

Jimmy wasn't here, not really. The District Three lead, Chapman, and Mark Compton were chasing down a couple of Gavin's possible friends. They'd present a photo lineup including Bowman to Lizzie. They'd made it clear Jimmy was to remain at HQ. And not make any calls.

"Three," Nina said. "Running back."

"He turns left," Bill muttered and punched at his keyboard.

The tech marked the map.

All four screens flickered. New cameras. The route was obvious now. The team had already mapped a stingy line of confirmation following Detweiler from the gas station where Stacy had turned on her phone.

By the first camera that they could pick Gavin up on, the friend with him was already in the car. No help there. And they hadn't yet found a time lapse where they might have stopped, where the team might collect better CCTV from a store to ID the friend. But damn if he wasn't built similar to Bowman.

Maddox ducked through the doorway. "Listen up, people. ME's confirmed Gavin Owens's death as a homicide. Chapman and Compton have been notified." He nodded at Jimmy. "Stay put until I come back for you."

"Yes, sir."

The burner vibrated against his thigh.

He ignored it.

OUT ON THE front steps of City Hall, a cold gust of wind fingered Taka's hair and lifted his jacket. Andrea, Karie, and Bowman were all inside with Taka's former co-workers, none of whom he could talk to now. Jimmy wasn't picking up. He'd already called the guard on Dewey duty and spoken to the home health worker.

He really wanted to call Scott. He slid his phone screen open. He'd taken Scott off his favorites list, so he had to scroll all the way down through his contacts to the S's. Scott Fergusson. The last name was almost certainly fake. Was Scott his real first name? Maybe his middle name. Or a brother's name. A name it'd be easy for him to get used to being called.

A geeky patrol officer came down the stairs and stood near him. "Detective Taka?"

"Not anymore." Taka glanced over at him. He looked familiar. "Corporal."

After pocketing his phone, Taka zipped his jacket up.

"I'm Chris Mendel, I—"

"I remember you. The highway. Your uncle saved my life out in Fivemile." He reached out and Mendel shook his hand. "Thank you."

Mendel blushed. "Happy to serve, sir."

"Taka, please." Their breath puffed white. Taka put both hands in his jacket pockets. "You've kept Andrea's secret."

"Is she in trouble again?"

"Afraid so. She might have to confess to seeing ghosts."

"Is she seeing them now, sir?"

"You didn't know?"

"No, but I heard the most amazing voice phenomena at her house."

"You know Karie?"

"The paranormal specialist at Waltham-Young, yes, sir."

"She heard a disembodied voice yesterday."

"Holy cow, no kidding?"

"No kidding."

"Well, you tell them, if there's any way I can ever help to please let me know."

"You can help by telling anybody who asks you if it's true that she communicates with dead people, that yes, it's true."

"Absolutely, sir."

"Only if they ask."

"Only if they ask, sir.

"Thanks, Mendel."

"Yes, sir." The young patrol officer went on down the steps, headed for the garage.

Taka didn't want to wait inside, but the temperature was dropping every minute. It'd be dark in an hour, hour and a half. He hunched his shoulders, wishing he had another layer on. Felt like snow again.

His phone buzzed. He tugged it out and looked at it.

Dewey.

Did he want to talk to Dewey?

He did but face to face.

The buzzing stopped.

Missed call.

Dewey called right back.

Shit.

Taka slid the call open. "Yeah."

26

"Didn't our agreement cover you answering the phone when I call?" Dewey said.

"I'm busy."

"Don't call my people. Call me."

"By definition," Taka said, wishing he hadn't answered. "My job is to call your people."

"Not when you're just checking up on me."

"I wasn't. Something's going on with Gavin Owens. I need you to keep your head down and I need your people awake."

"Is Gavin Owens undead? Coming back to haunt me?"

"I'm pretty sure he's still dead. Maybe he had a twin brother."

"If you were doing your job, you know already if he did."

"He doesn't," Taka said, rolling his eyes. "His parents are in shock, and he has a sister in Pittsburgh. But he also has an asshat friend that I'm guessing WVSP is still trying to track down and getting their ruff up about it."

"That's more like it."

A commotion began near the top of the steps. Taka turned. But it was just a wedding party coming out, whooping and yelling. A middle-aged het couple and six friends, all in their Sunday best, coats, and gloves. Dark pants and calf-length dresses fluttered in the wind.

Someone handed the couple a sign. They laughed, and held it up between them, "*Happily Married . . . Again*" and kissed. Two of the party filmed the moment with their phones.

Thursday was an interesting choice.

"Where are you?" Dewey said.

"You don't know?"

"No, William, I'm not omniscient."

"CPD."

"About?" His voice was lower, a warning.

"Right now? Andrea's friend, Karie, you remember her?"

"Yes, William. Karie Wilson, paranormal investigator, sidekick extraordinaire, possible arm candy for our commander friend."

"She made the anonymous tip on Detweiler's location. Andrea and Bowman were with her and CPD knows it."

For once Dewey was silent.

"Detwiler's car was off the side of an embankment," Taka said and suddenly he was mad. Unsuppressed, couldn't push it down, stompin' mad. He spun away from the wedding party, tucking his head down, and strode down the steps. "Not visible from the road," he bit out, knowing Dewey could hear the bitter anger in his voice, but it felt good.

He sucked a deep breath of cold air in through his nose and, finally, his chest opened up.

He wasn't cold anymore.

He strode across the driveway. Onto the sidewalk. Off the sidewalk and across the garage's entrance. An incoming brown van hit the brakes hard to avoid him. He was already on the exit side when the driver got his window down. Taka waved off the shouted insult without looking back.

Back on the sidewalk, walking he didn't know where, Taka unclenched his jaw. His words came out like a taunt. "Want to know how they found it?"

"Let me guess," Dewey said, his tone dry. "A ghost whispered in their ears."

"No." He stopped. There was no one near him. Cars rushed by on

Virginia Street. "Andy Detweiler's goddamn ghost stood out on the goddamn road with a goddamned hole in his head because of you and only Andrea could see him. And now she's back in that goddamned building trying to defend herself."

"Not because of me."

Everything stopped. Taka's heart, the blood in his veins, the cars on the street. And then it all rushed back in. "What? What did you just say?"

"William," Dewey said, in that whiplash voice that Taka hated, but every cell in his body responded to.

"What?" he spit, because it was all his brain would give him.

"I did not corrupt Detweiler, and you know it. Or you wouldn't have arranged CPD's little identification excursion."

Of course Dewey knew already. He was a fool to have thought Dewey wouldn't know. "Bowman?"

"No. Bowman's a wild card. Your petty cash account can't afford him though, so it's a good thing my lawyers keep their ears to the ground."

"Why didn't you arrange this kind of ID yourself?"

"Because, William, if Detweiler wasn't dead, those kids would have been a footnote on some vanished-into-thin-air website with no one the wiser and never in jeopardy of having their lives flayed open for public attention."

Like Dewey's own life had been as a senator's son. Or maybe . . . like it had been protected from attention if his mother had hidden his adoption. Taka had to bite his tongue to keep from asking. Now wasn't the right time. He shouldn't have even picked up the phone.

"And," Dewey said, filling Taka's silence. "I had hoped you'd at least consider keeping quiet once you knew they were safe."

"I did."

"If you had, it would've taken longer for you to spill. But you're you and although you probably don't believe me, I love you anyway. It was much better coming from you than from me. If it came from me, CPS would've been their first call and a judge for warrants their second." His voice softened. "Thank you for standing up for me."

Manipulated again. Taka pinched the bridge of his nose with his free hand to stave off the headache waiting behind his eyes. Two guys came towards him, slouching along. He dropped his hand and stepped back onto the squishy grass under a leafless tree. "Fine. I'm predictable. The point is, Detweiler's dead and Andrea's back in an interview room."

"I'll send Ryan." His lead lawyer, Ryan Merritt, so far batting a thousand keeping Dewey out of interview and court rooms.

"She's got Sweet Joe with her. He's going to let her tell them she sees ghosts."

"I'll send Ryan. She'll get some media splash and the cops'll go back to trying to nail her down and never getting anywhere. Just like me. At worst, they'll believe her and start asking for her help."

"I don't know why I answered the phone."

"Because you love me, too. And I own your ass."

Taka walked back to City Hall, more aware of his surroundings now. "I need to see you later. Jimmy's got an ask. And Andrea needs some answers."

"I know nothing."

"Expect us," Taka said and hung up. He took one more deep breath of cold air and trudged back up the stairs.

FIELDS SAID, "OKAY."

Tamarin, because of course he was there, gave Andrea his best imitation of a stink bug.

Sweet Joe said, "She's answered your questions about locating Sergeant Detweiler's remains. If there's nothing else, we'll be going."

"Actually," Fields said, "there is."

Sweet Joe inclined his head.

Tamarin opened a new folder, the other had contained photos of Andy's wrecked car. He slid a photo out.

Fields said, "Did you know Gavin Owens?"

"Only from the article I saw online."

"Did you know Stacy Owens?"

"No."

"How long have you known Commander Luke Bowman?"

She glanced over at Sweet Joe, and he nodded. "Since early December."

"You weren't acquainted with him prior to the incident involving the Conlons?"

"No."

Fields exchanged a brief, wordless conversation with Tamarin. Tamarin leaned forward. "Do you know if Commander Bowman was carrying a concealed weapon when he went down that embankment to Sergeant Detweiler's car?"

Andrea leaned forward as well. "If it were concealed, how would I know?"

Sweet Joe touched her hand.

She sat back. "No. I don't know."

No one said anything, which gave her enough time to consider the question. "Maybe I should be clear that Andy Detweiler was dead hours before the commander went down the embankment. I'm sure the ME determined his time of death . . ." Was Stacy Owens's time of death in question?

Tamarin raised his brows. "You didn't see Stacy Owen's ghost, too?"

"We're done here, gentleman," Sweet Joe said as he stood up.

"Maybe you should tell—" Andrea squinted at the detective in the corner's badge, clipped to his belt.

Frowning, he looked down, and then back up at her with a huge smile. He stepped out of the corner and slapped his badge down on the table. It immediately disappeared. He looked confused, his hand going back to his belt. He shrugged, pulled the badge back off and held it out to her.

"Thanks, Corporal," she said. But he again held up his finger, this time asking her to wait. He pulled out his wallet and flipped it open.

Andrea stood up and leaned over the table.

Glaring at her, Tamarin leaned back, away from her.

"Maybe you should tell Corporal J. G. Hunt, ID #632 how his last case was resolved and that he can clock out now." She stood up straight and looked Tamarin in the eye. "He'll be here waiting until you do."

J.G. Hunt nodded and put his wallet away. He gave her a thumbs up and stepped back into his corner, blood seeping through a slash torn in his wrinkled shirt. As it spread, he faded but remained, just barely visible.

"He was stabbed, just so you know."

Fields couldn't keep his gaze still, eyes going from the corner to her and back again.

They went out. In the hall, Sweet Joe kept his voice low. "Was that for real? Hunt was in the room?"

"I think he's been there a long time."

They found Taka and Karie downstairs.

"She did fine," Sweet Joe said.

Karie held her arms out and Andrea hugged her.

"Are you okay?" Karie said into Andrea's hair.

A rush of grief and relief welled up, closing Andrea's throat. Tears filled her eyes and her nose started running. Sniffing, she nodded. Taka hugged them both.

When they separated, Andrea swiped at her eyes. "Thank you, Joe, for coming so quick," she said. "Where's Luke?"

"He hasn't come down yet," Karie said.

Sweet Joe stood with both hands in front of him, wrapped around the handle of his bag. "I didn't like the direction of their questions. Does he have a lawyer?"

"He said he was 'good'," Taka said. "I don't know if that means he called someone before he found us or if he thought he could handle it."

"For his sake," Sweet Joe said, "I hope he has a good one. If he decides he needs me, you know how to contact me."

"Thanks again," Andrea said.

"Both of you know," he said, "you can just tell CPD to schedule an appointment with your lawyer, right?"

Andrea and Karie looked at each other. "We can?" Andrea said. "I never looked it up. I thought that was just TV making things easier than they really are."

"Unless they arrest you, yes."

"Good to know," Karie said.

They all shook his hand, and he ambled off across the lobby through the thinning crowd of staff leaving for the evening. They found a bench and sat. Andrea wasn't sure how she felt or what to do next. It wouldn't take long for word to spread about her through CPD. But would it go further?

"Fields has a poker face," Karie said. "He didn't react at all when I told him you see ghosts, that you saw Andy's ghost."

"What about Tamarin?" Andrea said.

Taka sat up from his slouch, scowling.

Karie shook her head, her mouth turned down. "I never saw him."

Well, that was weird. "He wasn't in your interview?"

"No."

"Huh."

"Why was he in yours?" Taka demanded.

"How would I know?"

"Considering what I told him," Karie said, "Fields probably went straight to him for back-up."

"Why are you so upset?" Andrea asked Taka, unable to stop the snap in her tone.

"Because he used you to get to that stupid Conlon kid!"

"You said you'd do the same thing."

"You're afraid of him."

They were leaning forward, barking at each other from either side of Karie. For the first time since Bowman tapped on the window, Andrea really looked at him. The tension in her chest let go. "You're afraid for me."

"Of course, I'm afraid for you. I'm afraid for you every day. But you're not usually afraid of anything. I hate that Tamarin scared you."

She looked down and swallowed the sudden moisture filling her dry mouth now that her body was standing down from high alert. "Uh, it's not Tamarin per se, that I'm afraid of, it's what he can do to me."

"Which is?"

"Put me in a cell with a really pissed off ghost."

"Oh."

After a second, Karie said, "We good now?"

Andrea sat up at the same time as Taka did. "Yeah, sorry."

"Nothing to be sorry for," Karie said. "They asked me a lot of questions about Luke, but Sweet Joe seemed more worried just now. What'd they ask you?"

"They implied Stacy Owens may not have died before we got to her. They asked if Luke had a concealed weapon when he went down to check on them."

Taka leaned forward again to look at her, elbows on his knees. Whatever Bowman carried was now in Taka's gun safe. Then his gaze moved past her, and he jumped up. "Merritt," he called out.

A sturdy man in his fifties veered in their direction. A sharp-edged woman in a tasteful navy-blue suit with a leather satchel on her shoulder and a guy who couldn't have been more than twenty-five followed in his wake. The man stuck out his hand, "Taka."

They shook and Taka introduced Andrea and Karie, whose eyebrows were pinched together, her face drawn. Ryan Merritt did not introduce his team. "I see Sweet Joe broke Andrea loose," he said to Taka. "Where's Commander Bowman?"

"They seem to think he played a part in this whole Detweiler-Owens mess."

Merritt breathed in sharply through his nose. "Hmm."

He pinned Andrea with his cold, blue eyes. "Dewey says you have a con."

She bristled.

"Did you tell them you see . . .?"

"Yes."

"I don't see how that can help," the woman murmured.

Merritt hummed again. He swung his focus back to Taka. "If he's been arrested, you'll arrange bail for him. If he hasn't, I'll shut him up and we'll hope the damage isn't too much to undo."

"What?" Karie said, the word high-pitched, as Merritt turned away on his heel.

His lackeys parted to let him through then fell back into step with him, a pace behind.

"What?" Karie said again, quieter. Andrea turned in time to catch her as she sunk, and then Taka was there, helping her onto the bench. Tears streaked her face. "How could they think that? How could they think that?"

WHEN A TROOPER CAME with a CCTV dump from several flash drives, Nina made Jimmy go sit at his desk to scan through it all. The bull pen was busy during the shift change. He studied the blurry outline of the tall, thin man in the shadowed interior of Gavin Owens's car. It was parked at a One Stop off I-64 on Friday before noon, a few hours before Detweiler was run off the road.

At eleven-fifty-one a.m., Gavin could be seen pacing in and out of frame, agitated, talking on his cell. Jimmy's copy of his phone records showed he was talking to a college buddy living in Charlotte. Copies of the interviews so far showed the buddy had only coughed up two first names for Gavin's local friends. That was better, though, than Gavin's co-workers managed. Neither friend was the man in the car with him.

Someone slapped Jimmy's desk. Chapman, back with Mark Compton. "No luck with Lizzie. She didn't ID Commander Bowman, but she didn't rule him out either. Said the guy had a cap on, pulled low, scruff on his face, and an oversized fishing coat, big logos on it. Zipped all the way up."

Which meant she couldn't see his port.

"She was more focused on Owens," Mark said.

Jimmy's burner vibrated. Andrea would try him on his regular cell, which was in Maddox's possession. It could only be Taka again. He shifted in his chair, making it squeak, and said, "CCTV along their route. Nothing clean enough to ID the guy yet."

"Keep at it," Chapman said, and headed for the team room.

As soon as he was out of sight, Jimmy threw a pen at Mark, who'd plopped down at his desk. He spun his chair around. "What?"

"Why is Chapman running Gavin's murder? Are they connecting it to Dewey?"

Long legs splayed out in front of him, Mark swung his chair in short arcs, side to side, looking pensive. "Ballistics say Gavin definitely shot Dewey, so my investigation is as good as closed. He out-ranks me. I think since there's a question about Bowman's involvement, the higher-ups wanted someone with more experience."

"What's the deal with Bowman, anyway?" Jimmy asked. "He retired?"

Mark shrugged. "I don't think Chapman's thinking any further ahead than he has to. No need to borrow trouble until we know he's our guy."

"Hopefully the commander's thinking the same way."

Mark threw Jimmy's pen back at him. "He walked into CPD of his own accord. He gets what he gets." He spun his chair back around. "I got work to do."

Jimmy fast forwarded through footage for forty minutes before he found another shot to study. He checked the trooper's log. Another One Stop, after Andy's time of death. Again, Gavin's friend remained in the car. Did he never have to pee? He leaned over the console, the sun lighting the side of his face, but it was just too blurry to make out his features.

Jimmy could see that he was still wearing the logo'ed jacket, though. He let the tape run.

The guy rolled down his window and lit up a smoke.

On New Year's Day, they'd all woken up at Andrea's in various states of hung-over. When Jimmy shuffled into the kitchen, Bowman was out on Andrea's back stoop, freezing in shirt sleeves and sweats, smoking.

After starting the coffee, Jimmy went to the door. The pungent smell of good weed drifted in. "Dude, you're gonna be a block, come inside."

Bowman took another hit even though he was shaking with the cold. He held the joint out in invitation.

Jimmy waved him off. "I'm not retired."

Bowman looked through him and then away. He took another hit, held his breath while he pinched the end out, then let it out slow. Very deliberately, he pulled a Ziploc with a couple of other unburned joints and a handful of pills and capsules of different colors in it and stuck the joint back in. "Coffee?" he croaked.

Jimmy pressed his fingers into his tired eyes. He opened them and looked again at the CCTV. Was that him?

Mark stood up, his chair rolling back, and turned around, looking at his phone. "They had to release Bowman. Ryan Merritt showed up, asked to see his client."

Dewey's lawyer.

Mark hurried out. Jimmy stretched. Only four people in the room.

Vasquez shook her fast-food drink at him. "Just looking at you makes me want more caffeine."

He crumpled the empty Mountain Dew can on his desk. "Don't need anymore of that," he said. "Maddox comes looking, I'm in the can."

"TMI," she said, already shuffling papers on her desk.

The men's room was empty. He went into a stall, pulled out his burner, and made himself comfortable.

The door slammed open. "Jimmy, you in here?" Chapman.

"Yes, for God's sake." Did they not trust him that much?

"Feds got some questions on the Sanderson stuff."

"I'll be out in a few."

"When ya gotta go, you gotta go."

He was over by the urinals.

Jimmy clutched the burner in his hands. "You scared it away."

Chapman grunted and zipped. "You got five minutes."

He did, at least, wash his hands before he banged back out.

Jimmy opened the burner. Taka had texted three times: *Call me, Wtf is going on, he's out*

Jimmy considered all the different information he could text. Prints and shoeprints at the scene of Detweiler's wreck. Stacy Owens's death. Gavin's murder. Had he changed his mind about committing suicide? Had his accomplice killed him?

There was nothing he could do with the burner. If someone found it on him, without the SIM card, his career would be done. Any text needed to be on the up and up. Plus— *Did* Bowman do it? If so, why? Was there some issue here beyond domestic abuse? Some dealing with Dewey that cost three lives and harmed another?

Were Andrea and Karie safe around him?

Jimmy used both thumbs to type his message. He hit send.

27

Taka's phone dinged. Jimmy.

At the next red light, he checked to see if Karie's headlights were still in his rearview. Andrea was riding with her.

He plucked his phone up out of the Yukon's drink holder and tapped the text.

Don't let him out of your sight.

Taka glanced over at Bowman in the passenger seat. Bowman looked back. He didn't look any different. He wasn't pissed. He wasn't scared. He had that same exhausted pallor he'd been sporting since they met, but that was normal at the end of the day. His gains were most apparent in the morning.

Except this morning. 'Cause, alcohol.

Green light. Taka set his phone back down and accelerated, going straight ahead.

"What'd he say?"

"That he can't say anything."

"You want to tell me why we're headed to Andrea's instead of my car?"

"Safety in numbers."

Bowman settled back a little. All he'd said when he came down with Merritt was that he'd told Fields the basics, corroborated Andrea's claim with his own eyewitness account, allowed his fingerprints and boots to be taken, and then invoked his right to silence as soon as they started pushing on his statements.

"Why didn't you ask for a lawyer?"

"I called my contact before I found you."

His contact, not his lawyer.

"They must have your prints on Detweiler's car."

"I'm sure they do."

"You knew Andrea wanted to stay anonymous. You didn't wipe your prints?"

"They planned to go into a store at a major shopping center off newly developed roads with high security features."

"You went with the probability they'd be identified."

"Cops go all out for their own."

That was fair. And if he'd wiped his prints, that'd be more suspicious when they were identified as the tipsters. So, what had Jimmy so wary?

They drove in silence. Bowman slouched down with his arms crossed and closed his eyes for the ten minutes it took to get to Andrea's exit. Taka turned left onto Greenbrier, which had Bowman sitting up. At Foodland, Taka threw his blinker on and waved at Karie behind him. She flashed her lights and went on when he turned in.

Bowman scratched both hands through his short dark hair. "We owe her, don't we?"

Taka parked and pulled the shopping list from his jeans pocket. "I got it."

"I'm coming in."

"You have no shoes."

Bowman held up one foot in the blue bootie he'd been given. "It's fine."

"Suit yourself."

The store was overly bright, after the dark roads. They both grabbed hand baskets. Taka threw lettuce and cucumber in his. Bowman picked up mangos. Taka raised his brows. Bowman shrugged. Tossed them and yellow bell peppers in his basket.

They cruised the meats. "Burgers?" Taka said, picking up ground chuck.

"Then we need mushrooms. And provolone."

"Good call."

They wandered up and down, filling the list. They argued over coffee and got two bags.

Piled everything on the same conveyor. Bowman's face was tight by then.

"Headache?"

"The lights and"—Bowman waved his hand—"all the stuff."

Taka picked up the Goody powders stacked next to the candy and tabloids. "Ever tried?"

"No."

He dropped them on the belt.

"How long before she trusts me again?"

The way Karie'd zipped up after her initial tears dried? Taka thought it might be a while. "Tell her why you didn't wipe your prints."

The cashier looked over with one eye, breaking her rhythm with a half-second's hesitation.

"Can you split the payment?" Bowman said.

"Why, you need an alibi?" she snapped, and then grinned at him.

"That was funny," Taka said to Bowman.

"No, it wasn't."

"Yeah, it really was," he said. And to the cashier, "You're quick."

"The booties helped."

"You saw those?"

"Everybody saw those."

"HEY," Taka said, coming into Andrea's home office. He held out a glass with two fingers of whiskey in it. "I can't drink this by myself."

She took it from him and sipped. He pulled the soft chair in the corner closer to her desk and she handed the glass back. She stole a glance into the kitchen. Karie was still at the table, staring intently at her laptop with her headphones on. She'd reset the equipment. The shower was running upstairs. Madeleine had yet to reappear. "All's quiet on the western front."

"Aren't you tired?"

"So tired. You hear from Jimmy?"

Taka stole his own glance at Karie, then palmed his phone and showed Jimmy's text to her. Kidnapping the barefoot Bowman for dinner and an overnight made more sense now. Taka's 'safety in numbers' had convinced Karie to just bring her bag in instead of going home after two nights away already.

Andrea didn't know how to feel about Bowman now. "You two make a great dinner team. Thank you."

"I just changed the sheets upstairs. I'm going to insist he take the guest bed tonight. I'll take the couch. You're okay sharing with Karie?"

"Sounds good." She took another sip of whiskey and passed the glass to him. "Do you think Stacy was still alive when he checked on them?"

"We've known him a while. After getting down on the ground with Harper and Bella, do you think he'd kill their mom?"

She didn't know how worried she'd been until it all rushed out of her. "No?" she said. She waited, seeing if that felt right. But, no, she really *didn't* believe he'd done anything to Stacy Owens. "I guess I should've thought that whole anonymous tip thing through. I panicked. When you think about, it was sweet of him just to let me think it was a good idea."

"How are you feeling about spilling now?"

She took the glass back and gulped a bigger swallow, then nodded. "I'm okay."

That slow smile he gave her was her favorite. "Liar."

"I'm dreading the fallout."

"I don't know. That ghost, Corporal Hunt, he may have helped you."

"How so?"

"Did you look him up yet?"

"I did. He was killed in an interview room in '91."

"There's no way you could've known it was *that* room or his ID number. I don't think Fields or Tamarin are going to say much when they figure that out. And you remember Corporal Mendel?"

"Yes?"

"He's gonna have your back."

"Thank you."

"I might be wrong. It could be a circus, but maybe not."

She handed him the glass. He slugged back the remainder and got up. "Do your thing. I'll keep Bowman occupied."

She was looking up at him and he bent and kissed her like he'd been leaving her with a kiss for years. But the ease of it, how easy it'd be to just sink into it, caught them both by surprise. He drew back a few inches, eyes locked on hers.

"Okay then," he said, mostly to himself, she thought.

He left. Andrea tried to remember how to breathe. She glanced again at Karie, but she had one headphone slid back off her ear and was saying something to Taka, who was out of sight. Okay then.

She was overtired and awake. After dinner, she'd done a quick google search for the Copper Ridge song. Nothing. Dropped a few hooks in various historical and reenactment forums. Found her way to folk music hangouts and saw Eddie had been there. His interest must've been piqued. She'd decided to leave it to him.

She shuffled through her notes. Skim Tess Albright's music files or see if she could find Madeleine through digging into the families? The song wouldn't solve how Madeleine was connected to Dewey. Genealogy it was. She googled on Dewey for ten minutes just in case she was missing something. His parents' marriage pre-dated his birth, his sister was younger. The property Madeleine and Dewey described as the homestead was the same one and Dewey said his grandfather owned it.

It seemed way more likely that Madeleine being connected to the property meant she was connected to the Sandersons in some way rather than to a random birth mother. Since she wasn't in Dewey's direct line, she might pop up in the families from the surrounding area that had married into the wider Sanderson family. Or Flynn Iverson might and give Andrea a different avenue to explore. It was looking like she'd have to get used to Madeleine talking at her for the foreseeable future.

Considering the red crossvine on his farm, she started with Roger Wright, gleaning his parents and siblings' names from an uncle's obituary. Put together his age and a basic bio from tidbits about him on social media. He didn't have a presence online himself. Beau Sanderson did, with a couple of articles on him related to ginseng picking. Roger Wright stood in the back of one photo, a digging spade in his hand and hundreds of roots in a pile between him and Beau in the foreground. Maybe that *was* Beau's red truck that passed them out there at Wright's farm.

She pulled up property tax maps for Greenbrier County, found Wright's place and looked at who currently owned the former Sanderson holdings to the west and north. She noted those last names. The north property was bounded by the Cranberry. Walking in to poach ginseng would be easy. The properties to the south and east were much larger, thirteen-hundred and eighteen-hundred acres.

It hadn't dawned on her how alone she and Karie would've been if they needed help and couldn't drive out. The Iversons' bones had been out there for months. Skye, the bloodhound, had been out there for months. If the trapper's cabin was out there somewhere on that huge acreage, how would anyone know? Tucker told Madeleine to go up to Leah Beth's in the holler, but the girls she needed to fetch were picking ginseng on Winslow Creek. Only . . . Andrea went back to her notes:

They've gone sanging (picking ginseng) down on Winslow Creek. Everybody knows that abandoned homestead's got haunts (pronounced 'haints', meaning ghosts) that'll scare the skin right off you.

Madeleine wasn't saying they were down on Winslow Creek *somewhere*. She was saying they were picking ginseng on Winslow Creek *at* that abandoned homestead. Where did ginseng grow best? In rich, moist soil facing east or north. In combination with black walnut, maples, and poplars, where there wasn't much understory. When settlers built homes, they cleared the brush away, but left or planted trees for shade and to block the wind.

She needed to be looking for a once populated site on Winslow Creek, not just somewhere near it. On a high bank above the creek, with the slope running away from it. If Toby hadn't flown over the right locations for the topographical maps, she might need to pull whatever had been collected in the course of genealogical research on all the area's oldest family surnames. Diaries, journals, letters, farm records, anything where some gossipy resident might have shared the best place to dig ginseng on the banks of Winslow Creek.

Or she could call Greenbrier County's king of ginseng and just ask him. She checked the time. Right on ten o'clock. A little late, but he could really fast forward her research if he had thoughts of where she should be looking.

It rang four times and voicemail picked up.

"Hey, Beau, it's Andrea Kelley from Waltham-Young. We spoke yesterday. I'm sorry to be calling so late. Someone in town mentioned in passing that you buy and sell ginseng and I have a separate question about ginseng you might can answer for me. Could you please call me back? I'd truly appreciate it." She rattled off her number, repeated her name, and thanked him again for his cooperation the day before.

Going back to Roger Wright and his dead uncle, she opened up Ancestry, FamilySearch, FindaGrave, Rootsweb, and the WV GenWeb Project just to get started and began typing names. Through link after link, she followed parent lines and sibling lines as far as anyone had traced. Here and there, the Wrights intersected with the Sandersons, as well as other prominent surnames in the area.

No Madeleines.

Rather than go any further, she opened a new document and went back to her Sanderson notes to make a list of related names through marriage. Then she went back online and start clicking through those known genealogies.

JIMMY STIFLED a yawn and signed yet another verification. He hoped it was the last, but the stacks of reports, statements, transcripts, and evidence inventory had migrated across the length of the biggest conference table at HQ so many times, he had no idea.

"Don't start," the blond Fed said, standing at the far end of the table, compiling files. Jimmy had never caught her name and she didn't offer it when he came into the room several hours ago. "I've only had short nights since your partner ignited this review."

By getting killed, Jimmy didn't say. Damn. Andy was really gone. "He's dead."

Her tone softened. "That was insensitive. I apologize."

"Thank you. Can you tell me the status of this investigation now?"

She cocked a hip and crossed her arms. "I don't know the state's final stance, but my division sees no further need to be involved in a criminal investigation of Dewey Sanderson at this time. Our tax evasion and fraud departments are still arms-deep in a review of the businesses he owns in partnership with the late Senator Sanderson." She waggled her head. "Allegedly owns."

Surveying the thousands of pages surrounding him, Jimmy blew out his breath. "Did we do any good at all?"

"Absolutely," she declared and went back to her organization. "Those small arms and drug deals your undercover reported and the names he collected have already or will help us make other connections. Either bigger links in the networks or filling in the information gaps. Having Sanderson in the mix isn't something we're worried about at this time."

"Some people are above the law?"

She stopped and considered him for a second. "You're one of those."

Jimmy scruffed his fingers through his hair. "I'm too tired for this conversation. What do you think I am?"

"One of those LEOs who has no idea how much he's accomplishing because he's focused on a single goal. One of those who doesn't care if a small fish needs to remain in play because in *his* town, that sardine is a white whale and you're Ahab."

"My town is the whole state."

"No, your town is this particular WVSP Detachment. And that's good. By being Ahab, you've helped your state and your country. So, keep an eye on your whale, but let him run the line out for a while. We could use a few more wins like hooking the Conlons and their contacts out of seven states and straight into the frying pan."

We could use a few more wins like hooking the Conlons. He'd met all four heads of the local, state, and federal investigation teams following up and coordinating other agencies as they mopped up the Conlons widespread organization. Dewey's participation had led them to the encrypted trafficking site that blew the investigation wide open. Did that "we" mean this woman worked for the federal investigative lead on the Conlon task force? "Has Kate Bolling taken over the federal Sanderson criminal investigation?"

The woman smiled at him, closed mouth, with a little shake of her head. "I just told you, we're closing up shop on further reviews at this time. The state will let us know if we need to revisit."

Looked like Bolling had taken an interest in Jimmy's white whale and bumped the former lead.

When he didn't say anything, she said, "I don't know about your partner's legacy, but this work will earn you a promotion. You'll see."

"Are we done?"

"*You* are."

KARIE DROPPED down into the chair Taka had left beside Andrea's desk. "Hey."

"Hey, what time is it?"

Karie yawned. "One."

"One? How is that even possible?"

"The guys went to bed hours ago."

"Did Jimmy call Taka?"

"No."

"Want to get in bed with me?"

Karie's mouth turned down.

"It's okay," Andrea said. "It's okay to not be okay with him."

"I thought I knew him."

"You do. We don't know that he's not completely innocent."

"But I should, right? I should believe him."

They were speaking in hushed tones, but Andrea lowered her voice to a whisper, "Has he said he's innocent? Or that he didn't do it?"

"Not in those words," Karie whispered back. "He said again that they were both dead when he got down there. There was no way not to touch the car. The hill was too steep. Why hasn't Jimmy called?"

Andrea closed out all her open windows. "I don't know."

Karie rubbed her eyes. She dropped her hands and sighed. "Maybe it's just that I know he's killed people."

Andrea saved her documents and closed them. She turned off the monitor and the room went dark, lit only by the distant stove light still on in the kitchen. "Taka's killed people, too."

And then she remembered the pressure of the trigger under her finger, the blood mist hanging in the air, the awful thump of Oliver Fitch's body when it hit the kitchen floor. "So have I."

The memory of witnessing that death crossed over Karie's face. "It's funny how the brain works to protect itself."

"Self-preservation. It's not just the brain, it's the whole body."

"Now that we're awake again, let's bring the music files up with us."

While Karie used the bathroom upstairs, Andrea got herself a glass of water, turned off the stove light, and peeked at Taka sprawled uncomfortably across the couch. Karie slipped out just as Andrea came up. She took the files from her and headed into the bedroom while Andrea got ready for bed. But as soon as Andrea settled under the covers, Karie sighed and dropped her head back on her pillow to stare at the ceiling.

Andrea held out her hand for the file Karie was holding. "He's the same Bowman right now that he was yesterday. If he turns out to be a bad guy, he's a bad guy. Are you afraid of him?"

Karie rolled her face towards Andrea and really thought about her answer for a long moment that stretched into two. "No. I'm sad. I'm worried that he's not the guy I think he is, and I'm worried he's exactly the guy I think he is and I'm hurting him."

"He's probably neither of those guys, you know that, right? But if he at least falls on the right side of that equation, he'll understand."

"Do you really think so?"

"You can always blame it on Taka. Tell him Taka said to stay away from him."

That at least got a smile out of her. "Hey, know what I was looking for tonight?"

"What?"

"Any folklore or ghost stories about trappers or settlers in the area of the Cranberry or Cherry River. There's several, mostly related to buried treasure or Native American encounters, or murder of one kind or another but nothing that checks enough boxes yet."

Andrea threw her arms around her and gave her a big squeeze. "I've never had a friend like you. Not just anyone gets to hide in my bed from something we don't actually know anything about!"

28

Jimmy hit pause on the Coliseum's security cam footage he was watching in the team room. They'd lost Gavin within blocks of the club, but they also knew Gavin had lost his passenger about two hours before that. Nina and the two other techs were long gone, scheduled to be back early. Jimmy was working backwards through the CCTV patrol had collected along Gavin's route so far. "Need coffee, Bill?"

"Black, please."

Like Jimmy hadn't been handing him black coffee for years now. "You got it."

"And a Red Bull if there's any in there. I don't care whose name is on it."

In the break room, the cases of water and soda had dwindled as the extra manpower trickled out of the building. No Mountain Dew. Jimmy pulled the fridge door. Five out of a six pack of Red Bull. A post it on top read, *I don't mind getting life if anyone touches my Red Bull-V.*

Vasquez.

Jimmy didn't doubt her, but Bill got what Bill needed, so he plucked a Red Bull out. And then another for himself. The coffee was still hot. He rinsed out two mugs, filled them, and carried it all back to Bill.

He'd finished his coffee and was half-way through his Red Bull when he saw it. Gavin Owen's Acura pulled to the curb outside an old ice cream shop and grill on 7th Avenue with a walk-up window. The Bowman look-alike got out, and Gavin drove off. The guy walked into the shop's flood light and looked up at the menu. Jimmy hit pause. "Got him, Bill."

Bill spun around and leapt off his chair. He skidded around the table Jimmy was working on. "That's not the commander."

"No, it's not." His throat was tight. He swallowed hard. "Let's find out who he is."

"Move, move," Bill said, already sitting down as Jimmy vacated the chair.

Jimmy lifted both arms, running his hands through his hair, and linked his fingers behind his head. He pushed back into the hold, stretching his back and neck.

"That is a beautiful shot," Bill said. "Though I could wish he didn't have the cap on."

He got up, went back to his own station, and called the screenshot up on his monitor. Fingers flying, he labeled it and began the process of uploading to their database for facial recognition and then sending it to every immediate team and task force member, then out to the Kanawha County agencies to issue BOLOs to all their officers. If that didn't scare him or his name up within six hours, they'd issue alerts to every agency in the state.

Seven forty-five p.m. put the stop hours after Detweiler had been run off the road and then executed, but before the shooting at the Coliseum. Jimmy flipped through the log. Afterward, they had Gavin headed eastbound on Route 25, alone. They'd lost him only blocks from the club. He'd probably parked, found a good vantage point, and bided his time. But they hadn't found his escape route yet. If he'd stuck to side streets, stayed off the bigger roads and highway, they might not have him on any traffic cams at all in route to where he died.

"Hey, Bill," Jimmy said. "Maddox has my phone. Can you call Chapman?"

Bill finished whatever he was typing and then snagged his phone and made the call. Then he put the grill's CCTV up on his monitor and they watched it again. Asshat friend ordered, was handed a drink and a white bag, then made a call.

"Time?" Jimmy said.

"Eight-oh-two."

Jimmy flipped through Gavin's call log. "Not to Gavin."

The guy waited a couple more minutes before a dark-colored Camaro pulled up, passenger door to the curb. He yanked the door open and got in. The camera angle couldn't catch the plate. Bill started typing hard. Jimmy scrabbled in his pile of papers, coming up with the list of traffic cams. "Next view is Route 25 at Virginia, camera code GH561 to the east. Or west on 25 at Route 62, camera code LM283."

Bill pulled the cameras up. He fiddled, running them to eight o'clock on Friday night, then let them play. The Camaro passed the Virginia camera onto Route 25 headed westbound, and they got a perfect view of the license plate. It continued westbound, away from the Coliseum and Gavin.

Bill ran with the license plate and got Chapman's okay to send units out to the registered owner with Chapman and Mark Compton rolling out to meet them. Jimmy wondered how much longer he'd be sidelined. He stalked to the bullpen and back, then went for a piss. He went into a stall but didn't go through the charade again with anyone who'd check on him out of the building. He jerked the burner out and texted. *He's good.*

It was almost four a.m. He didn't expect a reply, but one came.

You okay

His heart clenched. *Yes,* he sent. He couldn't seem to stop lying to these people who he'd never considered would become his . . . Just his. They were his people. *No,* he sent.

Brkfst @ Andrea's

Okay

He pocketed the phone, did his business, and went back to Bill.

"All good?"

"That was a good find, Jimmy. You headed?"

"Naw. Told Maddox I'd stay."

"When's he come back on?"

"Haven't the foggiest." He sat and finished the Red Bull and then went on reviewing footage. About five, Bill went for more Red Bull.

He came back and handed one to Jimmy. "You watch Fergusson go down yet?"

"No."

"You were totally justified, Jimmy. You'll feel better if you see it."

"You think?"

"C'mon, I'll watch it with you. If you look hard, you can see your hit on Gavin Owens, too."

"No. I'm good."

Bill flopped down in his chair. "I get it, dude."

But there was no way he could. Jimmy wasn't at all sure Bill had ever fired a gun, period. He'd definitely never shot a police officer whose safety was his responsibility.

"Oh, yeah." Bill tugged a large manila envelope from under the mish-mash of papers on his desk. It was too big to toss. Bill walked his wheeled chair over. "Nina said to give this to you when you came up for air."

He pushed off Jimmy's desk and slid back to his own. He spun around, took a swig out of his can, and then settled back down. Jimmy opened the envelope. On top of the pile of documents he slid half-way out was a note from Nina: *All I could find on the '81 murder of Ellen Shannon Westfall*. He was way too tired. He shoved the case back into the envelope. Looked at his watch again.

The team would be back in at six. If he was going to man up and watch himself shoot Scott and hit Gavin, but not hard enough, he'd rather do it alone. He cued up the video, from three different cameras. One on each back corner of the club, one wide-angle over the back entrance. The views were disorienting. He closed his eyes and envisioned what he remembered to orient himself.

The Coliseum was on a corner lot, a standalone building with its entrance on Quarrier. There was parking on and across the street. Wide sidewalks allowed a crowd to gather outside on Quarrier and Summers. Coming into the private back lot off Summers, through a lift-arm restricted entrance, you could go right into a large outdoor residents' lot, which served the condos next door, or left, into six spots directly behind the club for Dewey, his security team, and whichever of his managers was on.

The entrance area between Dewey's parking and the residents lot formed an extra wide alley of sorts. It accommodated delivery trucks, a dumpster, and a pedestrian entrance into the condo's covered parking and elevator entrance. As far as Jimmy knew, the pedestrian's gate stood open twenty-four seven. It was part of the condo's ornamental wrought iron fence that blocked off access to both the garage and barely-there alley between the Coliseum and the condo where a few scraggly bushes grew.

He'd been out on the sidewalk on Summers, headed for his car on the street when the first shots cracked through the air. He drew his gun as he ran forward. He rounded the corner of the building with his gun raised, and body lowered, into the meager cover of the landscape bed there, a few large evergreen bushes trimmed round like big green balls and a leafless tree. Dewey's Mercedes idled in the middle of the alley, facing the exit, two dark lumps on the ground near the passenger door. *Civilians down.*

Jimmy remembers that exact thought.

No recognition of names, just 'civilians down' in the bark of Bruten Wilder's training voice in his head. A silhouette with a raised gun in both hands stood at the rear of the car, shrouded in the steam rising from the car's exhaust pipe. The silhouette turned, pointing the gun right at him and there was no thought at all. He pulled the trigger as recognition flooded him. Ears ringing, movement drew his eye and the muzzle of his gun. The shooter. On the edge of the club's floodlights. Gun aimed at Scott. He pulled the trigger, followed the shooter's stumble, fired again. He rubbed the memory of the pressure from his index finger, blew out his breath to rid himself of the quick bite of propellant from his nose, shook the phantom buzzing silence that followed the shots from his head.

Before he chickened out, Jimmy made sure the sound was off and hit play.

His belly rolled. He flinched with the muzzle flash from Gavin's gun back near the pedestrian's gate. Chet spinning away from Dewey.

Another muzzle flash. Dewey folding onto the ground. Scott turning, firing at the flash, then, blinded, searching for Gavin in the shadows. Himself, coming around the corner of the building. Scott swinging around, gun still raised. Muzzle flash from Jimmy's gun—once, twice, three shots. Scott going down hard. Past him, Gavin stumbling against the condo's fence when Jimmy's bullet hit him, then scuttling along it, through the pedestrian entrance and out of sight.

Jimmy ran it back, gaze flicking between the three screens. Ran it back. Watched each one all the way through. Watched them all at once again. There, a flicker of light. Six times before he saw it for what it was. There, behind him, a shadow. Jimmy didn't know how he couldn't tell before whether Gavin's accomplice was Bowman or not.

Because he knew without a doubt that this was Bowman. Jimmy ran it back, over and over, piecing out Bowman's movement. He came around the corner of the Coliseum off Summers right behind Jimmy. Up into the landscape bed. Half-crouching among the balls of green. His movements mirrored Jimmy's. Exactly. He moved with stealthy grace, utterly at ease with the scene playing out in front of him. With rock hard discipline, he didn't fire. When Jimmy ran forward to the men on the ground, Bowman covered the pedestrian entrance, then stepped back around the corner, like he'd never been there. He might be nothing but a dark reflection.

Jimmy ran it back.

Between the second and third shots, the Coliseum door banged open, bouncing off the back wall, almost shutting again. Scott swung around, Jimmy fired. He moved forward, Bowman slid back. Dewey's bouncers came spilling out the back door, the only reason Dewey didn't bleed to death.

Voices coming down the hall.

Jimmy reached out and pulled the flash drive out without ejecting it.

He dropped it in the small box among the others.

"Hey, Boss," Nina called out. "You got him!"

"Bill got him," Jimmy said. "He got the license plate."

Bill spun around and Nina and the other techs high-fived him one after the other. Jimmy picked up the cold case and moved out of their way.

Nina pointed at the envelope. "You read that yet?"

"Haven't had a chance yet." He shook his thumb at the doorway. "I'm gonna go get some sleep."

"You deserve it!"

"Keep me up to date."

"You know it."

He went down the hall and through reception and into Maddox's office and sat down. In his mind's eye, he kept seeing that shadow fade as he stepped forward. It could almost be his imagination. Almost. He'd just closed his burning eyes when Maddox swept in, bringing the cold air in with him.

"Jimmy. Good catch, I hear. They pinned him down already."

"That was fast."

"He was sound asleep." He slid his desk drawer open and tossed Jimmy's phone at him. Jimmy fumbled the catch against his chest. "Get out of here. I'll see you at the memorial tomorrow."

"Yes, sir."

Outside, ice crystals hung in the crisp air, making it sparkle in the rising light. Jimmy's shadow stretched across the parking lot.

Why would Bowman retreat from a fight?

He wouldn't. He'd also know immediate help was at hand.

What an experienced operative might do is slip around the far side of a building and cut off a shooter's escape.

If Gavin was like any other disrespected abuser, Jimmy could hear him sputtering now, spitting out how he'd taken care of that cheating bitch and her boyfriend and that asshole Sanderson for interfering. Even assuming Bowman didn't know Detweiler was protecting the man's wife, what might a man used to a different kind of justice do then?

ANDREA WOKE to the tune of Madeleine's fairy song. Fairies stealing babies. She stretched. Surely the Sandersons hadn't stolen Dewey? No, he looked too much like his dad. And with his prominence, someone would've unearthed that a long time ago. Likewise, if Flynn had been stolen from them. That'd be widely known.

Maybe they'd managed to keep a surrogate private? Was surrogacy a thing yet in '80? 81? But then why do it again and not keep the second one? Flynn Iverson was either Dewey's brother or his doppelganger and he hadn't been raised by Mrs. Sanderson.

Maybe the senator had always had a woman like Anna Lansing on the side and her pregnancy wasn't the first whoops. Or maybe Andrea was on the wrong track altogether.

She rolled over. Karie was facing her, out for the count. In the low morning light, her dark red hair shone as it fanned out over her cheek. Please, please, Bowman, be a good guy. Andrea didn't know much about Karie's previous relationships. It wasn't something they'd talked about much. She'd had a couple. Nothing serious. Andrea knew Karie had given her a lot of time the last few months, but not that, like Andrea, she didn't have many close friends.

Which reminded Andrea that Lauren had texted yesterday. She slid out of bed and eased her walk-in closet door open. She checked the weather app, texted Lauren that she didn't know if Skye the bloodhound would be hers yet, and pulled on sweats and a Henley. Taking her socks and tennis shoes with her, she padded to the bathroom and hoped flushing wouldn't wake everyone up.

Checking on Taka, she found him awake, but still staring vacantly at the ceiling. He caught her movement though and propped himself on his elbow.

"I'm going for a run," she said, keeping her voice down.

"Bowman's out there. Jimmy texted the all clear a couple hours ago."

"Oh!" More relief wicked through Andrea than she expected. "That's good. I wanted to believe him, but . . ."

"But he's got scary stoneface."

She stifled her laugh and grinned, glancing up the stairs. "He really does."

"Go." Taka dropped back down and wiggled to get comfortable under his blanket. "I'm just gonna lay here and contemplate my life choices."

"Are we going to see Dewey later?"

Taka sighed. "Don't make him add more weeks to my sentence."

"Got it. Negotiate my own answers."

He sat back up. "Oh, God. Please don't. He'll have you researching vintage cars or whatever business he's *consulting* on next and writing gun descriptions for the website. Never mind, I'll take the bullet for you."

"My hero," she said, clutching her hands to her heart.

His sleepy face sharpened, and his eyes narrowed.

Oh. Heat filled her belly. They'd flirted since they were thirteen. She'd had everything he had to offer except this one last facet of himself. She'd shared him with both girlfriends and boyfriends and seen him through happiness and heartache. They'd waxed and waned and waxed again. They'd come close more than once. But now she knew she'd never before experienced the focus of his full attention. It was like walking into the sun.

"You better go," he said.

Right. Wrong time. Wrong place. But—this was really happening between them.

Her heart soared.

She backed out of the living room's threshold, turned, grabbed her thin down jacket off the rack, and opened the front door to a blast of cold air. Bowman sat on the top step, smoking a joint. She closed the door. "You had pot on you at the police station?"

"Left it in Taka's gun safe with my meds."

"Ah." Pulling on her jacket, she sat down next to him.

He nodded at his feet and Taka's old tennis shoes. "Good enough fit for me to run."

She eyed the joint. "If you feel okay."

"Better now."

"Running in jeans won't bother you?"

"Nah. Wet fatigues are worse."

"I've gotta warm up."

He stubbed the joint out and tucked it into his jacket. "Everyone should."

She went down onto the drive, unusually self-conscious. But Bowman didn't say anything, just warmed his legs up, then followed her lead with her usual jumping jacks and did lunges alongside her. He did small arm circles while she did large.

Out on the road, he kept an easy pace with her, falling behind her when they had to go single file. She circled them back from her two-mile mark, picking up the pace on the way home. The air was just a little too cold for any sprinting, but she stretched her legs a little. Bowman stayed on her shoulder. A couple of hundred yards before Double Branch, she said, "Walk the rest?"

He dropped to a walk in response. Concerned, she turned back, but he smiled at her. Breathing hard, it took him a minute of walking to recover enough to speak. "The cold air's been kicking my ass."

"Just—keep being a good guy so *I* don't have to kick your ass."

He stopped and took a couple more big breaths before he slowed his breathing.

Andrea turned again to face him.

"I don't know why they thought what they thought," Bowman said. "And I understand that for as welcoming as you've been, you don't know me well. I hope I've never given you the impression I'm not somebody different than how I've presented myself. There's things I can't talk about, but I've never lied to any of you.

"As a matter of fact, it's been a very long time since I could be myself and have people accept me the way you all have. I don't want to lose that. And I especially don't want to lose Karie before we've figured out if there's an *us* or not. I didn't think I wanted that. Never have before. And after seeing what Cole went through when my sister disappeared? No. Just no.

"But now? I do want it. And I want all of you with it. I want it all. The ghosts, the weird place you guys work, the way meals come together, and everyone pitches in to figure out what needs to happen next and doesn't complain about it? It's crazy. Maybe you guys don't know this, but this kind of working unit? I didn't know it was possible to—"

He threw his head back, opened his fisted hands and put them deliberately in his jacket pockets. He watched the heavy grey clouds scud across the sky, but Andrea knew he wasn't seeing them.

"I came here on a lead," he finally said. "To find Becky. I was already sick and skipped out on treatment and almost died a second time. But I couldn't. Because I have to find her. For Cole." He sniffed hard. His voice came out tight. "For Elsa. I lived, and I found a way to stay employed so I could stay longer, but I didn't want a life."

He lowered his head and met Andrea's eyes.

She couldn't look away now if the earth dropped out from under her.

"I wasn't planning to have one after I find her. Already decided how and where. And then you guys inserted yourselves into my vendetta because of a murdered woman who was a complete stranger to you. And you showed me what life could be. And if Karie and I don't work out? If I have to go back to the Navy? If we have a falling out and lose our friendship? That's fine. I'll always want a life because of you guys. But I don't want any of *that* to be because of *this*, whatever they thought I did."

The wind gusted, tugging at their pants. Bowman's jaw was clenched, braced against whatever reaction he thought she'd have. He looked miserable and cold, and she was almost sorry she'd hurt him. She had no idea what to say, but then she was saying, "I don't know what they thought they had on you, but we were never going to abandon you. I don't know how this happened, this family we've made, but you're a part of it. Scott's still a part of it. They'd have to come up with some damn solid evidence before we'd believe them over you. Taka brought you home with us because you're one of us."

"He brought me home because Jimmy hadn't called yet and he didn't want me disappearing."

"Tell me you wouldn't have disappeared."

He suddenly found the threatening darkness on the horizon very interesting. Then he said, "We're attracting attention."

He started walking and Andrea fell in beside him. Her across the street neighbor, Dr. Huntley, wearing an oilskin coat and carrying an umbrella, had just turned off Double Branch, and was walking towards them at a brisk pace.

"Luke," Andrea said.

"I'd have come back. I meant everything I said."

"So did I. And thank you."

"For what?"

"For letting me have my panic attack and pretending that anonymous tip would stay anonymous."

And there it was, that sly, amused smile as he glanced over at her. "What are friends for?"

She surprised herself by threading her arm through his and leaning into him. When had she become this friend? The physically affectionate one? But she liked it. "Hi, Dr. Huntley, have you met my friend Luke Bowman, yet?"

29

As soon as they turned the corner, they saw Jimmy had arrived. Andrea could practically feel Bowman packing himself back down inside his armor. Not full mental shields raised mode, but back to the wariness of not over-sharing and watching where he stepped as the new guy that he'd slipped back into after the other night and the discussion about Scott.

The lovely rich aroma of strong coffee met them at the mud room door. Taka and Jimmy were juggling eggs and sausage patties, while Karie was piling cathead biscuits from a baking sheet onto a plate.

"See, what'd I tell you?" Taka said.

Jimmy laughed.

"What'd you tell him?" Andrea asked.

"That you have a sixth sense and you'd be here right before everything was finished."

"Absolutely," she agreed. "I like my food hot."

Outside, thunder rumbled in a low, rolling boom.

They toed their shoes off in the mud room and left their jackets on the wall hooks. Andrea pulled a T-shirt she knew was Scott's from the pile of Taka's clothes folded on the dryer and slapped it against Bowman's chest. "Don't get weird."

He nodded.

She smiled and shook her head. He'd probably used up most of the hundred words he allotted himself each week on his little speech. She opened the cabinet above the washer and found the box of large waterproof bandages she'd picked up after she saw the ones he used over his portacath.

"You bought me bandages?"

"I know you don't change it every day, but just in case. You need one?"

"Please."

"We'll be right back," she yelled as they passed through the kitchen. Bowman hit the half-bath and Andrea ran up the stairs.

Her room was dark. She flipped the light on, half-expecting to see Madeleine, but the room was empty. Karie had made the bed. Mrs. Albright's folders were gone, probably down in the kitchen. She slid her closet door open. The dog inside leaped forward, barking furiously. Andrea caught the shriek in her throat. She bent over, trying not to hyperventilate.

"No one's so bright as them dark-headed lads what's been gone from Winslow's crick so long."

"Hush," Andrea said to the dog. The dead dog barking at her. If her heart weren't thumping so hard, she'd yell.

"None's them touch don't feel it. Them bleeding-vines don't lie."

Wait. This sounded vaguely familiar, but Andrea didn't have it in her notes. She whipped her phone out.

"Tucker sez they's just a'moved, gone away."

"Wait, wait, wait," Andrea whispered. Using both thumbs, she typed as fast as could. "Quiet, dog."

"But Leah Beth heard tell how's that one's a wraith and ain't it been seed a'sanging in the holler . . ."

"Leah Beth," Andrea breathed, typing,

". . . diggin' and pickin' like it was still a'this world."

Madeleine and the dog both fell silent.

Andrea looked up. They both had their heads raised, listening.

The still air in the closet pressed close.

Goosebumps crawled up Andrea's back and neck and spread down her arms.

Madeleine turned her head, looking past Andrea. "He's coming."

Lightning flashed and a crack of thunder made Andrea duck and the house shake. When she recovered, Madeleine and the bloodhound were gone. The windows rattled. Rain ricocheted off the glass like thrown pebbles and drummed down on the roof.

DOWNSTAIRS, everyone was making biscuit sandwiches at the table. The heavy rain outside the large window painted the room in wavering shadows. Sitting close to Bowman, Karie looked happier this morning. Andrea decided her encounter could wait. She grabbed coffee and settled between Taka and Jimmy. Taka scooped eggs onto her plate while she selected a biscuit. These were too big to be the Grands she had in the fridge. "Did you make these, Karie?"

"I did," she said, spreading jam on hers.

Jimmy held out the plate of sausage patties.

Lightning flashed.

Andrea plopped two patties onto her biscuit. "So, tell us what the heck was happening last night."

The thunderclap that underscored her words grumbled away.

Jimmy set the plate down, eyes going to Bowman, who kept his head down and took a huge bite of his sandwich. "Pass the jam, please."

Karie handed it to him, and he took his time spreading it on his biscuit top.

Andrea had her breakfast assembled before he said, "Screw it," and looked around at each of them. "No need to say for your ears only. I know you won't share. Gavin Owens had an accomplice. Being down the embankment the way it was, the first responders were surprised at the number of tracks around Andy's car. They sent one guy down to confirm death, which allowed them to keep the scene mostly intact. There were three different unknown shoe prints, but only two whole prints, both on Stacy's side." He lifted a finger at Bowman. "Bowman's and Gavin's.

Stacy died a long time after Andy did. Ballistics proved the gun recovered with Gavin killed Andy and he did shoot Stacy in the head, but it was the third bullet she took that killed her, and that was from a different gun."

Jimmy bit into his biscuit.

Taka cleared his throat, then coughed, then took a big swallow of coffee, then didn't say anything.

"Taka," Andrea said, covering her full mouth with her hand. "What?"

"Fields asked me if I knew anything about Bowman's guns. I told him I had possession of two of them in my truck, but he'd need a search warrant if he wanted them."

Forearms on the table, biscuit in both hands, Bowman straightened up, his mouth open. He closed it and set his breakfast down. "You did that for me?"

"It was the right thing to do."

"They didn't ask me. About my guns."

"They might still get a warrant," Jimmy said. "It's unlikely anyone who didn't know where that car was to start with would've found it as fast as y'all did. They'd have only been found by air search or drone flyover or an accidental sighting from a different ridge. They found Gavin's car mid-afternoon Friday on the same traffic cam y'all went through on Saturday. The problem is, there's a guy in the car with the same build as you. And you probably knew Detweiler through your connection to Dewey. And his connection to Dewey is under a microscope right now."

That'd be a problem, Andrea could see that.

Bowman frowned at his biscuit. Karie reached out and grabbed his hand.

"Except you're a decorated Navy SEAL. You walked into CPD on your own to share what you knew. You have no known ties to either Gavin or Stacy Owens. And you gave CPD what they asked for, so they gave you some leeway."

Silence.

Jimmy's throat clicked when he swallowed. "Plus, Horton called me this morning and said Andrea walked in and told them how y'all found the car. Apparently, she spooked them by pulling a name, ID number, and cause of death out of thin air for a cop who did actually die in that room they were in." He slid his gaze to Andrea. "That was very brave. I'm proud of you."

"But they might still get a warrant for Bowman?"

"A search warrant. 'Cause, 'ghosts' isn't really a legal defense. But we ID'ed and located Gavin's passenger. He's being held because he was in the car when it was seen in Westridge. They did get a warrant for his place and all his weapons and ammo are now at the ballistics lab. And they're trying to find any vehicles related to him on the two traffic cams out there. If he came and went out Sugar Creek without ever going to the highway, then they won't find him. At least not on a road that a defense lawyer can't argue reasonable doubt on his direction of travel."

Bowman opened his free hand. "Why are you telling us this?"

"Because most of it will be given to the media this morning. Because Fields already went to Taka about the guns, so he knows Taka would tell you they were interested in them. Because if you did shoot Stacy, that gun is long gone, and they know that."

"I didn't shoot her. She was dead."

Jimmy rolled his eyes. "Good to know. Eat your biscuit."

Bowman shot a glance at Andrea. Taka and Jimmy had just proven her point. She smiled and took a big bite out of her biscuit. Through the rain pounding the window and vinyl siding and roof, a familiar clicking came through the mud room into the kitchen. It sounded just like a dog walking across the floor.

She concentrated on her biscuit and took another bite.

She was starving.

A dog shook, the tags on its collar clacking, and then she had to look.

Madeleine's bloodhound, wet from the rain. He snuffled the air, barked once at her, then turned and sat, watching the carport door in the mud room with an expectant air.

"Why is it so dark in here?" Taka said and got up to turn the overhead lights on. "What are you looking at, Andrea?"

They were all looking at her. "I . . . y'know the bloodhound with Madeleine? The ghost one?"

"Yes," Taka said.

"He's—I think he's—"

The massive dog tipped his head back and bayed.

"I think he's here."

The dog leapt up, barking wildly, escalating in seconds to ready to tear into whoever stood on the other side of the carport door.

"The dog is here?"

"Yes. And the trapper."

The carport door shook under the force of three blows. The dog kept barking.

Andrea was aware of Jimmy, Karie, and Bowman all standing up behind her at once, a chair falling over.

Taka came to her side.

"Did you hear that?" she yelled over the dog.

"Someone's knocking," Taka said. "Should I answer it?"

"Who is it?" Andrea called out as loud as she could.

No answer. Or none she could hear.

She looked over her shoulder at the others. But there was someone else standing in the door frame between the kitchen and her office. Andy Detweiler.

The door shook under three more devasting blows.

She tore her gaze away from Andy.

Enraged, the dog rushed into the mud room, barking and growling.

"Step aside, Andrea," Jimmy commanded from behind her, voice calm.

Andrea backed to the side, knocking over one of the cameras on its tripod. She got a hand out to catch it but missed. It hit the floor. The camera broke into a scatter of pieces.

Jimmy had his gun drawn at low-ready. Taka slipped to one side of the framed entry to the mud room.

"Who is it?" Taka yelled at the carport door. "Answer now!"

Detweiler drew Andrea's focus back to him by stepping up just behind Jimmy, off his shoulder. He flashed nine fingers and then two. Ninety-two again. But what did it mean?

The carport door shuddered, the boom of another blow echoing through the house.

The bloodhound attacked the door, nails scrabbling and scraping through the paint, leaving long gouges of raw wood.

Wild-eyed, arms out, and half-crouched in self-defense, Taka shouted, "What the hell? What the hell, Andrea?"

Again, the door shuddered, the booming knock louder than the dog.

On his hind legs, his huge head at the top of the frame, he barked and growled, tearing onto the door, flinging slobber in his frenzy to get to the other side.

"Andrea!"

Her head snapped around at the unfamiliar voice.

Bowman ran by her. Karie still crouched by the kitchen table, eyes wide, staring past her. Jimmy stepped forward with one foot, dropping into ready fire, both hands raising his gun. But it was Detweiler who'd spoken. He stood tall, looking right at her. Unnaturally still.

He lifted his right hand, drew his index finger in a line under his eye to the outer edge, up his temple to his forehead, and then flicked it down to the top of his cheek.

The next booming knock fell.

Fire jumped from the muzzle of Jimmy's gun.

From the corner of her eye, Andrea saw Taka lean forward as she turned her head. The bullet blew splinters from the door, the crack of the gun filled her ears. Then there was only ringing silence.

Taka darted through the mud room and threw himself to the left side of the carport door, pressing himself into the hanging coats between the dryer and the wall. He looked back, face pale, mouth open, lips moving. He ducked, grabbed the door handle, and straightened, yanking it back against himself.

Storm light and a mighty wind swept in, brushing a frigid, wet, earthy moisture over Andrea that smelled like the open grave at her mother's funeral. But the memory that came wasn't hers.

She's wet and cold but exhilarated. Her hand is warm in his. They must have thirty wild men between them. There. The place is right where he said it'd be when the rain started. They run out from under the lashing trees into the pummeling rain. He ushers her through the whipping, tall grass onto the overgrown porch, brushing through the fall of the crossvine flowers. The door is open. The push through it. It's dark inside, the windows are covered. The rain is loud on the roof shakes above.

He strikes a match and holds it up. There's little furniture, a broken chair, a rickety table. He shakes the match out and using the wan, watery light from the door, breaks the chair and tosses it onto the cold ashes in the stone fireplace. He hooks the pot crane and swings it out of the way. "I need something to build the flame, see anything that'll burn?"

She does look but sees nothing.

He strikes another match and wanders into the adjoining room. Something clatters and he curses. She hears him strike another match. "There's a pile bones on the floor in here."

"What kind of bones?"

"Oh, uh, just animal bones, I'm sure. The door's been open." Something rips, like fabric. He comes back with a handful of straw, and it dawns on her he must've torn a mattress open. He drops his sling bag of ginseng. In a few minutes, he has the fire going. He takes his wet jacket off and lays it on the floor for her. She lays her bag next to his and sits down.

They talk about nothing for a while and after she warms up, she decides the fire has made the cabin cozy. She imagines fixing the place up and watching his face in the flickering light, the way his dark hair curls around the backs of his ears, she wonders how it would be to live with him. Eventually, he leans over and kisses her.

Her daddy would kill her if he knew, but they've been together before. She likes being that close to him. She likes the must that rises off him, the way he nuzzles into her neck and breathes into her mouth and fills her up. She pushes him over and straddles his hips. The rain and the scent of the flowers and the feel of him under her just makes her want more.

He holds her tucked into her side when they're done. The fire dies down. She's starting to get cold. They get up and dress. Now that the rain has stopped, the late afternoon light is stronger through the door. They grin at each other and kiss again. He picks his jacket up and slings it on.

The door slams shut.

"Hey!" he yells.

He runs to the door and pulls at the wooden bar that's dropped into place, but it won't lift. It's stuck in place. He yanks and kicks and then bangs on it with his fists. Then he bangs on the door itself with the flat of his hand.

"Tucker! This ain't funny! Let us out!" he yells at his brother, who must've locked them in. But there's no laughter outside.

"Try the windows," he says and starts scrabbling at the door's wooden peg hinges.

The glassless windows are shuttered. She shoves at them, but they're stuck fast.

Trapped.

They're trapped.

A thunderous rapping against every surface of the house sent Andrea to her knees, hands over her ringing ears and foggy mind.

Then it stopped.

The silence rang inside her head.

She opened her eyes without having known she'd closed them, but Taka's arms were already closing around her. His hand covered her head, holding her close. She clung to him and burst into tears.

All their phones started ringing at once.

30

Taka ignored his phone. Andrea hugged him harder. The hairs on his arms and the back of his neck were still standing on end, making the cold air pouring through the open door almost painful. His ears rang from the trapper somehow knocking on all the doors, the casings, the floors, the roof, the counters, even the kitchen table, which had jumped and shuddered under the blows, sending two of the dishes and a glass crashing to the floor.

Now the phones kept ringing, a chaos of ringtones, long past when voicemails should've kicked in.

"Mia," Jimmy finally said.

Bowman cleared his throat. "Fields."

"Someone from Greenbrier County," Karie said.

"Shit," Jimmy said, his voice coming now from the mud room. Just thinking about the rip of the wood as invisible claws raked the door made him pull Andrea in just that much more tighter.

"Fields," Bowman said again, his tone an address this time. His voice retreated down the foyer to the living room. "What's up? Luke Bowman. No, you called me."

"Hey, Mia," Jimmy said, going out the carport door. He shut it behind him.

"This is Karie Wilson," Karie said, and a long pause later, "Oh, why am I calling? I thought you called me?" She drifted into the office.

Andrea snuffled into Taka's chest and pulled back. He let her go with reluctance, and both of them climbed to their feet. Skirting the broken glass and ceramic, she went to get her phone off the table. He pulled his from his back pocket. Dewey.

"It's Beau Sanderson," she said, sounding remarkably pulled together, and thumbed it open. "Mr. Sanderson? It's Andrea Kelley. Thanks for returning my call." She frowned, shooting a glance at Taka. "Oh! I'm sorry. I didn't realize."

Taka finally answered his own phone. "Yeah?"

"That was good timing," Dewey said. "You got a camera on me?"

"No. What do you need?"

"Right now? A yacht. And an ocean to sail it in. What do you need?"

"You called me."

"No, I really didn't, but that was your one chance. My cousin Beau called saying Andrea was out in Winslow Creek on Wednesday asking about homesteaded Sanderson property and now she was calling him about his ginseng operation. Beau isn't big on anyone knowing exactly what he's up to."

"Must be genetic."

"Speaking of, there's a pair of sheriff's deputies sitting in my great room right now, asking about a brother I don't have and his missing wife. I need you to come talk cop to them."

"His missing wife?"

"That's your takeaway?"

"Just tell them you don't know anything. Unless you do."

Dewey's tone turned sour at Taka's insinuation that he knew more than he was saying. "They're asking me about a certain Andrea Kelley and her friend, Karie Wilson."

Taka lowered the phone six inches and only cursed in his head. He put it back to his ear. "We'll be there in fifteen."

Dewey cut the call.

"Yes," Andrea said into her phone. "Yes. I understand. I'm happy to sign a non-disclosure. No, I'm looking for a property directly on the banks of Winslow Creek that is or might've been an ideal location for wild ginseng in the past."

Karie came back into the kitchen.

"If there's an abandoned cabin on the property or nearby," Andrea said, "that might be the one I'm looking for. It doesn't have to be related to the Sandersons, just any property matching that description and then I'll find the history." She drew circles on the top of the kitchen table with her finger. "Thanks for asking. No. Nope, no luck."

And then Bowman came back, looking pensive.

"Do you remember the name Tucker in stories from the area? No? Okay. I'll look forward to hearing from you. Thank you." She lowered her phone and hit the end button.

The carport door opened, with another rush of cold air. Taka tensed, but it was just Jimmy. And just cold February air.

"He agreed to help me," Andrea said.

Jimmy closed the door, turning to examine the gouged wood again. "Who?"

"Beau Sanderson."

"The cousin out in Winslow Creek?" Bowman asked.

"Yes."

"My call was from Dewey," Taka said. "Well, he said I called him—"

"Same," Bowman said at the same time Karie said, "Me, too."

Andrea nodded as well, and Taka looked over at Jimmy, who had come to the mud room doorway. "Same," he said.

"Andy was here," Andrea offered.

"Do you think it was Andy?" Karie said. "But why?"

"It was the trapper," Andrea said. "Who was your call to?"

"Roger Wright. He was upset I called. And upset we were out there because the law's still there, poking around in the bushes, and that's what poachers get for disturbing treasure."

"Treasure?" Taka said.

Karie shrugged. "The Iversons were wildcrafters. I think he meant whatever they were collecting out there. He said he's sure the sheriff thinks he killed them, but if anyone did, it was the wraith."

"The wraith?" Andrea said, and Taka recognized that energy that surged through her. An archivist catching a promising scent in her hunt.

She scrolled through her phone. "Madeleine says, 'That one's a wraith and ain't it been seed a'sanging in the holler'"—she looked up at them but was deep in thought—"when she's talking about the dark-haired boys that have been gone from Winslow Creek so long. Her husband, Tucker, thought they'd moved away, but I think Madeleine thinks they were connected to the cabin with the red crossvine. 'None's they touch don't feel it.' She thinks blood feeds the crossvine and makes the flowers red. In my vision—"

"You had a vision?" Taka said. It came out harsher than he intended.

Karie glared at him.

"When the trapper came in," Andrea said, her attention still connecting dots.

Jimmy had come all the way into the kitchen to stand next to Taka. "What'd you see?"

"Saw, heard, felt . . . everything. It was raining," she said, her voice dreamy. "Tucker's brother and a young woman ran onto the porch, which the crossvine covered like a bower. They'd been picking ginseng. They went inside. Tucker's brother found bones in the bedroom, but he said they were animal bones. He started a fire, and they made love. But when they tried to leave, the door slammed shut. It wouldn't open. The windows were shuttered and overgrown. They were—"

"Trapped," Karie said.

Andrea came back to herself. "The trapper."

Taka wanted to carry her upstairs and wrap himself around her and hide forever.

"So Wright might be able to tell you more about the wraith," Bowman said. "And might be able to narrow down the search for the homestead."

"If he'll talk to us again," Karie agreed.

Bowman looked directly at Taka. "You said Dewey called you?"

"We have to go over to his place. He has Greenbrier deputies at his house. They told him his brother's dead, and his sister-in-law is missing."

"Missing?" Andrea said as Jimmy said, "He knows he has a brother?"

"Missing," Taka said. "And he claims he doesn't have a brother which is why he wants me to come speak 'cop' to them."

Jimmy tilted his head, his eyes narrowing. "He's going to let them stay long enough for you to get there?"

"Only if he really doesn't know and wants me to flush out as much info as I can. Which would also mean he isn't totally sure if he does or not. Also, they're asking about Andrea and Karie."

Bowman crossed his arms. "Or he just wants to see how fast you'll jump, and they'll be long gone when you get there."

"That, too," Taka conceded. But Dewey would win in that case, because he was going, but first . . . "Who called you?"

"Apparently, I called Fields. He'd just gotten off the phone with Horton, who's at WVSP HQ. They got a confession from an accomplice to Gavin Owens this morning." He and Jimmy exchanged glances. "When he didn't hear from Gavin on Saturday morning, he got worried Stacy and Andy were alive and had talked. He had his girlfriend drive him out there and found Stacy still unconscious but alive. He killed her about noon."

Karie covered her mouth with both hands, like a prayer. "Poor Stacy."

Andrea reached out and Karie took her hand.

"Putting you in the window for her time of death," Jimmy said.

"Yeah. Wish we'd been a little sooner."

"Beau agreed to help me," Andrea said. "Mr. Wright confirmed at least the rumor of a wraith that's been haunting the area of Winslow Creek since Madeleine's time, Dewey's relationship to Flynn Iverson's been revealed to him, and Fields reported both Andy and Stacy's murders have been solved."

"Sounds like Andy was helping us," Karie said. "Who was your call to, Jimmy?"

"Mia. She needed a shoulder. The team investigating Andy has asked a lot of questions. And she's worried about what happened to the kids he moved, if they're safe."

"Since I was cleared, Fields and I are still leaving Tuesday to collect ID on the kids. Since they were transported across state lines, the

Conlon task force is insisting on sending a federal agent with us, who's also a psychologist. They want to meet this morning."

Not what Taka wanted, but he'd known he was handing over any control the second he gave the kids up. If push came to shove though, he'd fight to let the kids stay where they were if no family was looking for them.

Andrea held her hand up like she was going to grab something. She closed it into a fist. "I almost have it. I just can't quite put together what Madeleine's trying to communicate. And why would the trapper have followed her here?"

Taka could practically hear the bell ding in his head. "He did, didn't he? Madeleine's connected to Dewey and the trapper's followed her vapor trail all the way here."

"But why?" Karie said.

Bowman turned his head and Taka followed his line of sight past Jimmy to the claw marks on the carport door.

"To stop her," Jimmy said, swinging their attention away from the door.

"From communicating with Andrea," Karie said. "But what escalated everything this morning? I mean, three ghosts were here at once."

"Rachel Iverson is missing," Andrea said.

Karie raised her brows. "She's been missing seven months, and she was with her husband."

"Who's been declared dead," Taka said. "And wasn't trapped in a cabin, if that's what you're thinking, Andrea."

"They're going to be looking at Rachel as the main suspect in her husband's murder," Jimmy said. "And whoever else that was out there with him."

"Then we need to find her first," Bowman said.

Jimmy shook his head. "Why? I don't see why the news that someone who's already been missing seven months is missing would cause"—he waved his hand over his shoulder at the door—"that. What would suddenly be important about it?"

"Let's go find out," Andrea said.

NOT KNOWING where the day would lead, Andrea and Karie both called in to say they'd be out of office but available. Karie cancelled her ten o'clock. Outside, Bowman unselfconsciously strapped his weapons back on under the shelter of the carport. Taka said, 'yippee-ki-yay' under his breath as they watched, making Andrea hide her smile.

She'd carried daily since Oliver Fitch and still thought it was over the top. She hoped she never felt as unsafe as Luke obviously felt every day. Jimmy was taking him to his truck so he could meet with Fields and the special agent. Jimmy was going home to sleep, if he could, to be ready to help if they went looking for Rachel.

Andrea and Karie rode in the Yukon with Taka.

Andrea dove right into looking up the Iversons on her phone. She hadn't felt so scattered in her research in a long time. So many angles, and this pressure in her chest like she was facing a test no one had told her about until just now and she didn't have enough information to pass it.

The thunderstorm had passed, but rain beat the windshield. The Yukon's wipers swished across the glass on steady fast, barely clearing it.

About halfway to Dewey's, Taka suddenly said into the silence, "How big is that ghost hound anyway?"

"Huge. Well over a hundred pounds," Andrea said. "He was flinging ghost slobber all over, too."

"I've been looking up wildcrafting," Karie said from the back seat. "I wonder whether the Iversons used their bloodhounds to hunt mushrooms and roots."

"There's not much about their disappearance," Andrea said. "Rachel's dad and sister seem to be the extent of any family. They weren't missed for a couple of weeks until a couple of small restaurants they supply couldn't reach them. One of the chefs went out to their farm to collect an order of wild greens and found their goats and chickens in distress. They don't have a website, but they have a small list of dried and preserved stuff they keep on hand and then they take requests or post what they've found fresh in season."

"Like what?" Taka said.

"Various mushrooms"—she looked at her phone—"ramps, onion and garlic, slippery elm bark, goldenseal, cherry bark, black and blue cohosh, sassafras, ginger root, lots of stuff in season. Looks like they were starting to cultivate, too."

"Ginseng?" he said.

"Yes. Dried."

"They hadn't been in business long," Karie said.

Taka slowed at a red light. "I'd be afraid of poisoning people."

Karie scooted up and thrust her cell between Andrea and Taka. "Here's their YouTube channel. They were afraid of that, too, so they were learning and teaching plant ID along the way."

On the screen, Rachel was holding a detailed botanical book up while Flynn pointed out the parts on the plant they hadn't yet picked. They were maybe thirty, both comfortable in loose grubbing pants and hiking boots. She wore a light hoodie, and he was showing off his muscled arms in a practical T-shirt. The epitome of a living off the land couple, like dozens of others with YouTube channels. He was a taller, less barrel-chested Dewey with dark hair. The resemblance was undeniable.

Taka hit the gas. Karie pulled her phone back and said, "They weren't hiding their business, so they couldn't be poaching everything, that's for sure. Oh, here's a thank you to landowners for granting foraging permission and ten minutes on how to approach a landowner."

"It doesn't sound like they had permission from Mr. Wright to be on his land."

Taka made the final turn to Dewey's house. "Maybe somebody dumped them there."

"Dumped him there," Andrea murmured, still looking at her phone. "She's missing."

"Maybe she dumped him there," Taka countered.

"Maybe not," she said and held up the phone for him to see a Facebook post.

He glanced over. "They found their car?"

"Five months ago."

"Where?" Karie asked.

"Downstream, at a property they had permission to forage. The owner rarely goes out there."

"Then she didn't just drive away," Karie said. "Maybe her bones were scattered further away from his. Mr. Wright said there's still people out there with the sheriff's department. Maybe they'll find her."

And maybe not. Andrea punched in Waltham-Young's number as Taka pulled up along the curb. A Range Rover and a marked Greenbriers County Sheriff's Office Tahoe sat in the drive. Marji answered the phone and patched Andrea through to Toby. He didn't pick up.

When his voicemail kicked in, she said, "Hi, Toby, this is Andrea. My project's taken a turn and I kinda need those maps on priority rush if you have them. Something's come up that might be urgent. If you could maybe let me know what you might have along Winslow Creek today, I'll owe you a big favor. Thanks." She disconnected.

Taka turned the engine off but didn't move. "Andrea, if you're thinking Rachel's still alive out there . . ."

"It's been seven months," Karie said.

"I know. It's just, like Jimmy said, why is the trapper here? Why the drama now? If Andy's trying to help Madeleine by helping us connect with the people we need to talk to, the reason must be urgent."

Taka held up his hand. "Or it might be because of some urgency on the ghosts' part, that doesn't have anything to do with the living." His gaze shot up to the roof of the Yukon. He took a couple of measured breaths. "I can't believe this is my life now."

"I'm sorry," Andrea said.

He met her eyes and dropped his hand on her thigh. "Don't be sorry. Not that being an archivist doesn't change the world, but because of this *ability* you have now, in just a few months, some very bad people are no longer operating and that's a very good thing."

"A very good thing," Karie echoed. "We're all on your side."

Andrea never could've imagined everything that had happened since she started seeing Billie Mae last spring. Or the support she had around her now. "I just have this terrible feeling that all this has something to do with Rachel."

Taka squeezed her thigh. "I'm just saying slow your roll a little.

Maybe Rachel had a second car. Or a friend. Let's find out what the deputies have to say and beat some info out of Dewey before we go storming back to Winslow Creek."

"That's what we're going to do, isn't it? Go back there."

"Damn straight," Karie said softly, and opened her door, letting the rain sweep in.

31

The Range Rover turned out to be Ryan Merritt's and one of the Greenbrier deputies a detective. After hanging up their wet coats and introductions, Andrea studied the wary look on Detective Hendry's face.

"Could you excuse us, please?" Detective Hendry said, looking between Dewey and Taka. "Mr. Merritt can stay if it suits."

"It does," Dewey said. "We'll be in the kitchen."

They left, Dewey using a cane and limping heavily.

"Please sit," Hendry said. "Mind if we record?"

Without waiting for their response, the other deputy turned his phone recorder on and stated the date and time and all their names.

They sat down on two leather couches facing each other over a grey slate coffee table. The deputies on one side and Merritt, Andrea, and Karie on the other.

"I've read the report and understand it's the first time y'all have been out to Winslow Creek," Hendry said, addressing both her and Karie. "What brought you there?"

"I've been upfront with CPD in another matter," Andrea said. "So I'm going to tell you the truth."

"I'd appreciate that," he drawled.

"Dewey Sanderson has a ghost very interested in him and she seems to be from Winslow Creek."

Merritt coughed into his hand.

"Excuse me," Hendry said. "You said a ghost?"

"I'm sure you're aware your sheriff spoke with me yesterday morning. You're aware that recently I've come across more than one body."

"And shot a man," he said.

She winced before she could stop herself. "Yes. No apologies on that one."

"Ms. Kelley," Merritt said.

"It's okay, Mr. Merritt, it's true."

"But it bothers you," Hendry said.

"Of course, it bothers me."

Hendry shifted his gaze to Karie without turning his head. "You were there."

"I was. Andrea saved my life."

Hendry's eyes slid back to meet Andrea's. "Did that man also have a ghost *interested* in him?"

"Not in the same way Mr. Sanderson does."

Hendry sat back on the couch, regarding her for a long moment. "It strikes me as odd that you two know Mr. Sanderson. You go to Winslow Creek, for the very first time, looking for property owned by Ezekiel Sanderson, and end up on Mr. Wright's property, where you follow a dog to a pile of bones that turn out to be the mortal remains of Mr. Sanderson's brother, who he claims he did not know existed."

"Please refrain from spurious insults directed at Mr. Sanderson," Merritt said.

Hendry didn't even look at him.

"How did you learn about their relationship?" Karie asked, which Andrea was grateful for since Hendry's attention was pinned on her.

Hendry redirected his next question. "Are you interested in ghosts, too?"

"I'm the lead investigator of the paranormal division at Waltham-Young."

"Waltham-Young Community Library, a bastion of research even for the paranormal." He pursed his mouth and then popped his tongue against the roof of his mouth while he thought. "Who'd have thunk it?"

They were silent long enough that the deputy had to restart his recording. Hendry leaned forward again. "Okay. I'll bite. Who is this ghost that's interested in Mr. Sanderson?"

"Her name is Madeleine."

"You're an archivist. I assume you've figured out where she fits in Mr. Sanderson's life?"

"No, I haven't. Do you know who Flynn Iverson's mother is?"

"Yes."

"Is she still living?"

"Like Mr. Iverson's wife, she's considered a missing person."

Well, that was interesting. "Did she go missing in Winslow Creek?"

"As a matter of fact."

"Does she still have family there?"

"Maybe you can tell me?"

"I'm not a medium, I just see ghosts. Some ghosts, not, I'm sure, all ghosts."

"You see them? Or you perceive them?" He circled his hand in the air, and lowered his voice into a spooky tone, wiggling his fingers as he continued. "Receive symbols from the beyond that you interpret using some intuitive guidance?"

Karie gave him a withering look Andrea had never seen her use before. "Sounds like you've watched too much TV, Mr. Hendry."

Without the woo-woo tone, though, he was basically describing the techniques Miss Ava and other true mediums used. It was too bad there were so many fake ones.

"Detective," Hendry said.

"A detective would show more respect," Mr. Merritt said, his voice pinched.

Hendry dropped the act. "Come on now. If I subpoena your credit card records, and your work schedules, and ask around Winslow Creek, am I going to find one or both of you there in August?"

"No," Andrea said as Mr. Merritt said, "A mere coincidental connection is not probable cause, no matter how odd it strikes you, Detective."

"They found the bodies, Mr. Merritt."

"They found bones, one set of which is suspected to have been there decades longer than the other."

Detective Hendry shrugged and let it go. "Mr. Sanderson and Mr. Merritt have pertinent contact info for Mr. Iverson's family. They can decide how much they wish to share with you." He opened the leather portfolio he'd been holding on his lap and extracted paperwork and two pens. Separating the paper into two stapled packets, he slid them across the coffee table to Karie and Andrea along with the pens. "These are the statements you gave at the scene. Could you please review them for accuracy?"

DEWEY'S KITCHEN was all open shelves and black drawers and sleek marble countertops. A huge island with a built-in cooktop separated the functional from the ornamental and the heavy built kitchen table that sat eight. He pulled out a chair and fell into it with a very unlike himself lack of grace.

Taka hated that he cared. He went straight around the island, slung the teapot from the cooktop and filled it with filtered water. "Where's your help?" he asked, setting the teapot on its back burner and flipping the gas on with a practiced twist of his wrist.

"Sam's outside."

Security. "And your home health aide?"

"Let her go."

He opened the coffee and tea drawer. As usual there was a wide variety of tea. "The agreement was a week, Dewey. It's been less than three days."

"So hire her back. Tell her to be here at two."

Taka chose the Lipton's. "Why two?"

"'Cause I'm freakin' tired. I need an undisturbed nap when these guys get outta here."

Taka put one regular tea bag back and selected chamomile instead. "I'll have them send someone else."

Snagging two black mugs, he set them on the counter next to the tea. The kettle was already steaming. Turning on his heel, he snagged a bottle of Jack Daniels from the walk-in pantry.

"Good man," Dewey said and laid his forehead straight down on his hands folded on his cane.

"I see the old man you're going to be," Taka said, tossing the chamomile bag in a mug and ripping the Lipton's open.

"Fuck you."

Before the tea kettle could whistle, Taka pulled it off and filled the mugs. He tippled whiskey into both and brought them to the table. "You take your pain meds?"

"I did, because I'm not an idiot."

"Antibiotics?"

"Upsets my stomach."

"Dewey." He made toast and buttered it and filled a Ziploc with ice. Shoved the toast in front of Dewey and pulled a chair out and lifted his leg onto it, pretending not to notice the sweat of Dewey's forehead when he did. Then laid the bag over his thigh. "Anti-bs?"

"Nightstand."

Taka retrieved the antibiotics, noting the closed drapes and the unmade bed and the towel slung over the bathroom door instead of the drying rack he knew was mounted on the wall. "You weren't supposed to shower yet. You get that dressing changed okay?"

"Yes, Mom."

Taka pulled his own chair out and sat. Dewey ate his toast and threw his pill back with his tea.

The voices in the great room went silent, but there was no movement.

"What," Dewey said.

Taka looked up at him. "You knew, didn't you? That you had a brother. You were surprised he's dead."

"You weren't."

Taka shook his head.

"How'd you know?"

"Remember that ghost that's attached to you?"

"My brother's name wasn't Madeleine."

"Madeleine's how Andrea and Karie found him out there by the creek. One of his dogs was still alive, so identification was assumed. We looked him up. We knew right away."

"You didn't tell me."

"Assumed ID, Dewey. Not confirmed until now and here I am. They didn't do DNA from bone this fast, so how'd the sheriff's office know he was your brother?"

"Apparently he had a deathbed letter from my papaw Sanderson with his papers."

"He was given up for adoption? Or you were adopted by your mom?"

"No, not officially, I'm sure. And, no, my mom's on my birth certificate. She lost a baby. Dad's girlfriend was already pregnant with me. He did what he always did and threw money at a couple of medical staff, and voila! Instant baby, no scandal. It was early days for him in politics. He could afford most everything except scandal."

"When'd you find out?"

"I've always known."

"How could he risk that? He wasn't afraid you'd blurt it out?"

Dewey stared down into his tea. Taka didn't think he was going to answer, but then he did. "I was terrified of my dad. My dad was terrified of her. She was a strong woman. I think she must've blackmailed him into staying with her. When Flynn was born, she was four years older, and she wasn't going to give up another child. Not that my mom was going to take on another of my dad's mistakes, anyway. And she'd had my sister by then. She must've been about a year old."

"You knew her? Your biological mom?"

He nodded. "The homestead? That was my grandfather's place. Her dad." His gaze wandered away to the floor. "Or maybe her grandfather?"

"You know where it is?"

Finally, he looked up. Taka couldn't remember ever seeing him unsure before. "No."

"His last name?"

"I don't know. I don't know her name. They gave Merritt copies of the papers Flynn left. Maybe it's in there."

"It's not Iverson?"

"No. Detective Whatsit out there said he took Rachel's maiden name."

"Why would he do that?"

"He was two and my dad dropped him off with my papaw Sanderson in the dead of night and I never saw him again. I doubt he thought Sanderson was a great name. Or maybe they gave him some fake name. That'd be my dad's style."

"Why?"

Dewey blinked hard, tears filling his eyes.

Taka frowned. He had no idea how to handle this Dewey he'd never seen before. Maybe he should give him another oxy and some more whiskey and ask about the Beretta while he was on his back foot, though.

Voices drifted in again from the great room, then out into the foyer. The front door opened and closed. Dewey wiped his eyes and drank his tea. By the time Andrea, Karie, and Merritt came through the doorway, he was himself again, only paler.

Merritt had an old-fashioned hard cover briefcase in one hand and a manila envelope in the other. He held up the envelope. "I'll go through these papers, Dewey. And have the information verified."

Dewey, who hadn't looked up from his tea, glanced over at Taka. "Could you take him into the office and help him copy those?"

"I can have copies sent over," Merritt protested.

"I want them now."

"If you like, we can go over them together."

"No, Ryan, I don't like. I've been shot, I've lost two of my security team, and a friend, and now the brother I didn't know I had is dead and his wife is missing. As a matter of fact, just give that here." He held out his hand. After a slight hesitation, Merritt gave him the envelope. "I'll call and make an appointment next week if I need help, capiche? And send me a list of private investigators who'll go to Winslow Creek."

"Sure, Dewey," Merritt said, keeping his voice smooth. He pulled his jacket down and straightened his shoulders. "By end of day. And I'll see you next week."

He saw himself out while Dewey stared at the closed envelope and Taka made more tea and put the whiskey and a honey bear from beside the bread box on the table. Andrea looked askance at the whiskey. Taka shrugged and tilted his head at Dewey.

After the tea was doled out and doctored up, they all sipped for a few minutes.

Taka watched Dewey watching Andrea, who kept looking up and catching him.

"Is she here now?" Dewey said.

"Madeleine? No."

Taka spun his tea mug around. "The ghosts put on quite a show this morning. You aren't the only one in need of whiskey."

"That wear them out?"

"Sometimes," Karie said.

"You believe they're really ghosts?" he said. "Souls of the dead?"

"Honestly?" Karie said. "I have no idea if they're remnants or souls or people on another plane that are bleeding through. I'm still a skeptic. I'll test everything I can. I still have no verifiable proof of life after death. The energy we've been observing always saps the batteries on my equipment, or causes static, or could be a passing shadow, or the circumstances break cameras and recorders. Waltham-Young's going to have to increase my budget for replacements. And they will, because I get just enough evidence to make it worth it. And the things I've witnessed the last few months? This morning? Incredible."

"I called them both Mom," Dewey said. "My mom, and my biological mother, my dad's girlfriend. I think my dad thought that'd minimize any screw-ups on my part, but he trained me well. Winslow Creek was a secret I never spilled. I adored her. Always cried when we came back here. When I was six and Flynn was two, I watched my dad kill her at the homestead. I think she was pregnant again."

Thinking of the Beretta, Taka said, "He shot her?"

"No. My grandfather's dog had puppies, so mom and dad took us over to see them. Before we left, we drove down to see the sheep behind the big barn. And saw this old tumble-down cabin in the woods. It was covered in these huge red flowers, so we went to look at it. They had a fight on the porch there, yelling about a baby. He must've knocked her down, because he was on top of her, and she was choking, and then she wasn't anymore. I remember her lips were swollen and cherry red and her nose was bleeding. I can see it now. Clear as day. I was holding Flynn and we were up under the vines. Dad dragged her inside and we left.

"We drove and drove and drove. But when I woke up, we were at Papaw Sanderson's house, which wasn't all that far from my grandfather's. Dad took Flynn inside and that was that. We never went back. My mom's place was just across the street. A short enough distance that I was allowed to walk between them. But when I got older and hired people to find Flynn, the property records didn't lead anywhere."

"Your mom's place," Andrea said. "It was two story? Had two big oaks on either side of the porch and a big barn to the left?"

Dewey squinted, staring at her, but lost in thought.

"Maybe a couple of rusted out cars and an antique truck?"

"I loved that truck," he murmured. "Mom was afraid I'd get cut on the rust."

"The old Bennett place," Karie said.

"How'd you know?"

"Beau Sanderson gave us directions to your papaw Sanderson's, but he told us the wrong side of the road. Your mom wasn't a Bennett?"

"No. They had a son who died and a daughter, who'd have been fifty-something when I was born. But she never took over the trust and then the money ran out. I, uh, bought the tax lien years ago, but I just renewed the trust under an LLC named Bennett."

Karie picked up her phone and started scrolling as Andrea said, "No wonder. Maybe your mom was a renter?"

Still looking at her phone, Karie said, "Mrs. Tyson said something about the Bennett's daughter, right?"

"Yes," Andrea said, and picked her phone up, too.

Dewey opened the envelope and slid a sheaf of papers and a couple of letter-sized white envelopes out. He picked up the letter with "Flynn" written on it in script. He tilted it towards Taka. "My papaw Sanderson's handwriting."

The other was newer and had Dewey's name on it in a different hand.

"Here it is," Andrea said. "The daughter lived there a few years before she passed. The granddaughter ran off."

"The flat-footing ghost's husband thought she ran off, too," Karie said.

Dewey put both the letters back in the envelope. "I don't think I want to ask," he said.

"Sound decision," Taka offered and finished off his tea, so he didn't have to see Andrea and Karie's reaction to that.

Dewey flipped though the papers. "Mortgage, car titles, marriage certificate, will, birth certificates. Flynn's has no father's name. Mother's name, Claire Susan Westfall."

"None of the properties I've looked at are owned by Westfalls," Andrea said. "I was looking at places owned by Sandersons and properties surrounding them. We were only on the Wright property because of the red crossvine." She tapped her fingers on the table as she thought. "I haven't seen that name in any of the family trees. If her father owned the property with the homestead on it, and it's on Winslow Creek, I need to look at all the properties with creek frontage. If it's not still under that name, it could take months to research past owners."

"Westfall might be a married name," Karie added. "Or she was being raised by someone else and just called him her father."

Andrea jumped up. "I need my laptop. You want yours?"

Taka stood, his chair sliding out, and dug his keys out of his pocket.

"Yes," Karie said. "It'll be faster if we both look. I'm going to call the number that guy at the diner gave me. Maybe Shawnee brave guy has heard something about the wraith."

Dewey tensed, pulling his leg back down. The ice bag plopped to the floor. "What's the rush?"

"Rachel's still missing," Andrea called over her shoulder as she left.

"Detective Whatsit said all her stuff was in the car or at the house," Dewey said. "None of their accounts have been accessed since they disappeared. They think Rachel's still out there, but they haven't found any remains yet. They're going to drag the creek."

Karie, digging through her little wallet, came up with a scrap of paper. "Andrea thinks she may be at the homestead."

"The ghosts this morning," Taka said. "Put your leg back up."

Karie took her phone and went back towards the great room.

When Dewey just looked at him, Taka got up and helped him get re-situated. "How many ghosts we talking?"

Taka took the bag to empty and refill with fresh ice. "Madeleine, Detweiler, and some crazy Andrea's calling the trapper. I think she thinks he's the wraith haunting the homestead."

"Detweiler?"

"Yeah. Detweiler," Taka said coming around the island. "He was there at the hospital when you were in surgery. Andrea didn't realize he was de—"

Dewey's hand shook as he poured a healthy slug of Jack into his mug.

Taka crouched down beside him, set the bag of ice on his thigh, and took the bottle from him. "I'm sorry. That was thoughtless of me."

"Y'know? Andy saw his father kill his mother, too. I hated my dad for that. I wanted out of his house from the time I was six years old. I'd have gladly gone to live with Papaw Sanderson and Flynn. That's what I thought, for years. Even when Papaw came to visit without him. I was ten before I understood that Flynn was gone. Andy, his dad went to prison. He went from foster home to foster home, which is probably what happened to my brother. Makes me wish I could kill him all over again."

Taka froze, still face to face with him.

Dewey didn't look away, daring Taka to call him out on it.

"I know," Taka said. "Would tarnishing his legacy work instead?"

Dewey's gaze darted away and came back. "How?"

"You still have that Beretta 92 of his?"

32

T he rain was letting up. Andrea hugged the laptops to her under her coat to keep them dry. Karie was talking on her cell in the great room when Andrea came back in. She came over and took the laptops while Andrea stripped her coat off again. After she set them on the coffee table, she waved Andrea over. Lowering the phone, she hit the speaker button and an excited older man's voice leaped into the room.

"I'd never seen an apparition like that before. I tell you, when he stopped and looked straight at me, my blood curdled. If looks could kill, I'd be a dead man."

Andrea sat down and Karie followed.

The man talked on. "I could see the hate in his eyes in my headlights. And I don't blame him. Talk about germ warfare, and the Europeans didn't even know it. They just thought their prayers had been answered. Why if—"

"Mr. Montpelier," Karie said.

"Bob, please."

"Bob, would you mind very much writing down your account and everything you remember about the apparition? His physical description, his clothes, what he might have been carrying on him?"

Andrea opened her laptop and linked her hotspot.

"Oh, sure," Bob said. "I can do that."

"Also, the location and your circumstances at the time."

"Sure. Like why I was there?"

She checked her email. No maps from Toby. No NDA from Beau Sanderson.

"No, more like the time and your vehicle description. The height of your headlights would be useful."

Pulling up the statewide property tax map site, Andera crossed her fingers that she'd find the name Westfalls along the course of Winslow Creek.

"Well, sure."

Andrea did a quick Google search and found Mr. Wright's street number on Charter Woods.

"Maybe you could record yourself telling the story as well? All in one take, just like you'd tell your friends, and send it to me?"

"Sure."

Putting the address in the search bar resulted in a twist and zoom to the tax map of Greenbrier County and Charter Woods Road.

Then Karie asked the money question. "Have you ever heard of a story involving a wraith in your area?"

Andrea paused to listen more closely.

"Well, not in my area, but up north of here, sure. You don't hear stories about wraiths much. Haints, sure, and ghosts, but wraiths not much. Or maybe nobody remembers the term anymore 'cause you see titles like, 'The Vengeful Ghost,' when what they're describing is a wraith."

"And by 'north,' you mean?"

"Oh, gosh, I heard tell it's been seen on the upper fork of Winslow Creek, near the border of the Cranberry. You know the Cranberry Wilderness?"

Yes. Maybe this was finally the person they needed.

"I do," Karie said.

"My friend Gary's friend, Robin, said her papaw saw it while he was fishing in the creek up there. He thought it was an animal at first, diggin' up the bank, but then it stood up and it was a dark-haired man. He thought maybe it was a wildlife officer down from the Cranberry checking licenses and he splashed outta the creek and snatched up his gear real quick. But that man jumped down off the bank and he was all transparent like. And mad, angry as a hornet.

"Then he flew across the creek. Gary said Robin said like a cloud, like his body was streaming off behind him, and hit her papaw hard enough to lay him out. Course, he jumped right back up, but that wraith, he swirled all around him, all around him, til her papaw had run clear down the creek a mile or so and then he left off."

"Thank you, Bob," Karie said lifting her brows at Andrea. Andrea lifted her hands, palms up. It was interesting, but not helpful. "I haven't heard that one before. Anything else you know about it?"

"They say you can't be picking ginseng up there on the upper fork or that wraith'll be right on you."

"But Robin's grandfather was fishing?"

"That's what she said."

"But maybe he was really picking ginseng?"

"I don't know. Maybe. I've heard there's a lot of it out there, on the upper fork. In season, you can get a right pretty penny for a few hours digging and papaws might need the, uh, love boost, if you know what I mean."

Stifling her laugh, Karie met Andrea's glance. Yes, Andrea did know that some touted ginseng for its effect on the libido.

"But it's all private property up there and the ginseng leases last forever."

Ginseng leases? Like oil or mineral rights? She thought of Beau Sanderson's red truck barreling across the creek on Charter Woods behind her. Maybe he had cornered the market in ginseng leases on the upper fork. Hopefully he'd send that NDA soon and she could ask him.

"Have you ever heard of a trapper's cabin up that way that's haunted?"

"Sure, its connected to the wraith. Every kid knows 'bout it round here. It's our Bloody Mary story, but not anyone knows where it is."

Andrea's disappointment pricked her gut. Like a knife, as Bob would say. She rolled her eyes at herself and started clicking on the properties on the tax map that were up creek from Mr. Wright's. Please let there be a Westfall.

"What do the kids say?"

"A long time ago, two brothers lived up there on the upper fork. They were out sangin' in the rain with their sweethearts when they got separated."

Andrea stopped breathing. Karie shifted, holding the phone closer to Andrea.

"The trapper lures the unwary inside so he can steal their harvest. He caught one of the brothers with his girl and skinned him in his cabin while she watched."

In her head, Andrea heard Madeleine saying, *They's gone a'sangin' down on Winslow crick. Ever-body knows that 'bandoned homestead's got haints that'll scare the skin right off'n yourn..."*

"Her screams alerted the second brother and he come running," Bob said, his accent thickening. "But right when he got to the trapper's, boom! Lightning struck him dead. His girl saw the whole thing. She listened to her friend beat on the inside of the cabin door the rest of that day and all that night, screaming and crying that she couldn't lift the drop bar inside. She never did come out and she stopped screaming at dawn. The second girl couldn't lead a search party back to the cabin. She couldn't find it again.

"She wandered the woods alone, searching for her love until she died of a broken heart. Her love, the brother killed by lightning, has taken revenge on the trapper ever since by scaring off ginseng hunters so the trapper can't hoard it and satisfy his hunger."

Andrea frowned. His hunger for . . . ginseng? Karie mouthed, 'what?', but then asked Bob, "What's the Bloody Mary part?"

"You go out in the neighbor's yard and steal a flower. Crossvine's the best, but any bloom will do. We scared ourselves silly all summer long, daring each other to do it."

"And?"

"With your back to a mirror, in a dark room by yourself, you prick your finger, or, you know, pick a scab, and let a drop of blood fall on the flower. Then you close your eyes and whisper, 'Tomorrow. Tomorrow. Tomorrow.' Then you turn around three times, yelling, 'I wanna go home' three times."

Behind her, Madeleine said, "Tomorrow is what Tucker always sez.

Tomorrow. Tomorrow. Tomorrow, Madeleine. I'll be a'taking yous home."

All the hair on Andrea's neck stood up, sending an icy shiver down her back.

"All the kids outside the room, of course," Bob continued, "are a hooting and hollering so no parents catch on."

Madeleine drifted out from behind the couch, her train still fluttering through it. "I wanta go home. A'want, a'want, a'want."

Andrea grabbed Karie's wrist and pulled her up so Madeleine wouldn't drag her dress right through her. Taka was standing in the foyer, shoulder propped on the door frame. He stood up, gaze darting around the room.

Bob's voice remained steady and unperturbed. "When you face the mirror again, you'll see your true love's name written in blood and the date you'll die."

Madeleine stopped. Her head tilted as she listened to something Andrea couldn't hear. Uh-oh. Andrea stopped, too. No thunder. No dog.

"Course the trick is sneaking in and screaming right when your victim's turning around or, like Marty Simonsen's brother did, hiding with some meat juice and while they're yelling, splashing it up on the mirror." He laughed.

The click of canine nails came across the foyer tile. The big bloodhound appeared slowly, in patches. An ear, then a hind leg, then a shoulder, until he was fully realized. Standing next to Taka, he wagged his tail, and doggy smiled at Bob's laughter.

Andrea eased up on Karie's wrist.

"Hello?" Bob said. "Still there?"

"Yeah," Karie said. "Just writing all this down. It's great stuff, Bob. Y'all must've had fun with that story."

"We really did."

"Do you think there's some truth to it? Not the Bloody Mary part, obviously, but the rest?"

Bob's tone sobered and his accent softened with it. "Yes, I do. This area was the frontier for a long time. A lot of hard things happened here.

I'm sure Winslow Creek isn't the only meat camp to have a mentally ill trapper in its history."

"You think the cabin's real?"

"Real enough. Something probably happened on the upper fork in a little log shack and got talked about forever, the story evolving as the generations re-told it."

The dog wandered over to Madeleine and leaned against her legs. She relaxed a little and bent to stroke his head and rub his ears. He closed his eyes and groaned in pleasure.

"What do you do for a living, Bob?" Karie said and then mouthed, 'Anything else?'

Andrea nodded, but she was still focused on Madeleine, who wasn't talking, but instead seemed unbelievably in the moment, carefully studying the room and its furnishings. True to its name, Dewey's great room was large. The facing couches were situated near the massive front window, with drapes that hung heavy and rich from just beneath the high ceilings.

"I teach history at the high school in Rupert."

Andrea heard the pause in Karie's response, but Madeleine was gliding past the mahogany and burgundy felt pool table in the center of the room. Beyond it, a wood-burning fireplace, windows to either side of it, and another seating arrangement ate up the far wall.

"How'd you like to bring your classes to Waltham-Young on a field trip?"

Madeleine headed to the side wall running along the foyer. She threaded between a couple of comfy reading chairs with small round drink tables beside them and stopped before the second of three floor to ceiling built-in bookcases. They were situated between the opening Taka stood in and the opening into Dewey's formal dining room.

"Really?" Bob exclaimed. "I'd take you up on that in a heartbeat."

The bloodhound simply walked through the chairs. He snuffled the air.

"I'll arrange it and make sure you get the invite."

"Are you okay?" Taka whispered.

Andrea nodded.

The bookcases held a compelling array of books and mementos. A double row of two large drawers bisected each case across its center, breaking up what could have been an overwhelming display.

"Thank you," Bob said. "I'll send you what you asked for on the ghost I saw. I'll write down the wraith's story, too, if you'd like?"

What was Madeleine looking for? She was present, aware, hungry for something she needed.

"That'd be great."

"What's the trapper hungry for?" Andrea asked.

"That's my colleague, Andrea," Karie said to Bob.

Bob raised his voice, as if Andrea were further away than Karie and would have trouble hearing him across the speaker. "Blood is my understanding, Andrea."

"What does that have to do with hoarding ginseng?"

"Everything. The legend of ginseng is the long life and virility it grants. The wild men bleed red, like blood, when steamed and grant virtual immortality through a strong immune system. Maybe it's granting him spiritual immortality."

"Why not let the people he lures in leave and just keep the ginseng?"

"Ghost stories handed down over generations have logic barriers, for one thing," Bob said, as Madeleine said to the bookshelves, "Ever-body knows why them crossvines a'grow so thick down there at the homestead."

Blood. For the crossvine.

"And two," Bob carried on saying. "Remember how the crossvine's the recommended flower for the true love ritual? The wild men feed the trapper and the blood he drains from the ginseng pickers feeds the crossvine that hides the cabin from the broken-hearted girl so she can never reunite with her true love, the wraith, who's still out there sanging and pissing off the trapper by keeping him from feeding. Well, mostly, anyway."

"Mostly?" Karie said.

"Lots of people go missing out there. There was a couple just last year. Wildcrafters. Just, poof. Gone."

"Oop," Karie said. "My next appointment just walked in. Send me that stuff and I'll get that invite out to you."

"Sure thing. Bye now."

"Bye!" Karie thumbed the call off. "Oh my god. How crazy was that?"

"Not as crazy as Madeleine being quiet and here."

"Like here right now?"

"Yes, and here, looking at Dewey's furniture here, not off in her head somewhere."

Madeleine said something quiet to the dog and he went to her. Blood seeped from the skin of her chest, running into the bodice of her gown. The dog snuffled the air and then lifted his head and howled, his front legs coming off the ground in his exertion. Again, a quiet word Andrea couldn't catch.

The dog snuffled along the bookcases, to the end and back, lifting his nose here and there. At the case nearest Taka, he reared up, placing his front paws on the top two drawers and drawing in breath after breath before he threw back his head and bayed, a totally different sound than his barking at the trapper.

"What's happening," Taka said, voice tight.

"I don't know," Andrea said. "Madeleine gave the dog her scent from, I don't know, her death wound? And he's baying at the bookcase."

She walked over to the bookcase. Baying, the dog scrabbled at the drawers. Andrea opened the left one. Books. Photo albums. The dog scratched and scrabbled, leaving faint marks on the wood. Stretching his nose up, he bayed again. Madeleine drifted over and looked up, staring at a plain wooden box, pushed to the back of the shelf above the dog's nose. Andrea reached her long arms up and pulled it down. The dog dropped, quiet.

"Those are my dad's ashes," Dewey said from the doorway into the dining room. "It was the box he kept his cufflinks and rings in."

A box he handled a lot. Maybe it still smelled like him.

Madeleine had been staring at it, now she looked up sharply. "He's coming." She shot her hand out and grabbed Andrea's arm. "My sister . . . He's coming."

Falling. Wind knocked out as she hits a hard dirt floor, stinging warmth against her neck. Her hand comes away bloody. She lays there, the blood wet dirt filling her nose with metal and earth. Her heart's thumping, pushing itself out her throat. Then he's there, daylight dropping through the door.

He flings the bloody crane arm back against the firebrick so hard, the rusted joint breaks into pieces and the arm drops halfway to the floor, the pot hook clanking when it hits the hearth and then the heavy pot she was trying to set on it.

He scoops her up. Another contraction hits her, doubling her over. Sending them both back to the ground. Blood gushes over her straining belly.

"No," he moans over her. He wraps his arms around her.

She opens her mouth, but nothing comes out. I tripped, she wants to say, the baby. He's coming. But she can't and a heavy stillness starts in her toes and spreads up her legs. Her blood's so hot, but she's so cold.

"I meant to fix it," he cries. "Please, God, no."

She's closer than she thought. It's so much faster than last time. More gushing warmth, this time between her legs. The baby. Her belly contracts and she folds up with it. Her blood's so warm, thank God, because she's so cold. Somehow now the ceiling is above her. The ground hard beneath her back.

"Push," her love implores, one big hand upon her belly. So warm, hot with life.

Isla's upside down. Silly little girl. She pats her cheeks with her pudgy little hands. So warm.

"Mama," Isla says.

She opens her mouth, but only her breath slips out.

And then the baby slips out with her.

Her baby.

The light surrounds them.

It's blinding,

She opens her eyes to darkness.

She's in the corner of the ceiling.

Her love is huddled on the ground in front of the cold hearth. He's skin and bones. His clothes are ragged and crusted in mud.

"Where's Isla?"

"They took her," he says.

"Who?"

"The fairies. The fairies stole her away from me when I wasn't looking."

It must be true.

She's not here with her wherever here is now.

"Come with me," she says.

"I meant to fix it," he says. "All I needed was another sack before I had a full load. Just one more sack."

He stays.

She goes.

The hip-high seed heads slap against her open palms, there's laughter in her ears, blue sky above, it's their own little mountain paradise . . . and Isla, running for her from the cabin, all covered in blooms. She catches her and swings her high and hugs her hard.

"Where's the baby, Mama?"

And here he is, a tall, fine young man. And Isla hugs him, laughing.

They hold hands and walk through the meadow. And as they walk, Isla grows into a beautiful young woman. "I was an old lady," Isla says. "I had four lovely little babies of my own. They'll be along soon. I'm so glad to see you, Mama. Is Papa here yet?"

"Soon, my love. Not yet."

Falling. Wind knocked out as she hits a hard dirt floor, stinging warmth against her neck. Her hand comes away bloody.

"He's coming!" Madeleine shouted in her ear.

Andrea jerked back and fell sideways. Taka's arm kept her from smashing her head on the bookcase, but the box fell, scattering the senator's ashes across the floor.

"What the hell was that," Dewey said.

"Madeleine," Andrea bit out, trying not to cry, as Taka steadied her. But the memory wasn't Madeleine's. "We have to find Rachel."

"Andrea," Taka said.

"No," she said, stopping him before he could start. "Don't tell me again it's been seven months. And I don't have the luxury of months to research. Come on, we're going. We're calling in all our favors right now."

Dewey leaned on both hands on his cane. "Where are you going?"

"Winslow Creek. He's coming and we need to be there."

"The trapper?" Karie said.

"No. I think Rachel's still alive and she's having a baby."

"That's—"

"Crazy, I know, but isn't all of this? Dewey, will you call Beau for me?"

"Why?"

"He's the ginseng king," she said, stalking back across the room. "I'm guessing he has a deal with Mr. Wright. I'm guessing he has a deal with everyone on the upper fork. I think he knows exactly where the trapper's cabin is and whether he knows it or not, he has a deal with him, too."

Karie came over to grab her laptop, too, and her phone. "What did you see?"

"I don't know what that was," she said, heading into the foyer, an icy niggle of unease setting up camp in her gut. Taka snagged her wet coat before she could and held it up for her. She shoved her arm into the right sleeve, shifted her laptop, and shoved the other arm in.

"Slow down a second," Taka said, pulling on his own coat.

"Wait for me," Dewey yelled from somewhere back in the house.

"You're not coming," Taka yelled back.

"You want Beau, you got me."

"Shit," Taka sighed.

"Just go get him," Andrea said.

Karie pulled the front door open. The day was grey and dripping, but the rain had stopped. "Who do you need me to call?"

33

"Hang on, let me check my email." Andrea felt better out in the fresh air. She pulled her phone from her back pocket and tapped on it with her right thumb. No Toby. No Beau. She turned to Karie. "Can you light a fire under Toby?"

"The topographical maps?"

"Yes." She'd leave Beau to Dewey. She could take a run at Mr. Wright. That red crossvine had to mean the cabin was close, but she could wait to see what Beau said. She listened for a second to Karie talking to whoever answered the phone at Waltham-Young as she walked down the driveway. She dialed Eddie.

"Andrea," he said, obviously pleased she'd called. He sounded so . . . normal.

"Hi. I saw you dropped some chum in the internet music waters yesterday. Any news on the song?"

"As a matter of fact, your timing is perfect. Someone hooked me up not thirty minutes ago."

Andrea suppressed the urge to suggest 'hooking up' might not be the best phrase to use anymore. "Thank you, Eddie. I can't tell you how grateful I am."

Taka and Dewey came out of the house, Taka carrying a small black case. Dewey on crutches. He looked a lot more comfortable.

"You just did," Eddie said. "Want the back story?"

"Hit me."

"Old song, 1790 or thereabouts. There was a little holler somewhere near Slaty Fork called Copper Hollow. There was a young woman there who gained a reputation of telling futures."

"Let me guess," Andrea said. "Rolling bones?"

"Lucky guess. Maybe you're the witch."

Taka held out his hand and she handed him her laptop, then hooked his keys out of her jeans pocket.

"Oh, no. Did they hang her?"

She could see Taka wanted to ask, but then he shook his head and ushered Dewey onward.

"Stoned her. She'd married a young man, planning to join him in his medicinal herb business, but then predicted his death and refused to travel with him into the wilderness to help make his fortune. He worked his way down the Cherry River and up Winslow Creek. He sold a small collection of dried herbs and roots to the west meat camp and then headed back up Winslow Creek and disappeared."

"Never to be seen again."

"They did find his camp and journal, but no sign of him."

"Was his name Robie Dawkins?"

"It was."

"His poor parents. Could you shoot me the lyrics, please?"

"Just sent."

She put him on speaker and opened her email.

THERE BE LOVE,
  and there be fate,
  But then there be
  That one from Copper Ridge.
  Sing now, Robie Dawkins,
  Afore she sets your future,
  Sing now Robie Dawkins,
  Afore she claims your soul

Sing now Robie Dawkins
Afore she kisses you.

THERE BE LOVE,
    And there be fate,
    But then there be
    That one from Copper Ridge.
    Dance now Robie Dawkins
    Afore she rolls your bones
    Dance now Robie Dawkins
    Afore she calls you home
    Dance now Robie Dawkins
    Afore she declares her love

THERE BE LOVE,
    And there be fate,
    But then there be
    That one from Copper Ridge.
    Run now, Robie Dawkins
    Afore she builds your casket,
    Run now Robie Dawkins,
    Afore she destroys your future
    Run now, Robie Dawkins,
    Afore she eats your heart.

"CHEERY." Was he a victim of the trapper? "Any idea what her actual prediction was?"

"If my source is accurate, yes."

"Do tell."

"Quote, 'Don't pluck of the vital root or be forever trapped as a fly under glass.'"

What would she say if she didn't know exactly what that meant? "Kinda vague for a root collector to take seriously."

"Interesting story, though," he said. He had a symphony on in the background, something with a lot of foreboding crashing of cymbals. "I hope that helps."

"Thank you, Eddie, I owe you."

She jogged to the Yukon, surprised to see Dewey in back with Karie. Taka started the engine as she got in up front. "I got one of the trapper's victim's names. Robie Dawkins, from the song."

"One," Taka said. "Madeleine?"

"I don't know about her. But if my vision at home was correct, Tucker's brother. No name. And his girlfriend, no name."

"Still counts," Karie said.

Taka glanced in his rearview at Karie. "Three, then."

Plus, the bones of Dewey's mother, since the senator had left her in the cabin.

"Toby said to give him another hour," Karie said. "I asked him to work as fast as he could."

Dewey leaned forward. "Why was she so interested in my dad's ashes?"

"I have no idea," Andrea said.

"You can't just ask her?"

"No. Did you call Beau?"

"Left him a voicemail."

"Will he call you back?"

"No. He'll do what I told him to do."

"Which was?"

"To meet us at Uncle Solomon's place out on Charter Woods. Do you think she was interested because she's my mom?"

No, how could she be, the way she talked about Tucker? "Did she have red hair? Slender build?" Was she so very young? Then again, Madeleine's version of heaven made everyone young.

He sat back. "I don't think so? And I remember her having a solid build. But I was six."

Andrea turned in her seat to look at him. And saw Karie had offered her hand and he had taken it. "I'm really sorry that happened to you, Dewey."

FIFTEEN MINUTES INTO THE RIDE, Madeleine wedged herself in between a drowsing Dewey and Karie. She wasn't chattering incessantly, but every few minutes, she'd run through her litany of phrases. Almost muttering, but just loud enough that Andrea could hear every word. Twenty minutes in, the dog had wandered through the Yukon's rear door, announcing himself by shaking vigorously, his ears slapping his head. Then he walked through Dewey, veered over, and parked himself in the console between Taka and herself. Only the upper half of his body showed. He panted, smiling out the windshield, flinging ghost slobber every few minutes as he licked his chops.

Forty-five minutes. Karie had her headphones on and her laptop open, working on a client report. Andrea was contemplating all the pieces of info she had, rolling them around her head like the clattering bones of the girl from Copper Hollow, seeing how they fell every time she tried re-sorting them.

Taka's hand and phone went right through the dog and tapped her forearm. "Take a pic of him for me." The dog whined and laid down, his head going through the radio, which Taka had on, but turned down low. "Dewey," Taka said, tilting his head at the man in question.

She took the phone and twisted around. Dewey was gone in a heap against the door, mouth hanging open, his jacket wadded between the window and his head. She took three shots and Taka grinned when she held his phone up for him to see. The restless dog shifted, sitting up again. She moved back in reaction and Taka noticed.

"The dog is here between us," she said, pulling her knee up, shifting around to sit more sideways and give herself a little room from the dog. "Madeleine's in the back seat, talking."

He tucked his phone back into its holder and turned the radio off. "What did you see at Dewey's?"

She shivered and pulled her coat closed, tucking her hands into the pockets. "It was like the memories Aaron gave me, but—"

"But?"

She explained the first part, a labor contraction catching her off balance, bleeding out because she caught her throat on an iron extension meant to hold pots sticking out from the wall of the fireplace. "I think it was the start. The reason why the trapper's the way he is. He was going to fix the pot crane, but he kept putting it off until he had just one more sack for a full load to sell. Maybe to replace it?"

"A full load of what? Ginseng?"

"It'd have to be, right? It's what he hoards? The other episode I had—"

"We're calling them episodes now? Like ghost TV?"

"The last *vision*, the couple both had, like, old-fashioned sling bags holding the ginseng they'd picked."

The shush of the wet road and Madeleine's quiet murmuring filled the silence.

The dog panted.

They were almost to Summersville, where they'd take the winding road to Richwood.

"So, what's the 'but' part of this vision?" Taka said.

"She died and I didn't move on to someone else's memory or come to. I died with her." She shuddered. "She was at peace, in the meadow behind the cabin, running through the tall grass, the open, blue sky above. And then she was back in the cabin. It was dark and the trapper was nearly dead, skeletal. Her daughter Isla was gone, but not to heaven with her. He said the fairies took her. He refused to come with me. He said he meant to fix it, the fireplace crane, that held the pot, but he just needed the one more sack. And then I went back to . . ."

"Heaven?"

She shook her head. "I think it was Madeleine's version. It felt different, not detailed. Except . . ." The wild joy of reuniting swelled inside her.

"Except?"

He looked over when she did, their eyes meeting. "The joy. It was overwhelming."

"Maybe it's what Madeleine wants, what she's dreaming of. Maybe she can only touch it through whatever this common pool of ghost remembrances is that she and Aaron have accessed."

"You make it sound so reasonable. Logical. The guy telling us the trapper's story was the same way."

"Bob."

"Bob." She lowered her voice in imitation, "Ghost stories have logic barriers, Andrea."

"He's right."

"He is, but I want it all to make sense."

"I don't think we'll ever get all the details we want, but I know one you don't."

"What?"

"The number ninety-two Andy was referring to? Dewey's dad owned a Beretta 92 that was linked to a murder in '80 or 81. Jimmy was going to try and pull the case."

She checked the time on her phone. "Minus travel time, he's had at least a couple of hours to sleep, think that's enough?"

"I doubt he's sleeping after this morning."

Still. She texted him. Checked the time again. Checked her email. "Hallelujah! Toby emailed." She opened it. "They didn't have the data processed for the drone footage in the area we needed, and it took all night to render. But since he was waiting anyway, he analyzed each portion as he went. Oh. Dang. He didn't see any features that matched what we need. The whole length of Winslow Creek we chose is heavily treed. He sent the maps that have fields, though."

Karie pulled her headphones off and leaned forward. "Did you get Toby's email?"

"Yeah. He sent about four maps."

Taka slowed the Yukon for the right out of Summersville onto Route 39.

"Forward the email. You look at the first two and I'll check three and four before the road gets too curvy to look."

"Or we lose signal," Taka said.

Andrea looked up from her phone. "There's no signal out there. If Rachel needs real help, we're in trouble."

"That case Dewey gave me? Satellite phone."

How many times was Dewey going to shock her today? "He believes me."

Taka glanced up at the rearview mirror before he spoke. "Dewey's motto is be prepared. That sat phone is always in his car."

"She's alive, Taka."

"It's been seven months, Andrea. I can buy a ghost trapping her in his cabin, but it's not like he's shopping at Kroger every week. And it might take days to find the cabin."

"What's this?" Karie said, passing her phone forward through the yawning dog. A darker patch of woods. Andrea zoomed the map out. The road name was Charter Woods. "See the crossvine house in the field?"

"The red crossvine a'grows so thick down there, on the homestead," Madeleine murmured.

"Yes." The dark spot was to the left and closer to the thin ribbon of the creek. She clicked through the layers from the menu at the top of the page. The land fell away from the dark spot towards the creek, but there was no pond-like feature or cooler temperature and no notations from Toby. She zoomed back in. Ponds filled in. Trees grew in meadows. "I don't know. It's a possibility, but look for land falling away from the creek, not towards it." She handed the phone back and picked her own up.

Toby had circled an artifact on map three. It was on the north side of the creek, barely visible under the untrimmed trees. The land fell away from the creek. The photo layer showed a flash of red through the bare branches. "Karie, how long do crossvine flowers last past summer?"

"Some til first frost."

"This is October." She passed her phone back. The dog shook his head and laid down again, only the hump of his shoulders and part of his neck visible.

Karie fiddled for a few minutes. "I think it's a fallen-in shed. Watch the video."

After watching a couple of times, Andrea could see it. She poked around a little more. Zooming way out, she could see the faint trace of an old road, the suggestion of a barn. There'd have been only a wagon road to the trapper's cabin, no worn in road from car travel. She swayed against a curve in the road and her stomach turned. She looked up. If only they had more time. She could use Toby's tech and lay out a grid search. "Damn it."

"If Beau doesn't know where it is, he'll find out," Dewey said.

Andrea tilted to peer around the back of her seat. Dewey's eyes were still closed, his head still resting on his jacket. He'd crossed his arms. He looked a little better than earlier.

As if sensing her watching him, he opened his eyes. "You're smart, so work smart. You said this trapper guy's living on Winslow Creek. He hoards ginseng, picks off anyone who gets close enough for him to get ahold of. You did your work, you found Beau and you found out he's the area's largest ginseng dealer. Does it proper, right? Buys and sells. Grew up here. You're done. He either tells you or he doesn't."

"Are you telling me to delegate?"

He closed his eyes again. "If you're going to succeed at anything, even ghost wrangling, delegation is the game. Do your work by finding who you need, not what you need."

"What if he doesn't tell us?"

"Who, not what."

Karie held her hand up and pointed at Dewey, flexing her index finger, open and close.

Andrea rolled her eyes. "Dewey, can I delegate the responsibility of making sure Beau locates the trapper's cabin for us to you?"

He smiled. "My pleasure," he muttered.

"Them bones don't lie," Madeleine said.

34

Jimmy couldn't sleep. He rolled over and felt around on the floor until he found his handball. He slouched back against his pillows and headboard and threw the ball at the wall. Caught it. Nope. Not going to work.

He picked up his phone. Andrea had texted a half-hour ago. Taka wanted to know if he'd pulled the Beretta 92 murder case.

He got up and padded through the doublewide to the chair by the door where he'd dropped everything when he came in. He yawned and snatched up the envelope. He threw it on the kitchen counter and reheated yesterday's coffee before he sat down at the island and opened the envelope. Ellen Shannon Westfall née Bennett was fifty-six when she was shot and killed at her home on Falls Branch Road at about three p.m. on a Tuesday in unincorporated Winslow Creek.

Well, shit.

Widowed with one daughter, age twenty-two, also of the home. They'd recently moved from Philadelphia to care for Ms. Westfall's aging father. He had Alzheimer's and was transferred to a care facility. No forced entry, no robbery. Sheriff's Office suspected a disagreement over the daughter's pregnancy out of wedlock. She would not name the father and stated he was out of their lives. Daughter was cleared on the strength of her alibi. No other motive was discovered. Filed as a cold case.

Jimmy wondered if, even with the gun, they could build a case against the senator.

Nina had included a copy of a marriage license for Ellen Bennett to Jeremy Westfall, of Winslow Creek. He'd been declared dead seven years after disappearing with a male friend on his family's property bordering the Cranberry Wilderness. A large search was conducted to no avail. At the bottom of the stack, were articles from the Winslow Creek and Richwood papers as well as the Charleston Gazette and Daily Mail on Ellen's murder, all with a headshot and a photo taken at her wedding. And then, from the Richwood paper, two articles detailing Jeremy's disappearance and the search, including a map of the search area. And his family's property.

Jimmy called Andrea. She didn't pick up.

He called Taka. No answer.

He texted the info to both of them, then took photos of the search map and Ellen's wedding pic and prayed they'd receive them.

He jumped up to get dressed.

TAKA TRIED to ease the bounce of the Yukon over the rough gravel road by not driving into every pothole but couldn't do much to stop the rattle. Dewey's jaw was clenched tight as he hung onto the grab bar over the window with one hand and pressed down on his thigh with the other. In the front passenger seat, Andrea kept flinching away from the nothing that was the non-existent bloodhound sitting between them. He was just glad those mighty ghost claws weren't leaving scratches on the console.

"Is Madeleine still here?"

"Yes."

"She can't give you directions, but maybe she can point the way?"

"If I can break her thousand-yard stare. She's never responded directly to me." She turned in her seat. "Madeleine? Are we going the right way? She's humming the fairy song. I don't think she's going to be any help." She settled back into her seat. "The turn's right up there onto Charter Woods."

Ten minutes later, as she and Karie were agreeing that Roger Wright's farm was on the left, Andrea lunged at the console with a high-pitched yelp, grabbing at air. Taka jerked the wheel and the Yukon swerved hard towards the trees.

"Fuck me," Dewey yelled.

Taka yanked the wheel back around and the Yukon fishtailed on the loose gravel.

"Sorry," Andrea said. "The dog just like, dove into the engine. I guess he wanted out. Madeleine's gone, too."

"Are we sure," Karie said, "the Wright cabin isn't the trapper's?"

Trying to slow his pounding heart by sheer willpower, Taka drove around the curve and crossed a bridge over Winslow Creek. For all the build-up, it didn't look like much, just another West Virginia creek.

"Next drive on the right," Dewey croaked.

He should've said, drive another mile to the next drive. The farm was bottom land, acres and acres of the brown stalk remnants of the feed corn harvest, in the process of being turned under, and what he thought was winter wheat. The drive brought them to a huge barn, where several trucks and ATVs were parked. He parked at the edge of the crowd.

"That's Beau's truck," Andrea said pointing at a red Chevy.

"Step one, check."

"That's why I love you," Andrea said. The words were simple, she'd told him that before, but it hit him differently this time. The smile rose from his chest.

"Optimism is an inheritable trait," Karie said, and dropped out of the truck. "Just saying."

"What *is* she saying?" Taka said.

"Nothing, I'm sure," Andrea said as Dewey said, "That you've been a dumbass for way too long."

Whatever. He was onboard now, that's all that mattered.

He retrieved Dewey's crutches and by the time they were situated, a big man was coming out of the barn. And with him was Bowman.

Which made Taka think of what he'd found in Dewey's locked drawer at Kirkby Road.

"Wait," Karie said. "How'd you get here?"

Bowman's mouth turned down like he was confused. "I flew?"

"Ha-ha," Karie said.

"He's useful to have around," Dewey said. "I called him from the house. Moving on."

"Dewey," Beau said. "I told you before I don't know where any abandoned cabin is up here on the creek."

"None."

"Well, not none. There's quite a few 'bandoned places round here in the woods."

"Any where you're cultivating ginseng?" Andrea said.

"Who said I'm cultivating?"

"You did, in an article I read online," Andrea countered. "Mr. Wright was standing right behind you in the photo."

"I told you I need an NDA signed for I take you anywhere. I don't share my proprietary information with just anybody."

"Can it, Beau, or we're done."

"Dewey," he said, his tone wounded. "What do you want from me?"

"What do I want from him, Andrea?"

Andrea's gaze wandered past the barn to the low roll of the land beyond. "Where do you *not* pick ginseng, even though there's plenty?"

Beau shifted, his eyes darting past Taka.

"On the Wright farm?"

He shook his head. "Old Westfall place. Some third cousin owns it now, but my lease is still good."

Andrea closed her eyes and breathed in. Dewey hung his head.

"Why do you keep the lease if you don't dig there?" Karie asked.

"Because there's so much ginseng there."

"That makes no sense," Taka said.

"It's old growth. Potent. I go in and dig in season."

Bowman, arms crossed and feet square in his usual manner, lifted his chin. "That's what you're cultivating from."

"Yeah."

"You know where the abandoned cabin is?" Dewey asked.

"The trapper's cabin. Ain't nobody know that."

"It doesn't move," Dewey ground out between his teeth. "I've been there. You don't know where it is?"

"Is that the homestead y'all are looking for? Never been Sandersons there."

"Mom and Papaw Sanderson took me there to buy a puppy," Dewey said, pissed now and talking around the truth in that incredible way he had of doing so. "I was six! I couldn't remember who's place it was, but I do remember the shit cabin on its last legs and the red flowers all over it."

"You don't have to get so fired up about it."

"So, you do know where it is."

He held up his hands, palms out. "It's hard to find."

"Andrea," Dewey said. "What do we need in order to find this place in February."

"A sacrifice," she said, looking right at Beau.

Taka almost felt sorry for him.

"Okay, okay. Y'all obviously know something. I dig me a bagful, and I dig him two."

"And the wraith?"

"He don't scare me. He tries. He don't like me feeding the trapper, but that ginseng's worth a few scratches."

"Now that we're all on the same page," Dewey said.

Bowman lifted his hand. "Someone'll fill me in later?"

Karie smiled at him. "I will, sweetie. Just go with it for now."

"You got it."

"You've got dried ginseng here?" Andrea asked.

Beau clapped Bowman on the shoulder. "We'll throw two sacks in the chopper."

The chopper? Dewey's small chopper? Did Bowman fly?

"Wait," Karie said. "You flew here?"

Bowman cracked that smug, one-sided smile out.

Andrea turned and hugged Dewey, almost knocking him over. Taka stepped in, just in case.

"The rest of us will go by ATV," Beau continued. "It's the only way in there, since they let the farm grow up."

Taka handed Bowman the sat phone case and the medical bag that lived in the Yukon. Then Bowman and hop-along Dewey made their way around the barn while Beau set the three of them up with helmets and gloves. Karie climbed on behind Beau. Taka waved Andrea on to their ATV as driver. He wanted to be able to keep an eye on their surroundings and he couldn't do that watching the ground. They rode over to another barn and Taka and Karie held the large sacks of dried roots on their laps over to the chopper.

A four-seater, the senator had bought it twenty years ago to allow him to better meet his constituents, but it had seen its share of purely social outings of another kind. Taka tossed the sacks across the back seats. By the time they drove past the barn and headed down the drive, Bowman had the engine fired up. When they turned left onto Charter Woods, the chopper swooped low overhead and out across the field, following the creek.

They rumbled down the road, over the bridge, and onto the Wright property. Beau bore left through the field from the drive, all the way to a barbed wire fence, and turned right to follow it west on a rutted trail over several small hills before Taka could tell they were climbing over a ridge.

Dropping down into a small hollow, they cut north towards the creek across a field matted in long brown grass. Through another patch of woods, they bore left and rode straight down an overgrown road to the abandoned Westfall house. A large rabbit scrambled out of their way. The house wasn't in bad shape yet, just desolate.

They wound between several outlying buildings and then Beau picked up speed down a lane between broken board fences and unkempt pastures. Back into heavy woods and a right turn north again through yet another field took them across a shallow ford on what Taka's sense of direction told him was Winslow Creek. A rising track to the left carried them past another barn and out onto a small bluff. A brisk wind blew off the creek. It was wider and looked deeper here, with a tumble of whitewater.

Bowman had the chopper high, circling, until he spotted them. He swooped down and away again. They went another quarter of a mile before

Beau held his arm up and slowed down, gradually bringing them to a halt. In front of them, the bluff fell away from the river to the north, along a shallow meadow where a small barn stood among a jumble of fallen posts and split rails that may have once formed pens around it. Three massive black walnut trees towered over a good mix of smaller hardwoods forming the far tree line. Taka suspected the deer hunting here would be very good.

Bowman flew low along the creek, checking the meadow out, before he circled away and came back again straight above it and set the chopper down with skill. He was, indeed, going to be useful to have around, if he stayed. He shut the blades down and Beau waved them on. On the other side of the chopper, he shut his ATV off and Andrea followed suit. Taka got off and then helped Andrea. They pulled their helmets off. The wind bashed the backs of the heads.

Andrea caught her hair and pulled it back, wrapping one of the multitudes of hair ties he found everywhere, even his truck, around it. Bowman already had the sacks of ginseng on the ground. Dewey's door was open, his attention locked on the barn, but he made no move to get out. Andrea straightened, coming to alert.

Taka followed her gaze. There was nothing but the trees. The grey light shifted through them. There was little understory. These woods were old growth. "Is it the wraith?"

"Yes. He's sangin'. He's just a boy."

Karie came over, watching where Andrea was looking. "Does he have dark hair?"

"He does."

"Wraith's not here," Beau said, standing next to Bowman. "Nothing to be afraid of."

"Oh, he's here all right," Karie said under her breath.

"You carry those sacks down through the woods there," Beau said, "and you might find the cabin."

Andrea shook her head. "Maybe I was wrong about that. Dewey and his mom weren't picking when they were at the cabin."

"That's why they're still here. The reason anyone still knows it's here is 'cause people seen it. Random-like. Always in full bloom, though. They come back, it's gone. Can't find it nowhere."

"Hey, Dewey," Beau said, leaning into the open door. "You said there was flowers all over that cabin when you were here, right?"

"That's the only reason I remember it."

Yep. The only reason.

"Why you want to find it so bad now?"

No one answered him.

He wagged a finger at Andrea and Karie. "You lookin' for more skeletons?"

Bowman swatted Beau's hand down and bent to heft a sack up on his shoulder in one smooth motion like it'd been an accident. "We going or what?"

35

Andrea didn't see any point in avoiding the wraith. She wondered if he was just an echo by now. He didn't react until they were under the trees, then he rose up to assess.

To her right, Bowman stopped. He lifted his arm to block Karie, keeping her behind him.

Andrea walked forward a few more feet, aware of Taka flanking her.

The wraith stood still, watching them with a curious regard.

"Tucker," Andrea said.

He looked as surprised to hear his name as Bowman had been to see him.

"Tucker, Madeleine wants to go home."

Tucker looked back over his shoulder, then back at her. "Tomorrow. I have to get my brother first."

"It's been a thousand tomorrows, Tucker, and more than a thousand more. I can help you get your brother." Was lying to a ghost a sin? "Leah Beth's up the holler. She's waiting on her girls."

"Tomorrow. I'll take you home tomorrow, Madeleine."

"We're taking this root to the trapper now, so he can make his sale. I'll get your brother for you." She struck off into the woods, acting more confident than she felt.

Rachel needed them.

The others crunched through the leaves after her.

Tucker screamed, a bellowing roar of outrage and pain.

Andrea jolted forward, her hands over her ears, and ran. He blew around them in a blustery gust, punching and slapping. Tears sprung up in her eyes with the sting of his touch on the skin of her face and ears and hands. *None's them touch don't feel it. Them bleeding-vines don't lie.*

She stumbled, hitting the ground with one knee. Bowman and Karie, hanging on to each other, kept going. Taka's hand closed on her bicep, and he propelled her up and forward. It seemed like forever before she noticed a thinness to the woods around them. The ground sloped down under her feet. She held a hand over her eyes. They were at the top of a gentle rise. There at the bottom, the woods were thick with a riot of young trees and undergrowth.

"Here!" she shouted. "Put them here."

Bowman and Taka dropped the sacks one atop the other. The wraith bit and kicked and pummeled them with his storm of fury. Andrea crouched, her arms over her head. Taka knelt over her, protecting her with his own body. A man's rough and weathered hands reached out and grabbed the top sack, yanking it into thin air.

Andrea shook, certain he would grab her next.

Taka's arm came around her chest and pulled her up and back.

The man's hands reappeared, grabbed the second sack. Yanked it away into nothingness.

The wind stopped. Just stopped. The still air felt strange after the fury of the last minutes.

Andrea opened her eyes.

"It's an echo," Karie breathed.

The cabin was decrepit but standing. Hundreds of red flowers covered it, leaving only a bower-like entrance onto the gabled porch. It was too dark and narrow to see the cabin door, but Andrea knew it'd be standing open. Nothing moved in the woods. No birds sang.

Bowman lifted his head, listening. And there's where she'd seen Madeleine's stillness before. She didn't know how she hadn't recognized it before now.

"What do you hear?" she said.

But it was Taka who answered. "A hound on the hunt."

And then she could hear it, too, the bloodhound's distinctive bay, far away.

And then a cry, from the cabin.

They all looked at the entrance at the same time. "Rachel," Andrea said, and bolted up the rough-cut steps, afraid if she didn't, she never would.

"Andrea," Taka yelled and followed her.

She brushed through the vines, petals showering down on her, and through the open door.

Wearing only a dirty, blue hoodie, Rachel squatted next to a flattened blue-tick mattress in the middle of the floor. Her stringy hair hung to the floor, covering her face. Andrea turned back to yell, but Taka was already striding across the porch. Karie and Bowman right behind him.

The door slammed closed with a sound deeper than should have been.

The drop bar fell into its brackets.

Rachel cried out again and half-stood, her hands on her huge belly. Her bony legs trembling.

Andrea ran back to the door and grabbed the bar to lift it. It stuck fast. She pulled up but couldn't lift it. She pounded upward with the heel of her hand. It didn't budge. She spun around, lifted her right leg and mule-kicked the center of the bar with all the force she could drive through her thigh. Pain shot up her leg. She screamed and hopped forward.

Rachel was staring at her, panting with little expulsions of breath. She cried out again and bent over, then dropped back into a squat.

"Are you pushing?" Andrea said.

Rachel nodded hard, whining from deep in her chest.

There was no sound from outside.

No pounding at the door.

No Taka yelling her name.

What had she done?

Rachel stood, actually crying now, with little sobs of breath. Tears streaked her cheeks and dropped off her chin. Then she grunted and dropped again. Andrea knew nothing about childbirth. With their first responder training, Taka and Bowman knew more than she did. That's why they were here.

"It's coming," Rachel said, the words exploding out of her.

"I know," Andrea said. "That's why I'm here."

"No, it's coming," she panted.

"Oh!" Andrea limp-hopped over, but the sting of the kick was already fading. She slid down to the floor and Rachel pushed back up again, half-standing. The crown of the baby's head peeped out from between her shaking legs.

"Don't let him fall," Rachel gasped. "Don't let him fall on his head."

Andrea laid down on her side and stuck her hands out under the baby's head. Would the trapper's hands reach out and snatch the baby away into nothing like the ginseng sacks? Rachel groaned and squatted, the baby's head hitting Andrea's hands before she could move. It was so soft and wet and warm. He had hair already. Rachel grunted and a rush of hot fluid gushed over Andrea's hands and suddenly she had the weight of a whole baby in her palms.

She drew her arms back, and sitting up, brought the baby to her, the umbilical cord still tethering him to Rachel.

"Oh, god, oh god," Rachel cried. She crawled forward, nearly bowling Andrea over and flopped down on the mattress.

The baby lay in her hands, quiet. Staring up at her. It blinked.

Why wasn't it crying? Didn't all babies cry when they were born?

The trapper's hand appeared, reaching out.

Andrea pulled the baby up, against her chest, and it launched into a full-throated tantrum, turning red and kicking. An arm appeared, attached to the hand, then a shoulder, a full beard. Andrea looked up and the trapper slowly materialized.

"Let him touch the baby."

Andrea couldn't close her mouth as she snapped her head around.

"Let him touch the baby," Rachel said again and then closed her eyes.

The trapper crouched in front of her, his gaze on the screaming baby.

He had kind eyes. Brown eyes.

She slowly lowered her arms, revealing the baby girl to him.

He ran a calloused finger over the baby's forehead and down her cheek. The baby turned her head to the touch and quieted. Andrea found herself bouncing her arms in a slow timeless rhythm.

"Thank you for the wild men," the trapper said, and Andrea looked up to see him meet her gaze straight on. He seemed so very human. "I'm going to market now."

He stood up, the light breaking through him.

Andrea brought the baby back up, huddling over her and closed her eyes against the brilliance as he flashed over.

"Oh," Rachel cried, full of wonder. "Oh! Look at them!"

Andrea opened her eyes to see dozens of spirits glowing all around them.

Voices rose up, all different tones, heavy and soft accents, women, men.

"*There's love and then there's fate and then there's Robie Dawkins and that slip of a girl from Copper Ridge.*"

"*You know that's real, don't cha? A girl from Slaty Fork, they say.*"

"*That girl from Copper Hollow sees the future. Ever-body says so, but I don't believe that.*"

"*And that spotted hound sniffin' the breeze?*"

"*Tucker!*"

"*Now throwin' the bones, that there's different, but just a'closing your eyes and saying sumpthin' what rise up on your tongue...*"

"*Them bones don't lie.*"

"*Tucker sez tomorrow, Madeleine.*"

"*. . . what's this? 'nother fair-haired boy. They's be a nickel to every dark-haired dime down's Jackson way.*"

"*Since when does you all think you can have the run of the holler, child?*"

"*But he's not a'one. Not a'one them those bones be chatterin' and clatterin' on aboot.*"

"*Build that fire higher.*"

"*Those girls, I told them now, you watch out for them dark haired boys.*"

"*And then I sez to her...*"

"I'll be a'takin' yous home."

"My sister. . ."

"None's them touch don't feel it. Them bleeding-vines don't lie."

"No one's so bright as them dark-headed lads what's been gone from Winslow's crick so long."

"Tucker sez..."

"They's just a'moved, gone away, but Leah Beth heard tell how's that one's a wraith and ain't it been seed a'sangin' in the holler, diggin' and pickin' like it was still a'this world."

Their glow ignited, lighting up the air as they passed over one by one, like white light firecrackers.

———

SHE WAS BEING JOSTLED, roughly. The roar of an engine filled her head. She struck upward, to make it stop, and jammed her hand into something hard. The rough movement stopped. The roar ran away from her.

"Andrea?" Taka said.

"What is happening?"

"They took Rachel in the chopper with the baby."

The roar, having run away, came rumbling back again and then fell silent.

"She wake up all the way?"

She scrunched her face up at the familiar unfamiliar shout.

"Beau," Taka said.

She gave him a thumbs up.

"You were loopy!" Beau shouted. "You missed it all!"

Not quite.

What was on her head? She shoved at the heavy thing again.

"Hey," Taka said. His arm tightened around her middle. "Stop. Hang on."

His warmth left her back and then his arm lifted. He pulled the helmet off her head.

Helmet. That's what that was. She looked around. They were in a field. Grass. Trees.

"Where are we?"

"Almost off the Wright property."

An old gold truck with the windows down came growling across the field from the direction of the house.

"I've been trespassed."

Taka smiled at her. "I know."

"I'll go talk to him," Beau said, still half-yelling. He was fired up, half-wild with what he'd witnessed. He went charging away to intercept Mr. Wright.

Taka put his hands on his knees so he was eye-level with her. "Do you remember what happened?"

"Yeah. Trapper. Baby. Liiights."

"Lights?"

"Peweh! Peweh! Like firecrackers."

"Are you high on ghost lights?"

She frowned, trying to think. "Maybe? Did Tucker leave?"

He grinned. "Yeah. The cabin just . . . dissipated like it was being disassembled. But I think we saw some of the spirits rising from it as it went. Not like you did. Just wisps of white fog, blowing away, some of them together. But Tucker reappeared right near us as the cabin fell apart. Two wisps drifted over and circled him and rose. He was looking up, watching them go, when this barely there girl, a teenager, walked out from the woods and wound herself around him and everywhere she touched, he wisped, too, and then they just blew away."

She sobered up as she listened to his strong, firm voice. She pointed up. "Look."

There were patches of blue-sky peeking through the grey, shafts of sunlight spreading down to touch the ground between them and where Beau was talking through the truck's window to Mr. Wright, waving his hands all around.

"Stairway to heaven," Taka said.

Madeleine walked out of one of the shafts, the sun striking her red hair and making it shine, the long train of her dress blowing behind her. A handsome dark-haired young man—*Those girls, I told them now, you watch out for them dark haired boys*—walked beside her in a black tux. A striking woman with long dark hair materialized next to Madeleine and the three of them hugged, their joy evident.

Andrea clutched her hands together at her chest watching them. "Can you see them?"

"Are those three more wisps in the field?"

She held out her hand. "Try holding my hand."

The warmth of his hand shocked her. He laced his fingers between hers.

"This time," she said, "instead of not focusing, concentrate really hard on where I'm looking."

Flynn Iverson came over the hill, laughing, the big bloodhound chasing and leaping along beside him.

"It's Flynn!" Taka said. "And that dog is huge. Is that Madeleine? That's how you described her, but I thought she was with Tucker and that guy's definitely not Tucker. And I'm pretty sure Madeleine's the one who wisped him."

Flynn joined the group hug, the big dog leaping around them.

"They're Flynn's family," Andrea breathed. "They're Dewey's family. Her name was never Madeleine."

A shout drew Andrea's attention away from the reunion. Mr. Wright had thrown his door open, and he and Beau were standing side by side, watching the spectacle. "Oh, my God! Jeremy!" Mr. Wright yelled. "Jeremy, Ellen! Oh my God!"

The man in the tux lifted his hand and not!Madeleine, Ellen, apparently, blew a kiss at the old man. She threw a grin at Andrea as the other young woman nodded and mouthed thank you. They grew more brilliant, and Andrea and Taka ducked a little, shielding their eyes.

"Oh, my God," Mr. Wright shouted, clutching at Beau. "Did you see that? Did you see that, Beau?"

The dog ran to Taka and Andrea, ears and tongue flopping, grinning. Flynn disappeared and reappeared in front of them, hands on hips. "My big brother?"

"He'll be a good uncle," Taka said. "Rachel will be cared for no matter what."

Flynn smiled.

Andrea nodded. "We'll tell them you love them."

He placed a hand over his heart and bowed, a gesture so similar to something Dewey would do that her heart ached for him. He patted his thigh and as the dog came bouncing over, the shafts of sunlight reached them and then they were gone in an explosion of light.

Beau and Mr. Wright had almost reached them, but now stopped, looking confused. "Who were you talking to?" Mr. Wright demanded. Andrea guessed him to be in his eighties, if not older. "Were there more, did you see Jeremy and Ellen? Oh my God, I saw them. Jeremy Westfall lived next door. He was a few years older than me, but not much. He and Ellen got married and not long after he disappeared with a friend. Right there on the farm. Lordy, that was Jeremy and Ellen, clear as anything. Oh, my Lord. Who were you talking to?"

"Flynn Iverson."

"That wildcrafter? He died here on this property, you know. Some other woman was with him, but the sheriff told me her bones might be mor'n a hundred years old. Maybe lots older."

That made sense. Maybe they belonged to Tucker's Madeleine, who Bob said died of a broken heart trying to find the trapper's cabin again. She stuck her hand out. "I'm Andrea Kelley. My friend Karie and I—"

"Found those bones on my property. I would be mad at you, but—" He waved his hand back at his field. "And Beau here says y'all just found the wife back there at the Westfalls. Still alive! And ain't that something! Maybe I'll be mad tomorrow. Oh my God, gives me hope for my day coming. Beau says he's meeting the sheriffs, collect all those other bones back there y'all found. Wanta leave the four-wheeler here and I'll drive you back to Beau's?"

Andrea looked over at Taka, who was still holding her hand.

"Beau's taking care of it," he said.

"You've been trespassed," Mr. Wright said. "I never saw you here."

Despite coming out to what felt like half the law enforcement in the state in the last two days, including the Greenbrier Sheriff's Department, Andrea nearly sagged in relief that she wouldn't have to explain what she still didn't understand about the last few hours.

36

Taka sent two of Beau's men back to meet Beau and the sheriff's deputies.

Andrea hugged Mr. Wright good-bye, carefully, when she felt the frail wings of his ancient shoulder blades under his flannel jacket.

"What a gift, what a gift," he said, and wiped his eyes. "I'm driving straight over to tell Eulalia what we can look forward to."

"Eulalia?"

"Eulalia Tyson. She and Jeremy and Ellen and my big brother were great friends a long time ago."

"I've met her. Give her my regards."

"I will. I'll do that."

They waved him off down the farm drive, then raided bottles of water and protein bars from the stash in the back of the Yukon and left Winslow Creek in silence, lost in their own thoughts.

Almost into Richwood, Andrea still half-high and drowsing, their phones started dinging, their text messages downloading.

Jimmy. She held her phone up. "Jimmy found the property. We'd have gotten there one way or another."

"That was a given," Taka said, and grinned at her.

God, he was beautiful.

She lowered her phone and scrolled back to where Jimmy had started sending. "Oh, my god. The gun, the senator's Beretta, it killed Dewey's grandmother when his mom was pregnant with him. That's why she was staring at his ashes."

She stared at the photo of Dewey's red-headed grandmother in her wedding dress, her handsome new husband at her side. She held the phone up again for him to see. "Not!Madeleine was Dewey's grandmother, Ellen."

"Not!Madeleine?"

Andrea shrugged and scrolled to Ellen's headshot. She was older, but still recognizably the young woman who'd been so determined to make Andrea understand her, despite her ghostly limitations.

The voices in the cabin echoed in her head. Ellen was murdered in 1981. Her accent probably wasn't the heavier accent of the past. And she was never trapped in the cabin. Her husband had been with a friend, which meant she was never anywhere near the trapper at all. "She was speaking for the trapped ghosts."

"What?"

"Think about it," Andrea said, waving her phone in the air. "The senator killed Ellen. At the Bennett place. When he strangled her daughter, though, he left her in the trapper's cabin, where she probably actually died. And the trapper got her husband Jeremy right after they were married. Rachel probably got locked in the same way I did, so Ellen's grandson, Flynn, kept looking for the cabin until he died, just like Madeleine did after Tucker was hit by lightning and his brother trapped inside. All of her family except Dewey died one way or another because of the trapper. Ellen was repeating the things she heard the trapped ghosts say. Giving them her voice."

"So you could find Rachel and her great-grandson."

"So *we* could find them."

Shooting her a sideways glance, Taka nodded. "What was her full name?"

"Ellen Shannon Westfall."

"Ellen Shannon Westfall," he repeated. "Was that Dewey and Flynn's mom we saw with them in the field?"

"With the long, dark hair? I'm sure."

"Her name was Claire. Claire Susan Westfall. I don't know if there'll be enough evidence to make a case against the senator, but we'll make sure they're never forgotten. Maybe we should start making some sort of scrapbook for each ghost you help and a list of the others you come across."

"Ahead of you on the list, but scrapbooks would be nice, especially when we're old like Mr. Wright and Mrs. Tyson."

"Think we'll get that old?"

"I'm planning on it. You better be there."

"I told you I'd never leave you."

"But are you going to be with me or beside me?"

Again, he glanced over, but this time held her gaze long enough to say, "We pulling the pin on that conversation?"

"After how hot you made me this morning? God!" Andrea said, throwing her arms up. "Was that just this morning?"

Taka turned his full attention to the headlights on the road, the night rushing past them.

Just when she thought he was going to let her question go, that they'd just go on the way they had, he said, "I'm tired of being scared of moving forward for fear of losing you. I want all of you for as long as I possibly can. I love you. I've known since middle school. I've known since I left for the Army that we're soulmates."

Soulmates. They'd thrown the word around, occasionally introduced each other as their soulmate, but the firm way he said it now sobered her.

He swallowed hard. "The way that hurt to leave you then, I couldn't imagine ever letting myself fall for you. If we didn't work out, I'd be torn in half. But I fell a long time ago. Just because I kept you at arm's length didn't stop everybody else from seeing it. Shit, Chuck checked in with me before he asked you to marry me."

"To marry you?" she said before she could stop herself.

Taka rolled his eyes.

She hoped he'd never stop doing that.

"To marry him." He glanced over, hands at ten and two, knuckles white. "Let me get this out."

She nodded. He watched the road unfold for a few minutes.

"Every one of my relationships has been jealous of the way I look at you. I love you the way those spirits loved each other all those years. I'd wait a thousand years for you if I had to, but what am I waiting for now?"

"I don't know," she said. "What *are* you waiting for?"

He looked over again and then away. "Maybe for you to ask me one last time."

"My offer stands. I always said I'd give it a rip with you if you ever wanted to. I said I wouldn't wait, but I have. I can't help myself. You're the only one I want, body and soul."

"Then I'm in. Body and soul. Are you going to keep me this time?"

"That's a stupid saying, the 'if you love it, let it go' one. If you're in, I'm not ever letting you go again. I'm keeping you."

"I was never going anywhere."

"I know."

"I kinda like high!Andrea."

"I heard that exclamation point in there."

"I wish we could start exploring this new aspect of our soulmatiness, but your former boy and mine need us to get home."

"I know." She stretched and then took the hand he offered her and held on to him all the way back to Charleston.

JIMMY AND DETWEILER met them off the elevator at the hospital. They walked down to Rachel's room, but didn't go in. She was asleep, an IV running. Dewey sat in the room's recliner with his leg up, a hospital freezer pack on his thigh, and the baby in his arms.

They walked down to the waiting room where Bowman and Karie were sipping hot chocolates and trying to decide if they should go home. They were still wired, but Detweiler's funeral was in the morning.

"Did she say anything?" Taka asked.

"We had to keep her awake, so Karie asked her all the things," Bowman said, beaming at Karie.

"It was seven months," Taka said. "And she was pregnant. How'd she stay alive that long?"

Karie handed Andrea her hot chocolate. "She collected rainwater from leaks in the roof."

Andrea wrapped her cold hands around the cup. The warmth slid down her throat and spread out in her belly. She looked up in surprise. "Yeah," Jimmy said. "I have a flask. Thought y'all might need warming up."

"What'd she eat?" Taka said, holding his hand out.

Jimmy dug the flask out of his jacket pocket and slapped it into his hand.

"He let small game and birds in," Bowman said.

Karie nodded "She'd find piles of greens and berries and wild carrots around the cabin."

Andrea shivered. "Wasn't she cold?"

"She said the cabin stayed the same temperature all the time. She got used to it. Obviously, she didn't eat enough. She's malnourished, and dehydrated from the labor, but the baby's healthy. Small, but healthy."

"Her family?"

"They're on their way," Jimmy said. "With an escort."

Andrea begged off for the bathroom and Detweiler walked beside her.

"Good job on those phone calls. So, are you ready to move on tomorrow?"

He shook his head. At least he looked like his regular self. Still in need of coffee, but not injured.

"Need me to tell Mia or Leon or Jimmy something?"

He shook his head.

"Waiting on the kids to get ID'ed? See if CPS pulls them?"

He nodded.

"You want to know how your investigation will wash out?"

He shook his head no again.

"Just want the kids where they wanted to be?"

Yes.

"You know there's nothing you can do if it doesn't go that way."

He shrugged.

"Don't follow me into the bathroom."

He gave her a lopsided smile and blipped away.

37

They got through the funeral. Detweiler wasn't there. Andrea figured he stayed with the kids rather than come watch himself be eulogized. They spent Sunday speaking carefully with Rachel's family. Then they rode with Dewey to WVSP, so he could hash out all the complications and issues of turning over the Beretta 92 with Jimmy, Maddox, and Merritt.

After that they ate lunch back at Dewey's, making sure he had help for the week so Taka could concentrate on the businesses and the club. And they discussed, endlessly, whether he should admit to seeing his father kill his biological mother.

That would involve a huge family mess and Dewey didn't want to hurt his mother or his sister. In the end they back burnered it and swore they wouldn't tell anyone else. Taka headed to the Coliseum to back up a manager over a disputed tab and Andrea went home. In the middle of the night, when she got cold, she found Taka there, throwing all the heat and snuggled up to him.

They got through the week. Karie mourned the loss of any video footage from the kitchen, but the audio gave them the chaos and a singular EVP of the trapper saying, "Mine." The video and audio from the Strange Creek trip was pretty powerful, though. Nothing that couldn't be faked, but Karie's reputation was strong enough to allow it a little publicity.

The trip to ID the kids went off without a hitch after Bowman refused to give CPD and the Conlon task force the addresses when they finally made their move to sideline him on Tuesday morning. Fields called Taka Friday morning to say the school and neighborhood moms confirmed the photos were of the kids they knew. The fingerprints and DNA were being processed.

When Taka called her from the Coliseum that night, Andrea was already half asleep and knew they needed a break, but after talking to Karie, she knew there was one more thing she needed to take care of in Winslow Creek. "Hey, I know it's a long drive, but will you go with me to the Bennett place tomorrow?"

"I've got Dewey set for the weekend. He's doing the club tomorrow and I have Sunday off. Want me to ask him since we know he owns it now?"

"No. Don't bother him with it."

"Guess what?"

"What?"

"He's closing on the Westfall property next week."

"Seriously?"

"Yeah. He found some old pics online. The grandfather he remembers was actually his great-grandfather."

"Wow. He's going to own half of Charleston and half of Winslow Creek, too."

THEY STEPPED over the chain with the "No Trespassing" sign and walked up the muddy drive. Andrea couldn't believe it had only been a week and a half since she'd been here last.

"It's in bad shape," Taka said.

"Maybe Dewey will want to restore his grandfather Bennett's truck."

"Maybe. Not that the drive over wasn't nice, what with getting to sit for a while and just chill with you, but what are we doing here?"

She pointed at the sentinel oak on the left. "Dewey's great uncle fell from that tree when he was fourteen and broke his neck."

The transparent teenage boy in question appeared feet first again. High-waters, suspenders over a grey and white striped shirt. He looked up into the closest oak tree, showing Andrea his crushed skull once again, then blipped right out.

She looked up. "And there he is. You can look, I need everything loud if you can turn up your dial."

"My dial?"

"You know what I mean."

"Where am I looking?"

She pointed. "That branch."

The boy fell.

Andrea couldn't help the little yelp that climbed her throat as she followed him down.

He disappeared but the book hit with a puff of ghostly dust. With Taka there, she could read the title.

"Did he just fall?"

She got busy on her phone. "Over and over."

Frowning at her, Taka stuffed his hands in his pocket. "Really?"

"Hang on."

She watched one more time, got a good idea of where he'd lost his place in Thoreau's *Walden*. "God, he was like, two pages from the end!"

"And?"

When the boy's feet reappeared, followed by the rest of him, Andrea took Taka's hand and started reading. The boy did not blip away. After a few lines, he looked up at her, then at Taka, then out at the abandoned farm. When she finished, she said, "It's okay. Your family's been waiting for you."

"Thank you, I wanted to know how it ended," he said in a clear, strong voice. "How do I go now?"

"Just think about your mom and your dad and your sister, and how much you want to see them." Before she even finished talking, he was breaking apart and flashed over as she finished.

Taka swung her around to face him and kissed her hard. "I'm so proud of you. Are we done here?"

"Yes."

He kissed her again, thoroughly, making her spine tingle and her belly ache for him. When they broke for air, he said, "I know where Dewey's spare key is at the lake house."

"Are you ready to explore this new aspect of our soulmatiness?"

"I can't believe you remembered that."

"I wasn't that high." She ran her hand down his back and then lower. "I've been ready since I met you."

"Summersville, then," he said, letting go of her to capture her wandering hand and steer them back down the driveway to her FX.

"If I let you drive, how fast can we get there?"

He stopped, pulling her in close again. "If you let me drive? I'm gonna get you there so slow," he murmured, his lips barely touching hers, the heat of him making her as incandescent as the ghosts, "we'll be there for years."

THANK YOU FOR READING WRAITH!

Andrea Kelley will be back in
The Archivist Book 4

READ ON for an excerpt of ghost mystery,
Blind Mice Bite, AVAILABLE NOW from your favorite bookstore.

**To sign up for notifications of new releases, giveaways, and free
books: www.elleandrewspatt.com**

Please consider telling a friend about Wraith
and maybe leaving a review or posting on social media. Both help other
readers find the book and that helps authors.

I truly appreciate you! ~ Elle

Giving up your ghost is harder than
you think. Just ask Matt Loose.

Elle Andrews Patt

BLIND

MICE

BITE

A Matt Loose Mystery

BLIND MICE BITE

Prologue

2015 ~ New York City

"Can you tell me your name again?" the quiet voice said.

In the dark, Matt lay still on the cot, not aware until then of having spoken. What name had he given her?

"Could you please confirm your name out loud?"

Everyone was forever asking his name here, even after they checked his wristband. But he was leaving soon. Going to—

"I need your name."

"Yeah," he said, hearing the slow in his voice, tasting it on his tongue.

Daytona. That's where he was going.

He had a different name there. But not even the company knew that cover. He'd never said the name out loud. That wasn't who he was right now.

"Your name?"

"My name is Matt Loose."

"Are you married, Matt?"

"Divorced." Anna left him two years ago for an investment banker. That's what he got for moving back to New York. This line of questioning seemed familiar to him, but he couldn't remember anyone else asking about Anna since he'd been here.

"Kids?"

An image rose in his mind's eye. Dakota spinning around to greet him, dark brown hair swinging over her shoulder, big brown eyes shining, a grin spreading across her freckled face that broke his heart with happiness. God, he wanted to wrap his arms around her and bury his nose in that hair, snuffle up her scent of baby shampoo and little kid sweat and crayons and horse and her. "A daughter."

"Tell me about your daughter."

No words would come. How could he describe her? "She reminds me of my sister."

"And your sister is . . .?"

"Lily." Lily would be coming to get him soon. To take him to Daytona Beach, let him adjust.

"Your nephew?"

Did he say he had a nephew? "Ethan."

"How old is Ethan?"

He had to think about it, but Ethan was born a year before Dakota. "Nine."

"When was the last time you saw him?"

"When he was three."

"Has your daughter met him?"

Dakota knew she had a cousin, but Lily couldn't afford to fly up and they didn't have the time to fly down. Anna's job was as busy as his own. Though that was different now, wasn't it? It wasn't like he had a job anymore. Not that he could watch Dakota anyway.

"Matt?"

"No. Maybe next summer."

"Does your daughter live with you?"

He lifted his right hand, opening his fingers wide, only then aware that both his hands had been fisted on his stomach.

"What?" the woman said, sounding honest-to-god curious about what he might be thinking.

"No," Matt said, letting his hand indicate his condition and his tone convey his irritation. "She lives with her mother."

"You could learn to care for her."

He let his hand drop onto his chest. "Maybe."

"When was the last time that you saw her?"

"Her eighth birthday." He'd brought her a chocolate cake from a little bakery near his place in Tribeca and a cross-eyed stuffed unicorn. Anna's boyfriend banker had been away somewhere on business. After candles and cake, Dakota fell asleep sprawled across the couch, trying to anchor herself to both of them at once. When he came back from tucking her in, Anna had a glass of bourbon in her hand.

She tilted her head in invitation, and Matt plopped down beside her.

They'd finished watching The Little Mermaid for the umpteenth time, taking turns adding random lines between the dialogue and sipping from the one glass like they used to before Anna left him. He'd gone back to his apartment instead of staying, but it had been a near thing.

Matt rolled his lower lip under, tasting the ghost of Anna's cherry-cola chap stick under the gentle scrape of his teeth.

"What's your daughter's name?" the woman asked.

"Her mother named her. I was deployed."

"How old is Dakota now?"

"Who?"

"My mistake. What's your daughter's name again?"

"I wanted to name her Sophie, but she'd have hated that. She's a tomboy, through and through."

"How old is she now?"

"She likes horses, you know? She takes riding lessons in Central Park."

"When will you get to see her again?"

"Soon, I hope. I have to get better first. And I'll have to wait until a school break."

"Okay, Mark—"

"Matt. My name's Matt."

"*Seguro que te llamas Matt?*"

What?

"Matt?"

"I, uh, Spanish isn't my strongest language. Are you asking for my name? It's Matt. Loose."

"Okay, Matt. I know you're tired. You're relaxed. Your eyelids are heavy."

His muscles were heavy, too. His head hurt in a vague way. He let his eyes close.

"When I count backwards from three," the woman said, "you'll sleep until I wake you, okay?"

"Sure."

"Three, two, one."

"Is he out that fast?" a man said, too loud, too deep, too close.

Matt tried to close his fingers in his shirt, hold on to himself.

"Hang on," the woman said.

The words distorted, pulling at the edges of him.

Cool fingers closed on his, stilled his scrabbling hand, stilled his mind.

"You've done," the man said, each syllable stretching and stretching as Matt hung on to them, "a remarka—"

Matt fell into the silent darkness where he'd been living for too long.

Fell and fell and fell.

Chapter One

2017 ~ Daytona Beach

Matt Loose lay in the dark, listening to cicadas buzz at one other in the meager landscaping outside his apartment. At nearly one a.m., he'd normally be nestled within the ordered intensity of the Daytona Beach Racing and Card Room, pouring drinks for the regulars who muttered their orders at the bar girls in smoke-grizzled voices. But Ed only let him work ten nights on, before he made him leave for two.

He noticed the cars first, three in a row, coming in the complex entrance that lay beyond his second story window. Just after the cicadas picked up their rhythm again, two more rolled in. Matt waited for the slamming of doors, the alcohol fueled voices that would signal a party in the making, but neither came.

He sat up, his foot hitting the laptop he'd left near the middle of the bed. The slight odor of cheese pasta lingered in the humid air. He felt around in the folds of his duvet and found his cell phone. A thud echoed up from the other side of the single apartment-wide building, near the stairs. And then boots were coming up the stairs, several sets, sounds familiar from Matt's Marine Corp days.

A raid maybe. There'd been a couple of drug arrests in the parking lot in the past couple of weeks. He set his cell phone on the shelf above his bed and lay back down, glad he'd not yet fallen asleep, prepared to hear what he could hear. It wasn't just a couple of men, it was a team. The boot steps hit the top of the stairs and passed his door, but stopped even with his bedroom wall, waiting out there on the other side of his closet as others continued pounding up the stairs. They must have been lining up along the walkway, waiting for the full team to make the second floor before they continued past. Why anyone thought they were safe behind wood framing and drywall was beyond him.

There was a pause, a held breath, and then a resounding crash from his living room that catapulted Matt straight up again, heart thumping. A woman shouting, but he couldn't tell what over the rush of blood in his ears. Were they really in his apartment? He scrambled over, his hand brushing over the holster attached to the side of his bed.

"Police, police, police," a man yelled in the hall outside Matt's closed bedroom door.

Cops. Matt drew his hand back.

Another voice, hollow, from his bathroom. "Clear!"

Swinging his legs over the side of the bed, Matt stumbled up, the blanket catching his leg.

"On your knees, on your knees, on your knees," the first man yelled again as Matt's door burst open, bouncing off the stop as men rushed into the room, filling it with the fury of their movement, rank sweat, leather, gun oil, shouting, "Down, down, down."

Matt fell to his knees, bringing his hands up behind his head, elbows out. Hands grabbed him, dragging him forward, pushing him face-down onto the musty carpet.

"Stay down," the first man said, although another had a knee planted in the small of his back. The man sitting on him yanked Matt's right hand out and down, snapping the cuff against his wrist bone hard enough to bruise and then grabbed the other.

Unable to breathe, a chilling wave of familiarity crashed into Matt's chest, and he tensed, resisting the pull on his wrist.

The man above him snapped, "Don't. We're cops. Police. *Policia*."

Matt closed his eyes tight, fighting the instinct to roll, lay this man flat out on the floor before he could stop Matt from doing it. He hitched in a stifled breath and then relaxed his shoulders, let the guy tug his arm down to his lower back.

Detective Lucinda Troy strode forward, alert for trouble as more men disappeared into the bedroom. In the doorway, she fetched up against the SWAT team leader's back. From inside the room, she heard a quiet grunt and the unmistakable sound of cuffs being closed.

"Clear," someone said.

She peered over Latham's shoulder into the dark room. His acne-scarred cheek caught the reflection of his men's hooded flashlights before he hit the light switch to his right. He turned sideways, swinging his right arm back to both invite her in and let her by.

In a glance, she registered that the bedroom was as spare as the rest of the small apartment. Boxy headboard with built-in bookcase, bare except for a handful of stacked CDs, half a bottle of water, a cell phone. No lamp. Laptop sitting half-buried in the crumple of dark red sheets and beige comforter. Three-drawer dresser. No mirror. Nothing on the walls. A hat rack looking thing that held a button-down shirt, slacks, a dark jacket, a tie, and a single pair of black dress shoes.

A blonde bulldog of a white man in boxers and a black tee shirt lay on his belly on the beige wall-to-wall carpet, arms cuffed behind him, face turned away from her. From what she could see, he matched the description of their suspect. That was a good start.

SWAT team giving way, Cin crossed the small room to the foot of the bed and crouched down to address the man. "Doug Moultrie?"

"No."

"Excuse me?"

". . . loose."

"No, sir, I can't do that. Are you Doug Moultrie?"

"No."

Sighing, Cin looked up at Latham. "You ready to hand this over, let my team find out who he is?"

Latham leaned back a little to look down the hall. "Already flipping the living room."

"I'm Matt Loose," the bulldog said.

"Excuse me?" she said again.

"Is my tongue not working?" He lifted his head. "My name is Matt Loose."

"You're not Doug Moultrie?"

He pressed his forehead down onto the carpet and growled.

"This guy for real?" she said to Latham.

Latham shrugged.

She sighed. Their witness, one of her CIs, a criminal informant, had sworn up and down the man they wanted for the murder of a local drug dealer lived here and was headed out of town. He'd provided a bloody shirt for DNA evidence and said their suspect had taken drugs and the murder weapon from the scene.

After cursory checks and speaking with the lab, she'd convinced the judge on duty to sign out an arrest warrant for murder on Doug Moultrie as a flight risk and a no-knock premises warrant in search of Moultrie, electronics, weapons, and drugs before they could be destroyed. Her CI had proved reliable, but he'd been jumpy on this one. "Where's your ID, Matt?"

"Kitchen drawer," he said into the carpet. "Closest to the hall."

Latham turned to retrieve it without being asked.

Talking to the back of Matt's head, she said, "You know James Shad? Jimmy?"

Silence.

"Got it," Latham announced. He pulled a card from the top of a small wad of cash held together by a rubber band. "Florida ID card. Matthew Anthony Loose. Got a carry permit here, too."

"You don't drive?" Cin asked. After another moment of silence, she leaned forward. Matt's eyes were closed. She frowned at him. His breathing was rapid, and his jaw clenched. Sweat beaded in his hairline. "Sit up," she said, looping her arm through his.

Latham stooped to grab Matt's other elbow and help him kneel upright before they steadied him as he maneuvered around to sit cross-legged. Latham stepped back as Matt took a deep breath. Cin let go of him but remained crouched at his side. "Little tense there, Matt," she said. And he was ripped under that tee. "Your name's not on the lease."

"I sublet."

They always had a pat answer. "Want to look at me?"

He shook his head slightly, but opened his eyes, turning his face to her. His brilliant blue eyes stared through her, unfocused.

"You take something, Matt?"

He took another deliberate breath and swallowed before he said, "Panic attack."

She looked up at Latham. He shrugged. Stepping to the side, he keyed his mike and asked dispatch to run the ID for outstanding warrants.

Charlie, the other detective on Cin's team, stepped into the room. "Nothing."

Cin lifted her chin, indicating the rest of the room. Charlie eased by them to hit the far side of the room first, the direction in which Matt was still staring towards the blind-covered window. He blinked, drawing her attention to his long eyelashes. Wide forehead, a faint frown dipping between thick, curved brows, high cheekbones above a strong jaw. Plump lips drawn together in a tight line, solid chin. Attractive. "Why you nervous, Matt?"

Rolling his eyes, he shook his head again. "I'm not Moultrie, but I'll let you do the search you're already doing despite the forced entry on the wrong address, unless, of course, my address isn't on the warrant in the first place. If you have a warrant."

Charlie scooted back past them.

"Got all our duckies in a row, Matt," Cin said, pulling the warrants from her back pocket. "Doubt you can read them strung out the way you are."

Pills rattled from the head of the bed. Charlie had already bagged the phone and laptop. He held up a prescription bottle in his gloved hand. "Oxy."

"Jesus Christ," Matt muttered.

"Focus on me, and I'll lay off," Cin said.

He huffed and dropped his gaze.

The sound of Velcro tearing proceeded Charlie's announcement. "FNS nine mil." He dropped the magazine out and racked the slide to remove the chambered bullet.

"Where's Doug Moultrie?" After a moment of silence, Cin continued. "How do you know James Shad?"

"You're in the wrong apartment."

"Come on, Matt, if we're in the wrong place, so be it. You want to answer my questions, prove you're on our side, or you want to spend your night in jail?"

"I've provided picture ID, you haven't found anything to justify arresting me," Matt said, his voice rising with each word until he was shouting. "And you're at the wrong address for whatever it is you're after!"

"ID's clean," Latham said.

Cin stood up, relieving the ache in her thighs. "That bottle labeled correctly, Charlie?"

Rifling through the closet, Charlie didn't turn. "If he's Matthew Loose."

"You on oxy right now, Matt?"

Matt shook his head.

"Verbal answer, Matt, speak up so we can all hear you."

"No, I have not taken any oxy tonight."

"What did you . . ."

"Shit," Charlie said, spinning around. "You blind, man?"

Blind Mice Bite is NOW AVAILABLE at your favorite bookstore!

ABOUT THE AUTHOR

Elle Andrews Patt writes speculative fiction and works in telecommunications and data migration. In the past, she has made her living as a vet tech, pizza maker, and horse breeding farm manager among many other ventures.

Her short fiction and novels have been recognized by The National Indie Excellence Awards, Killer Nashville's Silver Falchion Award, The Writers of the Future, and the Florida Writers Association.

Elle currently lives with her family in Tennessee.

Read a free story, sign up for her newsletter, connect with her on social media, and visit her website from one easy link:

https://linktr.ee/elleandrewspatt

Or visit www.elleandrewspatt.com

www.ingramcontent.com/pod-product-compliance
Lightning Source LLC
Chambersburg PA
CBHW031314280626
47169CB00019B/1538